W9-BMT-935

PRAISE FOR NIGHT SKY

"With a little something for everyone and a hip sense of humor, dialogue, and teen angst, this is a gripping page-turner from first to last. Particularly nice is the full integration of wheelchair-bound Calvin, who is far more than his disability. The start of something that can only be described as 'greater-than.'"

—*Kirkus*, Starred Review

"Original and exciting, *Night Sky* propels readers into a dangerous future where even the police are powerless, but softens the harsh blow with tender romance, powerful friendships, and intense loyalty. Loved it."

—Melissa Marr, *New York Times* bestselling
author of the Wicked Lovely series

"I have been a Suzanne Brockmann fan for years, and I am delighted to say that I am now a fan of Team Brockmann! *Night Sky* is full of adventure, humor, and just the right amount of Brockmann wit and humor. I love this book!"

—P. C. Cast, *New York Times* bestselling
coauthor of The House of Night series

"Action packed, mysterious, charming, and witty. I'm ready for more!"

—Gena Showalter, *New York Times* and *USA Today*
bestselling author of *Alice in Zombieland*

WILD
SKY

SUZANNE BROCKMANN
AND MELANIE BROCKMANN

sourcebooks
fire

Published by Sourcebooks Fire, an imprint of Sourcebooks, Inc.
P.O. Box 4410, Naperville, Illinois 60567–4410
(630) 961–3900
Fax: (630) 961–2168
www.sourcebooks.com

The Library of Congress Cataloging-in-Publication data is on file with the publisher.

Printed and bound in the United States of America.
VP 10 9 8 7 6 5 4 3 2 1

Suzanne

For Ed.

Melanie

This book is for Kat Varela—humble wife, gift giver, food maker, empathizer, organizer, listener, family event coordinator, dog lover, and mom to one of the greatest men I know. Your superpowers do not go unnoticed.

CHAPTER ONE

Milo was gone.

Correction: Milo had been *taken*, just like Sasha had been taken. Just like Lacey had been taken.

And even though it didn't make a bit of sense that a healthy, muscular nineteen-year-old boy could have been kidnapped as easily as two tiny, defenseless little girls, I believed what Dana had just told me when she'd called and woken me out of a deep sleep.

Milo is missing.

I'd gone from pajama clad and snoring in my bed to fully dressed and moving fast as I used my Greater-Than homing powers to race to find him. First, I'd hopped onto the back of Dana's motorcycle, because she'd called me, ready to roll, from the midnight-dark suburban street outside the house I shared with my mom.

But now we were on foot. We were running on a trail through one of Coconut Key's many abandoned town parks as I felt the familiar tug of Milo's presence calling to me, getting stronger by the second.

He was here. I was getting close, I knew it, so I ran even faster.

I can run pretty fast.

But right now it didn't seem nearly fast enough, as thick branches from the overgrowth of the tropical, beachside brush crashed against my sides like horse whips, reminding me of the way that Sasha and Lacey and dozens of other kidnapped little girls had been herded together and tortured like farm animals.

"Slower," Dana huffed from behind me. "Bubble Gum! You need… to go…slower."

My heart pounded manically in my chest, which had nothing to do with how fast I was running. I needed to find Milo. I *needed* to find him. I glanced back to see Dana lagging behind, pumping her arms furiously by her sides.

She'd ditched her knee-high leather stiletto boots and resorted to bare feet. Still, she was clearly winded and struggling. But I was already going far more slowly than I wanted so she could keep up.

My hair slapped me in the face, and I had to spit out several long, red strands to tell her, "Faster! We both need to go faster!"

Dana tried, her red-leather bomber jacket making squeaky sounds as she moved. "Remember," she called breathlessly as I pulled farther ahead. "Remember…that…there wasn't…blood…"

Oh! And that was supposed to make me feel *better*?

Apparently, there'd been no blood when Dana returned to Milo's campsite, but she'd told me that there *had* been signs of a serious struggle. And Dana had such a bad feeling about it, she'd woken *me* up in the middle of the night to help find him.

That was saying something. Because Dana was way better at this

Greater-Than-slash-superhero thing than I was. Also? It took a *lot* for her to ask for any kind of help.

So no. I didn't slow down.

The thick, wild brush opened up to the toddlers' playground, long deserted and vandalized. Bent and twisted swings creaked drunkenly in the warm wind, and what had once been whimsical rocking animals listed forlornly on their springs. I leaped over the still-noxious residue from a pair of split-open port-a-potties, shooting a quick "Don't step in that" back to Dana.

Back in the fall, just a few months ago, before we'd rescued Sasha, Dana and I had been in this very park. Tonight that seemed like forever ago.

So much had changed since then.

"Skylar…*please*!" Dana huffed. Even her use of my real name instead of one of her vaguely insulting terms of endearment didn't slow my pace.

But then my foot caught on something, and I looked down to see a decapitated head grinning up at me from the gravel of the path. I screamed but tried to swallow the sound, because I immediately saw that it wasn't Milo. It wasn't even human. It was the head of a stone statue of a little girl, complete with pigtails and a button nose. She'd once adorned the park, along with a little stone boy and their little stone dog. I might've been able to keep my balance if I hadn't then tripped over her dismembered stone legs. I was going too fast, and now I was going down, and that gravel was gonna hurt.

But Dana caught me with her powerful telekinesis, and for a few short moments, I knew what it felt like to fly. It was nice to have friends with Greater-Than superpowers. But then she put me down and pinned me in place as she finally caught up.

"You need to breathe. Take a moment and think." Dana's voice was low and intense, and in that moment, I realized how quiet the rest of the world was too. The loudest sound was my own labored breathing. I could hear the creaking of the swings and the wind in the leaves of the trees that formed a canopy overhead.

But Milo had been *taken*. It was all that mattered to me right now.

I felt like I was going to throw up.

"Use your brain, Sky. Signs of a struggle. But no blood. What does that mean?"

I looked around me. *Still thoughts. Still thoughts.* "It means he's probably still alive."

"Good," Dana said in a gruff whisper. "What else does it mean?"

I didn't know. I just wanted to find him. Now. I could feel him. He was somewhere nearby. I shook my head as I struggled to sit up, but Dana held me securely in place.

"If someone's taken Milo," she asked again, less patiently this time. "What. Does it mean?"

But the moment she said Milo's name, a barrage of images exploded inside me like a rapid slide show of the most heart-wrenchingly magnificent photos I'd never taken. His dimples. His skin. The way his eyes softened when he smiled at me. The crazy feeling of his thoughts in my mind whenever we touched. The sweetness of his lips, the heat of his body against mine...

It was then that I smelled it.

Vanilla.

Vanilla, coming from somewhere nearby.

Milo.

And Dana could no longer hold me back. In fact, as I launched myself to my feet, I knocked her onto her ass.

"Sorry," I hissed as I took off running again.

I could hear her cursing and scrambling to follow as I spotted a dark, squat building in the distance. It was a typical Florida hurricane-proof, concrete-block, fugly one-story structure, its outline illuminated by a full moon peeking through the thick branches of the banyan trees.

But as I got closer, something told me to slow down. It wasn't necessarily a danger—just a presence. I could smell it, along with Milo's familiar vanilla. And yeah. I know it sounds crazy. But I can smell things like evil and fear and anger and even love. It's one of my biggest Greater-Than skillz—being able to smell intense emotions. Frankly, I'd rather be able to burp deadly lightning bolts, but you are what you are, and that applies to Greater-Thans like me and Dana, too.

This time, though, I couldn't quite pinpoint the other non-vanilla smell. It wasn't unpleasant. It was just—*there*. And the familiarity of it, lingering around me, was irritating.

I was about to tell Dana that someone else was with Milo—but then that vanilla scent—the unmistakable, lovely, perfect scent that I *knew* belonged to my almost-too-perfect boyfriend—enveloped me like a fleece blanket around my psyche, and I was certain about the most important thing in my world at that moment.

"Milo's in there," I said, pointing at the building. "We have to get to him. *Now.*"

Dana nodded and pressed a deliberate finger against her lips, instructing immediate quiet. She then began moving closer to the structure with the stealth of a cat.

I followed alongside her, longing to simply race inside the building to where Milo most certainly was being held. I could feel him now, his presence pulling me like a rope pulls a boat to shore.

It was all I could do not to call out his name in the darkness.

But Dana kept her movements deliberate and slow, and I knew, despite everything vibrating inside of me, that this was the safest way.

Dana tapped me twice on the arm as we continued toward the building. I looked over at her, at the intensity in her eyes.

"What do you see, what do you think, what are you feeling? What should you be paying attention to?" Dana's whisper was so quiet, I wondered if maybe I was simply reading her lips instead of actually hearing her voice.

What did I see? Concentrating, I gazed ahead. The building was dumpy and gray looking, a soiled and windowless stucco mass. On the left-hand side I could see the sad remains of a fabric awning, its colors a faded candy-cane-striped pattern. Underneath it, a ledge jutted from the outside of the wall, and an ancient sign with the words "Hot Dogs 6.99" was festered and yellowed against closed aluminum.

Snack kiosk.

The side we were approaching had two open doorways, although I couldn't see inside to where they led. To bathrooms, maybe. And yes, there on the wall were the vandalized remains of the familiar signs, with the woman's icon a now-headless triangle with legs.

I squinted as we edged closer to the abandoned snack kiosk, as if somehow that would make it possible for me to see inside the building without actually *being* inside.

But while I could literally smell trouble, X-ray vision wasn't on my superpower résumé. And the visions-comma-psychic I was sometimes able to have were still about as reliable as the phone and Internet service these days—which meant they were seriously hit-or-miss. And, to make everything ten trillion times worse, I have even *more* trouble capturing important visions when I'm stressed out or scared.

Like right now. When, for all I knew, my perfect, wonderful, amazing boyfriend was in mortal danger.

Stress level on a scale of one to ten? Yeah. It was hovering between thirty-seven and thirty-eight, with occasional spikes of five million.

Dana, on the other hand? *She* had some G-T powers that could help us out. "How many people inside?" I hissed, my super-quiet whisper not quite as super-quiet as hers.

As a seasoned Greater-Than, Dana had excellent control over her unique powers—one of which was an ability to sense all of the living beings around her, both visible and hidden. Most of the time, if she focused hard enough, Dana could tell me the number and proximity of the rats in the nearby palm trees. Or of the number of bad guys in a makeshift Destiny farm. It wasn't X-ray vision, but it was pretty close.

This particular talent of Dana's had helped us out a *lot*, back when we rescued little Sasha from an Alabama Destiny farm. It wasn't foolproof, of course. There were times when Dana couldn't access her power. Like me with my fledgling psychic visions, her ability ebbed and flowed, with no clear rhyme or reason. But right now I wanted at least an *idea* about what we were fighting here… Were two bad guys holding Milo prisoner in that kiosk? Or twenty? I looked to Dana, hoping for the answer.

But she shook her head and grabbed at her temples. "I can't—" she started.

"Yes! You can. *Try!*"

"Trying." Dana shook her head. "No go."

I opened my own eyes wide and threw my palms up in the air, staring at her like maybe if I looked pissed enough she'd snap out of it and make things happen. But Dana's eyes were narrowed and intense as she nodded past me at the building that squatted in the darkness. Taking one hand, she nudged me against the side of the nearest banyan tree. It was the last large object keeping us hidden before we reached the clearing surrounding the kiosk.

It was kind of obvious that Dana wanted me to suggest a game plan.

I shrugged again, exhaling in exasperation. I didn't know. How was *I* supposed to know what to do? Dana was always the one with the plan.

But I didn't care anymore. Milo's presence here was drawing me like a magnet, and, for all I knew, he had mere moments left to live.

Dana was watching me, waiting impatiently, so I used both my pointer fingers and waved them in opposite-moving circles, to signal that Dana head to the left and me to the right. We'd check for other entrances or windows, and meet up around the other side.

It was all I had to work with. I didn't know what else we could do.

For a second, I thought about channeling my water-based tele-kinesis and overflowing the toilets inside—maybe that would make whoever was in there come running out. I could *definitely* do that, providing there was water in the long-abandoned pipes.

But it seemed like a ridiculous, stupid plan compared to actually going inside.

I didn't tell Dana this because I knew she'd think it was too dangerous and try to talk me out of it, but once she turned that corner, I was planning to say *eff it* and run right through the men's room doorway. Because I didn't care who—or what—was waiting in there anymore. All I cared about was finding Milo.

Dana looked unhappy, but she nodded, and together we backed away from the banyan tree. Her movement was still silent, but I immediately stepped on a branch. The crack underneath my sneaker might as well have been a gong, and I winced.

Dana glared at me but kept moving to the side of the building with the awning. I took several more baby steps, keeping my pace excruci-atingly slow as I pretended to angle right.

Once Dana rounded the corner and could no longer see me, I stopped crawling and started sprinting, moving like lightning toward the doorway that was now directly in front of me.

Milo. Milo. *Milo.*

"Freeze or I'll shoot you, your boyfriend, and your little dog, too!" The

distorted voice rang out—deep and authoritative, but computerized with a metallic filter. Whoever had spoken was about eight feet to the right of me.

Harmless.

It was more of a feeling than a thought, and it came to me immediately, even before I stopped and sharply turned, twisting my neck so fast that nerves shot painfully down my spine.

Shadowy shape—low, almost square, and solid.

Nope, not a threat.

All those hours of training paid off as I moved instinctively into a defensive crouch, even as I strained to see more clearly in the darkness.

Black male. Seated. Five foot eleven, one hundred sixty-four pounds. Definitely not a threat.

"Calvin?" I called out, my voice clear as a bell in the darkness.

The figure inched forward—or, I should say, *wheeled* forward—out of the shadows.

It was definitely Calvin.

"*Order me to blast him with my power!*" And *that* was Dana, rocketing herself around the corner of the building with the intensity of a SWAT team member, minus the whole humongous-gun-and-Kevlar-vest thing.

"What?" *Order* her…? And double-what because… "No, Dana, it's Cal," I told her. "It's"—I searched for the words—"*robot* Cal."

My best friend, Calvin, was wearing a ridiculous-looking padded jacket, along with a helmet that seriously resembled something Darth Vader might rock on a fashion-flunk day. His legs, bent and resting against the sides of the wheelchair, were covered in what looked to be oversized steel pants, of all things. And even though I couldn't see Cal's face, thanks to his helmet, I knew he was grinning inside that absurd costume.

I realized at that moment that if Cal was here and safe…

"That is *not* Cal!" Dana insisted as she continued barreling toward us. "That is an *evil, terrible monster!*"

I ignored her, because if *Cal* was safe… "Cal! Where's Milo? Did you already find him?" I asked, but then refused to wait another moment for an explanation. I turned and again charged toward the doorway of the snack kiosk men's room—

—and crashed directly into my perfect, wonderful, and very-much-alive-and-safe and *smiling* boyfriend.

Why was he *smiling?*

Oh my Lord you're okay you're all right oh Milo Milo Milo…

As soon as we collided, my super-special Greater-Than telepathy-with-Milo-and-only-Milo clicked on, and I felt my thoughts echoing in Milo's mind.

He'd turned the collision into a bear hug, and as he wrapped his arms around me, I felt his confusion. *Skylar, of course I'm all right. What did Dana tell you?*

I wrenched myself from the embrace to turn and glare at Dana, even as I instantly understood. This was a *training exercise?*

"Are you *kidding me?*" I said.

Dana ignored me as she stomped around and muttered choice words that started with *F* and ended in *-ing*.

11

Calvin removed his helmet. And yes. He was grinning, although his smile started to fade when he saw the thunderous expression on my face.

"Fail! *Fail*, Sky! This was *not* good!" Dana paced furiously back and forth in her bare feet as she plunged her hands through her short blond hair and glared back at me.

"*Excuse* me?" I exclaimed. "Not *good*? You got *that* right! This was not good at *all*!"

I sensed Milo directly behind me as he chimed in. "You didn't tell her this wasn't real?" he asked Dana. His voice was low, but that didn't mean he wasn't angry. The more upset Milo was, the quieter he got.

I, however, got louder. "This was really just a *game*...?"

"Of course I didn't tell her. Why would I tell her?" Dana answered Milo before she stopped pacing and planted herself directly in front of me. "This was no game, Princess. This was a test. A pop quiz."

I could feel my jaw drop. "A *pop quiz*?"

"And you flunked," Dana declared. "Miserably."

Calvin started giggling into his steel-encrusted sleeve. He always giggled when he was nervous or uncomfortable, so I forgave him.

Dana, however, was a different story. She'd gotten me out of bed with the heart-stopping news that Milo was in grave danger—to give me some kind of twisted test?

"First off"—she was still barking at me—"you didn't acknowledge your weaknesses. This was a potentially highly dangerous situation, and you know damn well you suck at stealth. And you also know that *I'm* just as capable of being stealthy as you are *not*. Yet your *master plan* had us *both* circling the building. What you *should* have done was assign the task of perimeter sneak-and-peek to *me*, while *you* stayed put, which is your best shot at staying silent—although that's questionable, too. Instead, by crashing through the brush the way you did, you put us all in harm's way. Lover-Boy included!" Dana jabbed at the air in Milo's direction.

Milo opened his mouth as if to speak.

"*Then* you didn't even stick to your shitty plan," she continued, cutting him off before he even began. "Once you went all Rambo by making a run for it like you did—which I could hear, even from around the corner, P-effing-S: you basically turned yourself into a giant target. No, not *a* target, *the* target! *You're* the target, Bubble Gum!

"That is a truth that you must never, ever forget! If and when some nasty-ass em-effers grab Milo or Calvin or your mother or the sweet little old lady who lives next door…? They're doing it to *get to you*! So what did you just do here? You put a freaking bow on your head and gave yourself to them on a silver platter, special delivery!"

"You're, um, mixing your metaphors," Calvin pointed out.

"You not only didn't stop to think about the bad guys' motives or goals"—Dana ignored him as she continued to skewer me—"but you also didn't take that butt-ugly truth a logical step further. Because if you *had*, you would've realized that if and when someone grabs Milo in order to get to you, once they have you, they're not gonna just let him go, like *thanks for your help, bro, here's money for a cab*. No! Once they get you, he's dead. So congratulations, you just killed Milo!"

She was right. To some degree. But I had to blink hard to keep my tears from escaping. I was still *that* angry that she'd let me believe that Milo was really in peril.

And I might've muttered an apology for failing her little late-night class in Abducted Boyfriend Rescue 101, if she hadn't piled on and continued her rant about everything I'd done wrong.

"And what the hell was that with Calvin anyway?" Dana huffed at me. "You just stop in the middle of a clearing"—she gestured to the open space we were standing in, between the kiosk and the jungle— "and have a *conversation* with someone who potentially wants to knock you unconscious, throw you in the trunk of their car, and take you to a Destiny farm where they'll bleed you dry?"

"I wasn't—" I started.

"He says *freeze* and you freeze?" Dana asked. "What were you thinking? *Why* were you thinking? You should've at least *tried* to blast him with your telekinesis before you even turned around!"

At this, I exploded. "That's *bullshit*!" I exclaimed, the foul word exiting my mouth like a glob of poison. "And you know it! I *knew* it was Cal!"

"His voice was disguised," she argued.

"I knew it was him," I insisted. "And yes, his being here made me a little confused, but—"

"All the more reason to send out a mental shock wave," Dana insisted. "I mean, yes, considering your limitations, it probably wouldn't've worked—"

"You seriously are on my case because I didn't hammer my *best friend* with a big ol' telekinetic left hook to the balls?" I laughed humorlessly, because last time I'd checked, Dana had been adamant about not letting me use my extremely limited water-based TK to try to move people—not even in a no-stress training session, let alone one like this. Although as I looked at Cal, I realized his robot suit wasn't just for visual effect.

He knew what I was thinking and tapped on his chest. The sound he made was similar to that of a drum kit's hi-hat. "Pretty sure this technology makes me Skylar-proof. Not only did we crash-test both the suit and the chair, but we're pretty sure *you* can't move me because you can't access the fluids in my body. The metal shields me. Neat-o, huh? The suit's just a loaner—we've got to give it back—"

"As in, we need to return the stolen goods?" I interpreted.

"Semantics," Dana said dismissively as I shook my head.

"It's not the easiest thing to move around in," Cal continued, "and I gotta admit it's toasty warm in here, but…" He shrugged as he glanced over at Dana. "Hot blond chicks can talk me into things."

That pissed me off even more. "Dana! Seriously! Did you mind-control Calvin into doing this?"

Dana shook her head. "Cal signed up willingly. The point here is that whether you knew it was Calvin or not, that was *not* the right time to stop and have a freaking chat!"

I shook my head, exhausted and angry, but also tremendously relieved. I turned to look at Milo, who was still standing slightly behind me. The important thing was that he was safe.

I didn't think the moonlight was bright enough for him to see the tears that were brimming in my eyes, but he reached out and took my hand and our connection immediately clicked on.

15

I'm so sorry. His thoughts immediately filled my mind. *I love you.*

I kind of laugh-sobbed as I nodded and squeezed his hand. *I love you, too.* I had to let go of his hand, or I would've started to cry. And I was *not* going to cry in front of Dana. She was my friend, yes, but these days she felt more like my worst frenemy.

She was still stomping around, trying to turn this farce of a so-called test into a teaching-and-learning moment. "You know, Bubble Gum, if you'd waited for me—your teammate—you could have given me the command to move him." She pitched her voice higher. "*Dana, zap the monster!* And I would've…" She nodded, her brows furrowed in concentration, and we all watched her use her powerful telekinesis to blast Calvin's chair high into the air. He whooped like he was on an amusement-park ride, and she twirled him a few times before she gently set him down on the other side of the clearing. "Done that."

"Oh, snap!" I heard Cal call from the distance. Then, "Hey, can I come back now?"

Dana's grin flashed and then faded so fast, I might not have seen it if I wasn't looking directly at her. But then she nodded again, lifting Calvin back through the air and placing him in the exact spot where he'd been before. Along with Calvin came the return of Dana's scowl, as she once again tried to stare me down.

But I held her gaze and lifted my chin as I stood my ground. The biggest *fail* here was hers. "Dana, you made me believe that Milo was in *serious* danger! I honestly thought he was going to be killed!"

"That's exactly what I was going for!" Dana insisted. "A truly emotional response from you—so that you could learn to perform under pressure. Hell, if I'd had someone train *me* this way when I was first honing my skills…? I'd be *thanking* them, not *bitching* about it."

Bitching. *Bitching?*

Once again, Milo took my hand. *She doesn't understand,* he told me through our telepathic connection. "Let's talk about this later," he told Dana, even as he silently told me, *After Lacey was taken and Dana's father was put in jail…it's been hard for her to let herself love anyone.*

He'd met Dana in a really shitty foster home when they were both in their early teens, after her dad had been convicted of brutally murdering her little sister, Lacey. But Dana had recently come to believe that Lacey was still out there, somewhere, held prisoner by horrible people but potentially still alive. And this knowledge was making her extra crazy. We were all trying to be considerate of her feelings, but tonight she'd pushed me too far. And to call *me* bitchy, to boot?

I was thinking in emotional whirlwinds rather than clear sentences, but Milo caught the gist of it anyway.

Still thoughts. He sent what had become our calming mantra back to me, even as he told Dana, "It's late. Sky needs to get some rest. We all do."

Dana looked from Milo to me to our tightly clasped hands, and she scowled. It bugged her that we could communicate this way— she said it was rude, like whispering in someone's ear at the dinner table—so we tried not to do it so blatantly in front of her.

But right now, I didn't give a crap. I held tightly to Milo as I glared back at her.

"Whatever," Dana said impatiently. Then, as she turned away, she said more quietly, "What a disappointment."

I felt a pang at that, and I realized that at least part of me felt bad about letting her down. I wanted to be a warrior—in many ways, I longed to be more like her. But at the same time, I was still so angry at what she'd done. The two feelings battled their way through my chest in the form of a solid lump that wouldn't go away no matter how hard I tried.

"Well," Cal said as Dana stomped off down the trail on the other side of the kiosk, opposite from the way we'd run in. I knew from a brief telepathic blast from Milo that Calvin's car was strategically hidden about a quarter mile away, near another hole in the fence. I also realized that Cal's robot suit really was unwieldy. He wasn't rolling along the root-covered path—Dana was using her TK to float him along behind her. He turned to look back at me. "I know it was a little too real for you, Sky, but I gotta confess, *I* had fun."

Fun? I heard myself make another one of those vaguely sob-like sounds. I was still so upset, I just wanted to get away from *everyone*. I wanted to go home so I could be completely alone to curl up in my bed and cry...

And yeah, I'd sent that thought straight to Milo. I felt him realize that I'd lumped him in with the generic "everyone" I wanted to get away from, and then I caught a very solid wave of his own distress. *Skylar, if I'd known she wasn't going to tell you this was just a training exercise, I never would have agreed—*

I know, I thought over him. *I really do know that. I was just so scared—I don't know what I'd do if I lost you.*

Holy crap, had I actually thought that aloud? Well, no, of course not aloud, but I'd certainly expressed my feelings in an orderly, easy-to-understand sentence with a verb and a noun, instead of the messy and wonderful wave of emotion that Milo and I swirled around in when we shared our precious and too-infrequent private time.

I pulled my hand away from him to cut our connection. I didn't want to be *that* girlfriend, needy and terrified, desperately clingy and relentlessly weepy.

But Milo's eyes were intense as he grabbed my other hand and stopped to pull me gently in front of him. We stood facing each other for a moment as he held my gaze. *You will never. Ever. Lose me. I promise.*

You can't promise that, I told him, fighting to keep my tears from escaping. But I couldn't do it. I could feel them start to roll down my cheeks. If Dana were there, she'd have been yelling "Fail! Fail!"

Yeah, Milo told me. *I can.*

I shook my head. He couldn't promise that the same way *I* couldn't promise that someday *I* wouldn't be grabbed and made to disappear the way that Dana's sister, Lacey, had. I was a Greater-Than, as were both Dana and Lacey, and there were lots of very bad people out there. People who would harm and enslave us, and use our blood to make a dangerous and addictive drug called Destiny—if they discovered our powers.

I would find you, Milo told me as we stood there in the silence of the night. *You know that, right? If they take you, I will find you.*

His face hardened, and I couldn't help but shiver. My boyfriend was sweet and gentle—with me. But he'd survived a terrible childhood that I still didn't know all that much about. Somehow, despite our telepathy, he managed to keep those thoughts and memories walled off from me.

He added, *But no one's taking you anywhere. As long as I draw breath, I won't let that happen. That I can promise you, Sky.*

And *that* I believed. Milo would fight to the death to protect me. And to protect Dana, too.

She'd vanished down the trail with Cal, but now she backtracked and tossed a key ring with a jangle and a thump into the dirt at our feet.

It startled me, and I jumped apart from Milo, quickly wiping any traces of tears from my face.

But Dana had already turned and started walking away. "Take her home on my bike," she commanded gruffly, and then vanished again into the shadows. She didn't bother to ask if I remembered where we'd left her motorcycle. She knew that I did. She also knew that I hated riding it, even with my arms wrapped around Milo's waist. The only thing that had gotten me on it earlier was my need to find him as quickly as possible.

"Shit," I muttered.

As we both looked down at Dana's keys gleaming in the moonlight, a breeze swept Milo's long hair into his angular face—a beautiful face so familiar and dear to me, even though we hadn't really known each other all that long. He pushed his hair back and pulled me into another embrace as he smiled at me—just enough to make his dimples appear.

I'll walk you home, he told me. *And come back later for the bike.*

It would take us an hour to get to my house on foot, another hour for him to get back here…

It's okay.

And despite all of the craziness of the past few hours, and all of the craziness that had occurred in my life before tonight—and there had been a *crap*load of crazy in my seventeen years so far on planet Earth—despite all of that, I knew that as long as Milo was with me, it *was* okay. It was and it would be.

So I took a deep breath, pulled Milo with me into the shadows of that fugly snack kiosk, and kissed him with all the passion of a girl who'd just thought the love of her life had come back from the dead.

Little did I know that this latest deadly round of craziness was only just beginning.

CHAPTER TWO

"We need to load up on ammo before we start this party," Cal said as he steered his car into the gas-station parking lot.

"Good call," I agreed, glancing into the backseat at the collection of multicolored water pistols stacked in an ungraceful pile. Only a few of the guns were filled, but I could hear the water sloshing around inside the plastic as Calvin went over a speed bump and then turned his car into a parking spot near the pay machine for the water hose. "I mean, even if our weapons *are* more Fisher-Price than Smith & Wesson."

"Girl, it's far less to do with the weapon and more with the person wielding it." Cal nodded to me, since I was the person who'd be doing any wielding. "Plus you've always got the advantage, 'cause no one knows who they're dealing with until it's too late." He gave me his best super-villain cackle as he tried to smile ominously, but it just turned into one of his world-famous toothy grins.

I responded with a snort. "Yeah. Right. I'm *soooo* deadly."

I'd learned a few months ago, the hard way, that the objects I could move with my mind had to have a high water content, or no go. I could move people, true, but only if I imagined them as walking sacks of H2O, which wasn't always easy to do.

Which was why, even though Cal and I were both still tired from last night's training-exercise-slash-disaster, and even though our private school was out for three whole weeks of winter vacation, we'd both gotten up at our usual way-too-early time to train.

Every morning before dawn, even on school days, Cal helped by standing guard while I worked out my Greater-Than skills, which included running superfast and practicing control over my limited telekinesis.

And because that training involved what Calvin referred to as *cah-razy shee-it* like running three-minute miles while keeping the waves at the beach from reaching the shore, I had to be careful to train privately, in a secluded place where no one could see me and start shrieking, *Look at the freak!*

Dana had been right about at least one thing last night. There were plenty of nasty-ass bad people living in this broken-down, messed-up world who would come after me if they found out I was a G-T with super abilities.

And she was also right about the fact that they would hurt or even kill my family and friends to get to me and my Greater-Than super-blood. And that scared me most of all.

I had to be ready for anything and hone my powers to the best of my still sadly limited abilities.

So, Cal and I had done our training thing this morning as usual, then gone home and showered. We now were on the verge of heading out of our wealthy, gated community of Coconut Key, in southwest Florida, and into the destitution of neighboring Harrisburg.

We were scheduled to meet Dana and Milo near the old Lenox Hotel at eleven o'clock, which meant we had to be relatively swift with our "ammo resupply."

That was why I looked over as Calvin hit the button to unlock his car door.

"Hey. I wouldn't complain if I were you," he told me. "Your abilities are greater than any normie around...and way more impressive than anything *I* could ever do." He glanced pointedly down at his wheelchair-bound legs. "Anyway, Dana's gonna be there, so refilling the guns is really just a precaution."

But as last night had reminded me all too well, Dana wasn't infallible. "Don't you mean *your High Goddess Dana the Magnificent?* She of pure sexy sexiness, for whom you, her lowly minion, would gladly lay down your life?" I teased him, adding, "I got this." Meaning, no need for him to take the time to get out of the car.

But Cal pressed another button, and the wheelchair ramp slid out from the driver's side, gently nudging his chair out of the car and onto the ground. "*Lowly minion* sounds about right," he said with a grimace that made me realize I'd struck a nerve. "Fill 'er up. I'm getting the *other* ammo." He nodded toward the store's adjoining CoffeeBoy.

I didn't know what to say. "You're not anyone's minion," I blurted as he started to wheel away. Although we didn't talk about it all that often, I knew he had a huge crush on Dana, but he was convinced she'd never go for a guy in a wheelchair. "I was just kidding. You know that, right?"

"Just a normie," he agreed. As usual, he refused to get too serious. "With a caffeine addiction. Who desperately needs a little java mojo to be alert. Quicker reaction time and all." Cal sliced through the air with a stiff palm, ninja style.

"Just go." I waved impatiently for him to continue toward his beloved CoffeeBoy. "Hurry." But I also smiled despite myself. "Goofball," I added.

"I heard that, even with my incredibly average normie ears," Cal called out gleefully without turning around as he wheeled through the entrance.

I opened up the back door to Cal's car, picking up the first plastic gun in the pile. It was the size of a double-barreled shotgun—the kind I pictured being used by old men who lived in log cabins as they "greeted" intruders at their door. Except this particular shotgun was neon pink. It was also made from the same kind of thick, dorky plastic as my mom's lunch Thermos.

A lethal weapon, clearly.

But I ran my debit card through the water machine, punching in a full gallon purchase, and filled its holding tank. I put it back in Cal's car, then started filling the next—an orange power blaster.

As much as I rolled my eyes over our colorful arsenal, I felt more secure venturing out of Cal's car and onto the streets of Harrisburg with a pair of these babies cradled in my arms. I'd learned to use my TK to provide significant velocity to the water that shot out when I pulled the triggers. That, plus my rapidly improving aim, could send a blast of water at an unfriendly's head, knocking him down so that we could run away.

The truth was, I didn't like going into Harrisburg. It was dangerous and depressing. And Dana had been going there, day in and day out, for the past few months. She'd been trolling the crumbling streets, searching for any and all information about the Coconut Key connection to the Destiny farms in Alabama where we'd found and rescued Sasha.

As I filled gun after gun—buying a second and then a third gallon of water—I thought about how much my life had changed since that night last autumn when Sasha's mother had pounded on my front door, desperate because her daughter had gone missing. I'd babysat for Sasha at least once a week, and I loved that little girl. In fact, I loved her entire family—Sasha's mom and dad were both warm and wonderful people. And I still don't know if it was sheer coincidence or somehow connected to my feelings of grief and loss, but at the same time Sasha went missing, my Greater-Than powers had begun to awaken.

Yeah, *that* had been weird.

But just a few days after Sasha was snatched from her bed, the police found blood in the back of her father's truck. There was so much blood that the little girl was immediately presumed dead, and her own dad was arrested for a murder that I *knew* he didn't commit.

It was right around then that Cal and I first met Dana and Milo. They'd come into town because they'd heard about Sasha's kidnapping— because Dana's own little sister, Lacey, had been similarly kidnapped and presumed dead, *her* blood found in the back of *their* father's truck. The parallels were striking—right down to Dana's unswerving belief that her dad had been framed and was on death row for a crime that, like Sasha's dad, he couldn't possibly have committed.

Dana told me that someone—*someones*—were kidnapping special little girls like Sasha and Lacey—and even older girls like Dana and me. Those very nasty people held girls captive in so-called "farms" where they stole our very special blood and used it to cook a dangerous drug nicknamed Destiny.

Last fall, even though Sasha had been declared dead, I remained convinced that she was still alive and out there *somewhere*. We finally used my Greater-Than psychic homing ability—the same power I'd used to find Milo last night—to lead us to little Sasha. It pulled us north, all the way to Alabama, where we found her chained up in a barn along with twenty other girls. Sasha was battered and abused but still alive.

And—this is the part that's both wonderful and awful—when Dana used her G-T powers to break Sasha's chains, the little girl had looked up at her and called her by Dana's little sister's name: *Lacey*.

We never got to question Sasha because she immediately went into shock and started to scream. Dana mind-controlled her back to sleep, and the next time Sasha awoke, she had no memory of *any* of it. No recollection of the entire terrible ordeal—or of meeting Dana's long-missing sister.

But Dana now had hope that Lacey was still alive, that her little sister was still out there, somewhere, like Sasha had been, even after all these long years since she'd vanished. And Dana was doing her damnedest to track down any possible clues to try to find her. And Cal, Milo, and I were doing *our* damnedest to help. If that meant going into Harrisburg, we'd go into Harrisburg, whether we liked it or not.

I finished filling a blue plastic pistol and was reaching into Cal's backseat for an identical green one when a voice startled me.

"What *are* you doing?"

I jumped and hit my head against the inside frame of the car door. "*Ow!*"

"I've been standing here, watching you for a while, and I just can't figure it out." The voice came from behind me, clear and deep and disturbingly familiar. "I keep thinking you and Williams both come from money. If you're looking to war-game or play whatever the hell you're going to play, you *should* be able to afford paint guns. I mean, they're just *not* that expensive."

It was Garrett Hathaway.

As in *the* Garrett Hathaway who had claimed his spot at the tippy-top of my ish list, mainly because he had proactively, albeit quietly, tortured "Williams," a.k.a. Calvin, for years.

Yes, it was the same douche-tastic Garrett Hathaway who had hit on me relentlessly a few months ago—mostly to piss off Calvin, but also because he truly believed that all he had do to was point his finger, and whatever girl he wanted would fall at his feet. I could tell that he still didn't quite believe that I'd turned down the fantastic opportunity to sleep with him. He was rich; he was tall, dark, and handsome; he was a football player and insanely popular—*and* he was an incredible douche.

He stood in front of me now with his blue eyes, his ever-present spray tan, and his rippling muscles. Beneath his football jacket, he wore a snug-fitting designer T-shirt that probably cost more than most Harrisburg residents' entire annual salaries.

As usual, I wasn't impressed.

And since I'd managed to whack my temple on the door frame of the car, Garrett was no longer just a pain in my ass; he was also a pain in my head.

"You've got to be kidding me," I muttered as I focused on finishing the task at hand. Cal and I needed to hit the road sooner rather than later. Dana wasn't exactly a patient soul in the best of times, and in her current searching-for-Lacey state, she'd be really unhappy if we were late for our date in Harrisburg.

"Are you and the Cal-ster going gunning for old people down by the duck pond?" Garrett asked. "I did that once—it was awesome." He held up his hands as if to block his head as he did a quavering and insulting imitation of an elderly woman. "*No, no, I just had my hair done!* Today would be super-diabolical because it's so cold."

"Oh Lord," I said. "No, we're not gunning for little old ladies." But I was standing there with a neon water gun in my hand, and it occurred to me how absurd I probably looked. Especially since Garrett was right—it was cold today, for Florida. This morning we'd been hit with a front, bringing the temperature down into the fifties. It definitely wasn't Arctic—having lived for most of my life in New England,

I knew what cold *really* was—but even in my fleece hoodie, I felt chilly. It *was* a decidedly weird day for the most epic of epic water gun attacks that Garrett clearly believed Cal and I were on the verge of perpetrating.

Garrett's smirk was enough to bring my irritation to a semi-boil, and I felt my cheeks heat up. Maybe I wasn't so cold after all.

"So, you're filling that Super Soaker to…?" He let his voice trail off.

I had nothing—no reason, no excuse—to give him, so I stood there silently, just staring at him.

It's possible he thought I was speechless from his hotness, because his smile turned a little too *I know you want me*, and then he ran his hand through his perfect hair in a move that made his muscles flex.

"Ew!" I said it aloud even as Calvin saved me.

"Car radiator has the tendency to overheat," he told Garrett flatly as he wheeled up. "Water bottle I was using sprang a leak. Needed something to put water in, and these were in the garage."

He'd returned from the 'Boy with an extra-large travel mug of coffee steaming in his chair's cup holder. As I sent him a silent thanks, he shot me back a WTF look.

I shook my head. I had no idea why Garrett had stopped to chat. His car was parked on the other side of the lot—he must've pulled in while Cal was in the CoffeeBoy and I was busy with the water machine. I definitely would've noticed if the midlife-crisis-mobile that he drove—his plastic surgeon father's sports car—had been parked there when we'd arrived.

I did know, however, that I needed a confrontation between Garrett and Cal about as much as I needed a hole in the head.

"Oh! Hey, Cal," Garrett said nonchalantly, as if he were greeting a casual acquaintance he hadn't seen in a while, instead of a victim of his relentless bullying. "'Sup, bro?"

Calvin rolled his chair right between Garrett and me, moving fast enough that Garrett needed to take a quick step back to avoid getting his designer sneakers smushed. "'*Sup?*" Cal repeated disbelievingly. He chuckled. "Right. Okay. *Bro.* Sky? You about ready to get going?"

"Yup." I stashed the last water gun in the backseat and closed the door. The machine still owed me a few more cups of water that I'd already paid for, but I was willing to forfeit that in order to get away from here as quickly as possible.

"Where are you guys headed?" Garrett asked. His tone was weird. Something about Garrett being here at *all* was just off. He suddenly both looked and sounded less certain, like he was maybe going to ask if he could hang out with us.

I checked the sky for the coming apocalypse—negative, the world was still turning—and then went point-blank. "Aren't you supposed to be on some fabulous vacation right now? In some fabulous, far-off land?" Before we left school for the Christmas break, he'd made sure everyone had heard about his impending Swiss mountain getaway. I'd applauded the news—the farther Garrett was from Coconut Key, the better, as far as I was concerned.

Calvin rolled his eyes, clearly disinterested in Garrett's answer. He beeped open his car door and lined his chair up with the ramp that would pull him behind the wheel. "Girl, we need to get going, for real. Dana's going to be pissed if we're late."

31

"Wait. Dana, as in that hot-ass blonde with the leather?" Garrett cracked an obnoxious grin. And, just like that, we were back in familiar douche territory.

Cal gave Garrett his own obnoxious smile—which was really more like a hundred-watt expression of joy. "As in that *hot-ass blonde with the leather* who couldn't keep her hands off me at *your* party?" Some months ago, Dana had blown Garrett's tiny mind by pretending to be Cal's girlfriend, which had been epic to watch, but probably even more epic from Cal's perspective. He continued, "The *hot-ass blonde* who referred to you as *Tic-Tac dick*? Oh yes. *That* Dana. Yup."

I laughed. Our leather-clad Greater-Than friend's ability to be insultingly blunt in her brush-offs was an art form, and it was clear that hanging out with Dana was wearing off on Cal in an awesome way.

I waited for Garrett to try to put Cal in his place with a typically dick-ish response. Truth be told, the real whopper insults toward Cal were usually administered when Garrett thought no one was around to hear them. But bullies like Garrett didn't pull punches, especially when cornered.

The weird thing, though? When I looked over at Garrett's spray-tanned face, I saw nothing except an intensely grave, almost *humble* expression. And then, unbelievably, he nodded. "Yeah, man," he said. "Listen. About that. About everything. I just… Well, I wanted to say sorry, is all."

I think Calvin's jaw made a little clunking sound when it hit the ground. He was that surprised.

My mouth hung open as well. "Wait. *What?*" I said. "Did you just *apologize*? To *Calvin*?"

"Listen," Garrett said, and nodded his head some more, staring first at his sneakers and then up at Calvin. "I've been a real dick to you. I know that, and I *am* sorry." His hands were shoved into the pockets of his football jacket, shoulders hunched like he was freezing. But it wasn't *that* cold outside. The language of Garrett's whole body was humble. Meek.

Like he actually felt *bad* about all that crap he'd done.

I wasn't exactly buying anything that Garrett was selling, though. He wanted something from us. But what?

Garrett turned to me. "I also want to apologize to you, Sky. I've really been—"

"A total giant douche?" I finished his thought.

Garrett nodded miserably.

Calvin had finally picked his jaw up off the ground. He engaged his ramp, and his chair went up and into the car. "Well, awesome. Kumbaya and yippee-ki-yay! We still need to get going. Dana's waiting."

"Wait!" Garrett exclaimed. "I just… Can I talk to you guys for a second?"

Cal started the car as he shot me a look. "Another time, man, all right?"

I was about to get into the passenger side when Garrett kinda exploded. "*No!* This can't wait!" He actually threw his hands in the air in exasperation, which was such a strange posture for him, I wished I had my phone out to take a photo for posterity. "Look! I didn't follow you guys out to this sketchy-ass CoffeeBoy gas station for nothing! I *really* need your help! *Please!*"

"Wait. *Follow* us?" I narrowed my eyes as I stood there, looking at him over the top of Garrett's car.

Garrett, genius that he was, realized he'd said too much, and his face flushed with color. "Well, I mean… Let me start over—"

"No," I said, pointing a finger at him. "You said you *followed* us here. Why are you following us? And don't even *try* pretending that you wanted to apologize."

"Look," Garrett said again, playing it cool and failing. He couldn't have appeared guiltier if he'd actively tried. "I can explain everything."

"No time," Cal said without hesitation. "Call my assistant, Jane, at 555-Screw-you. She'll set up an appointment for… Hmmm, how's never? Does never work for you?"

It was an old and tired joke, but Calvin's delivery was pretty damn awesome, and I couldn't help but laugh as I climbed into the car.

But Garrett opened the back door and got in, too, pushing aside the water guns to make room. "Just—let me ride with you, wherever you're going, it doesn't matter, and I'll explain." And then he repeated that word I thought I'd never hear from his entitled lips. "*Please.*"

As I looked back at Garrett, I saw tight desperation on his usually too-cool-to-care face. I could smell Calvin's surprise, and then I caught a whiff of something else, too.

It was that god-awful fish smell. The smell of all-encompassing fear.

Yes. As I've mentioned, one of my unique *skills* as a Greater-Than, besides being able to move water around with my mind, is my ability to smell emotions. And yes again. It sounds crazy. But it's not made up. It's a thing.

I narrowed my eyes at Garrett again, because that fishy smell was emanating from his pores like stale BO. He was scared about something. But his fear smelled slightly different than what I thought of as the usual nasty dead-fish *Help, Mommy, I'm gonna die* smell that most people gave off when under duress. Garrett's fear had an overtone of lemon to it, which made it oddly less awful.

I realized that although Garrett was definitely scared about something, he wasn't scared for himself. He was scared for someone else. That was new. And he wasn't joking around. He *really* wanted our help.

"All right," I said. I looked at Cal. "Drive."

"Sky!" Cal scoffed. "For real?"

"You'll have about ten minutes," I informed Garrett. "Fifteen tops."

He was already nodding. "Okay. Yeah. I think I can—"

"Giiiiiirl," Cal growled warningly through clenched teeth. "What the fuuuuuh." He silently mouthed the words, "Dana's gonna shit monkeys if we show up with McDouche in the car."

"We'll get rid of him before that," I said aloud then turned to tell Garrett, "FYI, we're gonna drop you at the Sav'A'Buck. You'll have to find your way home from there."

That gave Garrett pause. "The *Sav'A'Buck*," he repeated incredulously. "You mean, in freaking Harrisburg?"

"In mother-freaking Harrisburg," I confirmed. "Or you can get out now."

Garrett looked from me to Cal, who was glaring at him in his rearview mirror, and swallowed hard. And now I smelled a more regular fish scent. Garrett was afraid of going to Harrisburg. Who wouldn't be? It was a dangerous place.

"Do I need to count to three?" I said. "One…"

I smelled that lemony smell again as he finally squared his football-player shoulders and simultaneously shook his head *and* nodded. I realized his concern for someone else—I couldn't wait to find out who—trumped his fear for his own safety.

"Okay," he said. "You can drop me at the Sav'A'Buck."

"Go," I ordered Cal, who grimly used his hand-controls to jerk his car into gear. He came the closest that he'd ever come to peeling out of the parking lot as I turned back to Garrett and tapped my watch. "Talk. Fast."

CHAPTER THREE

"My dad's latest girlfriend," Garrett said as we pulled onto the interstate heading for Harrisburg, "has a daughter named Jilly, who's kind of a freak show, and I think maybe Rochelle, her mother—you know, my dad's girlfriend? I think Rochelle did something bad to Jilly, because Jilly's just, like, gone. You know?"

I nodded. I got it, but what I didn't understand was what this Jilly girl being gone had to do with Calvin and me.

Garrett continued. "And it's doubly weird, because for the first, I don't know, five months that Rochelle dated my dad—her name's really Rachel, but she calls herself Rochelle, and I think it's because she thinks sounding French makes her hotter, and she *is* pretty hot for, like, a forty-year-old or whatever—"

It's possible my snort of disdain or maybe the expression of incredulity on my face got Garrett back on track.

"But see, the weirdness is that Rochelle didn't even mention she had a daughter until, like, I don't know, maybe a month or two ago, when she suddenly went up north and then came back with Jilly in tow. Like, here's my daughter, *boom*," Garrett told us. "It was freaking bizarre. And now, again, *boom*, Jilly's just gone."

"Maybe she went back north," I suggested. "If she was living there with her dad—"

"Yeah, no. She told me she was staying here in Florida," Garrett insisted. "That she was here for like forever—and believe me, she wasn't happy about that. And her crap's still scattered all around Rochelle's living room—she rents a beach house not too far from ours."

Garrett's dad's "beach house" was a castle at the water's edge in one of the extra-wealthy parts of Coconut Key. I glanced over to meet Cal's eyes, and the look he was giving me was pure *I can't even*.

"Maybe Jilly's super-rich," I suggested, "and she just left it all behind."

"No." Again Garrett was absolute. "She told me her dad didn't have any money—none. That's why she was living with Rochelle. Who calls their mom by her first name, anyway? And I know for a fact that Rochelle herself doesn't have a lot of cash. She's been sponging off my dad from day one—and it's gotten way worse. Remember how we were supposed to go skiing in the Alps? That shit got canceled because Dad just ran away to some weeklong medical conference up in New York—which is step one when it comes to jettisoning his girlfriend. Step two will be when he finds a reason to not come home. I'm pretty sure there's a trip to LA or Houston in his immediate future, during which Rochelle will discover that the credit card he gave her doesn't work anymore."

"Nice," Calvin murmured. "The stealth breakup approach."

Garrett missed that Cal's words dripped with sarcasm, and heartily agreed. "It's definitely easier that way, especially when the GF's crazy, and my dad *does* go for the extra-crazy. Anyway, before he left, I heard them fighting about money, and it was ugly. I'm not completely sure what happened, but I think Ro used his credit card for drugs, but I don't know for sure, 'cause she never seems strung out or high.

"In fact, ever since she brought Jilly home, she's been looking, I don't know, *better*? Weirdly younger and even hotter, like she's been taking Botox on steroids, but it's not just her face; it's her…" Garrett held out both hands, cupping them in front of him, making the international asshole's symbol for a woman's breasts. "But her bitchiness seems to be increasing, too. Radically."

I glanced at Calvin again. I had a bad feeling about this, a seriously bad feeling. It sounded a lot like Rochelle was, in fact, on drugs.

Cal knew exactly what I was thinking, and as he met my gaze he nodded.

Destiny. Rochelle sounded an awful lot like a Destiny addict, since the drug's biggest side effect was that it made its users literally younger. And no wonder she and Garrett's dad had fought about money. Destiny was insanely expensive. Even the cheapest, nastiest, impure Street D was thousands of dollars for a single dose. And the designer boutique version of the drug could run close to five figures. I'd heard that some heavy users needed an injection more than once a week.

"And *then*?" Garrett continued. "This is pretty crazy, so get ready."

"Ready," Cal said from the front seat. He'd ditched any and all sarcasm and was listening intently as he drove.

"I went over to her place after my dad left for New York," Garrett told us, "and Rochelle answers the door and I'm like, *Hey, Ro, I'm looking for Jilly*, and she goes, *I'm sorry, who?*" He falsettoed what had to be a terrible imitation of his dad's soon-to-be ex-girlfriend. "And I go, *Jilly? Your daughter?* And she starts laughing, like *Ha-ha-ha-ha! Oh my goodness, you thought Jilly was* my *daughter? She's my older sister's daughter. I'm* much *too young to have a daughter Jilly's age! Did you honestly think I had her when I was ten?* I was so freaked out that I just left, because I swear, she introduced Jilly to me and Dad as her daughter. *Her* daughter. I heard her say it. I know this."

"How old's Jilly?" Cal asked, looking back at Garrett in his rearview.

Garrett cleared his throat. "Fifteen."

That throat-clear meant something to Calvin that I didn't pick up, because it made him laugh a little, and not because he thought it was funny. His next question took me by surprise. "You doing her?"

"What? Jilly? *No! God!*" Garrett's indignation was over the top, and I suspected that he was way more into the girl than he was willing to admit. "She's fifteen! Besides, she's not... She's..."

"A freak show?" I finished for him, repeating his own words.

"Well, yeah," Garrett said.

"What does that even mean, *freak show*?" I asked.

"I don't know," Garrett said, and it was obvious he was lying. It was clear that he thought both Calvin and I were *freak shows*, too, and he was nervous about insulting us—which might've been a first for him. "I guess it's because, she's, you know, all punk and emo? First her hair's green and then it's purple. And she wears these weird sunglasses, and God, the music she listens to." He made a face like he'd just tasted bad milk. "It's bad. Like, screaming angry-girl rock. And…" He shook his head.

"And what?" Calvin pushed. There was definitely something Garrett wasn't telling us.

"Well—she's creepy. Like, instead of watching TV and stuff like normal people do, she sits around with her e-reader all day and actually uses it to read instead of play games. Who does that? And then, even the *books* she chooses are weird! Like, a few weeks ago, she and Rochelle were over at the house, I was on my way to take a piss, and before I got to the bathroom, I read a couple lines over her shoulder, just to see what the hell. And she was deep into this story about a beating heart under the floorboards. How spooky is *that*?"

So the girl liked to read Poe and dye her hair different colors. Jilly actually sounded way cooler than Garrett would ever be—in fact, I already really liked the girl. But Garrett was still clearly leaving information out.

"All right, doooode." I knew Cal had started to say *douche* but then changed it last minute to *dude*, in an attempt to be diplomatic. "Seriously. It's time to get to the part that you *really* want to tell us about."

Garrett sighed deeply. "See, I promised her I wouldn't tell anyone."

Who would've believed it? Garrett McDouche Hathaway was reluctant to break a promise. Maybe there *was* hope for him yet.

"If she's really missing," I told him as Calvin took the ramp for Harrisburg. We were almost out of time—the Sav'A'Buck was right off the exit. "Whatever this secret is might help us find her."

"Are you going to help me?" Garrett said eagerly, leaning forward in his seat at my inadvertent *us*. "You know. Find her? Jilly? Because I heard that you helped find that dead girl, Tasha."

"Her name is Sasha," I said wearily. "And she wasn't dead."

"And we didn't find her," Cal interjected as he braked to a stop at the end of the exit ramp. "She escaped her kidnapper and called Skylar's cell phone for help. She hid until we picked her up and brought her back home." He was sticking to our cover story—what we'd told everyone, my mom and the police included—about what had happened. Because *We used Sky's Greater-Than psychic homing superpowers to find Sasha, and then risked our lives going into battle against a giant, bat-wielding beast of a psycho-guard in order to free her and twenty other little girls* wouldn't fly, even though it was the truth.

"Yeah, well," Garrett said, "I also heard that *Sasha*"—he was careful to get her name right this time—"was kinda freaky, too. Like, um, Jilly freaky."

I shot another look at Calvin. Uh-oh.

"Because that day?" Garrett continued. "After I came back from the bathroom? I saw something deeply freaky."

My stomach did a somersault. I had a serious idea about where this was going.

"Jilly was still sitting on the couch, reading that creepy-ass story. Except, I'd left the football game on TV. She'd been complaining about how it was bugging her, it was super-distracting, whatever. And I told her to deal with it, since it's my house and stuff, and anyway, *everything* pisses her off. She was going all bitch-mode on me about how I could at least be considerate enough to turn the volume down. So I told her basically that she was SOL—"

"Shit out of luck." Calvin quietly interpreted the guy-speak for me, as if I didn't already know.

"—and to go read her creepy shit somewhere else." Garrett crossed his arms and sat back in Calvin's backseat as we pulled into the potholed parking lot of the low-end grocery store. "Anyway, I was only in the bathroom for two seconds. But as I'm walking back into the living room, the TV shuts off.

"I dunno if Jilly just didn't hear me coming—she definitely didn't *see* me at first, because the couch faces the TV and she had her back to me," Garrett continued. "But that effing TV goes black, just like that. At first I couldn't figure out how it happened, because Jilly was still sitting on the couch, and I'd put the remote way up high, on top of the entertainment center where she can't reach it since she's really short."

As Cal parked in one of the many open spots, he glanced in his rearview, his eyebrows furrowed as he listened to Garrett.

"But then I see the remote. It's fricking hovering there, right in front of the TV screen. Like, in mid-freaking-air."

I swallowed hard.

Garrett paused, and for a moment, there was silence in the car.

"So yeah," he finally said. "*That* happened. And I couldn't keep quiet. I literally said *What the eff.* And Jilly heard me and spun around on the couch, looking all terrified and shit. And when she did that, the remote *flew* from where it was hanging there in the air and went back onto the top of the TV cabinet. It freaking *flew*. And she did that. She made that happen with her freak-show mind."

"You're certain of that?" Cal asked, because I was too busy trying not to throw up.

Garrett nodded. "She said it was called telekinesis, and that it was no big deal. But then she kinda proved that it *was*, because she begged me to not tell Rochelle."

"Did you?" I asked, because *that* would certainly explain Jilly's sudden disappearance. A mother who was an addict wouldn't blink before selling her Greater-Than daughter to the nearest Destiny dealer—maybe in exchange for a half-year supply…? Oh Lord, poor Jilly!

"Hell, no," Garrett said, and I could smell that he was genuinely offended. "I was already worried that Rochelle was treating Jilly badly. I mean, yeah, she's a pain in the ass, but she's small and Ro's not, and…" He sighed. "I don't know, Jilly always pretended to be bored or tough or whatever, but I could tell from the start that she was scared of her mother or her aunt or whatever the hell. As for Rochelle, she started out a mega-bitch, and like I said, whatever yoga or Pilates workout she's doing, it's not only making her hotter, but it's making her meaner, too."

I glanced at Calvin to find him looking at me. Rochelle was *definitely* using Destiny. My heart broke for Jilly, who was probably already dead.

"So will you help me find Jilly?" Garrett asked again. He smirked a little. "Who knows, with a little luck, maybe *she'll* call your cell phone and ask to be picked up, too. Like Sasha. Right?"

I never would've thought dumb jock Garrett Hathaway would be the person to cry *bullshit* on a story that my mother and the police had swallowed whole. I was just about to deny, deny, deny, and then order him out of the car since we'd reached our designated drop-off spot, but before I could open my mouth, bullets started to fly.

CHAPTER FOUR

I wish I could say I'd never witnessed a windshield shatter before, but I'd been in a terrible car accident a few years back, so I knew exactly what it looked and sounded like.

There's a weird silence that happens immediately after something like that, in which everything seemed to occur in slo-mo. I forced my mouth to move.

"Gunshot!" I shouted, because I could see both Cal and Garrett looking wildly around, trying to process exactly what that noise was and what had just happened. "Bullet to car window! Over to the right."

The broken windshield belonged to a beat-up sedan parked two slots down from us in the Sav'A'Buck lot. Someone had fired a gun, just once, probably from somewhere near the grocery store's front doors, judging from that broken front window. Shards of glass made tinkling sounds as they careened off the front of the car and onto the pavement.

"Gunman at the store door, get down get down get down!" Calvin shouted, and I stupidly turned to look instead of diving onto the floor of his car, and he grabbed me by the shirt and yanked me down just as the shooter must've flipped the switch from *one shot* to *massacre*, and the gun began going off, popping bullets through the air.

BOOM BOOM BOOM POP BOOM!

I braced for them to hit Cal's car, covering my head as I prepared for a rain of glass, but the man with the giant gun must've been pointing it in a different direction, because I heard the ping of punctured metal and breaking glass, but it wasn't from our car.

I could hear someone screaming—high-pitched and frantic—even as Garrett yelled, "*What the fuck! What the fuck!* Calvin, drive, what the fuck!"

"Don't," I told Cal as I closed my eyes and focused on that glimpse I'd seen before he'd pulled me to relative safety.

Single gunman.

Carrying…

A *big* gun. And something else…?

I focused on calling up the image, and yes, he was carrying something under his left arm, some kind of brightly colored sack, with his assault rifle tucked into his right elbow—this tall, broad man, maybe twenty years old, buzz cut, scar above his eyebrow.

That screaming—it had been a child's voice. She was silent now, but I realized with a flash that I hadn't seen a colorful bag but instead the cheerfully patterned clothing of a little girl. That man with the gun was abducting a little girl. And I bet I knew why.

"Gimme!" I said and reached back to grab one of the water guns from beside Garrett.

"Sky!" Cal exclaimed. "Don't—"

I didn't wait to hear what he thought I shouldn't do. I'd yanked my hood up over my head, hiding my red hair and as much of my face as I could, and I was already out of the car and on the asphalt, heading toward the man who was still firing that gun. He was using it not to kill, thank goodness, but to keep the little girl's family from following him.

I could see with just one glance that she was unconscious, as he tossed her none too carefully into the passenger seat of his shiny black Bimmer.

He had a nice car. And I was pretty sure I knew how he'd paid for it—by kidnapping little girls like this one, like Sasha, too, and selling them to the Destiny makers.

Mother. Effer.

"*Hey!*" I belted out. But my voice was buried beneath the cacophony of his weapon. I had to move fast, or he was going to get into his snazzy car and that little girl would be gone.

I took a deep breath and concentrated. Water versus bullets? Not normally much of a contest there.

But I could do this.

Couldn't I?

Suddenly, I heard Dana's voice in my head, shouting *Fail! Fail! What are you doing, Bubble Gum? You have no backup, you have no plan!*

What *was* I doing? This was insane.

Still thoughts. I closed my eyes and pictured Milo. I breathed him, I felt him, I heard him. *Still thoughts, Sky. Just let it go…*

And in that moment in which I was specifically *not* thinking about what I was about to do or what the consequences would be if I failed, I felt and then saw my enormous pile of plastic water pistols—there were sixteen of them total—shoot out from the backseat of Calvin's car and through the passenger side window that I'd left open. They streamed toward me like metal particles toward a magnet.

Then, just as quickly, all but one—a little green one—swooped in front of me before lining up and hovering in midair, exactly as Jilly's remote must've hung in midair in Garrett's living room.

The little green plastic water gun zoomed over to the man with the real gun and smacked him in the face.

"What the hell…?" He fumbled his weapon as he turned to see me standing there—me and that collection of water guns—and his eyes widened.

"Holy shit, Sky!" With the noise from the assault weapon silenced, I could hear Garrett shouting, and I winced inwardly because he'd used my name.

But whatever he said next was muffled, and Cal's voice rang out instead. "Hoshitski, look out!"

It was an intentional misdirect, and I tried to stand like a Hoshitski might, no doubt surly from years of being teased. I pitched my voice lower and ordered, "Drop it! Now!"

The gunman's wide eyes narrowed, and we both knew he wasn't going to drop his weapon, so before he could turn and kill me, I let loose my TK and blasted him. All of those plastic guns shot water from their barrels with the intensity of sixteen narrow but powerful fire hoses, and it sent the man down onto the ground so hard that I heard his head as it smacked against the pavement.

The gun he'd been holding clattered to the ground.

All of my weapons ceased water-fire and dropped onto the pavement in front of the unconscious shooter.

The silence that followed was eerie. I felt a little dazed, standing there with a single, silly-looking pink water gun still in my hand, staring at the downed man and his big *real* gun, and then over at the bullet-riddled storefront of the Sav'A'Buck.

"Hey!" Calvin bellowed. "Get back in the frickin' car!"

But I wasn't done yet.

Part of my relentless training with Dana had been in the safe handling of real weapons, and I dashed over to that ginormous military assault thing (clearly I'd slept through the chapter on identification of make and model) and carefully picked it up. I knew enough to remove the magazine, and I tossed it as far as I could across the parking lot. I unloaded the round that was chambered and ready to fire, too. It sprang out and clattered onto the pavement. I kicked it under a nearby car.

I could see the frightened faces of the little girl's family as they finally dared to emerge from the Sav'A'Buck, and I shouted to them. "You're safe, she's safe, your daughter's safe. Take this weapon, you can sell it." I could tell with just a glance that these people—mother, father, older brother, and an infant—had next to nothing. They were skinny and shivering in the brisk morning air. "His car keys are probably in the front pocket of his jeans, you should take his car, too. Use it to get out of here."

The nearly kidnapped girl's brother was on the ball—his parents were still stunned. But he was maybe twelve, and he didn't hesitate;

he just reached in and found Gun Man's key ring. I spoke directly to him. "Have your mom and dad drive north. All the way to Boston, or, once you're out of Florida, head west, out to California. There are people there who can help you. But above all, make sure your sister hides her powers, do you understand me?"

The mother had started to cry as she dumped her baby into her husband's arms in order to scoop up her almost-abducted daughter from the front seat of that Bimmer and cradle her in her arms.

"He didn't hurt her too badly," I reassured them. "He needed her alive. Now, go. Don't stop, at least not until you get up to Orlando. There are places there you can sell a car like this for cash, too. No questions asked. But then get another car, a cheaper one, and keep going. Boston. Or California."

The boy nodded, and I knew at least he was paying attention.

"Come on, Hoshitski!" Cal called out, still desperately trying to keep my anonymity. "We need to *go*!"

"Keep her safe," I told the boy again.

I didn't want to leave my arsenal behind, but there was no water left in any of the plastic guns, so moving them with my TK was a no-go. I scooped up as many as I could, holding out my shirt and using it to carry them in a kind of a sling as I ran back to Cal's car.

Cal didn't wait for me to close the door. He just backed up hard with a squeal of tires, and blasted out of the parking lot, leaving the Sav'A'Buck in the dust.

———

The first few miles, we all were silent.

Cal put us on the highway, heading back to Coconut Key. Still, he kept his eyes straight ahead on the road, driving with the intensity of a first-year driver's ed student. His hands were at ten and two, his eyebrows furrowed in concentration.

I managed to slow my breathing down a little bit, after I realized that the one thing I *could* hear was the sound of my own rapid inhalations. Each time I took a breath, I heard something slosh, and I realized it was the windshield-wiper fluid under the hood of Cal's car.

I finally got myself calmed down, only to hear Garrett laughing from the backseat. Not funny-ha-ha laughing, but an occasional *heh-heh*, like he couldn't contain himself, *heh-heh-heh.*

I turned around to look at him, and he was gazing at me, his eyes very wide.

"*Heh-heh*," he said. "So what else can you do?"

Alarmed, I looked at Calvin. "Oh my God," I whispered as I realized exactly what I'd just done. "Did he see...?"

"Everything?" Calvin supplied a noun. "Oh yeah. Yup. Yes. He saw it all."

Garrett released his seat belt so that he could lean forward and drape himself over the backs of our seats. "Can you fly?" he asked. "Do you think *Jilly* can fly?"

"Oh, shit," I said to Calvin and then remembered, "Hoshitski." Would it work? When that man woke up, would he start looking for a deep-voiced thug named Hoshitski or a red-haired girl named Sky? Although, when I looked back at Garrett, I realized we had an even more immediate problem. The school himbo had witnessed my G-T powers firsthand.

"I called Dana," Cal told me. "On her burner phone." When we'd first met her, Dana didn't have a cell, but since our adventure in Alabama, she'd gotten a disposable. She didn't use it often, and she replaced it frequently. Milo got one, too. Mostly, I think, so he could text me and regularly check in. "She and Miles are gonna meet us back in Coconut Key. At the Twenty."

I nodded. The former multiplex theater at the long-deserted mall that was just on our side of the Harrisburg town line. That was where I'd first met Milo.

"God," Garrett was saying, "what I wouldn't give to have sex with a girl who can fly."

"*Ew*," I shouted. "That is not okay!"

"Are you kidding?" he said. "It would be *awesome*! Although, really, what I'd want is X-ray vision. Oh my God, do you have X-ray vision? Can you see me *naked* right *now*?"

"I'm sorry," I told him. "Did you miss the part where we were nearly killed?"

"Nope," Cal told me. "He didn't miss it. First he screamed for his mommy; then he tried to talk me into ditching you; then he started shouting your name for everyone to hear. I had to punch him in the face to shut him up."

Come to think of it, Garrett's nose *did* look a little swollen.

If it hurt, he didn't seem to care. In fact, he leaned forward, grabbing my head between his hands so that he could kiss me on the mouth.

I pulled away from his still-fishy lips. "*Ew! Stop!*"

"*Can* you fly?" he asked again. "Because I might have to propose marriage."

"No!" I tried to salvage this. "And I don't know what you *think* you saw—"

"Oh please, Skylar," Garrett said. "I saw it all. You're a superhero." He looked from me to Cal and back. "And, oh, my God, your friend Dana is, too, isn't she? You and Dana and Jilly…" He laughed. "Odds are *one* of you can fly."

I looked at Calvin, and Calvin looked at me.

I'd messed up, big-time. Rule number one of being a Greater-Than was: *Don't let anyone know.*

"How about telepathy?" Garrett was saying. "Can you read my mind? Do you know what I'm thinking? Do you?"

"That little girl," I whispered. "I couldn't not…"

Cal reached over and squeezed my hand. "I know," he said. "Dana'll fix it."

"She'll want to kill him," I said, and Garrett laughed. He thought I was kidding.

But I didn't need Dana to fix my mess. I'd gotten myself into this, and I'd get myself out. I held up my finger in warning as I turned back around to face Garrett. "Sit back," I told him. "Seat belt fastened. Now."

"Oh, yes, ma'am," he said and actually obeyed.

"Besides being stupid," Cal murmured to me, "you were also kinda badass."

I shook my head as Garrett watched me expectantly. I was grateful that my telepathy was restricted to Milo only. I honestly did not want to know what Garrett was thinking. Not now, not ever.

"You can't tell anyone what you just saw," I told Garrett. "And you can't breathe a word about what you think you saw with Jilly, or what you imagine about Dana. I will neither confirm nor deny any theories you might have, but I will tell you this. As long as you don't tell anyone what you saw—not a *soul*—then I *will* help you find Jilly."

"*We* will," Cal confirmed, glancing into his rearview mirror at Garrett.

Garrett was looking from me to the mirror and back, nodding slightly.

"Do we have a deal?" I asked. "Because you need to say it. You need to promise. You need to *swear*."

Garrett's nods turned to a head shake. "No, sorry, no deal."

"What?" Cal voiced my own stunned surprise.

"It's not a fair deal," Garrett told us. "I mean, would you take this deal if you were me?" He mocked my voice. "*I will neither confirm nor deny any theories…* That's bullshit."

I glanced at Cal. "I'm gonna let Dana kill him."

"Dana's not going to kill me," Garrett said. "She won't have to. I won't tell anyone. I'll take that part of the deal. But only if you tell me what the hell. I want info. I want explanations. Details." He smiled because he knew he had us over a barrel. "I want to know what your other superpowers are."

He didn't say it, and I didn't need Greater-Than telepathy to know what he was thinking.

Garrett McDouche Hathaway wanted to know which one of us could fly.

"You do that, as well as help me find Jilly, and I'll keep my mouth shut." He made an annoying little zipping motion across his lips and even did the whole pretend-to-throw-away-the-key thing before holding out his hand. "Do we have a deal?"

Cal made a very sad little noise as I reached out and shook Garrett's nasty hand.

I choked the word out. "Deal."

CHAPTER FIVE

Holy shit had become Garrett's catchphrase, and as we approached the old Coconut Grove Mall, he used it again and again. First, as we pulled onto the overgrown and crumbling road that led to the abandoned mega-mall, and next, as we drove around the back toward the formerly gleaming twenty-plex theater, and finally, as Calvin parked his car near a hole in the huge chain-link fence that surrounded the entire deserted mall complex.

"Aren't there, like, security guards?" Garrett asked, clearly uneasy about trespassing. Still, he followed Calvin and me, ducking to get through that upside-down-V-shaped hole in the fence. I held aside a particularly sharp and clawlike cluster of metal so it wouldn't catch on his precious letter jacket.

"They never come down here—they don't have time." Cal repeated info that Dana had told us back when he and I first came here, all those months ago. "Budget cuts limit them to about a five-second drive-by, way out on the main road."

"We've never seen a guard," I added, "all the times we've been out here. It's safe."

Relatively.

After leaving Harrisburg, we'd stopped at a gas station to refill the six water guns I'd managed to salvage, and Calvin now carried them with us, on his lap. I caught Garrett glancing down at them as he followed us across the disintegrating asphalt, and didn't miss the fact that he stepped up his pace to stay close to me.

The morning sun was bright, and it sparkled and reflected off patches of broken glass that dotted the long-deserted parking lot. When Cal and I had first come here to meet Dana and Milo, it had been late at night and very dark.

The lush tropical plants that decorated the outskirts of this formerly upscale mall had grown like mad without the squads of landscapers constantly cutting them back. Weird fingers of untamed branches and vines reached crazily for the sky. It was spooky even in the sunlight. In the hazy moonlight, it had been flat-out terrifying.

"I went to a *Firefly* marathon here when I was maybe, I dunno, twelve?" Garrett guessed as we approached the silently hulking mall. The twenty-plex entrance held the now-empty frame for a huge screen that had displayed showtimes and even previews of the films. "They showed all five of the movies in a row."

Cal nodded. "I remember that. I was still in rehab, so I couldn't go."

"Rehab?" Garrett said the word with such incredulity, I knew he was stupidly thinking of the thirty-day programs that people entered for drug or alcohol abuse.

"Physical therapy, after the accident," I corrected him, keeping the *You ignorant idiot* silent.

"Oh, right." Garrett eyed the Dumpster that sat outside the twenty-plex's heavily chained doors. He looked wary, as if someone might be hiding behind it. "I thought that happened back when he was, like, nine."

It was a too-common phenomenon that came with the chair—people talked about Cal in the third person when he was sitting right there. *He* instead of *you.* I wasn't going to do that, so I let Cal respond as I opened the doors. They were unlocked—the chains were just for show.

"He *was* nine when the gas line exploded," Cal told Garrett. "But he had a series of surgeries to attempt to repair the damage to his back until he was thirteen."

"Bummer that it didn't work, dude," Garrett said as I held open the door so Calvin could go in first.

"Who said it didn't work?" Cal glanced up at me before motoring forward, and I nodded my reassurance. Normally, we'd enter with supreme caution, but Dana had made a fresh mark on the side of that Dumpster, indicating that she and Milo were already inside. That scrape in the rust told me they'd already checked for stray squatters and had come up clean. At least in this part of the immense mall.

"Well, duh," Garrett said with all of the sensitivity of rotting road-kill as he followed Cal into the musty dimness of the lobby. His voice echoed off the graffiti-covered walls and ceiling. "If it'd worked, you'd be walking."

"If it *hadn't* worked," Cal told him, "I'd be hooked up to an oxygen tank, wearing a diaper, lying in some bed in some hospital—assuming I was even still alive. The surgery gave me back the ability to breathe

59

on my own, and a whole bunch of other handy-dandy tricks like being able to use my hands, arms, and upper body—and to control my bodily functions."

"Can you have sex?"

It was amazing. Within just a few short hours of becoming our "friend," Garrett put voice to the one question I'd never quite managed to ask Calvin.

"You don't have to answer that," I quickly interjected despite the fact that I was burning to know.

But even as Cal shook his head in disgust, he flatly responded with, "Yes, Garrett. I will be able to have sex—when the right time comes, with someone—for me, preferably a woman—that I love, cherish, and respect."

Garrett opened his mouth, but Cal cut him off.

"Don't say it," Cal warned, but we all knew what Garrett was thinking. *Wouldn't it be awesome, especially considering Calvin's limitations, if she could fly?*

I laughed despite myself, and Garrett added one of his *heh-heh-heh's* as even Cal smiled and shook his head, too.

"Could you *be* any noisier?" Dana's irritation cut through, and we all instantly sobered. We were also instantly blinded.

She was standing at the entrance to theater six and she was shining an old-school flashlight directly into our eyes.

"Sorry," I said, adding, "Do you mind?"

Dana lowered the beam to the floor in front of us, and Cal silently led the way past her and inside.

"Hi." Garrett held out his hand to Dana. "I'm—"

"I know who you are." She cut him off. "Shut up and get inside. Milo?"

"Got it. Hey, Sky." Milo appeared out of the gloom of the theater. He reached to close the door with one hand even as he briefly touched me—his hand against the side of my head, tucking my hair behind my ear. It was enough for our telepathic connection to snap on. *You're okay.* His relief was powerful, but he double-checked with a question. *Are you okay?*

I am, I told him and zapped him with a fast-forward version of the events at the Sav'A'Buck. It was meant to reassure him, like, *See how well I handled things?* But his reaction to seeing that deadly assault weapon was a rather loud *Dear God!*

"I'm okay," I told him out loud.

"She's obviously okay." Dana echoed me, her impatience evident in her tone. "Do you mind saving the big Hollywood kiss for later?"

Milo let go of me, and I sent him a rueful smile with an eye roll, but the smile he gave me back was forced, with only a flash of dimples, before he closed the theater door, leaving the boys inside and Dana and me alone in the lobby.

She stomped away from the door, gesturing impatiently for me to follow, and I silently went with her into the vandalized ladies' room. For a weird moment, it felt just like we were normal girls on an outing with our friends. Especially since Dana was wearing what I thought of as *normie clothes*—jeans, flip-flops, and a yellow Coconut Key long-sleeved T-shirt. Most of her tats were covered, and the only leather she had on was a motorcycle saddle bag that she wore over her shoulder like a purse.

Even her short blond hair, usually worn in intentionally disheveled spikes, was product free and soft around her face, making her look younger and sweeter. Her makeup, too, was intentionally muted. She wore almost none around her ice-blue eyes.

But as I watched, she set the flashlight on the edge of one of the few remaining sinks and glared at herself in the broken mirror above it. "What," she said, aiming a pointed look at me. "The hell."

"I'm sorry—" I started.

"*You* were supposed to help *me* today." Dana cut me off as she reached into her bag for a tube of hair gel. "That meeting in Harrisburg wasn't for my health, Bubble Gum. I needed you to come looking like your usual"—she gestured toward me—"Susie Goody-Two-Shoes or whatever, so that I could get this Shania girl to talk to me. Instead, she blows me off, and *then* I get a distress call from Calvin—"

"If Shania blew you off, if she didn't come to the meeting," I pointed out, "then my being there didn't matter."

"Maybe she was nearby," Dana countered, leaning in toward the mirror. With her hair back to its spiky normalcy, she began to apply her usual thick, black makeup around her eyes. The effect was striking. "Maybe she would've emerged if it hadn't been just me."

"You really think she knew something about Lacey?" I asked.

"I don't know," Dana admitted. "She was a user, but she was the closest thing to a lead I've had in weeks."

"Wait wait wait," I said. "Shania was a *Destiny* user? And you don't think she would have told you anything, any old BS, to get you to give her money? And forget about the fact that she could've jokered and killed you! Or, God, told her dealer about you!"

Destiny users are one of the biggest dangers to girls who are Greater-Thans. If we get too close, they can recognize that we're G-Ts, kind of in the same way we can tell they're users.

Dana didn't respond, which was her surly way of agreeing with me.

"You act so tough, and you're so judgmental," I continued hotly, "but you're just like me. You'll be in danger, too, if someone finds out about you!"

She stashed her makeup back in her bag and pulled off her T-shirt. She wore her standard white tank underneath it, a black bra beneath that. And when she turned to face me, all traces of Dana-the-Normie were gone. She was back to full-on kick-ass Greater-Than.

"My sister might be out there," she said flatly. "Somewhere. Still alive. And I don't have your homing skills, so I can't find her the way you found Sasha."

Dana was incredibly pessimistic, not just about our chances of finding Lacey, but of finding her still alive. *My sister might be out there* was the most optimistic language I'd ever heard her use. And that was not lost on me.

"Dana," I said helplessly. If she were anyone else, I might've moved in to hug her reassuringly, but…I'd tried homing in on Lacey, but since I'd never met her, I'd failed. Apparently I could only find someone using my G-T homing skills if I'd met them first. And even then, it didn't always work.

"But you *can* find Sasha," Dana continued. "Even though her family's in hiding—*you* can find her. And since Sasha's the one who actually saw Lacey—"

"We only *think* she saw Lacey," I countered. Unfortunately, Sasha still didn't remember anything about her abduction. Even after we'd brought her home, she'd continued to draw a complete blank about *all* of it—how she'd been kidnapped, where she'd been held, even how we'd rescued her. The one time we'd met with her and tried to gently question her, she'd gotten terribly upset and her mother had insisted that we leave.

But Dana and I had had this argument before. Dana wanted to find Sasha and question her again and, if all else failed, try to get me to use my limited telepathy to unlock her memories—and the various awful secrets that were trapped in the little girl's mind.

"It's been months," Dana pointed out. "Maybe she remembers now. Maybe it would be good for her to talk about it with someone who understands—with *you*. And if not, at least you can try to—"

"Read her mind, the way I can read Milo's?" I finished for her, because we'd already discussed this ad nauseam, too. Forget the fact that the only person on this entire planet whose mind I could read was Milo. I couldn't read Dana's mind, couldn't read Calvin's, couldn't read my mother's or the clerk's at the CoffeeBoy…

"You have a connection with Sasha," Dana argued. "You told me that she smelled that evil sewage smell up in her bedroom, while you were babysitting that time? I've been thinking about it, and I'm pretty sure the reason she could smell it was because she was touching you. That *has* to be it."

I shook my head in frustration and disbelief.

"You *have* a connection," Dana repeated. "I've been searching for months, Sky, and I've got nothing, and I'm out of ideas. And you're right—I'm taking risks that I shouldn't. Talking to addicts…" She shook her head, exhaling hard. "You're right. It's too dangerous. Sasha—and you—are my only real hope."

"Dana," I started again. I didn't want the responsibility of being Dana's only hope.

She cut me off. "Please." I'd only heard her use the p-word a handful of times in the months since we'd first met. It didn't come easy for her. But then she kind of messed it up by adding, "You owe me. After what you did today…?"

"Yeah." I got in her face. "Because *you* would've let that little girl get taken, right? You would've just stood there and let it happen." We both knew damn well that Dana would've done nothing of the sort. "I was careful. I covered my hair; I disguised my voice; I knew Cal had muddied up his license plate." We smeared dirt and mud on Cal's car's identifying plates every time we went to Harrisburg, along with loading our water guns. "We dropped disinformation," I added. "With a fake name."

"Hoshitski?" Dana asked, heavy on the *Are you effing kidding me*? "Yeah, that's awesome. That'll work to fool everyone. Especially Garrett freaking Hathaway, who is now blackmailing you into helping him to…what? Find some stupid girl he wants to sleep with?"

"I'm pretty sure Jilly is a G-T." I quickly recounted the story of the hovering TV remote.

"Better and better," Dana said darkly. "But apparently blackmail works with you, so I'm doing it, too. You want me to help you with your little Garrett McDouche problem? Fine. I'll help. But you have to help me find Sasha in return."

"I'm not sure that's technically blackmail," I started.

"Whatever," she said and took the flashlight off the sink, leading the way back out of the room. "Garrett can make it part of *his* blackmail. I'll get him to do it."

I laughed as I raced to follow her. "You wouldn't."

"Just watch me."

Dana was serious. She made a deal with Garrett right in front of me. She'd help me to help him find Jilly—but only if he pressured me into helping her locate Sasha. Which he immediately did.

"In return, I'll stay quiet about everything I've seen," Garrett promised.

"Nice," I told Dana, aware that Milo was shaking his head as he leaned against the far theater wall.

The really stupid thing was that Garrett didn't need to use blackmail to get us to help a fellow Greater-Than. Cal and I both had been willing and ready to help find Jilly from the moment Garrett had uttered the words *remote* and *hovering* and *in mid-freaking-air*.

And likewise, I was fully onboard with helping Dana find Lacey. I just wasn't convinced that re-traumatizing little Sasha was going to help. But that was a conversation we'd have again later.

Here and now, Dana was upholding the other part of our agreement by giving Garrett a crash course in both Greater-Thans and

Destiny addicts, on a "For Dummies" level. It was laden with f-bomb droppage, maybe in an attempt to connect on Garrett's level, or maybe because she was still pissed.

Just imagine the f-word inserted at every opportunity for an adjective, and in some other extra-creative places, too.

"Greater-Thans like me and Sky and presumably Jilly"—Dana was lecturing—"can naturally access more of our brains, due to an unusual enzyme in our blood. With practice, we can hone our individual talents and turn them into superpowers."

"Like flying," Garrett supplied from his seat on the bare floor. Someone had removed the rows of chairs from the theater, probably back when the mall first closed, and short metal spikes dotted the slanted concrete. He sat upright, cross-legged and alert, like the most attentive (and largest) kindergartener in the world.

"Yeah, I don't know any G-Ts who can fly." Dana dismissed that. "Although some of us can make people appear to fly." She demonstrated by picking up Calvin, chair and all, and gently whirling him across the room.

"*Heh-heh-heh*," Garrett said, springing to his feet. "Do me! Do me!"

"No one's *doing* you," Dana said with disgust.

"A warning next time, please," Cal said, motoring back to where he'd been. There was only one spot in theater six where we could sometimes get Internet access on his phone, and he was clearly using it to search for something.

"The biggest problem with being a Greater-Than," I told Garrett as he sat back down, "is that somewhere, somehow, some evil genius discovered that if they took that enzyme that's in our blood—it's actually in the blood of most girls, there's just significantly more of it in a Greater-Than—"

"With that enzyme and a bunch of other ingredients, they created a drug called oxy-clepta-di-estraphen," Dana continued, "nicknamed Destiny, which has the power to cure the most deadly forms of cancer, and return lost youth to the elderly."

"Sweet!" Garrett said.

"Including all of the ancient and gnarly twenty-five-year-olds who want to look eighteen again," I pointed out.

"Stupid people misuse just about every drug out there," Garrett argued.

"The catch here is that Destiny is instantly addictive," Cal interjected bluntly. "It's a death sentence. One injection, and you need more or you *will* die."

"It's also crazy expensive," I said. "A single dose might last anywhere from a week or two—three weeks if you're lucky—and it costs close to five thousand dollars."

"Whoa. That's harsh."

"It's more if you want the good stuff," Dana said. "And then, there's jokering."

"That doesn't sound good," Garrett said.

"Destiny users often develop some of the same superpowers that Greater-Thans have," I told him. "But it happens too fast, just *bam*, and it's too much for them. D-users lose their ability to empathize and become morally corrupt."

"They turn into crazy-ass super-villains who think they're above the law," Calvin translated for Garrett. "Sometimes it happens slowly, like with Rochelle getting hotter but meaner? And sometimes it happens suddenly—that's called *jokering*."

"A Destiny user can joker anytime," Dana explained grimly. "And when they do, they usually wreak a lot of havoc—kill their entire families, blow up buildings, take out a school bus filled with children…"

Garrett did the simple math. "So, if Rochelle's a Destiny addict…"

"We don't know that," Dana told him. "We won't know for sure. Not until we go and see her."

"But we think she is," Cal said. "I mean, honestly? While you guys were in the girls' room, Garrett was starting to tell us this story about how he heard Rochelle getting really nasty with Jilly once, calling her all kinds of names."

"She didn't know I was there, and the name-calling was off the hook," Garrett agreed. "We're talking c-word—but that wasn't the worst of it. They were in the kitchen, and Ro just starts screaming, and I heard this crashing sound, and Ro's going, *I swear, I will lock you in again, you little c-word*, and I come running, and Jilly's on the floor with all these groceries and broken bottles and shit, and I'm like, *Are you okay?* And Rochelle's all, *Ha-ha-ha-ha, silly Jilly!* She tripped, and I'm looking at Jilly, and she's already cleaning up the mess, and she's like, *Yes. Yes, I tripped. I'm so clumsy.*

"And I know she's lying, and I back off. But I ask her about it later, like, *Lock you in where?* And Jilly insists everything's okay, that it's no big deal. She tells me that *lock-in* is what Ro calls it when Jilly's grounded." He laughed ruefully. "I mean, if that

69

house had a basement, that's the first place I'd look for her. But it doesn't so…"

"It's got goddamn closets, doesn't it?" Milo spoke up for the first time in what seemed like forever. He'd been leaning against the wall, but now he'd straightened up.

We must've all turned to look at him—Milo rarely swore, and I wasn't the only one surprised by the vehemence in his usually soft voice.

He cleared his throat. "Sorry," he said. "I just… Houses have closets. That's all."

"Starting tomorrow morning, first thing, we'll stake out Rochelle's house," Dana decided. "And when she's out, and we know for sure that she'll be gone for a while, we'll go inside and look for Jilly."

"Thank you," Garrett said, and it was weird because he both looked and sounded like he meant it. But then he asked, "Do you think she's already dead? Do you think if Ro's a Destiny addict that she's already killed Jilly?"

Dana didn't pull her punch. "It's possible, yeah."

Garrett nodded, looking from her to me and back. "So, do, um, Greater-Thans ever joker?"

"No," Dana told him, but Garrett didn't look convinced.

Milo spoke up again from where he'd gone back to leaning against the wall. "If you dig around the Internet for info about G-Ts," he said in his soft, southern twang, "you'll find a bunch of frightened normies who claim that girls who are Greater-Thans lose their empathy and even their humanity. But that's just not true."

He looked directly at me and smiled, but it still felt a little forced.

70

Garrett's story about Jilly had bothered him deeply. Still, he knew that I was perpetually worried about what he called *the crap you read on the Internet.* Crap or not, I'd made him promise—no, *vow*—to stop me if I ever showed signs of losing my ability to empathize with other people.

"Speaking of digging around the Internet," Calvin said. "The police posted news on their website that a John Doe was picked up from the parking lot of the Sav'A'Buck in Harrisburg. He's been taken to Saving Grace Hospital, where he's regained consciousness but claims amnesia." He looked up, his dark brown eyes somber. "He says he doesn't know who he is or why he was lying in the parking lot."

Dana scoffed. "Amnesia my ass," she said.

"The police are keeping him in protective custody," Cal reported.

"Protective," I echoed. "Instead of arresting him...? Didn't anyone from the Sav'A'Buck see him firing that gun or trying to kidnap that girl?"

"If anyone saw it," Cal told me, "they're not admitting it. According to the police post, there were reports of shots being fired in that area, but no one from the grocery store—customers or clerks—actually saw what happened."

"Well, hallelujah for that at least," Dana said. I must've made a sound of dismay, because she added, "If they didn't see him, then they didn't see you either, Bubble Gum, and that's a good thing."

"I was kind of imagining him going to jail for, oh, I don't know, eight to ten years?" I said. "If nobody saw anything, the police will have to release him eventually, won't they?"

"So you *are* worried that he'll be able to ID you and find you," Dana countered.

"No," I said, but then admitted "yes," before quickly changing it to "maybe." I looked over at Milo. My uncertainty was usually his cue to come over, take my hand, and send me a silent but heartfelt *No one's getting near you as long as I'm around*. But he stayed leaning against the wall, and the only message he sent me was from the worry in his eyes.

"I'm putting a text alert on this story," Calvin announced. "If there's an update, like if they decide to release him, I'll know right away."

"Good," Dana said, then aimed her words at Milo. "Make sure she gets home safely." The *she* in question was me.

"I don't need to be babysat," I said quickly.

But Milo had already pushed himself up off the wall. "Nobody said anything about babysitting," he said, but he was heading for Garrett instead of me. "It can't hurt to err on the side of caution."

As I watched, Milo put his hand on Garrett's shoulder and gestured toward the theater doors. Garrett stumbled, his expensive athletic shoes catching on one of the little metal bumps that dotted the slanted floor. Milo caught Garrett's arm to keep him from falling as he moved with him toward the door. His mouth was close to Garrett's ear, and even though I couldn't hear what he was telling the football star, I suspected it was Milo's personal version of the riot act. In other words, he was letting Garrett know exactly what would happen should he accidentally let slip Dana's and my secret.

Milo's quiet intensity had scared the crap out of Garrett the first time they'd met, and it was clear that Garrett was still extremely wary of the older boy.

"I should go to the hospital," Cal suggested to Dana, even as he motored to follow Milo and Garrett, "and claim Amnesia Guy is my… Well, brother won't work. He had something of a white supremacist vibe, but—"

"Don't even think about it." She cut him off.

"It's one way to find out fast if he's lying," Cal noted. "About the amnesia."

"And if he *is* lying, and I'm sure he is," Dana argued, "then you'll have just given him another clue to help him track Hoshitski over here." She gestured to me with her head.

I held the door for Calvin, and after he went through, I stopped Dana with a hand on her arm and said, "For the record, you didn't have to use blackmail. Saying *please* and asking for my help would've been enough. I know how badly you want to find Lacey. I really do—"

"Yeah, see, with blackmail?" Dana extracted herself from my grasp. "We don't have to have *this* conversation. I want to find her. Fast. I don't have time to cry about it."

And with that, she walked away, taking her flashlight with her. I had to hurry to keep up and not be left in the dark.

CHAPTER SIX

After dropping off a very quiet and subdued Garrett at the CoffeeBoy, where his car was still parked, Milo and I asked Cal for a ride to the public beach.

Coconut Key Beach had become the unofficial spot to meet for Milo-and-me time. And, considering the day we'd had so far, I really needed some quality Milo minutes.

I knew Cal had a physical therapy appointment that afternoon—PT was a three times a week deal for him, and it would be for the rest of his life. He'd recently started lifting weights to keep his upper body healthy and strong, and it was starting to show. He'd always been wiry and strong, but now his shoulders were filling out.

"Keep your phones on," Cal warned us both as he pulled into the vacant beach parking lot. "Both your burner and your mom-phone."

"I will," I said. Because my overprotective mother sometimes tracked me via my cell phone, I'd gotten a burner like Dana's and Milo's. I'd become a pro at juggling them.

"And keep your eyes open," Calvin added.

"You, too," I said.

"Yeah, well, I'm driving, not…" He made embarrassingly loud smoochy noises.

Milo laughed as I slammed the car door closed. "Good-bye, Calvin."

But Cal rolled down the window. "How worried should we be?" he asked. "About Garrett knowing what he knows?"

"I believe him," I said. "You know, when he says that he wants to find Jilly, that he's worried about her…? He really cares about her—which is weird, I know, but he's not going to mess that up."

"I feel that he took me very seriously," Milo added.

"So…we trust him," Cal said.

"We kind of have to," I said.

"Hell just froze over. Would you rather team up with Garrett McDouche or suck the toes of a swastika-wearing neo-Nazi with a Hitler mustache and an aversion to soap and water?" He didn't wait for us to respond—he answered it himself. "A few hours ago, I probably would've at least *considered* the nasty toes thing." Cal pushed the button to send his window back up. "Eyes open," he said again before it closed and he pulled away.

"Ew," I said, watching as he drove out of the deserted beach parking lot. No one else was here. It was too cold. "That's one powerful hatred of Garrett McDouche."

"It is." Milo was laughing, and as I met his eyes, I knew what he was thinking, even before I touched him. I had kind of weird, skinny feet, but he claimed that he loved my toes. *Elegant*, he'd called them once, right before he'd kissed them. In fact, that same day he'd kissed me in a lot of unusual and interesting places. And I knew as he stood there smiling at me, hands in his pockets and shoulders hunched against the ocean breeze, that he was thinking about that, too.

We were alone at last, so I reached for Milo and he extracted a hand to intertwine his fingers with mine. And, yes, we finally shared that Hollywood kiss, as Dana had called it back in the Twenty. And no, despite Calvin's grim order, we didn't keep our eyes open.

Because sometimes you just *have* to let the entire world fade completely away.

───────

This close to the water, the breeze was relentless, and the wind chill brought the temperature down well into the low fifties. Which meant, here in Florida, that it was time to light your hair on fire and collapse sobbing on the ground before going inside to huddle beneath fleece blankets and turn on the stale-smelling electric heat.

But Milo and I didn't mind the cold. The sunlit and sparkling ocean, the cloudless blue sky, and the white sand were as gorgeous as ever. More so without the vacationing throngs to block our view. We sat on our favorite bench swing in a secluded little area that held picnic tables and ancient, boxy charcoal grills. Even though we held hands, we both just sat in companionable stillness and silence, our feet swishing back and forth as we both gently pushed the swing. But as the breeze gusted, I shivered a little bit despite my sweatshirt.

Milo peeled off his hoodie and wrapped it around my shoulders.

Won't you be cold? I asked.

His answer was immediate. *I'm good*, although I also picked up a stray thought that maybe I wasn't entirely meant to hear. *Maybe it'll help. I always run a little too hot around you...*

Is that a bad thing? I wondered as he gently ran his hands up and down my arms in an attempt to warm me more quickly.

Milo smiled ruefully and maybe even blushed a little. *Sometimes. Yeah. It can be.*

My boyfriend was impossibly handsome, especially when he was smiling. The dimples on either cheek only added to what was, in my opinion, an already perfect face.

As soon as the thought crossed my mind, I knew that Milo had caught it, too.

His smile broadened, and it's possible that he blushed again before leaning in to kiss me. But it was a quick one. He pulled away almost immediately, and although I felt a burst of that heat he'd mentioned, I caught his pointed *Got a few things to talk about* as he settled comfortably back on the bench, his arm still around me.

I nodded. The drama at the Sav'A'Buck, although I wasn't sure what more I could tell him. I certainly wasn't going to apologize for doing what we all knew was the right thing. But then my thoughts shifted to darker things, and I exhaled.

"Dana's crazier than usual," I said out loud, sending him a memory burst of the conversation I'd had with her in the movie theater bathroom. Setting up meetings with Destiny addicts? Forget about what I'd done as a knee-jerk reaction in the Sav'A'Buck parking lot. A scheduled heart-to-heart with a D-girl was *beyond* dangerous.

"I know." Milo's smile turned sad as he pushed a strand of hair back from my face. *Can't really blame her this time…*

As long as I'd known her, Dana had been intense. But last fall, when Sasha had looked up at Dana and called her by the name of her younger, long-ago-abducted-and-believed-to-be-dead sister, Lacey…

Dana's initial reaction had been one of sheer disbelief. She'd worked hard through the years to deal with the grief and the loss—and to put it behind her. But now…

She really thinks Lacey might be alive? I asked Milo. *Has she found any hard evidence?*

He shook his head. *None.* He smiled at me again. *I think she decided to go with her gut.*

Inwardly, I nodded. Greater-Than powers were so weird and mysterious, and often involved things like sometimes sensing snippets of the future. And even though Dana didn't include prescience on her personal talent list, it was a given to have faith in a G-T who was trusting her instincts.

If Dana really believes Lacey's out there, she's not going to rest until she finds her.

My thought penetrated Milo, who gazed off into the distance as he slid his hand down my arm and grabbed hold of my hand. *I know, Sky.*

She really didn't have to blackmail me to get me to help. I was still feeling wounded by that.

I know. He met my eyes. *And Dana does, too. But she knows how much you love Sasha, and she knows you don't want to bring any more trauma—even memories of trauma—into that little girl's life. If Sasha*

*gets upset by triggering her recall of her abduction, it'll be Dana's fault,
not yours.*

I shook my head. *So...you're saying that Dana's being cruel to be kind.
Maybe a little.*

*Also, this way, she doesn't have to ask for help—she just demands it. At
virtual gunpoint.*

Milo smiled. *Better than at literal gunpoint.*

I had to smile, too, but it wasn't *quite* because what he said was
ha-ha funny. We both knew that Dana was capable of making
demands at literal gunpoint.

I spoke out loud. "If Sasha was traumatized by just a few days
of being chained to a bed in a Destiny farm, isn't Lacey likely..." I
couldn't say the words, but I knew that Milo could read my thoughts.
*To be badly damaged? A little, innocent girl, held captive for years? I
mean, wouldn't she be completely traumatized?* I searched Milo's face as
he continued to focus on the shoreline.

Everyone's different, he told me. *Everyone's got their own personal
breaking point.* He glanced at me. *And she is Dana's sister.*

I forced a smile, but he wasn't fooled. He knew that I was worried
about what we might find.

We'll cross that bridge when we come to it, Milo reassured me. *Right
now we have to focus on locating and rescuing Lacey. Gotta do that before
we fix her, right?*

His thoughts blurred into more of a feeling than words—he was
thinking again about how glad he was that I was safe after today's
snafu—but somewhere in there I heard the phrase *needle in a haystack.*

He was right. Even if Sasha suddenly remembered everything about her abduction—including the exact location of where she'd seen Lacey—the odds of Dana's sister still being there were slim to needle-in-a-haystack.

I sighed because Dana was right. I was reluctant to bring turmoil back into Sasha's life. *I just don't want to make things worse for Sasha.*

What if we could make things better for Sasha? Milo asked me. And before I could ask what he meant, he explained by opening up and letting me see a memory of a recent conversation he'd had with Calvin.

It was weird how he could do that. It was kind of like he mentally lifted the lid of a closed box. I felt a sensation not unlike falling—but in a good way—as I passed through his carefully organized recall. Milo and Calvin were in the CoffeeBoy, and Cal was wearing a blue shirt. This memory was from yesterday afternoon, well before Dana's oh-dark-hundred "test."

Huh, I thought I'd gone inside the shop with them, too. No wait, this must've been when I'd hit the extremely grotty bathroom.

I focused on Milo's memory instead of mine, and as I watched, Cal leaned forward and conspiratorially said, "You know the thing I've been working on? Urban Legend Trackers R Us?"

It was weird seeing Cal through Milo's eyes and feeling the sensation of speaking through Milo's mouth as he responded with, "You mean Morgan."

As Cal nodded, I had a rush of my own memory of Cal finding information on the Internet about a legendary Greater-Than named Morgan, who apparently had world-class telepathic powers along with a crazy ability to shape-shift, if you can believe that. But she was best known for her ability to help people with PTSD—post-traumatic stress disorder. She would, supposedly, go into their minds and help them process the trauma. She was also known for helping people with repressed memories. Cal's hope was that she could two-birds-with-one-stone it and get the info about Lacey that was locked away in Sasha's mind, while simultaneously helping the little girl recover.

Dana, of course, had rolled her eyes and announced that the Great and Powerful Morgan was nothing but a myth. Cal might as well attempt to find Johnny Appleseed or the Wizard of Oz while he was at it.

Still, apparently he'd continued his quest. "I think she might be up in Tampa," he'd said to Milo in the CoffeeBoy. "And better yet, I think I've found a way to contact her. I posted this kinda cryptic message on a forum, and if I did it right, Morgan'll email me sometime in the next few days. I wanted to update you, but I don't want to tell Sky or Dana until I know for sure."

He didn't want to give you false hope, Milo interjected into the memory. *But he told me today...*

I now saw a flash of Calvin and Garrett at the movie theater, and Calvin nodding as Milo closed the door behind me and Dana, and saying briefly, "Got an email. I'm still working to verify it's really from You-know-who."

As in Morgan. But he didn't say more because Garrett was there.

Whoa. I felt Milo laughing a little as hope now literally roared through me. False or not, the idea that we could enlist the aid of another powerful G-T who'd help us find Lacey *and* heal Sasha...? That would be a win/win/win/win/win!

What it might be is a scam, Milo cautioned me. *Whoever emailed Cal might be looking to make money from just the promise of Morgan and her alleged powers.*

I know that. Still...

It might not work out, he told me.

But it might, I countered, and Milo smiled.

He was back to gazing out at the water. If I hadn't had access to his thoughts, it would have been difficult to read him, since his default expression was one of almost saintlike calm. I felt another wave—this one of gratitude—rush through me. Our telepathic connection meant that I was closer to Milo than I could otherwise ever hope to be, by a long shot. And since I'd never met another human being, besides Dana maybe, with such a huge wall built up when it came to showing emotions, this was a very precious ability.

Although, despite her tough exterior, even Dana was relatively easy to decipher. She had three basic settings that she allowed others to see: focused, semi-pissed, and flat-out furious. And it didn't take psychic powers to figure out where she was.

Milo, on the other hand, rarely exhibited any kind of anger. Still, I knew that, deep inside, there were so many complex thoughts looping through his mind. And, because of my telepathy, I now owned a precious key that allowed me access to at least a few of those hidden compartments inside him. He still managed to keep fairly large puzzle pieces from me—I wasn't quite sure how. For example, everything that had happened to him before he and Dana left their foster home and struck out on their own was a major mystery to me. There was a lot about Milo that I didn't know, even with my telepathic access key...

"An access key, huh?" Milo's spoken response was enough indication to me that when my own mind had wandered, his had followed.

It was my turn to blush. "Yeah, well. You know."

"I do," he said, smiling. "And I like that I do."

I shrugged and inhaled before beginning to more clearly explain what I'd meant.

But Milo moved faster than my words, and before I could form a single sentence, he cupped my face, leaned in, and kissed me again.

It was heaven.

There was no better word to describe it, although whenever Milo and I kissed, words were lost entirely, replaced instead by the rush of our emotions swirling together in a perfectly reciprocal pattern. It was weird and wonderful—I sometimes couldn't tell where I ended and he began.

I let him pull me closer, so I was almost sitting on his lap, and his heart beat even faster than my own. I knew this not from physical feeling but from *knowing*, from our unique connection.

I *knew*, too, in that moment—as Milo's sweet kiss continued, his hand running down the length of my side and then resting on the small of my back—that despite my sudden surge of hope, there was a deep sadness inside him today.

The moment I sensed it, I pulled away. That was always hard to do, but I wanted to gaze into his eyes. "What is it?" I asked. I reached up and held his face with both my hands.

Milo's smile was tinged with an almost-imperceptible melancholy. *It's nothing serious.* His thought was deliberate. Reassuring me. *Just... Lacey. And now this girl that Garrett's looking for...*

I nodded. *Jilly, yes.*

And there's also that little girl you saved today. It makes me crazy that you put yourself at risk, he told me, *but I'm also glad you did. Proud, too. But sometimes it seems that for every girl we save, a hundred more go missing.*

Milo exhaled loudly. He pulled me in close, his arm encircling me, so that my head rested on his shoulder. The bench swing rocked us forward and backward.

I just get sad sometimes, Sky. I wonder if what we do makes a difference. I know it's a terrible thought, but—so many G-Ts are out there being abused. Harmed. And most of them are just kids.

I was careful to keep concentrating on his thought until it was complete. I'd learned how to be polite and not interrupt—which *was* possible, even in telepathy-speak. When the last of his intentionally delivered words were through, I broadcast my own thoughts: *I get sad sometimes, too. But we have to believe that what we do makes a difference. All those girls in the barn? We made a huge difference for their families. You know? Sasha's parents. Think about how different their lives are, now that they have their daughter back again. We did that.*

Milo squeezed my shoulder. *Yes. We did. I know this. You're right.*

We're going to help Sasha even more, and we're going to find Lacey, I continued, *and everything will finally be normal and...great.*

Of course, I had no idea what *normal* would look like, other than *great.* I suspected it involved Milo and me going to prom or whatever the big school dance was called at Coconut Key Academy. It may also have included those elusive words that ended every romantic fairy tale—*and they lived happily ever after.* Dear Lord, what I'd give to live happily ever after with Milo forever at my side…

I realized with a rush of embarrassment that I'd let my mind wander again. I'd actually been imagining myself wearing a yellow ball gown like the one Belle wore in the Disney classic *Beauty and the Beast,* as I danced in the moonlight with a blue-coated and knickers-wearing Milo, his hair pulled neatly back at the nape of his neck.

Milo was back to gazing out at the water. Maybe his mind had been wandering, too, and he'd missed all of that.

Everything will be great, I thought again, and he glanced at me.

I wish this were a fairy tale, but I'm afraid it's not, Sky. It's real life.

Okay, so he *had* seen my fantasy dance in that yellow dress. I hurriedly continued: *We'll also find Jilly and we'll help her get away from Rochelle. Because that's what we do.*

Assuming, of course, that Rochelle hadn't already killed the girl. I hated to think that, but it was hard to assume Jilly was safe, considering that story Garrett had told us. The screaming in the kitchen, the broken dishes, the threats of "locking her in," whatever that meant—

Suddenly—like static interrupting a perfectly clear frequency—

A door. Slamming shut.

Darkness. Muffled yells and then crying. God, the crying…

Without warning, Milo jumped away from me, propelling himself off the bench. As our contact was broken, the sounds and image of darkness ceased. Just like that.

"Hey," I said out loud and stood up to take a step closer to a suddenly faraway Milo. "What *was* that?"

"Nothing!" Milo exclaimed with an urgent, almost-irritated tone to his voice. "It was—nothing. Sorry," he added.

"It wasn't nothing. Someone was crying. In a dark room. That was…creepy. Was that *you*? I mean, were you thinking about that?" If what I'd just heard and seen *wasn't* something Milo had been thinking, it was entirely possible that I was having some kind of psychic or prescient vision. And if I was, I needed to know.

"Yes. That was me thinking that. Sorry." Milo actually let out a nervous laugh, which was strange because I'd never heard him do that before. He crossed his arms over his chest and cleared his throat. "It must've been because…well, Dana's been downloading horror movies again, and I made the mistake of watching one with her. That must be it." He cleared his throat again. "I'm not a fan."

Dana lived on a constant diet of incredibly scary movies. And Milo was *not* a fan. He'd told me that plenty of times before. It kind of made sense.

Except that it hadn't felt like the memory of a movie. The whole thing had felt way too real.

And was it really a coincidence that I'd been sending out waves of childish Disney-prince fantasies, complete with my fairy-tale longing to live happily ever after, right before Milo took an express train trip to the nightmare-hell level of his mind?

I stood there, just looking at him, uncertain of what to say. "Sorry?"

He shook his head. "No, *I'm* sorry," he said.

I sat back down on the bench, but instead of joining me, he leaned against one of the ends of the frame that held the swing in place. He crossed one ankle over the other before he folded his arms over his chest. He was just far enough away from me so that we were easily able to talk to one another—without being close enough to touch.

"I got spooked." He attempted a joke. "Next time, I'll pick the movie and go for something a little less hardcore, like *Seven Brides for Seven Brothers*. Still terrifying in its own way, but…not…yeah."

So okay. Milo was acting super-weird, and I wasn't going to pretend otherwise.

"I also don't want to… I mean, man, all that renewed hope," he added as I struggled to understand him without having access to his thoughts. "I'm pretty discouraged," he continued. "I mean, yes, we rescued Sasha and all those girls in the barn that day, and that was a good thing. But it doesn't seem like there's an end in sight."

I didn't know what to say. I didn't want to make it all about me, but Milo's body language was weirding me out. And I couldn't help but feel as though it had absolutely nothing to do with him feeling discouraged. In fact, if anything, it felt like it had *everything* to do with me.

Had I made a mistake, maybe come on too strong with that inadvertent burst of hope that I'd hit him with—my faith that we'd help Sasha and find Lacey and even Jilly?

All that renewed hope, he'd said, like maybe it was something alien or unpleasant.

And I'd also told him how much I enjoyed having access to his secret thoughts, followed by that full-on fairy-tale fantasy filled with insane-girlfriend-type thoughts of happily-ever-afters and forever-by-my-sides.

Oh, my Lord…

"I'm sorry if I…" I started but didn't know how to finish. I wasn't quite sure what I'd done or how I could fix it, so I retreated to another simple "I'm sorry."

Milo looked at me with his intense, dark eyes. He took a deep breath in and then blew the air out slowly. I didn't need to be psychic to know that he wanted a cigarette—even though he'd quit smoking months ago. The cravings still haunted him, especially in times of stress.

"Are you out of nicotine gum?" I asked. He still hadn't kicked that part of his habit entirely, but it was much better than the alternative.

"I am," Milo said and shrugged. "It's okay."

For a moment longer, we locked eyes and said nothing. I longed to touch him. But I didn't move from the bench swing.

And he didn't move from where he stood.

"It'll be okay," I said out loud, finally. If nothing else, my words broke the silence, which had become too much for me to handle.

Milo nodded. "Yes," he said. "It will all be okay."

But for the first time since I'd met him, Milo made me feel anything but reassured.

"Come on," he said. "It's getting colder. I'll walk you home."

And he did. But he didn't reach for my hand, so I kept mine in my pockets, too, as I wondered how I could fix this—whatever this was that I'd somehow stupidly done.

CHAPTER SEVEN

"Would you rather eat fried cow eyeballs or drink a gallon of cockroach juice?" Cal asked me. He was leaning his head against the steering wheel of his car.

We were parked on the side of the road, half-hidden in the tall reeds as we staked out Rochelle's palatial "beach house," looking for any sign of her daughter-slash-niece Jilly. We'd been here since six a.m.—or as Cal called it, *the butt-crack of dawn*—and we were both feeling it.

At around ten o'clock, Rochelle had left the house, pulling out of her garage in her expensive convertible and vanishing down the street toward town. Milo had followed her on Dana's motorcycle. Meanwhile, Dana and Garrett had gone off in Garrett's car to do God knows what.

The idea that Dana was spending the day with Garrett was making Calvin cranky. Crankier, that is, than he normally might be from sitting in a car for going on eight hours now.

We'd run out of food a long time ago. Calvin now licked the inside of an empty bag of chips while moaning quietly.

I was extra cranky because Milo hadn't called. According to Dana's official plan, Cal and I were under strict orders *not* to leave the safety of Cal's car until Milo called to say the coast was clear, meaning that Rochelle had her head in a beauty parlor sink or was securely locked in a spray tanning booth. But it was fast approaching two o'clock, and Milo still hadn't called.

I checked my burner phone again—nope. No calls, no texts, no Milo. He'd been distant again this morning while we'd all shared breakfast, and I'd been using this endless stakeout to fine-tune my obsession. Why had he jumped away from me like that yesterday at the beach? And why had today's good-morning kiss ended so quickly?

"We *could* just walk down to the house, maybe peek into the windows," I started to say.

Calvin turned his head so that just his left cheek rested on the steering wheel. He lifted one eyebrow with deliberation as he glared at me. "Girrrrl, just because Rochelle McCrazypants isn't home right now doesn't mean she won't be coming home soon, and if she *is* a Destiny addict, she'll know right away that you're a G-T and she'll immediately try to suck your blood."

"She's not a vampire," I pointed out, although right now the idea of staking someone through the heart was extra appealing.

"I've been giving it some thought," Calvin countered, "as I sit here starving to death. D-addicts *are* freakily vampiric. The blood of innocents makes them stronger; they lose their souls; they're creepy as shit..."

He was being overly dramatic, but not about the *Rochelle will know right away* part. A Destiny addict *could* tell if a girl was a Greater-Than.

And vice versa. One up-close moment with Rochelle and—if she was a D-user—I'd be able to ID her, too.

Unfortunately, I hadn't gotten more than a hint of her shiny blond hair as she drove off this morning.

I aimed the binoculars again. What I was really hoping for was a glimpse of Jilly's emo-punk green-and-pink hair through one of the humongous sliders that led out onto the equally monstrous deck.

But nothing continued to move in or around the house.

I finally gave up, surrendering the last of my dignity as I tried Milo's phone again, but my call went straight to voice mail. I wrote another text: Would love a report. But then I backspaced and changed *love* to *like* before I hit Send.

Yeah. That's how inside my own head I was.

But again, all I got back was more nothing.

I was starting to worry about more than just my love life or impending lack thereof.

"Cow eyeballs or roach juice?" Calvin prompted me.

I set my phone on my lap, next to the binoculars. He'd been hitting me with Would You Rather questions all day. *Would you rather go on a stakeout or stick needles in your eyes?* was one I'd gotten more than once—and right now I wasn't in the mood. "Focus. Please. And PS, you're disgusting."

Calvin sighed mightily without moving a muscle. "I was trying *not* to focus on dying from terminal boredom. And PS, thanks for the compliment."

I matched Cal's mighty sigh and changed the subject entirely. "So when exactly were you going to tell me that you were tracking down Morgan-the-Wonder-G-T?"

He *still* didn't lift his head. "So Milo kinda sucks at keeping secrets, huh? One touch, and you instantly know everything." He made a rusty sound that might've been considered laughter among the undead. "That must be weird."

"That's not the way it works," I said, but then just shook my head. I didn't want to talk about Milo, even though I could think of little else.

Meanwhile, Calvin was waiting for me to continue. Or maybe he wasn't waiting. Maybe he'd just given up on anything ever happening. His eyes *were* starting to glaze over.

"Milo told me," I told Calvin, nudging him so that he'd snap to it and listen, "with his words, *intentionally*, that you'd gotten an email from someone that you think might be Morgan. The G-T girl who can get inside Sasha's head and help her, while also finding out what she knows about Dana's sister."

"Yeah, I dunno," Cal said listlessly. "For someone who's supposed to be like the second coming of Jesus with her super-telepathy, Morgan's kinda mercenary."

"Mercenary, as in…?"

"She charges for her services," Cal informed me. "Two fifty for a consultation, a grand for what she calls an *intervention*. That's what she would do with Sasha. And? The consultation is required before she'll do the intervention. And she's apparently scoping us out during the so-called consultation. *She* decides, *after* she takes our two hundred and fifty dollars, if she can be bothered to do the intervention."

"That's kind of…" I couldn't find the word.

"Bullshit?" Cal provided it for me. "Not just kind of. Absolutely."

"Does Dana know?" I asked as nothing continued to move in or around Rochelle's beach house.

"I told her this morning, when you and Milo were…" He made those obnoxious smooching sounds that I'd come to hate.

I socked him in the shoulder, more because Milo *hadn't* kissed me in a smoochy way. It had been more like a kiss for Great-Aunt Matilda.

"Ow!" Cal still didn't sit up. He just turned slightly and made a sad face at me.

"Milo and I were eating breakfast," I told Cal. "With Garrett."

My use of the G-word triggered even more pain than that pseudo-punch, and Cal's sad face turned tragic. "Why, oh why did Dana take *him* on her errands instead of me?"

"Probably because she didn't want to leave me alone with him," I suggested. "Which I appreciate. Also? I'm pretty sure whatever she's up to, she's paying for it with Garrett's credit card."

"Do you think they had lunch?" Cal moaned. "Someplace nice? Someplace delicious? Someplace where they'll get something to go, and bring it, here, for us to eat—and whatever you do, don't say no. Lie if you have to, but for the love of God, don't say no…"

"Yes, I think she'll bring us lunch," I obediently told him, although I had no clue if Dana would give us as much as a second thought. "So what did she say when you told her?" I added, "About Morgan?"

"She was pissed, and it got noisy," Cal said, perking up a little because Dana's creative use of f-bombs always delighted him. "She thinks Morgan isn't real."

"We pay two hundred and fifty dollars for a face-to-face, so Morgan can choose to *not* do the intervention with Sasha?" I asked. "Do *we* still think Morgan is real?"

"Our only other option is to let *you* try to surf around inside Sasha's head," Cal pointed out.

"So we need to find two hundred and fifty dollars," I concluded because we both knew that was a no-go, and we soon fell back into silence. It was possible that Calvin dozed off.

I alternated between looking at nothing through those binoculars, and watching my phone not ring.

Where *was* Milo, anyway?

And oh, yeah. Jilly. The girl who was missing. Where was she? Once we found her, we'd have Garrett out of our hair and this current awfulness could go back to normal.

"Would you rather," Cal mumbled, "have all your food smell like poop or everything you drink smell like urine?"

I had no answer. Both choices were too awful. The question was a true lose/lose.

And I realized then, with Milo acting so weirdly distant, and with Dana so frustrated and angry over our lack of leads in our search for her sister, I wasn't at all convinced that the *normal* we'd return to wouldn't be equally awful, too.

———

Milo's burner phone had died.

That's why he hadn't called.

He finally came back, roaring up the street on Dana's motorcycle, dust flying behind him as he approached, like some blockbuster movie hero.

Again, he didn't reach for me or kiss me hello after he pushed his bike into the reeds and then climbed into the backseat of Cal's car.

Of course, that might've been because I greeted him with a somewhat strident "Where have you been? Are you all right? Why didn't you call?"

"I apologize," he said as he handed his burner cell over to Cal, who was our unofficial tech expert. "When I left this morning, I had ninety percent battery and three hundred minutes left. But the first time I tried to call you, it was already dead. I'm so sorry, Sky. I didn't want to leave Rochelle."

Calvin handed the phone back to Milo. "It's dead, Jim. Looks like a case of POS-itis. You're gonna have to get a new one. Maybe go for a little *less* of a piece of shit this time?"

I exhaled hard. "Well, where's Rochelle right now? Do we have time to—"

Milo was already shaking his head no. "She stopped at the farm stand down by the public beach," he reported. "She'll be here soon."

So much for ringing her doorbell or peeking in the windows.

"We need to duck when we see her coming," Milo continued. He met my eyes. "I don't want her near you. She's definitely a Destiny addict. Her day was full trophy-spouse—tanning, facial, yoga—which

95

isn't all that different from lots of people here on Coconut Key, I know. But Garrett wasn't kidding when he said that she's mean. The way she treats other people…" He shook his head. "She's a user."

Cal and I were well aware that Destiny addicts quickly lost their humanity and empathy.

"She does have at least one friend though," Milo continued. "Someone she met for lunch over at Harbor Locke."

Harbor Locke was where the *really* rich people lived in Coconut Key— not just your average multimillion or billionaire, but full-on trillionaires.

"This woman could've been Rochelle's clone," Milo told us.

"So…another D-user," Cal concluded.

"That would be my guess," Milo said. "They had lunch there, at the club. It was all air kisses and hugs when Rochelle finally left. Happy-sounding *See you laters*."

"Did you get a name?" Cal asked.

"No, but the lunch took a full hour," Milo reported. "If it's something Rochelle does regularly…"

Then we'd have an hour to get inside her house—an hour that we *could've* used today. "When you get the new phone," I told Milo, "please also get a backup."

He smiled tightly. "I will."

"What was next in Rochelle's Very Important Day?" Calvin asked. "Maybe a stop at the local curling club or perchance a little horse dancing?"

Milo laughed. "No, but the next place she went was interesting," he told us, but then cut himself off to say, "Get down. Now."

Rochelle's car was approaching, and we all scrunched way down in our seats so Cal's car would look empty if she happened to notice it there.

But she pulled into her driveway without stopping, and I inched back up so I could watch as the automatic garage door opened. The car pulled inside, and the door went back down almost immediately.

I reached for the binoculars, hoping that she'd go into the kitchen, maybe open the sliders to allow the fresh ocean breeze into the house. It wasn't as cold today, so that was a real shot. Truth was, I was dying to get a look at her.

"Next place Rochelle went was…" Cal prompted Milo.

"A pawn shop near Harrisburg," Milo told us.

"What?" Cal said as I said, "Seriously?"

"Yes," Milo said. "She walked in wearing a lot of jewelry and walked out without it—carrying a thick envelope filled with cash."

"Why is she pawning her bling?" Cal asked. "If she has access to Garrett's dad's credit card…?"

"But she can't use his card to buy drugs—at least not anymore," I said. "So she uses the card to buy jewelry, which she then pawns for cash to buy Destiny. *Boom!*"

Milo nodded. "In theory, yes. That's what I was expecting. But then it got weird. After the pawn shop, Rochelle headed back across town for a…uh…" Milo held his hands out and pretended to paint his thumbnail with an imaginary brush.

"Mani-pedi?" I helped him out.

"That!" Milo exclaimed. "It was at a place called Beauty-holic Spa."

I listened intently, clutching the binoculars as I scanned the house again. So far Rochelle hadn't opened any of the doors to the deck.

"Before Rochelle went into the spa, after she parked in the lot out front—and first of all, there was a spot right near the door, but she didn't take it, which was odd, because earlier she nearly got into a knife fight with a woman over a prime parking spot," Milo told us. "This time, she parked way at the edge of the lot, and then she got out of her car and looked around. Hard. I had to duck behind an SUV, but she didn't see me. She pulls that envelope out of her bag—"

"The cash from the pawn shop?" Cal asked.

"Yes," Milo said. "And she's chewing gum, but she takes it out of her mouth, all of it, and puts it onto the envelope, and then sticks the envelope up inside the front tire well of her car and goes into the spa."

Cal scrunched his eyebrows together. "I was absent from school the day we studied Drug Deals 101, but what you just described sounds a lot like illegal activity to me." He shrugged. "I mean, cue the drug dealer, and...action!"

"Good guess," Milo said as he looked from Cal to me. "A few minutes later, a man pulls into the lot and parks next to her car. Mid-forties. Short, dark hair. Dark sunglasses. Dark suit. Nice suit. Nice car, too. Everything about him screamed money. He sat there for about ten minutes, checking to see if anyone was watching."

"Which you were," I pointed out with a mix of disbelief and irritation. "And you were worried about me, sitting here staking out a whole bunch of *nothing*?"

"There was a bus stop right across the street," Milo defended himself, "and Dana's e-reader was in the bike's storage compartment, so I pretended to read. Luckily the bus didn't come."

I stared at him, aghast. He was so casual about the fact that he'd been in serious danger.

"I'm a normie, Skylar," he reminded me quietly. "No one wants *my* blood."

"Yeah, but they might kill you for being a witness to a felony," I countered.

"That's not gonna happen," he said so absolutely that I almost believed him. Almost.

Calvin interrupted. "So our Man-in-Black, did he take the cash and leave the drugs? The suspense is killing me. Or maybe that's starvation I'm feeling—it's all starting to blur… Come closer, my children. I can't see your faces…"

Milo was still watching me, and I shrugged a *whatever* that I didn't really feel. And I'm pretty sure, even without our connection, that he knew that.

He cleared his throat again and told us, "He took the cash. But then he just drove away. No drugs left behind. No nothing."

That was not the conclusion that Calvin and I expected. And I understood now why Milo was perplexed. Rochelle had made only half of a drug deal. It didn't make sense.

"Are you sure?" I asked cautiously, not wanting to imply that Milo might've missed seeing the—what was it called in all those gangland movies I'd seen? The *drop*.

Calvin was less delicate. "Maybe you missed it, Miles. Maybe you blinked when he dropped the vial on the ground next to her car. Maybe—"

"I don't think so." Milo was pretty convinced.

"Check your math," Calvin suggested. "Use Sky's creepy telepathy thing to let her scan your memory. Maybe she'll see something you missed."

Milo looked at me, and I looked at him, and his *uh-oh* was nearly audible.

Cal didn't hear it though, and he had another question. "So did he rob her, then? Was Rochelle upset when she came back out? Like, did she start searching her tire well, or screaming, or…"

Milo shook his head. "She didn't even look. She came out of the spa focused on her phone, checking texts or whatever. She went straight to the car, got in, and drove away. I'd guess the guy who took the money texted her some kind of *got it* message."

I realized what Milo was saying. "Wait, you didn't follow the man in black? Wasn't he kind of a major lead? I mean, we know where to find Rochelle." I gestured at the giant house.

But Milo shook his head. "My job was to stick with Rochelle," he told me. "Without my phone working, I had to make sure I could get back here in time to warn you that she was returning."

Because apparently keeping me safe trumped everything. I hid my frustration by pretending to look through the binoculars at the house, but inwardly I seethed. And worried. What was *up* with Milo…? That unspoken *uh-oh* was freaking me out. Why didn't he want to touch me? What was he hiding?

"Do your creepy thing," Calvin urged us again.

I snapped at him. "I wish you wouldn't call it that."

He was unfazed. "I'll call it your glorious, fantabulous magical whoo-hah, if you want. But use it, ASAP, to check Milo's memory, so we can be sure she's not in there right now, shooting up."

"She could be doing that, regardless of whether she got Destiny from the man in black," I pointed out, still rather snittishly.

"Calvin's idea is actually a good one. It's possible I missed something," Milo said quietly, and I braced for him to touch my shoulder, but he didn't.

Instead, I turned back around, and he was just sitting there with his hand out, too-politely waiting for me to be the one to make the connection.

So I buried my frustration, tucking my anxiety in beside it—and tried to make my mind as peaceful and calm as possible.

Still thoughts. Still thoughts.

When I touched Milo's hand, I could tell that he was doing the same thing—prepping and bracing for the contact with a couple of soothing *Still thoughts*. It would've been funny if it wasn't so sad. Except it was confusing, too, because I immediately felt the warmth of his love. *That* hadn't changed.

But he was all business, leading me directly to the "box" for this particular memory. I felt the sensation of him lifting the lid, and I fell into the visual swirl of his recall.

A man. Dark suit. Leaning under the shiny silver convertible, making a displeased face at Rochelle's gum, but then sliding the envelope of cash

101

into his jacket pocket. As he quickly walked back to his car, got in, and drove away.

From where Milo had been sitting on that bus-stop bench across the street, he'd seen it all. He played it again for me, this time in slo-mo, and no, the man's hand had been empty when he'd reached for the envelope, and he'd dropped nothing as he moved back to his own car.

I froze the image—Milo had gotten a clear look at the car's plates—which had been artfully smeared with mud and grime that completely covered the numbers and letters. And *that* meant we had no way to track Man-in-Black.

As soon as Milo could tell that the memory had registered for me, he sat back, breaking away from my touch and leaving me in the dark.

But he loved me. Didn't he? That was love I could feel from him, wasn't it? Lord, I was overthinking all of this. Maybe Milo was just tired. God knew *I* was exhausted…

As I sat there and stewed, Milo recapped for Cal everything that we'd seen.

"What are we missing?" Cal asked. "Maybe he's her bookie. Or… maybe he's her ex and she's paying alimony—no, I'm not feeling that one. I dunno, guys. Bottom line is that Rochelle is into some sketchy shit, and the Jilly issue is looking not so great. Maybe the money is some kinda payoff. She killed Jilly, and Man-in-Black disposed of the body…?"

"Maybe she owes him a ton of money," I said, thinking aloud, "for hits of Destiny that she's already used. So she's paying him back in installments, but…that still doesn't make sense, because she's an addict and if she has any money at all, she'd use it to buy more Destiny. Except she's not strung out, she's not desperate, and I have *no* clue what's going on."

"She's getting the drug from somewhere," Cal pointed out. "According to Garrett, she's getting younger."

"Today she looked like she was twenty-five," Milo said. "Tops." Adding, "Car. Approaching."

And we all ducked down again in our seats.

"Please let it be Dana, and please let her bring lunch," Cal chanted. "Please let it be Dana, please let it be Dana…"

CHAPTER EIGHT

It was Dana.

And miraculously she'd brought lunch.

But she'd also been laughing at something Garrett said as they parked behind us and got out of Garrett's father's sports car, and the look of dismay on Cal's face when he heard her was one I'll always remember.

"Is she actually having *fun* with him?" he asked me, sotto voce.

"No," I told him. "She's not. She wouldn't." But I wasn't sure. Dana was…Dana.

We all got out of Calvin's car to greet them, and then we hunkered down at the side of the road for a little picnic of deli sandwiches and lemonade.

Cal didn't fall on the food as eagerly as I'd expected him to. His appetite was apparently gone.

Milo and I dug in though, as Dana explained what she and Garrett had been up to for most of the day.

"We got flowers," she told us, gesturing toward Garrett's car. We could see them in the back. "Lots of 'em. Three huge floral arrange-ments. The cards are signed from G's dad. *To Ro-ro. Yours forever, Dickie.* Anyway, they're so huge, G's gonna need his besties"—she pointed to Milo and Calvin—"to help him lug them up to her house. The three of you will bring them inside for her."

"Wait," I said. "You want Milo, Calvin, and Garrett to go inside· the home of a potential Destiny user to deliver flowers…?"

"Not just flowers," Dana said. "We also bought Daddy's crazy girl-friend a nice array of wireless micro-mics and Minicams, so we don't have to sit out here and wonder what's going on inside her lair. Once G gets those flowers inside, we'll have front-row seats to the Rochelle Show."

Calvin winced—just a little—every time Dana called Garrett "G." "And you're sure Rochelle won't find them?" he asked. "These minia-ture cameras and mics?"

"She's not very tech-savvy," Garrett said through a full mouth. "I thought it was worth a try. Besides, if she finds 'em, she'll think it's my dad spying on her." He laughed. "She'll probably think it's sweet. Proof that Daddy still cares."

"And this took *all* those hours," Cal said, trying to sound casual and failing. "A trip to the florist's and then to the Big Box media center?"

"We spent about two hours at my place," Garrett told him with a grin. "Your girl wore me out."

"Oh?" Cal said and his nonchalance was epically faux.

Dana and Garrett both laughed. "I told you he'd be jealous," Garrett said to Dana.

"You won that bet, G," Dana said before turning to Cal. "Calvin.

Baby. Garrett knows that you're my one and only." She widened her eyes a little as if to say, *Play along*. No doubt—to keep Garrett from relentlessly proposing marriage (with plans for a midair wedding night)—she'd reinforced the pretense that she and Calvin were a Thing.

"We went shopping in G's attic, looking for pawnables that wouldn't be missed when Daddy comes home. We need cash. So we got us some. Project Jilly can't be bankrolled entirely on a credit card."

"Although buying that wireless surveillance combo-pack put a solid dent in my plastic allowance," Garrett informed us through a full mouth.

"What's your surveillance operating system?" Cal asked, and while Garrett shrugged, Dana got up and fetched a tablet from the front seat of the sports car. She and Cal were soon deep into the tech of it all, heads together as they leaned over the screen.

Garrett picked up the binoculars and trained them on Rochelle's house.

I looked up to find Milo watching me. "Sorry about before," he said.

"I'm not sure what's going on," I confessed quietly. I wanted to take his hand, but I didn't dare. Instead, I rewrapped the second half of my turkey sandwich. Like Cal, I'd lost my appetite. "Are we okay?"

"Yes," he said. "We are. I love you—please don't doubt that. I'm just…I'm dealing with some…stuff. Hard stuff. Harder than I thought. And…I need a little space."

I love you, but I need some space. Milo didn't need to be inside my head to realize that I wasn't reassured by that at all.

"Sky—" he started.

I interrupted. "I can imagine how…weird it must be to know every little thing I'm thinking and feeling, and I want you to know that I'm learning how to control that. I am. I see what you do, with those… kind of…mental boxes—"

This time he cut me off. "Don't you dare!" He was loud enough that Calvin and Dana looked up from the tablet.

"Let's never fight," Dana told Cal. "Shnookums."

"Never," Cal promised. "Pookie."

Milo took my hand and pulled me to my feet as he stood up. Our connection snapped on, and I felt his embarrassment and frustration as he pulled me away from the others, back behind Garrett's flower-filled car. But once again he let me go almost right away. "This isn't about you," he told me. "I love being inside your head. I don't want you to change anything. It's me. It's all me."

I wanted to believe him. "Maybe I can help with…whatever it is…?"

"Yeah," he said again, but he shook his head no. "Eventually, yes. I'm sure of that. But right now, I just need…"

"Space," I finished for him as my heart sank. Still, I tried to understand. "I'm here when you want to talk."

Milo nodded. "I know that."

"It's time to do this," Dana called. "Guys? Miles, we need you."

"Rochelle's dangerous. Be careful in there," I whispered.

Milo nodded again, but I was hyperaware that he didn't kiss me. "I always am."

———

"She's a Destiny user!"

Dana and I blurted the words simultaneously as we sat in Garrett's car, hunched over the surveillance tablet.

I felt my heartbeat quicken as I realized that, with just one glimpse of Rochelle on a tiny little tablet screen, I'd known beyond a shadow of a doubt that the woman was addicted to Destiny.

"Abso-effin'-lutely," Dana agreed.

I focused, ignoring the urge to shudder as I watched the real-time play-by-play through the hidden cameras of the flower arrangements that Garrett, Milo, and Cal were carrying as they stood on Rochelle's doorstep.

All three bouquets contained Minicams, but Cal's definitely had the best view at the moment. Through his lens, we saw Rochelle as though we were gazing up at her.

Rochelle.

With her dewy, flawlessly tanned skin, lush blond hair, and petite stature, she was without a doubt the most absolutely drop-dead, stunningly, perfectly gorgeous woman I'd ever seen in my life.

And, more importantly, she was terrifying.

I'd never seen someone exude *mean* without saying a single word. But Rochelle was just that.

Scary mean.

Soulless, as far as I was concerned.

"What do *you* want?" Rochelle growled, her steely blue eyes narrowed as she crossed her arms over her ample chest.

She was dressed in an outfit that belonged on a tennis pro. And

Rochelle's physique matched that of an athlete's, minus excess muscle and plus enormous boobs. Her bleach-white pleated skirt complemented her figure-hugging pink polo shirt. None of the buttons on the shirt were being used. There was a lot of cleavage, even from this angle.

For a moment, no one said a word. It was almost like all three guys needed a beat or two to digest the epic view that was Rochelle. Meanwhile, her question lingered in the air like an odor—a question that had clearly been directed toward Garrett, who finally came into view as Calvin stealthily swiveled his wheelchair to his left.

"Special delivery!" Garrett exclaimed as he shifted the weight of the grotesquely huge bouquet in his arms. "*Heh. Heh-heh.*" His trademark nervous laugh was something I had, unfortunately, grown accustomed to hearing over the past few days. "Flowers! From my dad!"

Rochelle looked suspicious and none too pleased.

I couldn't see Milo, but I knew he was standing on Cal's other side, holding a similarly gargantuan floral arrangement. His voice rang out clearly though. "Sorry to bother you like this, ma'am," Milo said in his sweet, southern twang, "but your husband? He must really love you. There must be two hundred dollars of flowers here."

There were exactly two hundred dollars of flowers there—and it was good instinct on Milo's part to point that out. Things like that would matter to Rochelle.

As I watched, the woman's head snapped to her left to hone in on Milo. Calvin obligingly swiveled his chair again, and Milo's profile came into view. But I was still able to clearly see Rochelle's face from both Garrett's and Milo's cameras as she proceeded to give my boyfriend a full-on up-down check-out-the-hot-boy look.

In an instant, Rochelle's entire demeanor flipped from cold to hot. She smiled. "Oh, that's hysterical!" Her tinkling laughter was enough to send goose bumps up my arms. "Rick's not my husband, silly! I'm *definitely* too young to get married. Come in," she added and stepped backward, her hand still on the open front door in order to allow the three boys into the house.

Garrett led the way, with Milo right behind him. And through Cal's camera lens, I watched Rochelle unabashedly admire my boyfriend's ass as he strode into the foyer.

"Whoa, look at her eye-fah—" Dana stopped herself, no doubt because of the grim expression on my face.

Yes, I'd noticed the hideous and dangerous Destiny addict *eye-fahing* my boyfriend, thanks.

Then, to add insult to injury, Rochelle made a short sniffing sound before waving Cal inside impatiently—as though he were hired help rather than one of Garrett's friends. She could see that Cal's chair was getting hung up on the door's threshold, but she didn't move to help.

"Total bitch!" Dana hissed.

I nodded vehemently. "She is the *ugliest*. Beautiful person. I've ever. Seen."

"Well put, Cupcake." It was the closest thing to a compliment that I'd received from Dana in a very long time. I looked up at her for a second to acknowledge it. "Focus!" she barked at me as she stabbed furiously at the tablet screen with her finger.

Well, *that* had been nice for the zero-point-four seconds it had lasted.

The screen we were watching was split in three, each panel offering us a view from Milo's, Cal's, and Garrett's perspectives as they lugged the heavy bouquets inside. Milo and Garrett were both moving too fast, and the images from their cameras were dizzying.

Cal's point of view was better, but even his was a little bumpy for a second until he finally made it inside. Then things smoothed out and the front hallway was visible. It opened up into a cavernous-looking living room, complete with a collection of ugly, expensive-looking marble sculptures, ruby-colored leather couches, and a domed ceiling decorated with a gold-encrusted mural reminiscent of Michelangelo's Sistine Chapel. Meanwhile, Rochelle had clearly contributed to the already—ahem—tasteful decor, with enormous framed photographs of her own face hanging on every wall.

"Poor Jilly," I said. Despite Rochelle's denial, we all still believed that Jilly was her daughter. I couldn't imagine living in a house with *my* mother's giant face staring down at me constantly.

Inside the beach house, Calvin had slowed way down. He was clearly working on giving us a guided tour. The others had already gone farther into the house, Rochelle following hungrily behind Milo as he placed his bouquet on a low coffee table, camera aimed directly at the living room couch. It was a good call on Milo's part. The sofa was one of those huge recliners, facing an enormous flat-screen TV that hung on the far wall. Judging from the Chinese food containers, empty popcorn bowls, and lipstick-smeared wineglasses scattered around, it got a fair amount of use.

Since not much action was going to be happening on that couch right now, Dana reached over and tapped the tablet's window for Milo's camera. It shrank into a thumbnail, and the images from the other two Minicams took over the screen.

The flower-cam that Garrett carried was still moving—across that expansive room and down a hall, past what looked like a dining room.

Cal, meanwhile, lingered. He circled in his wheelchair, providing Dana and me with a panoramic view of the catastrophe that was Rochelle's living room.

Without warning, Calvin's face appeared in the screen, upside-down and humongous. "Would you rather eat five pounds of earth-worm poop or be forced to live with *this* crazy bee-otch?" he whispered into the mic.

I laughed. Dana scowled, but I could tell that her glower was only to hide the smile she wanted to crack.

"Calvin! Where you at?" Garrett's voice boomed through the speaker of the hidden camera in the bouquet he still carried. I refocused my attention to Garrett's POV. He had made it into the kitchen, where the perspective shifted when he set the floral arrangement on the counter.

Cal's face disappeared from his screen, and then his view was in motion again as he wheeled himself out of the living room and down the long corridor.

Despite the expensive wallpaper and intricate gold chandeliers, this part of the house was a disaster. Dirty laundry piled itself high on either side of the wide hallway, creating a narrow, claustrophobic feel. As Cal slowly motored forward, I spotted a set of ratty-looking pink sneakers and a pair of ripped jeans on top of a particularly large mountain of clothing.

"That's Jilly's stuff! It has to be!" I pointed to the clothes that clearly belonged to a teenager just as Cal passed it. Calvin was on the same page. He aimed his camera directly at the pile, then stuck his hand in front of the lens to give us a thumbs-up.

Dana nodded, her eyebrows furrowed as she studied the images on the screen.

"Do you think that means she's still living there?" I asked. "I mean, Rochelle would've definitely tossed that stuff if Jilly was…gone, right?"

By *gone*, I meant something far worse. But I couldn't bring myself to say the word *dead* out loud.

Dana shook her head.

Calvin continued forward, passing a formal dining room on the left—the table piled with more laundry—before he reached the kitchen. I had already noted, via the bouquet Garrett had set down on the countertop, that this room was even more cluttered and disgusting than that hallway.

"Apparently Destiny greatly improves your housekeeping skills," I said.

Garrett's bouquet was next to the sink, which held a leaning tower of food-encrusted dishes. He looked clumsy and absurd as he leaned in and fussed with the various stalks of flowers, no doubt making sure that the camera was aimed correctly. Meanwhile, through Cal's cam, I spotted Milo standing in the corner of the room, his back rigid against the mahogany cabinets as Rochelle worked on proactively popping his personal-space bubble. She whispered something to Milo.

Milo—*my* Milo—reached out, touched Rochelle's shoulder, and smiled back at her.

Ouch.

"*Here's* Cal!" Garrett exclaimed with over-the-top enthusiasm. "Thought we'd lost ya, buddy!"

"Yup! Here I am! With more flowers! 'Cause you definitely don't have enough of *those* now!"

Rochelle didn't turn around. Whatever she and Milo were discussing was obviously far more interesting.

She twirled a lock of blond hair in her fingers as she leaned even closer to Milo to hear whatever nugget of awesomeness he had to say to her in reply.

I hated her.

Hated. Her.

Even though I knew that Milo was putting on an act. This was not real. He was keeping her occupied so that Cal and Garrett could look around. Right?

Right?

"So, Rochelle!" Garrett said loudly. "Where's Jilly? I was gonna see if she wanted to…play some…Scrabble…?"

Beside me in the car, Dana threw her hands up in the air. "Oh, please!" she barked at the tablet. "Are you *kidding* me?"

Calvin, still lingering in the doorway of the kitchen, leaned forward into the bouquet-mic and whispered, "And the Academy Award goes tooooo…Garrett McDouche."

Milo stepped away from the wall, somehow squeezing past Rochelle's giant boobs. The woman turned to watch him, and I found myself thinking of one of those nature shows where a snake tracks its helpless prey. Except the warm and knowing smile that Milo shot back to Rochelle was anything but helpless. He joined Garrett, leaning against the kitchen island as he drawled, "That's right. Garrett's told me a lot about how great Jilly is. I really wanted to meet her. Is she here?"

The flowers on the counter were giving us a great shot of Milo and Garrett. Calvin motored forward a bit, deliberately angling his chair so that Dana and I could also have a good view of Rochelle's face.

And it was a seriously weird face. I couldn't quite pinpoint what was so strange about it, but Dana said, "Whoa, check out her insane micro-expressions."

"Her what?" I asked as in the kitchen, Rochelle gave a saccharine smile and said, "Oh, Garrett's told you about my niece Jilly, huh? She's a handful—with the pink hair one day, green hair the next! I never know what she's going to do!"

"Micro-expressions," Dana repeated. "Not everyone does it, and it happens really fast, but if you slow down a recording…" She accessed the control panel for the tablet's surveillance program, rewound the digital recording from Cal's camera and…

"She's at that age," we could hear Rochelle saying over the kitchen-counter floral-mic as on the other half of our screen we watched her face in slo-mo.

Her expression went from disgust to contempt to utter rage. Even when she smiled, her anger flickered through with slight downturns of her mouth or the baring of her teeth. As far as Rochelle's micro-expressions went, there was no misreading her feelings about her daughter-slash-niece. The fact that we could hear her trill of musical laughter as we watched the slo-mo made it even more surreal.

"I'm just trying to be patient," Rochelle continued telling the boys, "and let her, you know, find herself. If she can."

"Is she here?" Calvin asked.

With a flick of her fingers against the tablet screen, Dana had returned us to the real-time feed from his camera, so we caught the oddly blank look Rochelle gave Cal—again, as if somehow she hadn't expected him to speak.

"Jilly," Milo clarified. *He* got a smile.

"Oh," Rochelle said. "Of course. No. Nope. She, um, went to the beach. Yeah. She left about a half hour ago. You just missed her."

Dana shot me a quick *I call bullshit* look.

I nodded. "There's no way. We had a clear view of all the doors. Jilly didn't go anywhere today."

Cal knew it too. He stuck one thumb in front of the flower-cam and very slowly and deliberately turned it upside down.

Meanwhile Garrett was asking, "The public beach?"

Rochelle shrugged expansively. "Well, that's where she *said* she was going, at least." A giggle. "Teenaged girls. You know how *that* goes." *Giggle, giggle.*

"Excuse me!" Cal's voice boomed through the speaker of the tablet.

He still had the third floral arrangement on his lap. "Ma'am? May I please have, um, a glass of water? I'm parched."

We got more of those crazy micro-expressions from Rochelle. Now that I knew what to look for, I could catch little glimpses and flashes of bared teeth as she smiled, as if the woman had a snarling animal trapped inside her. For one horrible moment, I actually thought she was going to grab a knife and start slashing at Calvin as punishment for being thirsty. Or, more likely, thirsty while in a wheelchair and black.

But then, Garrett spoke up. "Yeah. Me too, buddy. Jilly's a Diet Splash addict—I bet there's a twelve-pack or two of that in the fridge. Ro, do you mind?" He started toward the refrigerator, but Rochelle rushed to cut him off.

"I'll get it," she said, and I immediately conjured up images of severed heads and body parts stashed in the vegetable drawers. "I'm not sure we have any Diet Splash though. Jilly's just decided to go, um, corn syrup–free…"

"She's a terrible liar," Dana announced.

Meanwhile, Milo was taking advantage of all of the energy around the fridge. He grabbed the flowers off Calvin's lap as he breathed, "Help Garrett."

For a fraction of second, Milo looked directly into the camera—directly into my eyes—but then he turned the floral arrangement around and the perspective changed to whatever Milo could see.

Calvin came into view. From his wheelchair, Cal shot the bouquet of flowers a sideways glance and blew a quick kiss.

"I'm gonna kill him when he gets back," Dana growled. "Doesn't he have even one serious bone in his body?"

"Nope," I replied confidently. "Calvin has exactly zero serious bones. Or mean ones. Nicest, goofiest guy in the universe."

"Yeah, well," Dana replied grumpily and then went on to grumble more unintelligible complaints about absolutely everything. I acted wisely and kept my mouth shut.

Calvin, however, did not. In that messy kitchen, he wheeled over toward Garrett and Rochelle saying, "Water would be fine."

On the other half of the tablet screen, Milo was heading down a hallway that led to the far wing of the big house. I could hear his steady inhalations even over the noise in the kitchen.

"Ah, there is one can of Diet Splash left," Rochelle announced as Garrett tried to get a look inside the fridge.

"Whoa, you've got a shit-ton of chardonnay in there," he said, busting my severed head theory.

"This stupid house doesn't have a wine refrigerator," Rochelle complained.

The hallway that Milo had taken looked similar to the other. It was a hot mess of clothes, hairbrushes, old ratty books, and even a haphazard pile of more framed glamour shots of Rochelle.

Milo leaned closer into one of the pictures with the bouquet, to offer Dana and me a better look.

I instantly knew what he wanted us to notice.

"Look at that!" Dana exclaimed, too.

I inhaled sharply. "Whoa. That's crazy."

The photograph had been taken a long time ago; Rochelle's hair and clothing choices were clearly dated. If I had to guess, I would've said the picture had to be at least ten years old, if not more. But the really crazy thing? In the photo, Rochelle looked like she was *at least* ten years *older* than she was today.

"Destiny is no joke," Dana said, and I knew she wasn't paying the drug a compliment.

I shuddered. It *was* creepy. "So she really is, like, forty." And she'd been hitting on my boyfriend. *Barf.*

Milo kept going, as in the kitchen, Rochelle realized he was gone. "Where's…your other friend?" she asked Garrett, who was getting two glasses down from a cabinet so he and Cal could share the single can of Diet Splash.

"Milo needed to use the men's room," Calvin volunteered. "He'll be right back."

"Milo." Rochelle said his name almost as if she were tasting a fine wine, and I couldn't not react. I tried to make it a laugh, but I'm pretty sure Dana wasn't fooled. "Oh, I should go find him and let him know that the one down here—the, um, toilet clogs."

"Lying," Dana intoned. I'd heard it, too—Rochelle's *um* that meant she was making things up. Like *Jilly's at the beach.*

Meanwhile, Milo was still moving down that hall, past a set of stairs going up and toward what must've been some kind of playroom or maybe a home gym. There was a pool table, along with an old-time pinball machine and an array of exercise machines and free weights. Milo stopped in the doorway and did a slow sweep with the flower-cam.

It was a little dark in there—kinda odd since the afternoon sun was shining so brightly. Milo noticed that, too, whispering, "Shades and blinds are all pulled down. Hmm."

He moved farther into the room, even as the sound of shattering glass pulled my attention back to the camera in the kitchen.

"Sorry!"

"Oh, wow, sorry!"

Garrett and Calvin apologized almost in unison as Garrett did an awkward little hop both out of the way of Cal's chair and over the glass that he'd just dropped onto the kitchen's tile floor. It was obvious they were doing some kind of Two Stooges imitation to keep Rochelle from chasing after Milo.

It worked, because now she wasn't even trying to hide her scary micro-expressions as she unleashed her exasperation. "Garrett, what the hell…?"

"Sorry!" he said again. "I'm sorry. I'll clean that up. Do you have a vacuum?"

"Does she *look* like a woman who has a vacuum?" Dana mused.

"Or a dustpan," Cal offered as he rolled over and opened the cabinet under the sink. "We could sweep it up with a dustpan—"

"Oh! The invalid wants to help!" Rochelle said, her tone tinged with disdain.

I gasped.

Dana's eyes narrowed. She pursed her lips until they turned white.

But, if Cal was equally offended, he did an awesome job of brushing it off. "I know," he replied, chuckling. "My invalidity is a total bummer! You're right. I'll just hang here, helplessly, and let way-more-valid Garrett clean up."

"Hey." Milo's voice pulled our attention back to his half of the screen. "You see this?" he breathed.

Oh yes, we saw. It was a tightly closed door on the farside of the playroom-slash-gym, with what looked like a brand-new and very shiny dead bolt—the kind that needs a key to unlock—right above the knob.

"Whoa," I said, because that was not the kind of door that normally needed a dead bolt. It looked like a simple closet door.

In the kitchen, Rochelle was still squawking about the broken glass as Garrett banged around and made noise about finding a broom.

From Milo's camera, we saw his hand reach into view as he tried the knob, but of course the dead-bolted door didn't open. It was securely locked.

Dana didn't budge. I think she'd stopped breathing.

Milo whispered, "Jilly."

Using two knuckles, he knocked lightly on the door.

"Jilly," he whispered again. "Are you in there? Knock back if you can hear me but can't speak."

Dana and I sat silently. I was holding my breath now, too.

"Jilly?" Milo was still whispering, but his tone had become agitated. Or excited.

Had he heard something?

I realized suddenly that the noise from the kitchen had dropped a few decibels, and when I looked over at that side of the screen, I saw that Rochelle had left the room.

"Rochelle's gonna find Milo," I started, but I stopped speaking when Milo's hushed voice rang through the speaker.

"I think…" he whispered. "At least I'm *pretty* sure I heard a noise—"

And then, just like that, the image of the door blurred and moved as Milo whipped his body to the left.

Rochelle stood there, arms crossed, her face looming huge and horrible in front of the camera lens.

I swallowed my scream.

"Oh! Hey," Milo said. "I'm sorry, I was just…"

"The powder room is back this way," she said, pointing behind her. And then her eyes turned molten with desire—which was truly creepy as she continued with those micro-expressions of near-snarling rage. She uncrossed her arms and took a step toward Milo. "Unless you're looking for a bedroom, handsome. They're upstairs. If you want, I can show you. Give you the hundred-dollar tour."

"*Ew!*" I recoiled in my seat, like I would have if I'd accidentally placed my hand on a stove. It was instinctive.

When I glanced over at Dana, I saw that she had done the same.

But Milo didn't back away from Rochelle. "I'd like that," he said in a low voice that triggered something dark and primal inside me. *Mine.* That was the way he spoke to me and only me. Or at least that's what I'd thought.

My vision actually blurred a little as I watched Rochelle reach out and place a hand on the bare skin of his arm to pull him away from that locked door. I could see her fingernails. They were long and bloodred.

Talons. It was the first word that popped into my brain. Right after *Get your fucking hands off of him.* It was possible I'd said that out loud, because Dana glanced over at me.

"Easy," she warned me, her eyes back on the screen. "She's dangerous, and Milo knows it. Let's keep her happy."

Yeah, but *how* happy? That one I kept to myself by clenching my teeth.

Meanwhile Rochelle was working to steer Milo down the hall, away from that bolted door. But I could tell, by the way the view through the camera lens blurred, that Milo was resisting her pull.

"Actually," Milo said, still in that low, flirtatious voice, "I'd love to start the tour here. A mysterious locked door…" He turned to the door again, and Rochelle's hand slid off his arm. It would not surprise me if later I found claw marks on his skin.

"It's nothing," Rochelle replied, impatience lining her voice as she came back into view and blockaded the door with her body.

She could've been holding a smoking gun. Her stance, pinned against the locked door, was just as incriminating.

"Jilly has *got* to be in there. Or else *something* bad is," Dana muttered.

I nodded silently. I couldn't look away from what I was seeing on that little screen.

"That's disappointing." Milo's voice was low and intense. And intimate. I tried not to squirm. Yes, Rochelle was beautiful, but in a really horrible way. Like Dana had said, Milo was putting on an act. Wasn't he? "A mysterious locked room in the home of Coconut Key's hottest, most beautiful woman, filled with…whips and chains and other…toys?" He leaned in toward her, just a little, to whisper, "Be still, my heart."

"Oh my God," Dana said aloud, laughing a little. "Miles, you bad, bad boy."

I still couldn't speak, but I'd made a noise that I again tried to turn into a laugh. Milo *was* acting. I knew he was acting—or at least my logical mind knew it. My heart and my gut, however, were gripped by an insane wave of jealousy. It was possible that I might throw up. This might be hilarious with a little time and distance, but here and now? No. Nope.

Dana was still muttering and even tapping at the split-screen window that showed us the kitchen. "Come on, Calvin, what are you and G doing? It's time for you to rescue Milo."

I spared them the quickest of glances—it looked like Cal and Garrett were going through piles of mail and papers that were scattered across the counters and the kitchen table.

On the other half of the screen, Rochelle had been standing with her back against the locked door, arms splayed to her sides like her body had been nailed in place. But at Milo's suggestive words, she turned the desperate stance into a seductive one. Her eyelids closed halfway and she gave Milo a come-hither smile.

"I wish," she whispered back. "But no. I rent this place, and this is the owner's closet. There's nothing exciting in there. Sheets and towels, bathing suits and flip-flops. Sunblock. They lock it up—as if I'd want to use their stupid stuff." Rochelle's nose crinkled with distaste, but then she smiled again at Milo and reached out to touch him. "I've got plenty of rooms upstairs that lock. And plenty down here that don't. Let's just get rid of your little friends."

I couldn't see where Rochelle's hand had gone, but it didn't take much imagination to picture her running her fingers through his hair. And again, Milo didn't move back. Instead he made a sound of pleasure, a quiet little *Mmmm* that was low and throaty. I was *definitely* going to be sick.

"Actually," he replied as Rochelle propelled herself off the door and moved in closer to him—on the camera she became grotesque and swollen—yes, that *was* her boob she was pressing into the lens, "there are rules for these things. I want to take you out to dinner first. Somewhere nice. Then we can come back here and…find a locked room or two."

I tried to take a deep breath, but it felt like there wasn't even air in the car anymore. My boyfriend had just asked out a fortysomething-year-old Destiny addict who also happened to be dating my former worst enemy's dad. I bit ferociously at a nail, my heart pounding out of my chest. I knew Milo was playing Rochelle. Like Dana had said, she was dangerous. He was making her happy. He wasn't really going to take her to dinner, was he? Or, Lord, *was* he? Maybe he was planning to do that so we could use the time to search the house, get into that locked closet…

I didn't want him going anywhere with her. And I was literally sick to my stomach from watching this. Rochelle was still standing much too close, but then, thank goodness, she stepped back and I could see her face again.

She pouted. "Tonight's no good, baby boy. I have…plans." Her talons had landed on Milo's arm again, and this time when she steered him away from the locked door, he moved with her. "Can we make it tomorrow night? Pretty please? With a cherry on top?" she asked.

"Tomorrow is perfect," Milo said. And then the view changed dizzyingly as Milo twirled the bouquet around before setting it down on some of the stacked clutter in the hallway, just outside the playroom. He somehow managed to aim the Minicam at that dead-bolted closet door, way across the room. But whatever he'd put the bouquet on top of must've been low to the ground because the only thing Dana and I could now see of Milo and Rochelle were sneakers and high-heeled sandals.

The two pairs of feet were facing one another.

"Good," I heard Rochelle tell Milo in a low, throaty voice.

I gnawed at my nail, held my breath, and listened.

"*Very* good," Milo answered. His sneakers scootched closer to Rochelle's sandals, so that their toes were almost touching. I hated to think about anything else of theirs touching too.

"If he kisses her—" I started in a shaky voice, but then I realized I wouldn't know if Milo had kissed her unless I asked him. And suddenly *not* seeing was worse than seeing. And I heard an echo of his voice as he told me, *I just need a little space.*

Was this what he meant?

The silence coming through the flower-mic was excruciating. I tasted blood and realized that I'd bitten my nail to the quick.

"'Til tomorrow," Rochelle said softly.

"I'll pick you up. Seven p.m. sharp," Milo responded.

Without looking at me, Dana reached over in the car, grabbed my hand—the one with the now-annihilated nail—and gave me an *It's okay* squeeze.

And even though I trusted Dana, I felt in my heart that everything in my world had turned to complete and utter *not-okay*.

The worst part about it? I knew that it was probably going to get worse before it got better. And I also knew that whether it truly *would* get better was one great big, fat, giant *if*.

CHAPTER NINE

"Jilly is in that closet. She's locked in there. I'm certain." Milo didn't bother with a *hello* or *how are you* as he swung open the passenger door to Garrett's car and leaned into the front seat. The expression on his face was as intense as his tone was urgent as he looked across me to Dana.

"Did you hear her in there?" she asked. "Did she answer when you knocked and called her name?"

Milo shook his head. "No, but—"

Dana cut him off. "Miles." She handed the tablet to me with an "Eyes on," command, then opened the driver's side door. She gestured to Milo with her head, like *Come 'ere* before stepping out and leaning her elbows on the top of the car.

Milo barely spared me a glance of apology as he straightened up as well, leaning his own weight across the passenger side of the car roof.

Seriously? I couldn't see either of their faces from where I sat, as Dana said, "Rochelle is definitely hiding something in that closet. Whether or not that something happens to be Jilly? It's debatable."

"Debatable?" Milo shot back.

"Yes," Dana said. "Look, I know this is…" She sighed heavily and started over. "You got that third camera in the perfect position. We'll know immediately if Rochelle goes anywhere near that closet…"

I was still sitting shotgun inside Garrett's car, which also meant that I had become officially sandwiched between Dana and Milo as they bickered over the top of my head. On the tablet, the kitchen camera gave me an excellent view of Rochelle as she uncorked a bottle of wine and poured herself a glass.

My heart was still pounding sixteenth notes inside my rib cage. I tried to focus on Milo and Dana's conversation, but when I looked to my right, the only parts of Milo that I could see were his pants and sneakers.

It was close to the same view I'd had just a few minutes ago, when Milo and Rochelle had stood in front of the flower cam and conspired to…rendezvous.

On the tablet, Rochelle took a delicate sip of her wine and then smiled, as if anticipating tomorrow's "date" with *my boyfriend*.

Garrett's car suddenly felt way too small. I needed fresh air. I needed to focus my thoughts on anything other than Milo—on a date—with a drop-dead gorgeous, big-bosomed Destiny addict.

I pushed my way around Milo and out of the car, still clutching the tablet.

"Excuse me," I said out loud.

The two-second touch between Milo and me was enough for me to read his thoughts.

Goddamnit, Goddamnit, God—He must've realized I was picking that up, because he quickly switched to *Sorry, Sky...* But I was already out of the car and away from him.

He reached toward me, as if to catch me and reconnect, but this time I was the one who didn't want him to know what *I* was thinking and feeling. Mostly because I wasn't sure exactly *what* I was thinking and feeling. It'd probably be good to figure that out for myself before I broadcast it to him. So I backed away.

But then I realized that his reach for me had been autopilot. As soon as he realized what he was doing, he pulled his hand back fast. And as soon as he did *that*, I stupidly *wanted* him to follow me.

But he didn't.

And then Garrett interrupted. "Hey! Everyone touching my car! Watch the paint, wouldja? I mean, that's an eighty-thousand-dollar vehicle right there!"

Cal wheeled himself toward us, too, keeping pace with Garrett. The two of them looked weird side-by-side like that—as though they actually were friends or something. But this was just an additional notch on today's bizarre-belt. We'd all been flung into the deep end of the strange pool—and yes, I knew even without Calvin to tell me, that I was mixing my metaphors. In fact, as I stood there clutching a tablet upon which played a video feed of the woman who'd recently hit on and possibly sucked face with my boyfriend—I glanced down to see Rochelle settling onto the couch, glass of wine in one hand, TV remote in the other—I could feel the panic that came from water closing over my head.

At Garrett's demand, Milo and Dana both stood up straight and stepped back from the car, each of them crossing their arms over their chests like belligerent bookends. I wanted to reach out for Milo—to beg him to reassure me that he hadn't enjoyed playing Rochelle. And, oh yeah, to also reassure me that's what he'd been doing—playing her. Right? *Right?* But I couldn't bring myself to do it. Instead, I leaned against the back of Garrett's car and stuffed my hands into my pockets.

Milo, however, had refocused his mental energy on Rochelle's locked closet. "It is *imperative* that we pick the lock to that door as soon as possible."

As pitiful as it sounded, Milo was *my* locked door. And despite my repeated efforts, these past few days felt a lot like I was getting that door slammed in my face by the same person who was supposed to *want* to let me in.

Calvin rolled up. "Maaay-an, that was some crazy shee-it." His eyes were wide as he pulled his chair up next to Dana. "Did you guys see all of that?"

He grabbed the tablet out of my hands and started rewinding the footage eagerly. Everything Dana and I had seen had been digitally recorded so we could review it if we needed to. But best of all, with those cameras left in place, we no longer had to lurk outside Rochelle's house, wondering what was happening inside. We'd be able to view the wireless feed from as far away as the comfort of Calvin's playroom, which was our unofficial headquarters, on account of my house being off-limits because my mom was insane.

"We saw everything," Dana replied. "And there is no lingering doubt in my mind anymore. That woman is a D-addict."

Dana was right about one thing—Rochelle was definitely addicted to Destiny. But we *hadn't* seen quite *everything*, had we? I glanced at Milo quickly before pulling my hand out of my pocket and chomping on a nail.

"And I'm just as certain that Jilly is *locked* in that closet!" Milo's voice actually wavered as he spoke. "That's why it's *imperative* that we—"

"We heard you the first time, Miles!" Dana barked.

"Tell me about it," I muttered, just loudly enough for Milo to hear me. Of course, I immediately regretted it. One corner of Milo's mouth twitched, and he gazed at me for a moment with raised, helpless eyebrows—a silent *Et tu, Brute?*—before crossing his arms more tightly across his chest and looking away.

"Milo is right." Cal added his two cents, even while he kept his nose to the tablet on his lap. "At least about checking that closet. We need to find out what's in there. Look-it that deadbolt. Whatever the wicked witch has locked up in there, it can't be good."

Garrett, meanwhile, had given up on lecturing about the value of his car and, instead, hopped up onto the back hood. He looked pretty freaked. "So, what does this mean for Rochelle? If she's an addict, is she just gonna… What?"

"She'll continue to lose whatever small portion of a soul she still has left, turn into a full-blown sociopathic narcissist—assuming she's not one already—and then die a horrible death. Most likely taking other people out with her if she's anywhere near them when she jokers."

Dana recited the words, careful to keep any lingering emotion from her tone.

Garrett swallowed hard. "Um? Wow. That's…harsh."

Milo nodded vehemently. "All the more reason for me to go keep Rochelle occupied so that you guys can get to Jilly. Let's do this before she's too far gone! If I went back there, knocked on the door…? She'd let me in."

What? "You want to go keep Rochelle *occupied*, right *now*?" I was incredulous "How? Upstairs, with the *hundred-dollar tour* while we sneak in and break into the closet—"

"Not you," he said. "Dana. And I wouldn't let her—"

This time I cut him off. "She's a Destiny addict, Milo! *And* a creeper! She wants *you*! Do you know for sure that she doesn't have any powers? Because if she does, she'll use 'em all to get what she wants. And oh yeah? Also? She's a *Destiny addict*! You *know* damn well she could joker at any second—especially if you don't give her what she wants! And—news flash! You're not a G-T! It's not like you can just *screw* the Destiny out of her!"

I'd shocked everyone—myself included.

"Sky!" Milo took a step toward me and grabbed my shoulders. I tried to shrug away—I was back to not wanting him anywhere near the too-noisy inside of my head—but he held on tightly. He moved so fast, I didn't have time to even try to blanket my thoughts.

Is this why he wants space, he wants space he said he wants space; she's a Destiny addict and she touched him and I'm pretty sure that she kissed him or maybe he kissed her and it's not okay not okay not okay he wants space is this why not okay he wants space—

Milo shook his head. "No, Sky. No." He spoke to me out loud, no doubt hoping to be heard over the noisy loop that was playing in my head. "No, that's *not* what I meant. *Shit*, I'm so sorry—"

Milo had said *shit*. It shocked me into a mental silence of sorts, which he filled with waves of apology.

Dana cleared her throat impatiently, and Milo looked up for a moment. It was long enough for him to relax his hold on my shoulders—and long enough for me to slip free from his grasp.

I didn't want him to touch me. Yes, I got that he was sorry, but I still wasn't sure quite what for. Because he'd said *shit*? Because he'd kissed Rochelle? Because he'd liked the dangerous game he'd been playing with her and was willing, under the guise of the mission, to take it even farther…?

"All right. Push the pause button on the lovers' quarrel. We have stuff to discuss here. Milo." Dana turned to face him. "The date-with-D-addict idea? That was a good call."

I laughed, and I confess that I sounded a tad insane.

Milo turned toward me. "Skylar, I'd appreciate it enormously if you'd trust me," he said.

Calvin was wide-eyed and I know he was trying to help when he chimed in with, "I think it's Rochelle she doesn't trust. You should check out this recording. The way she looks at you is…" He made a face as he shook his head.

Dana pushed the conversation forward. "You're not going back there now," she informed Milo. "That's a no-brainer. It'll be dangerous enough for you to meet her at some restaurant—and you are going to meet her, none of this picking her up. And while I wish that we didn't have to wait twenty-four hours, it is what it is, and it's better than nothing. In the meantime, it makes sense to continue the stakeout. Rochelle said she had plans tonight, so if she leaves, we're right here—to go in and see if Jilly really is inside that closet."

"She's in there." Even as Milo said the words, he gazed at me, his brow furrowed. I couldn't tell if the look he was giving me was a result of his concern for Jilly or simply a reaction to my incredibly uncool crazy-girlfriend outburst.

Trust me. I wanted to trust him. He loved me—I could smell it. At least I thought I still could… But why did he want so desperately to go back inside that house? And I knew he wanted to go, and *desperately* was putting it mildly.

As much as I wanted to look away, Milo's dark eyes drew me in and kept me there. Even though I couldn't communicate with him unless we were touching, I still felt a tiny charge shoot through the air—like radio static in a distant room.

Dana broke the spell. "Miles," she said in a carefully even tone. Milo looked away from me, and the dubious connection between us was gone. "I acknowledge your conviction. And part of me believes you might be right. Jilly *could* be in there. But…" She sighed. "I've been thinking. If you were a D-addict like Rochelle, and you discovered that your daughter or your niece or your whatever the eff this girl is was a Greater-Than…? What would *you* do?"

She looked from Milo to me to Garrett to Cal, who glanced up from the tablet to say, "Uh-oh."

"Oh no," I breathed as light dawned.

Milo just clenched his teeth.

"Yup." Dana nodded grimly.

"What?" Garrett asked, looking at us, then back at Dana. Because he was still new at this Destiny business, he was clueless.

"An adolescent G-T like Jilly," Cal told him. "That's not blood running through her veins; it's gold."

"Jilly's got blood that Destiny dealers need. It's an essential ingredient for their product." Dana broke it down for him. "Also? The dealers have the product that Rochelle needs to survive. Do the math. It wouldn't surprise me if Rochelle traded Jilly to her dealer."

"Traded?" Garrett still didn't understand. "Her own daughter?"

I made it as simple as possible. "Sold. You know. Like a prostitute or a slave."

"Slave?" His eyes widened. "Whoa! Really?"

"It's possible, yeah," Milo said, but then he shook his head at Dana. "It doesn't make sense. If Rochelle already received a supply of Destiny from her dealer in exchange for Jilly, then why is she paying off Man-in-Black in that parking lot—with money she got from pawned jewelry?"

Dana frowned. "Yeah," she muttered, almost as if to herself. "If he's her dealer? That part makes no effing sense."

Everyone paused and considered this for a moment. It was like a question mark just dangled there in the air.

"Unless she's paying down her debt for past purchases?" I suggested. "In weekly installments?"

"Maybe," Dana said, but she didn't sound convinced. "Hard to believe Rochelle wouldn't include that kind of settlement when she brokered Jilly's trade."

"Maybe the man in black has nothing to do with Destiny," I tried, but then Calvin cut me off.

"Yo! Guys! Check it out!" His eyes were wide as he smiled and held the tablet up and waved it around excitedly.

"What is it? Cal, we can't see what you're holding up if you move like that." Dana sounded like a teacher lecturing a student.

But Cal couldn't stop wiggling around in his seat and waving the tablet around victoriously. If he'd been physically capable of getting out of his chair and bouncing up and down, he seriously would have done it.

Garrett actually attempted to focus on the tablet screen as Calvin waved it through the air. His quick head movements reminded me of a cat trying to pounce on a laser light.

"Morgan! It's an email! Morgan-the-super-G-T actually emailed me back! She wants to meet us tonight!" Cal whooped and waved the tablet around once more. This time, in his excitement, he almost dropped the thing on the ground.

Dana used her own G-T powers to impatiently swipe the tablet away from Cal. It flew through the air and landed neatly in her own hands.

"Whoa," Garrett said. "*Heh-heh.*"

Dana scanned the screen quickly and rolled her eyes. "Wow. And she only charges two hundred and fifty bucks for this meeting, huh? What a bargain." Her tone was the opposite of enthusiastic.

Milo came around the front of the car and leaned against the driver's side door next to Dana, so he could read the tablet over her shoulder. I turned, wanting to look as well. But the last thing I needed to be doing right now was following Milo around some more.

"What's it say?" Garrett asked.

"She wants to meet up in Palm River," Milo read. He glanced up at Dana and Cal. "That's not too far, right?"

"Only half an hour!" Cal answered. "Twenty-five minutes if we hoof it…" He frowned. I knew it was sinking in, and he was thinking about the two hundred and fifty dollars that he most definitely didn't have. Two fifty—simply to meet this girl. It would cost more, guaranteed, if she agreed to help us help Sasha. "Should I tell her no?"

Dana locked eyes with Cal. And then she sighed mightily and reached into the pocket of her leather jacket with her free hand before pulling out a wad of cash and tossing it onto Cal's lap. "Tell her yes."

Cal beamed at Dana—who looked away, mainly because Calvin's grin was severely contagious, and I knew that Dana was in no mood for smiles because I wasn't either.

"You!" She pointed at Garrett. "Stay with me and help me keep an eye on the Rochelle-cams. Cal? Sky? Milo? The three of you can go to Palm River and get yourselves disappointed and scammed, for all I care."

But she *did* care—we all knew that. If Morgan was for real, and if she had the ability to get inside little Sasha's head, and if Sasha really *had* seen Lacey at some point during her abduction… There were a lot of *ifs* there, but after months of hitting dead ends, this *could* be the path to finding Dana's long-missing sister.

Cal's smile faded as he reached out to touch Dana's sleeve. "But maybe you should come with me, or…I could stay here at the stakeout with you, and let Sky and Milo go—"

"No," Dana interrupted. "You're the one with the connection to Morgan. You need to go. G and I will be fine here."

Garrett smirked. "Yeah, dude. We'll be *extra-fine*."

Cal shot Garrett the evil eye. I didn't realize my best friend had it in him. But he wasn't messing around.

Garrett knew it too. "Man, I'm joking," he added. "I'd never shoplift your lady."

Milo was gazing at me, and I looked up to lock eyes with him again. I didn't need telepathy to read his expression. He was dreading the drive to Palm River. I didn't blame him. A half hour there and a half hour back? The tension in the car would be thick enough to cut with a knife.

Of course we could both man up and have a grown-up conversation right here and right now. But the look on Milo's face was clear. He didn't want to talk.

And I wasn't going to force him.

"Milo should stay here, with you," I blurted, my heart breaking a little as I turned to Dana. "You'll need his help if Rochelle leaves. In case Jilly really is inside that closet." I swallowed hard and nodded, as if I needed actual reassurance from myself that I was making the right call. "Just…" I glanced at Milo again, and my voice grew softer. "Just stay here. Please?"

"Good call." Dana nodded approvingly. "Good with you, Miles?"

Milo looked miserable. He glanced from me to Dana, and then back to me again. "Yes," he said finally.

"Good."

Calvin let out a whoop, trying desperately to change the grim mood. "Lessssss goooo, beeeetches!" he exclaimed and clasped the wad of cash in his hands excitedly before doing a little happy dance in his wheelchair.

"Jesus." Dana shook her head, but her grin was impossible to hide.

Milo took a step toward me as I headed for Cal's car. "Sky." His voice was quiet. It made me want to run into his arms, grab him, and hold on tight.

Instead, I kept walking. "Not now," I replied without glancing up.

He wanted space. So I was going to give him plenty.

CHAPTER TEN

"Fag."

The beefy-looking jock spewing the hate word was standing by the door in the Palm River CoffeeBoy, but his voice carried like a bell. And the message was clearly directed at the boy standing right behind me in the long line.

On my left, Cal dropped his jaw and shot the offender an *Oh no you didn't* look.

But Jock-Boy most definitely had.

The kid standing behind us didn't even turn around. He did nothing except lift his head a bit higher and take a long, deep, cleansing breath.

But Jock-Boy wasn't finished with his abuse. "You are *such*. A *faggot*. God! What the fuck are you even *wearing*?"

As a matter of fact, the kid behind us was wearing an *extremely* cool rainbow-colored tank. He was stylish enough to pull off the look. He also had huge sunglasses and a designer bag that had probably required a serious down payment. And yes. Even without the Technicolor garb, he was also definitely setting off my gay-dar.

I turned to face him. His freckled face had darkened into a furious flush, and I caught a whiff of his anger. "Hi, I'm Skylar," I said as pleasantly as possible, holding out a hand in greeting. "I *love* your shirt." Translation: *Let's all ignore the a-hole and maybe he'll go away.*

The boy managed a smile as he took my hand. "Thanks," he said in a quiet, even tone. "I'm Ray."

The a-hole, sadly, did the opposite of go away. "*I'm Ray*," he mocked, as he came toward us. "Like a little ray of homo sunshine. I'm *so* cute."

The muscle in Ray's jaw clenched, and I pointedly turned my back on the approaching idiot and continued our far more civilized conversation. "Nice to meet you," I told Ray. "This is my friend Calvin."

"Ray." Calvin reached up a hand, and the two boys shook as well. "Cool bag, bro."

"Thanks," Ray said again. "You're not from around here, are you?"

"Just passin' though," Cal said in his best *High Plains Drifter* imitation.

Ever since Cal had sent the elusive Morgan-the-Wonder-G-T an email confirming that we'd meet her tonight in Palm River, we'd been getting instructions more suited to delivering ransom for a hostage than having a casual meeting. But with our two hundred and fifty dollars in our pockets, we'd followed all of her cryptic rules and instructions.

Get off the highway at the second Palm River exit, pull off the road at the ancient car-pool lot, and send her another email with an embedded photo of the view facing west. (Which happened to include three palm trees that, silhouetted against the night sky, rather strongly resembled male genitalia. Calvin pointed that out with appreciation. I was not as amused.)

In response to our email-with-photo, we got a text from an "unknown" number telling us simply to wait—which we did for twenty very long minutes. (Calvin asked me approximately twenty-four Would You Rather questions. I answered maybe half with "*Ew!*")

At that point, we got yet another text, telling us to drive to this local CoffeeBoy, go inside, and wait for further instructions. How? Who knew. Cal was hoping the message would come creatively—say, written in crayon on the side of our paper coffee cup. However, I was hoping Morgan herself would be there to greet us and end this farce of a scavenger hunt.

When we arrived, the little place was hopping. I scanned the crowd at the tables, searching for someone who might be a G-T. We didn't know if Morgan was my age or older—or possibly younger. She might've been twelve, for all we knew.

As a Greater-Than, I could often tell when another girl was a G-T. It wasn't foolproof, but it worked much of the time.

But aside from a table of hipster guys who ironically checked me out, there was no one in the 'Boy who even looked up at me, let alone who set my G-T senses a-tingling. Two exhausted-looking young women sat at a table together, but both had babies in strollers. An elderly woman sat alone, scowling at her laptop computer. A heavily tatted old man in camo simultaneously checked his phone and added a mountain of sugar to his coffee. Another man—golden haired and much younger, I think—hard to tell because his head was down—was at the table in the back corner, reading an actual printed book.

As for the other people in line with us, everyone else looked like they'd stopped in for liquid energy before dragging their tired butts home from a long day at work. Cal, Ray, and I were the only ones in our under-twenty age group.

And A-hole, of course. Who sadly hadn't become invisible simply from our desire to render him so. "Cool bag," he mocked. "For a homo."

When he uttered the ugly slur, he reached out and pushed Ray solidly in the chest.

Ray, half A-hole's size, took a wobbly step backward and nearly fell into Calvin's lap.

I could smell fear now—it was thick and fishlike and awful.

Enough was enough. "*Hey!*" I said, and very deliberately stepped in between the bully and Ray. "Get a life, will you? That's *not* okay!"

A-hole's varsity jacket had the name *Eric* sewn onto the front. He was a big dude. Big enough so that I had to crane my neck to lock eyes with him—which was saying something. My mom likes to describe me as *statuesque*. Which is code for freaky-tall.

Eric had surpassed statuesque a long time ago. He was gargantuan. Ginormous. Gozilla-esque. And he had muscles.

He also didn't scare me. Oddly enough, the fear that I smelled? It was coming from *him*, not Ray.

"What are you gonna do about it, Sugar-Tits? You gonna call your mommy on me?" He held an imaginary phone to his ear and spoke in a mocking falsetto. "*Hello, Mommy? It's me, Sugar-Tits! Come save me!*"

Eric laughed uproariously at his own words, as if he were the funniest person in the world.

But I wasn't laughing.

Cal wasn't either. In fact, he'd wheeled himself closer to the action as well. "Nope. She doesn't need her mommy. In fact, if you mess with her, you'll most likely end up going home crying to yours. And, stop me if I'm wrong—*Eric*—but I doubt that would help with your precious he-man reputation."

By now, the people in the 'Boy were flat-out staring. The line was still fairly long, with about three more orders to be placed before Cal and I made it to the counter. A lady in front of us whispered uneasily into her cell phone. I scanned the crowd again, because just then, I could've sworn that I felt it… It was faint, but it was back there. I was *not* the only G-T in this room.

"It's all right, guys." Ray put his hand on my shoulder and shook his head. "I'm just gonna leave—"

"What?" I said, pulling my focus back to the situation at hand. "No! You can't just let him bully you like that—"

"Or what?" Eric took another step toward me, and this time I was the one he pushed, his hand against my chest. It was not quite a boob-grab, but it was close. The *thwap* of his giant hand was enough to knock the wind out of me, and I almost fell on my butt.

Almost.

Instead, I dug in my heels and stayed right where I was. I crossed my arms and breathed, willing myself to keep my G-T powers securely under wraps.

I hadn't honed my abilities enough yet to use them *discreetly*, as Dana would say—and I'd proven that to be true yesterday at the Sav'A'Buck.

Here and now we were already drawing too much attention. The last thing we needed was for cups of coffee and little packs of creamer to start flying around the room. Until I had a stronger grasp on my abilities, the only safe time to plug into them was when no one was watching—or when someone's life was in imminent danger.

Eric was a bully and an a-hole, but he hadn't gotten to *that* point. Yet.

I'm pretty sure, however, that my best friend disagreed. "Oh, *now* you're in trouble!" Cal bellowed and wheeled himself directly between Eric and me. The left tire of the chair rolled over the top of Eric's sneaker. It didn't look like an accident.

"*Owww!*" The a-hole howled as he hopped up and down, grabbing at his foot. "What the *fuck?*" Just as fast, his pain turned to rage, and he pulled back his giant arm and turned his ham-sized hand into a fist.

I moved faster, throwing myself between them, using my back to shield Cal from the incoming blow. It was gonna hurt, but I had wicked-fast healing abilities in my superpower toolbox, while Calvin not so much.

"Eric, *don't you dare!*" I heard Ray shout.

I braced myself, but Eric didn't hit me.

And then, a heartbeat later, he *still* didn't hit me.

And then?

The weirdest thing happened. I felt it again. That sense that there was another G-T here in the CoffeeBoy with me. But it was so faint and…distant—like whoever she was, she was here, except she wasn't…

And I turned to look and saw giant Eric stand up straight, his hand relaxed and down by his side as he tipped his head back and literally screamed, "Ray, I love you and I always have and I just wanted to get up the nerve to be as brave as you are and ask you to the prom and I love your rainbow shirt and I think you're gorgeous and amazing and if I could, I'd kiss you right! Now!"

And suddenly, the fear I could smell made total sense.

There was a long, awkward pause. The sound of the clock on the wall was like a bass drum thumping.

"Wait-wait-wait. Come *again*?" Cal's voice finally broke the silence. He craned his neck to peer out around my shield-stance to verify that he really had just heard what he thought he'd heard.

He had.

We all had.

Someone in the CoffeeBoy started to applaud, and others joined in, like this was the ending of some sappy romantic comedy movie.

Ray was openmouthed. And rather horrified. Like, kissing Eric was on his ish list instead of his wish list.

Eric also seemed stunned. His chin wobbled for a split second before he turned on his heels and sprinted out of the CoffeeBoy.

"Whoa," Cal said. "Just whoa." He shook his head fast, as if trying to manually reset his brain in order to decipher the last five minutes of his life. "What *was* that?"

"I don't know," Ray replied. "But I'm pretty sure I no longer need any caffeine. Maybe not ever again." He extracted himself from the line as he pulled his cell phone from his bag. He'd already started to put it up to his ear when he turned back to us. "Thanks," he added. "Nice meeting you both."

I nodded and looked at Cal as Ray hurried for the opposite exit, already talking on his cell. "Holy crap, Lisa. You will not. Believe. What just happened."

"I saw it, Lisa," Cal called after him. "And I'm not sure *I* believe it." He looked me up and down with concern. "You okay? He hit you pretty hard."

I was about to say that I was fine. But I didn't have time to respond.

Because the young man who'd been sitting in the corner reading that book with real paper pages? He was standing right beside us. I glanced over and saw that he'd left the book on his table, spine up to mark his place.

Up close, I could see that he was younger than I'd first thought. Maybe Milo's age, maybe a little older. A college boy. Palm River had a handful of expensive private universities. In fact, my mother had already started making noise about taking campus tours, and was all *Wouldn't it be nice if you went to college somewhere close to Coconut Key?*

I'd given little to no thought to the future—my main focus these days was on keeping myself and my friends alive.

But this guy's photo could've been in the dictionary next to college-student-comma-wealthy. He was one of those too-handsome-for-his-own-good types: wavy blond hair, emerald green eyes, lightly tanned clear skin, average height with a lean, strong runner's build.

His shabby-chic wardrobe screamed—almost as loudly as Eric had—that his trust fund was at least eight figures.

Please don't hassle us, please don't hassle us…

Calvin was thinking the same thing that I was, although he put what I was thinking into words. "If you really need a piece of us, too, dude, can you wait until *after* we get the coffee?"

The young man shook his perfect blond head and smiled with a mix of exasperation and disgust. "You must be Skylar and Calvin," he said in an accent that I couldn't quite place. "I've been waiting for you. Get your coffee but then come. Join me in my corner."

He didn't say please. He just turned and walked back to his table.

———

"Who the hell are *you?*"

Cal's question was a good one, although it *could* have been asked a bit more politely with about half-a-boatload less attitude. But after our little escapade with Eric and his projectile vomit of an emotional outburst, I was willing to cut Calvin some slack. I even raised his opening bid with an elevated eyebrow and slightly narrowed eyes aimed at our new blond associate.

"My name is John Morningstar," the blond said. "Please. Join me."

I sat, and Calvin rolled closer, and it was strange—I wouldn't have labeled this guy as *sexy*, because one, wealthy college boys had never floated my boat. And two, let's face it, after Milo had come into my life, no one held a candle in comparison. But as I studied John Morningstar, the word *beautiful* popped into my head. And he *was*—in an ethereal, almost elfin way. In fact, he looked as though he had slipped out from the pages of a leather-bound collection of fairy tales. The kind of book with gold-edged pages and a red velvet page marker sewn into the spine.

And although he was attempting to maintain an expression of disapproval or disappointment or maybe even disgust as he gazed at us, he couldn't quite pull it off. There was something back there—a twinkle in his eyes—that he couldn't quite hide.

I thought about what Dana had told me about micro-expressions and tried to freeze-frame his.

But instead of bared teeth and snarling, I kept getting amusement and laughter and genuine joy, which was kind of weird.

"There's been a mistake," I started.

Calvin nodded. "Yeah, we're supposed to be meeting—" He cut himself off, because in her instructions, Morgan had made it clear that we were *not*, under any circumstances, to speak her name out loud. Cal cleared his throat. "Someone else."

"There's no mistake," John said. "You *are* Skylar and Calvin. Correct?"

We nodded.

"Well, there you go." He was satisfied.

"But you're not—" I also stopped myself. It was possible this was some kind of test. "The person with whom we're supposed to be meeting." If I was lucky, Morgan would give me extra points for my good grammar.

"It's okay. It's safe in here," John said. "I'm Morgan's advisor, for lack of a better term."

Cal scowled. "So you're, like, her *minion*?"

John laughed. It was just as supernal as the micro-twinkle in his eyes. I, however, didn't find *any* of this funny. But I didn't stand up and storm out, even though part of me wanted to. See, I still had that vague, way-back-there sense that another G-T was nearby—maybe monitoring this conversation, maybe lurking in the bushes outside...?

"Well, that's actually an even more perfect word," John said. "Minion. Yes. I do like that. I'm her minion. Indeed. Do you have the payment?"

Calvin had the cash in his wallet, in an envelope, and he leaned to the side so he could extract it from his back pocket and put it on the table.

John Morningstar immediately reached for it, but Calvin put his own hand down on top of it.

"So we give this to you," Cal clarified, "and you count it, and then...call the person we're meeting so we can actually, you know, meet her?"

"Of course," John said with a smile.

Calvin pushed the envelope toward him and lifted his hand off of it, complete with jazz fingers.

John pocketed it without any counting. "Also, of course, Morgan gives me permission to make this type of decision on my own, and I have to be honest, the odds of you making it through this first round of interviews...? Slim to none. You're terminal do-gooders—in fact, you drip with it. Morgan doesn't need the complications that come with entanglement with the likes of you. My recommendation—after I call her, which will be later tonight because she's very, very busy— will be RRAFAYC. *Run, run, as fast as you can.*"

This was just great. For once, Dana's cynicism had been spot-on. We'd been duped. Except…I could still feel that weird little…something, and I knew with a certainty that I trusted that Morgan was not only real but she was out there. Somewhere. Maybe even watching and listening to us right now.

"This is bullshit," Calvin announced.

"I *demand* to see her," I said. I was still being careful not to say her name.

"I don't understand," Calvin said. "How is trying to do something good a *bad* thing?"

John leaned in, motioning Calvin to do the same. He created a steeple with his fingers as he rested his elbows on the cheap CoffeeBoy table. I noticed how elegant his hands were. Everything about him was nimble and striking. Even the way he moved—as though he were made from pixie dust.

"It's not so much you as her," he told Calvin as he gestured to me with a tip of his head. "I mean, she's the G-T, right? And hello, not only is her best friend in a wheelchair, but she's not in here five minutes before she nearly gets beaten up defending a total stranger from a homophobe? Life expectancies of girls like that are… Well, her survival's got those same slim-to-none odds that I quoted you earlier." He leaned back in his seat. "Darlings, look, let's not waste any more of our time and just call it a night."

I stood up at that and squared my shoulders. "Then give the money back."

"Ooh," John said, winking at Calvin. "And she's feisty, too. They can chip that onto your gravestone. *She was a feisty do-gooder.* But you know what else drips off you, along with the little Skylar Do-Good vibe?" He didn't wait for me to answer. "The angst. Oh, my Gods, the teenage angst. Sweetheart, it radiates from you. And trust me, if *I'm* picking that up, then just being in the same room with you will make my poor darling Morgan's head *explode*."

I got right up in his face, both hands braced on the table. "Then I'll stay out of the room. And FYI? I'll take *She was a feisty do-gooder* over *He was a cowardly douche.*"

He looked at me with those emerald eyes as he laughed off my insult, but now his micro-expressions were something else. I caught flashes of sadness. Or maybe longing. And possibly even shame.

And because I could still feel it—that vague something I believed was Morgan—I pushed even harder. "A G-T named Sasha was kidnapped a few months ago," I said. "She's nine years old, but she's on the autism spectrum, so she seems younger. She's tiny. She's special. And she was taken from her bedroom in the middle of the night. We're not certain exactly who took her or where she was held during the weeks she was abducted, but we believe she was eventually transported north in a Doggy Doo Good truck, imprisoned in a dog crate along with dozens of other little girls."

He winced at that.

I continued. "Whatever happened to her, she's traumatized. We *do* know that she ended up in a low-tech Destiny farm in a rotting barn in Alabama. We found her there, *and* we got her out.

"And the night that we got her out, she said something that makes us believe that at some point during her captivity she'd seen a girl named Lacey, who's been missing for years," I told him and hopefully told Morgan, too. "Did Sasha really see this girl, or was it only some kind of psychic vision or dream? We don't know. But it's important that we find out. However. That answer is locked inside Sasha's head.

"She's back with her parents now, safely in hiding, and she's also struggling with PTSD, because *Jesus*. All we're asking is for your employer to go and spend a few hours with her, to help us in our search for Lacey, and maybe, please Gods"—I purposely imitated him—"give Sasha some relief. We'll get the money to pay her fee. Somehow. *And*, I repeat: I do *not* have to be there, as much as I'd like to be."

I straightened back up. "So there's the interview. Either take that information to your boss…I know she's here somewhere—I can feel her. Or give us our freaking money back." Only I didn't say *freaking*.

John's eyelids lowered a bit, but he continued to gaze into my eyes. "You can feel her?"

I nodded. "Yup."

"That's quite a powerful little talent you have there."

"If we could do this without her help," I said, "trust me, we would."

John looked from me to Calvin and back, and sighed heavily. "You win," he said, and for a moment I actually thought that we *had* won, and that he was going to help us.

But instead, as he stood up, he took the envelope of cash out of his pocket and tore it open. He took out a ten-dollar bill, saying, "For gas and my latte," and tossed the rest of it back to Calvin. It landed with a very unsatisfying *plop* on the table.

"Ta, kids," he said, and tucking his book under his arm, he walked away.

CHAPTER ELEVEN

I was locked in a closet.

Wait. I should back up.

My *dream self* was locked in a closet.

Ever since I'd first become aware that I was a Greater-Than, back just a few short months ago, my dreams-per-night average had increased exponentially.

Some of the dreams were incredibly amazing, like the ones that included Milo…and beds…and candlelight…

But some were the most terrible nightmares I'd ever had.

The craziest piece of it all was that, unlike your typical normie dreamer's, *my* unconscious mind had a habit of mixing random dream images with actual *meaningful* ones. In other words, my G-T talents included dreaming about things that had either already taken place in real life, or were yet to happen…also in real life.

Yup. I'm a little bit psychic. *And* a tiny bit prescient. *And* I can do something called *dream-project*, which means that while I'm sleeping, I often send my dream-vision mix directly into Milo's also-sleeping head. (But only Milo's, thank goodness.) But while I'm doing *that*, Milo's own creative dream-brain has the opportunity to chime in and add *his* random thoughts and images into the already-too-cryptic, mixed-up dream pot.

And yes. After months of this, I *still* thought it all sounded completely batshit crazy. And, as far as G-T skills go, its usefulness was questionable.

Let me give you an example of what I mean. Say I wake up to discover that I've dreamed about a pig who was eating my homework and who looked up at me to grumpily say, "Your spelling is atrocious."

It was possible that my *psychic* skills were letting me know—very cryptically—that there was an important, albeit misspelled document that would help lead us to, say, Lacey, and that we'd find that document hidden at a pig farm. Or maybe even just a farm. Or a farm stand. Or stuck between the pages of a book about pig farming.

Or it was possible that my *prescient* skills, which occasionally popped up to warn me of potential *future* events, were telling me that we might find a clue to Lacey's whereabouts near a misspelled sign that bore a picture of a pig—maybe for a barbecue place? So next time we ventured into, say, the wilds of Harrisburg, I'd be on the lookout for a misspelled sign for a barbecue "kichen" and, on that future afternoon, we'd meet someone inside who would give us information we needed. Maybe.

Of course, it was also entirely possible that I'd had the dream only because *Charlotte's Web* was playing on Animated Classics and *Milo* had caught a glimpse of it while flipping channels, *and* I was stressed about my English homework.

Sometimes freaky dreams were just freaky dreams.

Top this off with the fact that, like most G-T talents, my dream-skills were extremely hit and miss. I couldn't *make* myself dream about a future event. I couldn't make myself dream about *anything*. Few and far between are the G-Ts who can actually control their dreams and nightmares.

Anyway. In this particular dream, which occurred the night after we'd been rejected by Morgan's assistant, I found myself locked in a closet. Or at least I thought it was a closet. It was hard to tell because the space was so tiny. And it was pitch-black. I'm talking no sight whatsoever. I even tried to stick my dream-hand in front of my dream-nose and wiggle my dream-fingers a little bit.

Nope. Couldn't see a thing.

Luckily, I knew that I was in a dream. And luckily I'm not too claustrophobic. Otherwise, I would have been panicking.

Instead, I took a deep breath and reached my hands out to see if I could feel where I was. And *ow!* My knuckles rapped against wood way before I expected them to. Yeah. This room was small. It had to be a closet.

It made sense, considering all the noise Milo had been making earlier today about us having to go into Rochelle's house and find out if Jilly was locked in *that* closet.

Carefully, I tried to stand. I was crouching down, my knees close to my feet. My *bare* feet. I reached down to feel my legs—and they were bare too.

I was in my underwear.

Nope, make that underpants. Only underpants.

Oh joy.

I was able to stand up completely without hitting my head. But my knees felt weak—as if I hadn't eaten anything for days. My mouth was dry, and I tried to swallow, but it felt like my saliva was made of razor blades.

Things shifted then, the way they often do in dreams, and I was out in the bright sunshine, in Garrett's car with Dana, holding the stupid tablet and watching Milo and Rochelle over one of the flower-cams. Figures my subconscious would bring me back here. Thanks, brain.

"Tonight's no good, baby boy. I have…plans," Rochelle said as she pouted.

And then, instead of watching as the camera lens focused on Milo's sneakers and Rochelle's high-heeled sandals and manicured toenails, the dream shifted and burped, and I was sitting in Garrett's car, watching Milo and Rochelle actually kiss.

It was as awful as I'd imagined, seeing Milo lick his way into the elderly creeper's mouth, his hand firmly holding the back of her perfectly coifed head.

"I know what a man likes," Rochelle pulled back to whisper.

And I must've made a sound—a sob or a whimper—because I felt a hand on my shoulder and I turned to see Sasha—sweet little Sasha with her big, brown eyes. The little girl I used to babysit was standing behind me, and I quickly moved to cover the tablet—for some reason I didn't want her seeing it—but I realized I wasn't holding it anymore.

In fact, we weren't in Garrett's car anymore. We were back in that dilapidated barn in Alabama, and Sasha's head was shaved and she was wearing one of those thin, horrible hospital gowns that they made all the little girls wear. She shivered in the breeze and said, "Don't cry, Skylar. It'll be okay."

I reached for her, to hug her, comforted by her words, but she wasn't finished, and she stepped back to say, "We can play with my dolls soon—when we're both dead."

She smiled at me then, and her teeth were fangs that were dripping with blood and I recoiled, but the dream shifted again, and I was back in the closet, crouched in the darkness, my heart pounding.

But I was only there for a moment as the world slanted again, and this time Rochelle was leering at *me*, her hand on my jean-clad butt as she said, "If you want, I can show you. Give you the hundred-dollar tour."

It was almost as awful as Sasha's bloody fangs, but my sleeping brain made another sharp turn and I was back in the closet, where suddenly, I heard a noise to my left.

It was muffled. But it sounded like footsteps. On the other side of the wall—or door…?

There was a door to my left! The wood was smoother, and *yes!* I clasped the doorknob. It was old-fashioned and made of glass—smooth and cold beneath my fingers. Using both hands, one on top of the other, I muscled the knob to the left and then to the right. But it didn't turn.

It was, of course, locked.

The footsteps were getting louder and I started to shake with fear.

Another dream shift. And now I was in the kitchen with Rochelle and Garrett, who cheerfully said, "*Here's* Cal! Thought we'd lost ya, buddy!"

And here came Cal, wheeling into the room. "Yup! Here I am! With more flowers! 'Cause you definitely don't have enough of *those* now!" Except instead of flowers on his lap, he held a big cardboard box. He reached in and pulled out first one and then two of the cutest puppies I'd ever seen. They were pitch-black with long, droopy ears. Cal held them both up à la *The Lion King*—speaking of classic animation. Which really wasn't much of a surprise, since unlike Dana, I often watched Disney to de-stress.

Rochelle leaned in to me and whispered, "I'll cook them into a delicious, savory stew that you can lick off my body."

What? *Ew!*

Boom, I was back in the closet, and instantly I could smell it.

It hit me like a right hook to the nose. The stench of sewage—something I'd unfortunately become quite familiar with over the past several months.

You already know that my G-T powers allow me to smell emotions. But I can also smell a complete *lack* of emotion—which is also known as evil.

That sewage smell? You guessed it. Evil. Big-time.

The footsteps grew even louder, and then they slowed. My heart pounded in my chest as I realized that the evil I was smelling came from whoever—whatever—was standing outside that door.

Was I dreaming this through Jilly's eyes?

If that was true, then the person on the other side of the door was most likely Rochelle. In real life, I hadn't gotten close enough to smell her.

But in the other part of this nightmare, I had. Her perfume was disgusting but sewage free.

I stuck my nose into the crook of my elbow and took a deep breath, trying to filter out the awfulness as I continued to shake with someone else's—Jilly's?—fear.

Still thoughts. Still thoughts…

And then? The door swung open, and the light from the outside room blinded me—for just a moment.

"You piece of *shit!*" the voice roared…and it *definitely* wasn't Rochelle who yanked me out of the closet and tossed me onto the ground like a piece of trash.

It was a man. A big man. And he had a belt.

"You ready to stop acting like a selfish little piece of lying *shit?*"

But my heart was thumping hard in my chest, and maybe I'd misheard the man's words. I could see his face looming over me as I lay on the ground, helpless.

The first blow was excruciating.

As the belt came down and hit me on the rib cage, I tried to howl, the agony searing through my entire body like a shock of electricity. But the pain was so profound, I couldn't even find it in me to make a noise.

I didn't even know if I was breathing.

"*You little shit!*" the man bellowed again, and I tried my hardest to focus on his face. He was around my mother's age…with a tattoo of a... Was it a cobra on his forearm? Bald. Black V-neck T-shirt. Jean shorts. Scarred and scab-covered knees.

Still thoughts...Still thou—

Thwwwwwaaack!

The belt hit me again, this time on the side of my neck. The air I'd been holding in my lungs swooshed out of me with the force of the blow.

I wanted to inhale again, but the idea of pulling that terrible, noxious, evil air into my system again made my stomach churn.

"This time I'm gonna kill you!"

Just as the man raised the belt again, I heard the sound of my alarm clock—and, like a person pulled from the ocean to be saved from drowning, I charged out of the dream and woke up, *finally* able to scream.

And then? I sat there, in my bed, the incessant alarm sounding through the still-dark room, as I leaned forward, placed my hands over my face, and burst into tears.

———

"Skylar? What's wrong? Are you all right?"

Momzilla.

She'd obviously heard me scream, and now she was running down the hallway toward my room as if I were maybe being attacked by the vast collection of murderers, rapists, arsonists, muggers, and killer clowns who, in my mother's imagination, lurked around every corner, eagerly waiting for me to set foot outside the safety of our house.

Quickly, I reached over and slapped off my alarm clock. Somehow, my G-T powers had triggered it to ring and wake me up. But Mom would certainly wonder why my alarm was going at… I looked more closely at the clock. It was 3:48 a.m. I wiped away my tears and smoothed my hair down before sitting up straighter in my bed and planting an absurdly fake smile across my face.

It was just in time, too. Because Mom did exactly what I knew she'd do—she swung open my bedroom door without knocking and bounded across the room. "What happened?" Mom exclaimed, looking distraught as she wrapped her bathrobe tightly across her front.

I shook my head, my smile still plastered from ear to ear like a moron. "Nothing, Ma," I replied in my best nonchalant tone. I sounded shaky though. I couldn't help it. I was still out of breath from the nightmare.

"But I heard you scream! Were you—"

"Dreaming," I finished for her. "It was a nightmare. About…Sasha."

It wasn't *exactly* a lie, even though Sasha was, by no means, the star of that particular bad dream. That prize went to the man with the belt.

Was he a friend of Rochelle's? Brought in to torment Jilly or to stand guard, make sure she didn't use her G-T awesomeness to break free? Or was he the man who'd bought her from Rochelle? Probably not, because Destiny cookers kept rooms—or barns—filled with dozens of little girls. Unless Jilly was in some kind of solitary confinement…?

This dream was extra-cryptic, and I made a mental note to tell Dana and the gang about it.

"Oh, sweetheart," Mom said, her voice soft and thick with emotion. "It makes sense that you'd have bad dreams about Sasha."

"Yeah," I replied, attempting to keep my tone casual. I really didn't want a heart-to-heart with Mom right now. As nice as she'd been when I came back from saving Sasha—I'd only gotten a week's worth of grounding for what normally would have been an entire decade of no social life—I still wasn't ready for full disclosure. As much as I suspected that Mom knew, at least a little, about my Greater-Than status, neither of us had spoken of it. And I intended for it to stay that way for as long as possible.

Mom studied me, as if trying to read my thoughts. Thank everything holy that she wasn't telepathic.

I was still giving her my best *I'm fine* cheesy grin, and I raised my eyebrows a little to send her a silent *Are we done here, 'cause it's kinda sorta three in the morning* message.

Of course, Mom wasn't just not-telepathic. She was also pretty dense. Instead of exiting my room and letting me settle back into a (hopefully) dreamless sleep, she just sat there on the edge of my bed, smiling sadly back at me and not making a move to leave.

"It was a lot that you went through," she told me. "Seeing Sasha like that. I'm sure you need some time to process it all. I hope you'll let me know if there's anything I can do to make the healing easier for you."

Process. Healing. Sasha.

It occurred to me then, as I was trying to hurry my mom out of the room in the middle of the night, that maybe I could simply ask her to set up a meeting with Sasha, instead of using my homing powers to track down the little girl. I knew Mom was still in touch with Sasha's mother—I'd overheard them talking on the phone just a few days ago.

And, even without the elusive Morgan on hand to get inside Sasha's head, there was a chance that talking to the little girl might help us in our search for Lacey. It was a long shot—but better than nothing.

Plus, as annoying as Mom tended to be about everything, she was offering to help.

Now was as perfect a time as ever to ask her for that help.

What's the worst she could say?

Actually, I could think of a long list of cringe-worthy things that Mom would very likely say.

"We-ell," I started, "Now that you mention it? I... Well, I think I have an idea about how to help myself...process and heal."

Mom perked up so quickly and with such perfect posture that she looked like a prairie dog popping its head out of a hole in the ground. Somehow, I managed to keep a straight face. I tucked the sheets more snugly around my legs and studied the covers, as if what I was about to say was very difficult.

In truth, I was way past the point of needing to process and heal *anything*. As far as I was concerned, there wasn't any time in my life for *And how does that make you feel?* therapy. Because, as soon as one crazy, death-defying moment ended, I was on to the next before I could blink an eye. And, anyway, what had happened to Sasha had happened to *Sasha*. *I* wasn't the one who had been hunted down, kidnapped, and held in a dilapidated barn with dozens of other help-less little girls. *I* was just fine.

But I needed to really milk it for Mom. I stuttered a little as I started. "I-I... Oh, it's really hard to say. I just feel, more and more, like I don't have...closure."

Closure was one of those extra-magic *talk about your feelings* words. Mom nodded understandingly and waited for me to continue.

"I think that if I could just see Sasha again—just to talk to her and see that she's really okay—that I might feel better. The last time I saw her, she still looked terrible." I shuddered. Which didn't require acting skills on my part. Sasha *had* been a mess when Milo, Dana, Cal, and I had rescued her. All of those little girls—the ones we had managed to save—had been emaciated, eyes hollow and devoid, their heads shaved completely bald. Sasha had still looked like a concentration camp victim a month later, during my first and only visit.

Mom sighed deeply, and I braced myself and waited for the inevitable lame excuse for why I wouldn't be allowed to visit Sasha.

Instead, to my utter astonishment, Mom slapped the tops of her legs in a gesture of determination and then stood up. "I'll call Sasha's mother in the morning. I'm sure we can arrange something."

Momzilla actually said *yes*?

This was almost too weird.

But then again, maybe it wasn't. First Cal and Garrett had started getting along—or at least tolerating one another. Then, Milo started doing his freaky *I need space* thing. And now, Mom had said *yes* to something I was certain would get a resounding *no*. What was next? Was Dana going to start writing poetry or expressing her feelings through interpretive dance?

I covered up my surprise with a smile and reached out to catch and squeeze my mom's hand. "That would be awesome," I said. "Thanks, Mom. You're great."

And I honestly meant it.

CHAPTER TWELVE

"Get your ass in here, Bubble Gum," I heard Dana call out the moment I stepped into Cal's house.

Apparently I was the last to arrive—the entire gang was already here. We'd made plans to meet this morning, to debrief.

Although truth be told, Dana and Calvin had already exchanged a flurry of texts in which we'd reported last night's failure up in Palm River. In return, Dana had reported that Rochelle's so-called plans for the evening had apparently been to watch endless amounts of reality TV and kill two bottles of white wine before falling unconscious and snoring on her couch.

"You're late," Dana continued as I came into the playroom. She was crouching behind the table that held Calvin's video and gaming system, beneath his flat-screen TV, messing with some wires and cords. Cal had his chair right behind her. He was looking over her shoulder, micromanaging.

"That one," he said. "No no nuh no—the red one. The *other* red one."

Milo was on the sofa, and when our gazes met, he started to stand as if to come over and give me a hug. But then he stopped—as if he'd thought better about touching me—and my heart sank. Apparently, he still hadn't had enough space.

"Good morning," I announced to the room as pleasantly as I could muster. "I'm late for a very good reason."

"'Sup," Garrett said, coming out of the little bathroom. "I just took a dump that looks *exactly* like a manatee."

"Looks?" Cal said, on top of the details as usual. "As in present tense, looks? Dude, no one wants to see it, so go back in there and flush, *right now*."

Garrett turned back around, grumbling, "Well, if I *hadn't* saved it, then—"

"No one. Wants to see it. Flush!" Calvin repeated, although he was laughing and shaking his head, like the football player was merely zany, like Garrett was the Gilligan on our private desert isle rather than the douche that he'd long ago proven himself to be.

And okay, I was definitely biased when it came to Garrett. To fully overcome my negative view of him, he'd have to rescue a busload of orphans, puppies, and kittens from a fiery and certain death. In other words, never gonna happen.

Despite that, even *I* was convinced that his concern for Jilly was real. He cared about the girl—enough to put himself at risk to try to find her.

And that was not nothing.

Even Milo smiled as Garrett returned with a dramatic leap over the back of the couch. He landed with his feet already up on the coffee table and proceeded to give his full attention to his cell phone.

"So what's your good reason for being late?" Dana asked me, but then she straightened up and both she and Calvin looked over at Milo. "Try the wireless now."

Milo was holding both our surveillance tablet and the remote, and when he clicked the latter, the TV came on. Instantly, the three real-time shots from inside Rochelle's house—the ones that we'd previously only been able to see on the tablet—appeared on Cal's giant TV.

"*Yes!*" Garrett yelled out triumphantly from his spot on the couch. He'd done nothing to help, manatee removal aside. In fact, he was still busy scrolling through his phone and didn't even bother to look up. "Uh-oh," he said.

"What?" I asked, moving closer to the TV. Rochelle was nowhere in sight. The sofa was empty, as was the kitchen. The third camera was still focused through the open doorway to the home gym, aimed at that dead-bolted closet door. *That* was the side of the screen that Milo was watching.

"My dad's been texting me off the hook," Garrett announced. "He's pissed. Rochelle must've called and left him some big, long thank-you for the flowers and how nice it was that I'd brought them over, and he's basically all WTF. *CALL ME RIGHT NOW*—that one's in all caps, like he's gonna pop a vein." Garrett studied his phone for another second. "Eh." He shrugged and clicked his cell to silent mode and then dropped it onto the couch beside him. "Damage done. He'll get over it. Another two, three weeks, he won't even remember."

"Has Rochelle been up yet this morning?" I asked, looking around at my friends, uncertain whose turn it was to monitor the video feeds.

"She crawled off the sofa at around five a.m.," Calvin reported. "Hasn't been back downstairs since. But she and Miles have been—" He cut himself off, as if he suddenly realized that I might not welcome a sentence that started with the words *She and Miles have been.*

He was right.

"Texting." Milo quickly spoke up from the sofa. "Via my new burner phone." He held it up. "I told her I got her number off Garrett's phone and…I just sent you a text, too, with the new number."

After he'd exchanged texts with Rochelle.

Milo no doubt was able to read my mind despite our lack of contact, and he coughed. "I didn't really care about waking her, so…I was trying to get her to meet up earlier. For lunch instead of dinner."

My heart was pounding. "So you're actually going to go through with meeting her for *lunch* now."

"No," he said. "Well, *no* because Ro's not available until seven. Tonight. For dinner."

Ro? Give me a break.

"So," Dana prompted Milo to continue, "did you make solid plans with her?"

"We're on for dinner at seven sharp."

"Good boy. Rochelle will definitely be ready. She wouldn't miss it for the world."

Dana had *that* right.

"Gonna be interesting to see what's on her busy, busy schedule for today," she continued, settling onto the sofa between Garrett and Milo, and putting her steel-toed boots up onto the coffee table. *Thump* and *thump*.

Now that we no longer had to peer at the tiny tablet to monitor the feeds from Rochelle's house, Dana turned her attention to me. "Good reason for being inexcusably late?" she prompted with her usual tact and grace.

I definitely deserved bonus points for not taking my frustration with Milo out on her.

"Yes," I said politely instead of screaming at her. "It occurred to me that my mother's been in touch with Sasha's mother, so I asked my mom to give her a call, see if we could set up a visit. You know, instead of me homing in on her, and then Sasha's parents wondering how we found them and getting all freaked out and probably not even letting me see her—"

"A normie approach," Dana said, nodding. "Smart. When will we know if you're cleared to visit?"

"Right now," I said. "I'm cleared. Calvin, as well. I told my mom that he wanted to see Sasha, too—and that he could drive me. She already called and set it up. Well, almost set it up. We're working out the best day and time for Sasha, but it's definitely going to happen before the end of school vacation."

"Sooner is better," Dana reminded me. "Today, in fact, would be—"

"Yes, I know, but we're trying to find a time that's best for *Sasha*," I said a bit testily.

"Also?" Cal chimed in, aiming his words at Dana. "A delay gives us more time to meet with Morgan and convince her to go with."

To my surprise, Dana nodded. I looked at Cal, confused. "I thought that was a dead end."

After leaving the CoffeeBoy last night, Calvin had attempted to email Morgan, but his message had bounced. Her email account had been deleted. Just like that. Same thing happened when we tried to call the phone number from which we'd received those texts. It was disconnected. Even the Internet message board where he'd first made contact was shut down.

"Is her email working again?" I asked.

"Noooooo," Cal said, drawing out the vowel in a way that clued me in to the fact that he and Dana had done some strategizing without me. "But we've been brainstorming ideas for how to do a face-to-face."

He wasn't kidding. But before he could elaborate, Garrett pointed to the TV screen. "Guys! Heads up!"

Sure enough, Rochelle had come into view, via the kitchen-cam.

I sat down, tailor-style, on Cal's floor and held my breath, studying the Destiny addict's petite and perfect body. She moved like a dancer—all grace and elegant lines—and it was weird to think she was, in truth, a total monster. Today, she was wearing a pair of jean cutoffs, along with a white spaghetti-strap tank top. Her hair was, of course, perfect, too, and her tanned skin glowed as she went directly toward what looked like a programmable coffeemaker, opening the cabinet above it to get a mug.

But the cabinet was bare—she was going to have to give in and do the dishes. But as we watched, she took a mug from the pile of dirties in the sink, dumped out whatever had been in it, sniffed it, then poured herself some coffee.

"Ew, not even a rinse?" Garrett asked. Apparently he, of the toilet manatee, was squeamish about *that*.

That obvious discussion Cal and Dana had had about Morgan—and probably quite a few other things before I'd arrived—had left me feeling out of the loop. And last night's bad dream was still a vivid memory, so I asked, "Has anyone come out to the house? I'm thinking male, ginormous, hairy shoulders, scabby knees…?" I turned to look at Milo and found him staring at me as if maybe my words had rung a bell. "It definitely wasn't Man-in-Black from the spa parking lot money-drop. He was big, too, but it wasn't him."

Now Dana, Garrett, and Cal were also looking at me.

"Who wasn't him?" Garrett asked, confused.

"No one's come to the house," Dana said. She looked at Milo and Garrett. "Right?"

"Not that I saw," Milo said.

"Nope. It's been all Ro, all alone. So where do you get *scabby knees?*" Garrett asked.

"I had a weird dream last night," I reported.

"How weird?" Dana asked, eyes narrowing. "And was it a dream or a vision?"

Milo turned to look at me again, and now he was frowning too. But really, his expression was more sad than anything.

I studied the tops of my hands and shook my head. "I don't…know. I feel…felt…like it was real. But I don't think it was in *real time*, you know, like a psychic event. It felt more like a memory, but through someone else's eyes…if that makes sense. It wasn't *my* memory, but at the same time, it kind of was. For most of it, I was in a closet, so I was thinking I was picking up something from Jilly, because… Well. But there was this giant man with a belt and, yeah, really nasty knees."

Milo made a noise deep in his throat, like he'd been wounded. Just as quickly, he cleared his throat and reached into his pocket to pull out a piece of Smok'B'Gon gum.

Garrett did his creepy-laugh thing and looked from Dana to me and back again. "Do you seriously mean *visions*? Like, your dreams actually come *true*?"

"Not all of them," I replied. "Sometimes. It's kind of hard to explain." I then told Dana and the guys the details—well, most of them—about the dream, focusing on the man with the belt and the smell of evil. As I spoke, I was even more convinced that I was somehow seeing the world through Jilly's traumatized eyes.

"But since there's been no giant, hairy, scabby-kneed men showing up here," I pointed out, "maybe Dana's theory is right. Maybe Rochelle sold Jilly to her dealer, who sold her to some Destiny farm, where she's been thrown into their version of solitary because—"

"No." Milo interrupted me.

I looked over at him, eyebrows raised. "Excuse me?"

He shrugged helplessly. "I mean, maybe you were just, you know, dreaming. Jilly's in that closet"—he pointed at the TV screen—"in *that* beach house. I know it. There's no giant hairy man, just Rochelle, who, believe me, is awful enough."

"You *know* it," I countered flatly. "Because *your* G-T talents include omniscience—oh, wait, except you're not a Greater-Than. You're just a normie."

As the words left my lips, I wished I could take them back, even before the hurt flashed in Milo's dark eyes. There was no such thing as *just a normie*, and even if there was, he was anything but.

"I'm sorry," I whispered as Milo looked away from me. "I didn't mean that."

And there we were, sitting there in silence, while Dana, Cal, and Garrett all tried to be invisible.

"I know," Milo finally said, glancing back at me.

"Guys?" Garrett pointed to the TV.

Rochelle had left the kitchen, and for a moment, we all just stared at the video feeds, trying to figure out where she'd gone.

"There!" Dana said, pointing.

As we watched, Rochelle went into her playroom-slash-home-gym and headed directly for that dead-bolted closet door.

"She's going to open it," Cal started in a hushed voice, as if Rochelle could hear us from his rec room.

"Open it, dammit!" Milo hissed through clenched teeth. He was leaning forward in his seat on the couch, his eyes glued to the screen as though his life depended on it. "Open the closet, Ro!"

Dana also leaned forward as she, too, watched Rochelle. And we all heard the click of the lock as it opened.

The door creaked, and Rochelle quickly went inside. Despite the high quality of the camera, everything beyond the door was completely dark.

"Do you see anything—" I started. But Rochelle swung the door closed behind her, leaving us as clueless as we were a minute ago.

"*Shit!*" Milo breathed.

"She'll come back out again," Garrett said. "She did last night."

All four of us whipped our heads around to look at him.

"I'm sorry," Dana said in a normal voice, but then leaned in close to shout, "*What?*"

"*Heh-heh.*" Garrett thought she was kidding. "She went in, she came out; she went in, she came out. You know?"

"Rochelle went into that closet *twice* last night?" I clarified, and he nodded.

"When?" Milo asked.

"It was when I was watching the tablet," Garrett said. "Dana was sleeping in the backseat of my car and you—"

"Went to get dinner," Milo grimly finished for him.

"It didn't occur to you to wake me up?" Dana was incredulous.

"Or to tell me when I got back with the food?" Milo asked.

Garrett looked from Milo to Dana to Cal to me. It's possible I was making the least-angry-looking face, because he explained to me somewhat plaintively, "But we were looking for any sign of Jilly." He turned back to Milo. "You came back and you said, *Any sign of Jilly?* And there wasn't. Any. Jilly."

"And you didn't think the fact that Rochelle went into that closet— twice—was worth reporting?" Dana asked.

"Well, no," Garrett said, "because she didn't bring Jilly out with her."

"You told us about the *very important fact* that Rochelle farted,"

Dana pointed out. "You even wrote down the time code for when it happened."

"Well, yeah, because that was funny," Garrett said. "It was like a trombone solo." He imitated the sound, and out of the corner of my eye, I could see Calvin making a mental note to rewind to that part of the digital recording.

"What is she doing in there?" Dana asked. "And what was she doing last night?"

"I don't know," Garrett said. "All I know is, she went in and after a few minutes, she came out. And then she did it again."

What was behind that dead-bolted closet door?

I found myself leaning forward, too, but on Cal's TV nothing moved.

The waiting was terrible. Seconds passed, and then minutes, and nothing happened. And nothing happened. And...

"Here she comes!" Cal exclaimed.

Sure enough, the door to the closet was moving, Rochelle's talon-like fingers wrapped around the edge as she pushed the door open and came back out into the hallway. Her body was positioned so that, once again, there was no way for any of us to spot what lay beyond her, inside that very dark closet. Cal grabbed the tablet, opened a fourth window, and used it to rewind the footage from that camera's feed. He played it back and even took several screenshot stills, zooming in close in an attempt to see into the darkness. But all we saw were close-ups of darkness.

Milo was careful not to curse out loud this time. But I could tell by the way his jaw tightened that he was extremely unhappy.

Once the door was completely closed, Rochelle worked on checking and rechecking that the bolt was locked again.

"What're those thingies in her hand?" Garrett asked.

"What thingies?" Cal asked.

"There—" Garrett began to point, but Rochelle was already moving out of the camera's static view.

There was another pause, and then she reappeared again, this time in front of the sofa in the living room. The camera in the floral arrangement was positioned perfectly, and we had a clear shot of Rochelle as she sat down.

We could now see that she held not one but two syringes…along with a little vial of liquid and two rubber tourniquets—the kind that the lab tech uses before drawing blood. She set it all down on the glass coffee table in front of her. And, because of the camera in the strategically placed floral arrangement, in front of us, too.

"Wait. Is that—"

"Destiny, already in the syringes." Dana finished my sentence. "Street D, lower-grade stuff. You can tell 'cause it's red-tinged, from blood. That's processed out of the purer shit. Good eye, Garrett," she added.

"Is she… She's gonna—shoot up? Right now?" Squeamish, Garrett looked like he might barf.

Dana nodded grimly.

"What's in the vial?" Cal asked as Rochelle added a hefty amount of whatever it was to one of the syringes, then shook it as if to mix it up.

"I bet she's morphing it up," Dana mumbled.

Milo nodded his agreement.

I had no idea what that meant. Cal apparently didn't have a clue either. "Um, English, please?" he asked sweetly.

None of us turned away from the TV screen, but Dana ran an impatient hand through her hair as she watched Rochelle do the same to the second syringe. "Morphing it up. Morphine." She sighed, disgust tingeing her voice. "It's the latest thing. Soup up your Destiny with either morphine or dope. Heroin."

"I know what dope is," Cal said defensively.

I actually hadn't. But there was a reason why Dana always called me Bubble Gum and Princess. I didn't exactly have a ton of experience with drugs, and my street cred was zilch.

My stomach twisted as I remembered only a few months ago when Milo had reassured me that there was nothing wrong with not being street-smart. He had held my hand when he'd said it. It was right after we'd learned that we could communicate through touch, but before we'd become more than friends.

Now, Milo sat across the room from me. But he might as well have been across the entire country in California, along with my other ex, Tom Diaz. I caught myself. Milo wasn't my *other* ex. He wasn't my ex. Oh my Lord, was I really starting to think of Milo as my *ex*?

I willed my thoughts back to the present.

Morphine. Or heroin. Mixed with Destiny.

Dana was still talking. "The theory is that sedation makes it easier for the body to accept the dose of Destiny. So the chances of jokering are lower. At least that's what people try to convince themselves. Who knows if it's really any safer?"

"Wait," Garrett said. "Jokering is what, again?"

"When Destiny addicts go full-on, super-villain insane," Cal informed him. "It happens with a much higher rate of frequency when they shoot up."

"Kind of like overdosing, except instead of quietly dying, they kill everyone around them before they check out," Dana said.

"Destiny addicts develop their own unique superpowers," I chimed in. "Kind of the same way that no two Greater-Thans have the exact same abilities—like Dana has serious TK while mine is limited to moving liquids. She can mind-control people, but I can't. I can home in on them and track them, but she can't. Right? It's the same for D-addicts. Their powers are unique."

"And those powers get increasingly stronger when they joker," Calvin said.

"Which means it gets increasingly harder to kill a joker," Milo pointed out. "It's always best to do it fast."

"Good to know," Garrett muttered.

Dana pointed to the TV screen as Rochelle put down the second syringe. "What I can't figure out is, why two needles?"

I had been wondering the same thing.

We didn't wonder long though.

Because just then Rochelle's doorbell rang.

"Destiny party?" Cal asked in a grim tone.

"Or it's the ginormous man, come to stand guard while she's morphing it up," I suggested, and even though Milo shifted in his seat, he didn't contradict me.

"Come on in, Ash. It's open—but lock it behind you, 'kay?" Rochelle called.

"Hey, Ro. Ooh, looks like you're all ready for me!" Another woman walked into the camera frame and sat down on the couch next to Rochelle, giving her one of those weird not-quite-touching hugs and air kisses on each non-cheek.

"Aww," Cal gushed. "Demon lady's got a lil' buddy!"

"That's Ashley," Milo informed us.

"Lunch-at-Harbor-Locke Ashley?" Dana asked, and Milo nodded. "She's definitely a user, too."

Like Rochelle, this woman was blond, tan, and Barbie-doll perfect. She handed "Ro" a huge wad of cash that was immediately pocketed.

Garrett made a strangled sound, and when I glanced over at him, it was obvious he was torn. He looked like he couldn't decide if he should start drooling—the two women were, after all, movie-star hot—or puking, since they were also about to inject enzymes from the blood of innocent little girls into their veins.

We all fell silent as Rochelle helped Ashley tie off her arm above the elbow, and then Ashley did the same for Rochelle. All the while they were chatting about needing to shop for dresses for some upcoming gala and the color of their nail polish and Ashley's new shoes. They tapped the insides of their elbows on the tied arm with a casual air—it was clear they were old hands at this—then both women picked up a syringe and thrust their needles underneath their skin.

Garrett cringed and looked away. "This is so effed."

Milo chewed on his gum, his jaw working hard.

The two women instantly slumped against the couch. For a second, I actually thought that neither Rochelle nor her friend would possess the energy to extract the now-empty syringes from their arms. They were *that* out of it.

"Morphing it up, for sure," Milo said.

Dana nodded as Rochelle managed to rouse herself long enough to whisk both needles out of their skin and even pull off the tourniquets before carelessly tossing it all onto the glass tabletop. She then leaned back into the couch cushions and shut her eyes.

It was one of the most disturbing things I'd ever seen. Those two women—just fine moments ago—their eyes now heavy lidded and bodies now limp.

"Just say no to drugs," Cal offered.

But there was nothing funny about this.

Milo interjected, "We could go inside there now. Try to get into the closet while Ro and Ashley are...indisposed."

"No." Dana's response was fast and adamant. "They're not completely unconscious. And even if they were, there's no guarantee that one of them won't suddenly joker. Nobody's going into that house right now."

Milo's frustration was painfully evident. "So we're just going to leave Jilly in there with two ticking time bombs."

Garrett was the color of sour milk. I was feeling pretty freaked out myself. This *was* a lot to just walk into.

"We don't know for sure that Jilly is in there," Dana reminded Milo. "We're not going to put anyone else in danger for a maybe that leans heavily toward maybe-not. It's safer to wait 'til Rochelle leaves."

"We might be running out of time," Milo countered.

"We'll go in there *tonight*," Dana insisted. She turned to the rest of us, after deciding that since the Rochelle and Ashley Show now consisted of them lying on the couch like skinny, blond, beached whales, she no longer needed to keep watching. "Guys. Miles is right about not wasting time. We don't need to sit around and do nothing this afternoon. In fact"—she looked at me—"we'll use these next coupla hours to talk to Morgan."

I laughed. Really? Just like that? Snap our fingers and *talk to Morgan*—who didn't want to be found.

Dana continued without skipping a beat. "Clearly Cal and Sky couldn't get the job done. But *I* will. I should've been there in the first place. Mind-controlled that stupid John Morningstar into taking us to see Morgan."

"John Morningstar," Garrett scoffed. "Sounds like a porn name."

Dana ignored him. "Sky," she said instead. "You met Morningstar. That means you can home in on him now."

And *that* was how we were going to find Morgan even though she didn't want to be found. I looked at Cal, who shrugged. "It's true. We can track him."

"We?" I asked.

"You," he said.

And once again, everyone was looking at me.

It was always weird to perform under pressure, like doing a circus trick for an audience. I attempted to focus and search for the little flicker of awareness that was John Morningstar. He was out there, somewhere, and I *should've* been able to feel him…but I got nothing. I shook my head. "I don't know—"

"You can do it," Dana insisted.

I looked over at Milo, who was gazing back at me. His eyes were warm, for once. He surprised me by leaning across the couch and holding out his hand.

I didn't take it right away, and he smiled ruefully. "I know I'm just a normie, but maybe I can help."

"I didn't mean that," I said again.

"I know." He motioned for me to take his hand, so I did and our connection—warm, familiar, wonderful—clicked on. Lord, I'd missed this.

I have, too, he told me.

But I could feel the mental walls he'd put up—larger and sturdier than his usual barriers—and I got a strong sense that he was bracing himself. As if part of him expected me to take some kind of weird telepathic run at those walls, to get over them and see what was on the other side—to see exactly what Milo was hiding.

I wouldn't, I thought at him and of course he also picked up my hurt that he would think I would just go rifling through his mental underwear drawer, uninvited.

It's not you, it's me, he told me, adding quickly, *FOR me, I mean.* He knew I didn't understand, so he tried again with, *I'm trying to protect you, Sky. You don't need my chaos right now. You need to focus.*

I realized as I gazed back at him that I could construct my own walls—boundaries—to keep him from *my* chaos, too. It wasn't all that hard to do, although don't ask me how I did it. I just…wanted it to happen, so it did.

I felt Milo's sigh of frustration, even as I successfully hid my own burst of grief. As our relationship progressed, I'd thought we'd move closer, but this was a solid step apart.

Just for now, Milo promised, and I wanted to believe him, so I left all my doubts on the non-Milo side of my own sturdy mental wall. But believe me, they were there, stewing around plenty.

Focus, Milo told me. *Can you feel John Morningstar? Can you home in on him?*

Sure enough, with Milo's help, I realized that I *could* feel Morningstar. It wasn't a huge pull—not the same insistent feeling when I'd led us to Alabama to rescue Sasha. But that college boy we'd met up at the CoffeeBoy in Palm River was definitely present. I could feel him in the back of my brain, like little pieces of pixie dust floating around like cosmic breadcrumbs. If I followed them, we'd find John Morningstar.

"Okay," I said aloud. "Yeah, I got this."

Milo squeezed my hand before letting go.

"*Heh. Heh-heh.*" Garrett's obnoxious little snicker sliced through the air. "Superhero girls."

Dana cut the super-douche off with a "Yeah, yeah. The superhero girls need to go on a mission now. You get to stay here and monitor the two crazies. Call Cal's phone if there's any change. *Any* change. As in, if they move *at all*."

As far as assignments went, it was kind of lame. And Garrett knew it. But he nodded begrudgingly. "Fine," he said. "Calvin, you sure your parents aren't coming home?"

"Mom's on a business trip in Atlanta," Cal reported, "and Dad's got a project deadline. If he shows up, it'll be to grab a clean shirt and head back to the office. Just turn off the TV and tell him that I ran out to get pizza."

Dana clapped her hands. "Bathroom up, gang. We might be in the car awhile."

Cal rolled off to do just that, as Milo and I both scrambled to our feet.

"Although, let's just hope Morningstar didn't take a trip to Alabama," Dana continued. "I'd really like to stay at least semi-local here."

Out of habit, I reached for Milo's hand, and this time he only took a half a heartbeat to brace himself and reinforce his walls before he intertwined his fingers with mine.

Ready? he asked.

Let's do this.

And, for that moment, despite the mental walls we'd both erected, I almost felt as if I had my boyfriend back again.

CHAPTER THIRTEEN

"Guys?" Milo's voice was low but urgent. "Sky. Heads up."

The dogs had come out of nowhere, their growls ominous as they peered out of tunnels, from behind trash piles, and around the corners of abandoned midway booths. I'd been leading the way, but I now stopped and counted six sets of ferocious eyes locked on us. Dana was right behind me, with Calvin rolling beside her. Milo had our backs, trailing a few steps behind. But we now all froze.

"Whoa, they're pit bulls," Calvin said. "Big ones. Five of 'em."

"Six," I corrected him.

"Don't look directly at them," Dana said in a calm, almost too-quiet voice. "They'll read that as aggressive."

Currently, I was reading *their* growling as aggressive, oh and also? *Pit bulls.* They didn't need to growl—their simple existence here was enough to intimidate the crap out of me.

The four of us were on foot—or *in chair* in Cal's case—with the car at least a quarter of a mile away in the empty and overgrown parking lot of this abandoned amusement park called Adventure City.

The park was a sad, forgotten skeleton of what had once been home to an elaborate thrill-ride and water-play area. Looping slides, towering roller coasters, fun houses, and other garishly painted buildings jutted up toward the sky, creating castle-like silhouettes against the overcast horizon.

But my G-T homing skills had led us here, and we'd gone through a hole in the fence not far from the entrance arch. There, we'd passed a huge stone clown holding a sign that swung drunkenly on large, rusted chains, the lettering promising us that this place was *AWWWWWESOME*! Underneath were admission prices, the numbers crossed out repeatedly, the rates decreasing again and again until, eventually, it had been almost entirely free to pay Adventure City a visit.

Apparently, whoever had run this *awwwwwesome* place had been hurting pretty bad when it finally closed a few years ago.

Of course, packs of bloodthirsty canines running freely in the park probably hadn't helped business. Call me crazy.

There'd been no "Beware of Dogs" signs anywhere—at least not that I'd seen. That, along with that hole in the fence, hinted strongly that these dogs were feral and not part of anyone's security setup. Except they seemed oddly well-groomed—plus this pack was definitely all pit bulls. Surely some mixed breeding would've occurred by now if they'd been left completely on their own.

The other weird thing was that Dana's heightened G-T senses hadn't warned us about the dogs before this current face-to-furry-face (times six).

In fact, ever since Cal had attempted to high-five the stone clown as he'd rolled past, Dana had been grumbling about how she could feel absolutely zero signs of life in here. So why were we here anyway?

I was carrying my biggest plastic water blaster, and I held it now at the ready. I had enough water to hit one dog—and maybe slow it down at best. But against six? We were in trouble. I scanned the area because my homing abilities were still pulling at me—and telling me that wherever John Morningstar was, he was close.

"I'm good with dogs," Calvin said now, as we stood there in the middle of what used to be the park's midway, in an aisle between decaying booths of games of skill and chance where for five dollars you could win a toy animal stuffed with sawdust that would fall apart within minutes of bringing it home. "You know, I used to have a pit bull."

That news surprised me, but I didn't move to look at him, afraid my doing so would bring those dogs charging toward us. So far, since we'd frozen, they'd kept their distance. "You did?"

He cleared his throat. "Yeah. Lucy. She, um, died in the accident."

The accident, back when Cal was nine, when the gas line deteriorated and exploded, basically razing his house while he was home alone. Or at least I'd thought he'd been home alone. But apparently he'd had a pit bull named Lucy.

"Pit bulls are misunderstood," Dana said, at the same time that Cal said, "Pit bulls are vilified—if they're trained right, they're extremely sweet."

Dana added, "Miles, why don't you adios yourself while we deal with this."

"I'm not leaving Sky," Milo said, his voice tight.

I was confused. "Wait, what?"

"His stepfather had a Doberman," Dana explained. "Big dogs are kinda Milo's kryptonite."

If I'd had the time, I would've been irked. This was another of Milo's secrets—something that I didn't know but Dana apparently did.

"I'm seriously good with dogs," Calvin volunteered. "Why don't you guys just *all* back slowly away, while I—"

Dana cut him off. "Yeah, that's not gonna happen."

One of the pit bulls stepped slowly out from behind a cotton-candy stand, its rippling muscles spread taut beneath its short, tan-colored hair. If not for the insistent growl, I might have mistaken the animal for a horse; it was *that* big.

"Hey, girl," Cal said. "Who's a good doggy?"

At the sound of Cal's voice, the dog leaned its head down, bared its teeth, and growled louder.

This was bad. This was worse than bad.

In my head, I ran through our options, the first one being *run*. My G-T skills included superhuman speed. I had no doubt that, push come to shove, I could outrun this pack of dogs. But my friends sure as hell couldn't.

And Dana was already on top of option two, which was to get out of range of those powerful jaws and teeth. "Milo, Sky," she ordered, "get up on top of the Whac-A-Mole booth."

It *was* the sturdier-looking of the game booths that were on either side of us.

"Come on, Sky."

I turned to see Milo waiting to boost me up. He'd interlocked his fingers so I could step into them, which I did, hooking my blaster over my shoulder as I climbed the rotting wood and scrambled up to the booth's crumbling roof.

"Careful," I warned as my foot went through the shingles. I was able to scrunch my way over to make room for him, but I could feel the entire structure groaning under the weight as Milo joined me up there. Again, I scanned the area—I could see a bit farther from the added height, but John Morningstar wasn't lurking anywhere nearby. I did, however, see a seventh dog, even larger and lighter colored than the others, hanging back a bit. The dog seemed to look at me, but then slunk back farther into the shadows.

"There are seven of 'em," I announced. "Maybe even more that we can't see."

Meanwhile, on the ground, the six smaller giant dogs were slowly moving closer to Cal and Dana.

"Cal," Dana said, her eyes on the advancing pack, "I'm gonna lift you up onto the roof of that horse-race booth, 'kay?"

The rotting booth for a game where up to ten customers could use industrial-strength water guns to hit a little target and push their "horses" forward in a competitive race was directly across the midway from Milo and me. From this height, I could see the roof.

"It's not gonna hold the weight of his chair," I warned Dana.

"Dana, you get up there," Cal said evenly. "I'm telling you, I'm good with dogs—"

"I don't think anyone is *six* dogs good," Dana countered.

"Seven," I said.

"Go," Cal said.

"Sorry, I'm not leaving you," Dana told Cal, sounding anything but sorry. But then she turned to speak directly to the dog that was the closest. "I don't want to hurt you, Roverette, but I will if I have to. So just…run along home and take your friends with you."

I could tell from the way Dana was squinting that she was attempting to mind-control the pack leader, but the dog's stance only got more aggressive.

"Oh, shit," Dana said, and I knew she was out of ideas as the dog sprang toward her and Calvin, barking wildly.

All hell broke loose as the other dogs followed her lead.

Everything happened fast after that.

Dana was yelling, but I couldn't hear a word of it, because the barking and snarling was so loud.

I did the only thing I could do—I fired my blaster and propelled the water toward the pack leader. But if the equivalent of a small bucket of water in the face slowed the dog down, I didn't see it. And now, of course, I was unarmed.

Cal, meanwhile, had zoomed in front of Dana as if intending to use himself and his wheelchair as a human shield. Dana in turn used her G-T TK to fling his chair up and into the air, where it landed several feet back, away from the approaching pack.

Then the lead dog flew back through the air, yelping in surprise. But Dana set the animal down with as much care as she'd given Calvin, and it immediately charged forward again.

"Damn it, I *don't* want to hurt you!" she was shouting at the dog.

Cal also immediately gunned it back toward Dana. "*Get up on the freaking roof!*" he was shouting, and Dana finally did just that, clambering up onto the horse-race booth, which creaked and groaned beneath her.

But she was true to her promise and didn't leave Calvin behind. She lifted him up with her telekinesis, and instead of setting him down, she held him there, hovering in midair, a good ten feet above the snapping and snarling dogs.

"Now what?" Calvin shouted what we were all thinking.

"I can outrun them," I shouted. "I'll get them to follow me and lead them away from you—"

"No." Milo said it at the same time as Dana, but he added, "If you trip and fall, they'll tear you to pieces. You have no idea what a single dog can do—let alone *six* of them."

But I could tell from the look in Milo's eyes that he *did* know— that he'd witnessed it, firsthand. *God.*

Dana, meanwhile, was getting a workout. She put Calvin down about a hundred yards away, and his landing was bumpier than usual. The dogs raced toward him, and she picked him back up just in time and brought him flying back toward us.

"She can't keep that up forever," Milo said, and I nodded, looking around for a way to help. I needed water. A *lot* of water.

I reached out with my mind, seeking it, feeling for it. I sensed a lot of it nearby, but something was holding it back, keeping it from me.

On the ground, the remains of the puddle I'd left by firing my blaster at the pack leader shimmered and lifted up into the air—like droplets in zero gravity. But there was even less of it now—most had already evaporated, leaving me with maybe a half a cup. Yay?

"Skylar, WTF?" Dana shouted, and I realized that the booth she was on top of was shaking—because all ten of the water guns attached to the front counter were straining at the ends of their hoses! Water! From those hoses! Of course!

But I couldn't get the triggers to move to release the water—unlike my water guns, they must've been locked—and Dana was using all of her power to keep Calvin hovering away from the dog pack. I realized I'd have to go down there and do it by hand.

"*Milo!*" I shouted, and even though he was still carefully not touching me, I grabbed his arm. And there it was again—Milo's giant emotional wall. But I had no time to be mad or frustrated or sad. I just boxed up everything I was feeling as I stuck to business and telepathically told him my plan, even as I shouted to Dana, "Put Cal down again as far away as you can!"

"What the hell...?" she asked.

"Just do it!" I shouted back as I squeezed Milo's hand and sent him a quick *Stay here*.

Dana sent Cal flying, the dogs all bounded away, and I jumped down off the Whac-A-Mole and scrambled toward the water guns, keeping an eye out for that humongous seventh dog.

"What are you doing?" I shouted as Milo followed me. I'd told him to stay put. In truth, I had no idea if this was going to work—if the water guns really were attached to a still-active water supply or if there were only a few remaining gallons of water left in those straining hoses. If it was the latter, we were still up shit's very dried-out creek.

Milo didn't bother answering me. He knew what I was hoping to do, and he just grabbed as many of the water guns as he could. His fingers were big—he could squeeze the triggers on three of them with each hand. His only limit was the length of those hoses. I followed his lead and got three more guns spraying between my two smaller hands.

To my relief, the water came out with quite a bit of force and volume. It would've had to, in order to hit the horse targets that were all the way on the other side of the booth.

But Milo and I weren't trying to hit any targets. In fact, we aimed the water out into the midway, where I used my TK to catch and contain it, adding it to the droplets from the puddle. It hung in the air in front of us, a rapidly growing bubble of liquid.

Dana, however, was still not convinced this was going to do us any good. "Great," she shouted, as she lifted Cal's chair again and again, plopping him down like a giant dog toy, enticing the pack to lunge and chase after him. "Now they're not just gonna be angry dogs; they're gonna be wet and *extra*-angry dogs!"

"I'm not going to use it to get the dogs wet," I said, glaring hard at that water, stretching and elongating the bubble into a giant gelatinous worm.

I focused harder, attempting to stir it a bit within its confines, and it churned and splashed and gurgled. And still Milo and I sprayed those water guns, so it grew and expanded from a worm into a full-on water snake that I moved. I curved it and formed a giant, waist-high

circle—one that I wrapped around us, locking Milo and me inside…
and the dogs out.

It wasn't long before the gurgling became a roar.

"Holy shit!" Dana said—at least that's how I read her lips from her
perch on that roof. She brought Cal sailing back to us, landing him
inside my circle of water, and jumping down from the low roof to join
us in there, too.

The water rushing around us was louder than the dogs *and*
Dana, *and* Cal, who was hollering as he landed beside Dana. "Holy
Schnikeys!" At least, I *think* that's what Cal yelled.

Milo glanced at me for just a moment before returning his attention
to the glistening wall of water that swirled, low to the ground, around
us. The dogs were completely freaked out—they didn't dare approach.

My plan was to keep this wall spinning and moving with us and
around us as we headed back to the entrance arch. I had no idea
if I could maneuver it through the chain-link fence, or whether
attempting to do that would make it fall apart. But at that point, I
figured we could run like hell for Calvin's car.

I now had plenty of water to work with, so I released the triggers
of my water guns, and Milo did the same as I made a *move forward*
motion, pointing back in the direction we'd come. Dana nodded,
adding a *come closer* gesture. We huddled as tightly to Cal's chair as we
could—the footprint of our water wall had to be as small as possible
to fit through the midway alley. Bumping into a booth or telephone
pole could potentially send the entire thing splashing to the ground,
leaving us open to attack.

You okay? I realized Milo had taken my hand to send that question to me, and I nodded, again aware of his mental walls but grateful for his support.

I caught a glimpse of myself through his eyes and saw that my forehead was glistening wet. I felt trickles escape from underneath my bra, too, sliding their way down the sides of my stomach under my shirt. I knew what I was feeling wasn't splashing from the water wall though.

It was sweat.

Because this was hard work.

Six of the dogs were aggressively following us. Their barks and snarls were just barely audible over the roar of the current. When I looked back, I saw that the seventh—the biggest, super-blond one—was trailing silently behind, as if making sure we were heading toward the gate.

I could also see Dana eyeballing me as she motioned for the boys to move it faster. I knew she saw signs of my growing fatigue, so she also started looking around for Plan B options—where to run, jump, or roll to when the water hit the asphalt.

"I got this," I shouted, more to convince myself than her. We could see the archway and the gate behind it. We were going to make it!

But then I felt it. My homing ability had kicked back in, stronger than ever. Morgan's minion, John Morningstar, was not just nearby; he was ridiculously close. But where?

I looked back again—directly into the eyes of that giant seventh dog and suddenly the craziest theory popped into my head.

That dog is John Morningstar who is, in truth, the G-T Morgan.

Milo was still holding my hand—well, really, I was clinging to him so tightly that he hadn't been able to shake free. But because our connection was open, he'd been subjected to my brain explosion.

The big dog is who...? Milo was incredulous.

But I had a question for him. *Can boys really be Greater-Thans? I remember Dana saying something once about some G-Ts being boys and some are even grown men...?*

Well, yeah, Milo told me. *There's a really powerful G-T up in Boston named Dr. Joseph Bach. He's a monk or...something. I think. But it's pretty rare. And I'm almost certain that dogs can't be G-Ts.*

Maybe not, but rumor had it that a G-T as powerful as Morgan could change her appearance at will. And just maybe she—or *he*, since G-Ts could be boys—had managed to turn himself into a dog.

"Hold up!" I signaled for Dana and Cal to stop, and they both turned and looked at me as if I'd gone mad.

The archway was *right there*. But the dogs had fallen back a bit, as if to make it easier for us exit the park. Which completely made sense.

If I were a mysterious and powerful G-T who didn't want to be found, I'd make it easy for the people who were looking for me to leave, too. Because once we left, we wouldn't find him.

Morgan's a German word, isn't it? I asked Milo through our telepathic connection.

Yeah, I think so. Doesn't it mean...

We both thought it at the same time. *Morning.*

Yup, I was right. John Morningstar wasn't Morgan's minion. He *was* Morgan. Definitely.

Well, *maybe* definitely. But at least one hundred percent quite possibly.

If I'm wrong about this, I quickly told Milo, *get Dana and Cal out of the park. I'll run and lead the dogs away so you can get to the car, but then I'll meet you right by the hole in the fence. Make sure Cal pulls the car close, so I can get in, fast.*

He didn't like it, but he knew he wasn't going to change my mind. *Be careful,* he told me.

I nodded and let go of his hand before lifting up one side of the water snake so that I could slip out beneath it.

Out to where that pack of dogs was waiting. And yes, they'd backed off, but their snarling and barking got louder and some of them crouched down so that if and when they leaped toward me, they could reach me in close to a single bound.

Behind me, I could hear Calvin and Dana both shouting at me, variations on Dana's earlier WTF theme. But I'd locked eyes again with that biggest dog, who seemed to shake his head very slowly and sadly at me, and I knew I was okay.

"Call them off," I told him.

Cal almost messed it up by gunning his chair forward, directly through the water wall. He came out on my side soaking wet but ready to at least *try* to protect me.

I knew that Dana would be right behind him, and Milo right behind her, so I lifted the water snake up so that they wouldn't get soaked, too.

I was still holding the big dog's gaze, and the six other dogs all backed even farther away as they quieted and then lay down. Likewise,

I molded the rushing circle of water back into a static sphere, which eliminated the roar.

The sudden silence was deafening—I could hear my own heavy breathing as I shakily continued to work to keep that water aloft. No doubt about it—I was approaching my G-T limits. I could hear Dana and Cal and even Milo breathing hard, too—all three of my friends were still in fight-or-flight mode, with an emphasis on fight.

But then that big dog started toward us, his movement graceful as he said, "Color me impressed. Not so much about that…" He looked up toward the water bubble before smiling back at me.

"A talking dog! A talking dog," Cal breathed.

The dog continued, "But rather the fact that you figured out…this."

And on the word *this*, he transformed right before our eyes from a giant talking dog into, yes, the young man Cal and I had met in the Palm River CoffeeBoy the night before. He was definitely a Greater-Than. I could feel it now, the way one G-T instantly recognizes another—no doubt about it. And I also realized that one of his skills must've been an ability to mask his G-T-ness—and yet even with that, I'd felt something bleeding through up in Palm River.

"Holy shit," Dana whispered.

Cal's mouth had dropped open. "It's John Morningstar. So, *so* very much of John Morningstar."

He was golden and handsome and gleaming—and very, *very* naked.

"Otherwise known as Morgan," Milo said, pulling off his T-shirt and tossing it to the Greater-Than. "Sky figured it out."

But Morgan tossed his shirt back. "I'm good," he said, clearly completely comfortable with his body—why wouldn't he be? "But actually, you know, I haven't showered yet today, so...would you mind, Sky dearest?" He pointed toward my water ball that was still hanging in the air. "I know you must be getting tired, so...two birds with one stone, right?"

I nodded and somewhat jerkily moved the water over Morgan's blond head where I released it as gently as I could.

He lifted his face up as the water poured over him, arms raised to squeegee back his gleaming hair. He looked like a Greek god or a male model or maybe a movie star.

"*Holy* shit," Dana whispered again.

And now Cal was looking less amazed and even slightly grim. "I liked him a whole lot better when he was a talking dog," he muttered.

"Thanks," Morgan told me before sighing dramatically. "I suppose since you've come all this way, I have to invite you in. But I'll tell you right now, whatever it is that you want from me? My answer is *no*. Nope. *Nein*. Nada. Never gonna happen."

He turned and headed toward a huge building labeled "Gift Shop," and his dogs stood up, shaking before trotting away, back into the depths of the park.

"Come along," Morgan called over his shoulder to us. "Let's get this tediousness over with ASAP."

"Holy *shit*," Dana breathed again, before giving herself a shake similar to that of the dogs. Leading the way, she followed Morgan, whose bare behind was as gleaming and perfect as the rest of him.

"This is not okay," I heard Cal mutter.

Dana heard him, too, because she turned to glare. "What's *not* okay," she said, "was you putting yourself in danger. *Again.* What were you thinking? And now you're soaking wet."

"I was thinking, *I'm good with dogs*," Cal said for what must've been the twentieth time.

I just glanced at Milo and shook my head as they continued to bicker while we followed Morgan into Adventure City's gift shop.

CHAPTER FOURTEEN

"Whoa," I said. Because this place deserved a *whoa*. It was that insane.

This was like no gift shop I'd ever seen before.

To start, it was the size of a warehouse. All four walls were patterned like a gigantic candy cane, rising high up to a second-story loft that could be reached via four different sets of circular, winding red-and-white stairs. There was a long firefighter pole in the center of the room. It extended all the way to the ceiling and could be accessed from a series of catwalks on the loft. The red-and-white stripes that wrapped around the pole were rotating, although I couldn't tell if the pole was actually moving or if that was just an optical illusion. I sensed that, here in Morgan's world, illusions were a fairly prevalent theme.

In the far corner of the room, I spotted a long, curvy red slide. Beneath that was a gigantic pool of what looked to be multicolored plastic balls piled at least five feet high.

"This place is awesome," Cal said, but he sounded anything but excited. In fact he was uncharacteristically subdued as he added, "or so the sign claims." He was watching Dana, who was glaring at Morgan, who appeared to be in the process of shopping for a bathing suit among the round racks of clothing that dotted this part of the shop's brightly tiled floor.

Morgan looked up for a moment, shaking his head as he glanced around. "Pity. I liked it here. I'm gonna miss this place. Of course I have to leave now that you've found me." He clapped his hands together, the sound sharp in the big, echoey room, and we all jumped. "Well, it was fun while it lasted."

You'd think a guy who was naked after shape-shifting from dog back into human would've been in more of a hurry to pull on some clothes, but Morgan was taking his time and being selective.

He finally picked out a pair of board shorts patterned with a blue-and-aqua wave, but then took his sweet time removing the various tags.

"Can you give the guy at least a *little* privacy?" Cal finally said to Dana, who turned and looked at him with astonishment.

"If he doesn't care, why should I?" she countered as she strode to a pile of beach towels adorned with the Adventure City clown and threw one at Cal's head.

"It's a respect thing," he said stiffly as he caught it and started patting himself dry.

"Oh, you mean, kind of the way it's a *respect thing* when you ignore me and Skylar even though we're Greater-Thans and you're just a normie?" Dana countered. "Do you have any idea how hard it is to keep you alive when you won't even follow the simplest of directions?"

"Do they do this often?" I looked up to see that Morgan had directed his words at me. He'd pulled on the board shorts and was now shopping for a tank. He didn't wait for me to respond. Instead, he raised his voice and told Cal and Dana, "The dressing rooms are that way"—he pointed to the back of the building—"and they're *very* private. Practically soundproof, if you need a little alone time to—ahem—pound this out of your system."

Both Dana and Cal turned to look at him with near-identical expressions of *What?* And simultaneously Morgan's meaning dawned—he was telling them to *get a room*—and they both spoke at once.

"Oh, we're not, you know…" Dana cleared her throat and finished her sentence with "together," as Cal chimed in with an "Oh no. No, no. We're just…we're friends."

Morgan laughed. "You seriously expect me to believe—"

"Dana's single," Cal said with a grim sense of resoluteness that I'd never seen from him before. "Let's just be honest about it and not draw this out. She's single; you're Morgan. She's hot; you're hot; Greater-Than plus Greater-Than… It's inevitable that she's gonna hook up with you. In fact"—he turned to look at Dana—"I'm happy for you. I am. He's brilliant and perfect, with God knows what amazing G-T talents aside from the wicked awesome talking-dog thing, and you know for damn sure you won't have to struggle to keep *him* alive or get *him* to follow simple directions or whatever, so…congratulations."

We were all kind of stunned, maybe Dana most of all. She actually blushed, and I can't be quite sure, but I think she may have shot Morgan a look of apology.

But his eyebrows-up look back at her was pure amusement laced with micro-disgust. "What, no rebuttal? Calvin wants us to be honest, babe." When she didn't respond, he turned to me. "Seriously, the four of you are just a flaming clusterfuck of hormones. How do you get *anything* done?"

I was hyperaware of Milo, who was standing just slightly behind me. It *was* a very good question.

Dana spoke up. "Is this place secure?" She gestured with her chin toward the heavy wooden door we'd all just used to enter the building. "Is that the only way in—or out?" I knew what she was thinking. *Cool place, but it would suck to be trapped in here.* She scanned the room, focusing up at the loft railings that ran parallel to each wall.

In the corner opposite the slide and the ball pit was a collection of coffin-sized Russian nesting dolls. I saw Calvin eyeing them with an expression of vaguely horrified fascination. Cal hated dolls. They creeped him out big-time.

Particularly the kind of dolls that Sasha had collected.

I was struck suddenly by a vivid memory of the little girl I'd babysat nearly every weekend. One of the very first clues she'd given me as to her G-T status was when she told me that she liked to *make her dollies dance* in the middle of the night. Of course, at that time, I had no idea about Sasha's abilities—or my own, for that matter. I had assumed she was just a kid with an overactive imagination, trying to buy some extra time with the sitter before lights-out.

That had only been a few months ago. Sometimes it seemed like decades had passed since then.

"There's a fire escape up there, on the west side of the building," Morgan was telling Dana, although he was watching Cal, who'd finally pulled off his wet shirt and was drying himself with that towel. "And there's a tunnel from the men's room here on the first floor. It leads to the fun house, which is close to another hole in the fence. My girls guard all three egresses. I like that word. *Egress.* It's cheerier than *exit,* don't you think?"

Dana gave him her best dead-eye glare. "You don't mind if I check it out? The men's room and the loft?"

"Actually I do," Morgan said, "but that's not going to stop you, is it?" He turned back to Cal who was now pulling on an Adventure City sweatshirt. "Don't schedule the wedding date just yet. I suspect Dana and I are not entirely compatible, especially since we both find *you* a bit uncomfortably attractive. For me, the discomfort comes from your being straight."

"You're gay," Dana blurted.

"For Dana, it's more complicated," Morgan told Cal. He turned to Dana. "Cal said he wants us to be honest. Do be honest, Dana."

"I don't give a shit that you're gay," she blurted.

"Appreciated," Morgan said, "but I'm pretty sure Cal was hoping you had something to tell *him*…?"

Dana opened her mouth, but then closed her mouth. She opened her mouth again, and said, "Calvin, it's always been yuh—*What?*" She closed her mouth and even clapped both her hands over it as she continued to make some very strange sounds, her eyes wide. She turned to look furiously at Morgan.

"Don't fight it," he said. "Yeah, you're powerful, but, darling, you're no match for *me.* Let's make this easier. Look, Ma, no hands!"

"Hey," Cal said as Dana suddenly stood up tall. Her hands flew away from her face as her arms went down straight by her sides.

"Calvin," she said, "I really suck at things like love because I'm scared to let people get too close, but I'm so, *so* crazy about you." Her eyes welled with horrified tears. "I'd die for you, and I think maybe that means I love you because if anything ever happened to you, I'd fucking kill *everyone!*"

"Hey!" Calvin said even louder, his eyes hard as he rolled toward Morgan. "What the hell are you doing to her? You cut that shit out! *Right* now!"

"Suit yourself." Morgan shrugged, and Dana collapsed into herself, nearly falling to the floor as he released her from whatever kind of weird control he'd had over her.

Calvin was at her side instantly, but it was clear that he didn't know what to do. He awkwardly reached out and patted her shoulder, but she pulled away, her face hidden in her hands as she muttered, "Oh my God, oh my God…"

"That was you," I realized, turning to glare at Morgan, remembering the unexpected declaration of love from the jock named Eric. "At the CoffeeBoy! You can mind-control people into, what? Embarrassing themselves?"

"Into speaking the truth," Morgan said. "Your turn, Cal. Fair's fair. You said you wanted honesty…"

Cal had been leaning over Dana, but now he straightened in his chair as if a puppet master had yanked hard on his strings. "Dana, I thought I was in love with you from the very first moment I saw you," he said, "but as I got to know you, I realized just how incredibly special you are and—"

"Stop it!" Dana said, erupting up from the floor and getting directly in Morgan's face. "Whatever the hell you're doing, it is *not* okay!"

Morgan held his ground. "And whatever the hell *you're* doing? That *is* okay? Coming here, tracking me down, getting me tangled up in the rest of your drama? Helping Sasha, finding Lacey, saving Jilly? Gods, Calvin, your emails damn near wore me out with the details of your quixotic quests. Tell me, does it ever end? And do you *honestly* think any of that bullshit is going to matter in the long run?"

Dana was silent, and I knew admitting as much would be all but impossible for her. So I stepped forward and said it for her—and Cal did, too.

"Hell, yeah." He spoke over me as I said, "Absolutely—it matters."

Morgan laughed and threw a *Can you believe these crazy kids* look at Milo, who folded his arms across his chest and quietly said, "We all believe it matters. Whether we save one girl or a hundred. It matters."

Morgan shook his perfect head as he turned back to ask Dana, "How many years do you really think we have before *we're* kidnapped and bled dry, too? Those of us who are G-Ts, that is. The others, Calvin and Hot-Angst-Guy over here—they'll just be killed. Brutally, probably while we're forced to watch. Or maybe we don't have years before that happens. Maybe we only have months. Days. Hours. Hey, I have a good idea! Let's spend it doing something else—anything else! Okay?"

And that was something Dana could respond to. "I'll spend my last fucking *minutes* on Earth searching for my sister and yes, protecting my friends, if that's what I have to do." She glanced over at Calvin when she said *friends*, and Morgan laughed again.

"Oh, we're back to pretending it's just *friends*, are we?" he said. "I'll tell you what, Dana." He said her name mockingly, as if it were two separate words. *Day. Nah.* "I'll help you. I'll go meet little Sasha and fish around inside her sad, broken little head for any sign of Lacey."

"Sasha's not broken," I said, but I wasn't so sure about that.

Meanwhile, Dana's eyes had narrowed. "What's the catch?"

"Ooh, you heard that silent but deadly *if*, did you?" Morgan asked. "*If* you manage to do anything at all in the next, oh, let's say…ten minutes. Yes. Starting right now, you have *ten* minutes to do something that *completely* surprises little, old jaded me. Ready? Go!"

Dana laughed, but it was devoid of humor. "Figures you would make it into a game."

"It's life and death for us," I chimed in.

"Darling, we're G-Ts," Morgan chided me. "That's nothing new. It's life and death for us twenty-four seven. And it's nine minutes and thirty seconds now. Ticktock."

"Just tell me what you fucking want me to do," Dana snarled.

"Oh, anger and foul language," Morgan said, feigning a yawn. "*That's* no surprise."

In a sudden flash, I knew what Morgan wanted Dana to do—what would surprise him—and when Cal looked up at me, I realized that he'd figured it out, too.

"Hey, c'mere," Cal said, holding out his hand to Dana. He pulled her with him over to a bench shaped like a happy-go-lucky wooly

211

mammoth and tugged her down so that she was sitting at his eye level. "I know you're gonna hate this because it's so public, and you probably would walk away from me even if it was just the two of us alone, but…" He took a deep breath and exhaled fast. "I'm completely in love with you." She started to get up, but he didn't let go of her hand. "And that's me talking, that's not Morgan doing his voodoo, and I think from what you said when he *was* doing his voodoo that you maybe kinda like me, too, and I also think it would surprise the crap out of him if you were honest about that. To me. With me."

Dana was silent. She was just glaring down at her boots, muscle jumping in her jaw.

Cal reached out and gently tipped her chin up so that she had to meet his eyes, and he quietly added, "And if I got it wrong, and you really only want us to be friends, Dana, then I'm kinda trusting you here to break that news to me gently. I know that's what you'd do, but see, Morgan? He doesn't know you at all, so that'll surprise him, too. Either way, we win this."

Those tears were back in Dana's eyes as her mouth moved, half in a smile and half in refusal to cry.

"Winning is good," Calvin continued. "Helping Sasha and finding Lacey is better and we're gonna do that, regardless of—"

"Just shut up," Dana said, "and kiss me."

And Calvin did just that.

———

I pulled both Morgan and Milo away in an attempt to give Cal and Dana a little privacy.

"Surprised or not, you're helping us," I told the powerful G-T.

"Oh, I'm surprised," he said. "Beyond surprised. Fully flabber-gasted, in fact. So, fair's fair. You win."

"Thank you," I said grudgingly. "Although, FYI, you suck. And this is Milo, by the way." Not *Hot-Angst-Guy*, as Morgan had nick-named him.

I glanced over at Milo, who'd reached into his pocket for his burner phone. It was chirping. "I gotta take this," he told me before turning to include Morgan. "Excuse me." He headed back to the front door and stepped outside, probably hoping for better cell service.

All I could think was, *Who was calling Milo?* Was it Rochelle— *Rochelle—ROCHELLE! ARGH!*

Of course, now Morgan was eyeing me. One side of his mouth curved up into that now all-too-familiar impish grin. "Trouble in paradise, I'm sensing." He kept his voice low so that neither Dana nor Cal could hear him.

My stomach did a flip-flop, and for a second, I almost considered playing it off like I didn't know what Morgan was talking about. But his musical laughter was enough to let me know that not only did he more than *sense* the tension between Milo and me—he *knew* that it existed. And he also *knew* that I was trying hard, right then and there, to figure out how to pull a BS card on him.

"Yeah, fine, whatever," I grumbled. "It's not that serious."

"You don't believe that in your heart," Morgan replied. "And it's eating you up inside."

I felt my eyes well with tears but I blinked them back. Hard. I didn't want to talk about this right now. I didn't want to talk about this—ever. And the absolute dead-last thing I wanted was Milo being mind-controlled by Morgan and blurting out some horrible truth, like he thought Rochelle was a million times hotter than me, because let's face it, she was. Yes, she was also disgusting and dangerous, but… I shook my head and cleared my throat and stood up a little taller, my nose in the air.

"I'm fine," I said. "And he's fine. We're fine." I sniffed. "Okay? So don't even *think* about doing your truth-telling voodoo on Milo. *Or* me."

Morgan smiled. "I can see that you love him. With your whole entire rookie heart. But." His eyes grew solemn. "Of course, you know that love sometimes just isn't enough."

I opened my mouth to respond—*Gee, thanks for the pep talk, Coach*—but just then a series of huge cacophonous *BAMs*, one right after another, rang out in the corner. Instead of speaking actual words, I screamed. In my defense, while I screamed, I also leaped on top of a display counter in order to give myself the elevation I needed to scan the room. The first thing I noticed was that Dana and Cal were no longer smooching on the wooly mammoth bench. In fact…

"Oh God, sorry sorry sorry!" Cal jerked back from the pile of Russian dolls, all of which were now lying on their sides in a heap. Apparently, he had gotten too close to one of them and tipped it over—which had prompted the others to fall, like a series of enormous egg-shaped dominoes.

Dana, clearly spooked by the sound, cascaded down the firefighter pole from the second floor, where no doubt she'd been double-checking

Morgan's security. As always, making sure Calvin and the rest of us were safe. Her leather pants squeaked against the metal as she landed hastily on the tile. "What the eff?" she barked. As usual, she used the full f-bomb.

"Everyone's good!" Morgan exclaimed. "Just a minor doll avalanche. Kind of like global warming—the cause was human error."

Dana scowled at Morgan, but then looked over at Calvin and saw the gigantic mess that surrounded his chair. She tried her best to keep scowling, but instead she started cracking up. It wasn't every day that Dana belly-laughed. The sound was nice. Calvin thought so too. He smiled and shrugged. "I'll be here all night," he said and took a bow from his chair.

It was then that Milo came back inside. He looked concerned, his cell phone still pressed against his ear as he stepped through the doorway.

But Dana gave him the silent thumbs-up. He looked visibly relieved as he nodded and then said something softly into the phone receiver before hanging up and putting the cell back in his pocket.

"Who was that?" I asked. And then I felt like a complete idiot for prying.

But Milo didn't seem to mind. "Garrett, with an update on Ro and Ashley. Rochelle's still completely passed out—but Ashley's moving a bit, like she's going to be waking up soon."

"Rochelle *better* wake up. She's got a hot date with you in just a few hours," Dana replied.

Morgan's eyebrows were raised as he digested Dana's words.

"Fake date," Cal explained. "Crazy D-bag addict has the hots for Milo."

"I'll keep her distracted while they search a locked closet for Jilly." Milo finished the explanation.

"Ah, yes, Jilly. How very…valiant of you to distract the crazy D-bag like that." Morgan turned and studied me for a moment. His eyes looked as though they had changed color since the first time I'd met him in that CoffeeBoy. I'd remembered them as being bright green. At that moment, they were dark pools of hazel brown.

I narrowed my own eyes at him in a silent *Don't you dare*.

"Well, okay then," he said. "Since you've got *hot date* and *closet-rescue* plans for tonight, I'll assume you'll be in contact with a day and time for our special meeting with adorable little Sasha. Oh, and of course, it's still a thousand dollars. Payable in full in advance. Small bills preferred."

Dana looked at him with disgust.

"Seriously, darling," Morgan said. "Did you think I was running a charity here?" He didn't wait for her to answer. "Let me walk you to your car. My pups can get territorial."

And with that, he led the way out the door. I followed him, with Milo right behind me, into the overcast afternoon light.

"I really, *really* liked our visit to Adventure City," I heard Cal say.

"Shut up, Scoot," Dana grumbled, but when I turned around, Cal had pulled her down onto his lap and she was kissing him again as they rolled toward the gate.

Cal caught me looking, and he grinned so widely that I couldn't keep from smiling, too.

It was early afternoon when we got back to Coconut Key. We had several hours to kill before Milo's seven o'clock date with Rochelle.

I decided to use the time to wrangle my mom. I turned on my real phone, sent her a quick text, and found out that she was home. I'd use the time to have a pretend conversation about my top choice colleges with her. Win myself some extra points.

When I said I was going to do that, Milo asked to be let out of Cal's car while we were still downtown.

He didn't say it, but I knew he was closely monitoring the status of the John Doe with "amnesia" from the day-before-yesterday's Sav'A'Buck parking lot incident. The man had been in the hospital for more than two days now, and it was only a matter of time before the police let him go. And I knew Milo believed that the top bullet point on John Doe's to-do list was *Find the G-T who'd stolen his car and his assault rifle and had set free the little girl who was his latest intended payday.*

Of course, maybe I was wrong, and instead Milo was going shopping for a new shirt to wear for tonight's date with Rochelle.

I sensed Cal glancing at me in the rearview as he pulled into our neighborhood and approached our daylight drop-off place, right around the corner from my house. While I was now allowed to ride in Calvin's car, I was supposed to keep my mom updated about when I did it *and* where we were going. We had to stay extremely local. Today, with our trip to Adventure City, we'd gone far outside of Mom's ridiculously limited range.

With Milo out of the car, we'd driven the last mile in silence, but the tension between Cal and Dana was pretty intense. I suspected they were holding hands in the front seat. Tightly.

"Six thirty," Dana ordered as Cal pulled over to the curb. "Cal's house. Don't be late, Bubble Gum."

"I won't be." As I met Cal's eyes in the mirror, I was tempted to mock him with the same warning he always gave Milo and me. *Eyes open! Even when you're* (insert immature smooching sounds here). Instead, I said, "I love you both."

As Cal laughed and Dana turned to give me an *Are you a moron?* look, I shrugged. "Residuals of Morgan's speaking the truth. I'm happy for you. That's all."

Dana made a disgusted noise. "Just get out of the car."

I did, but first I blew Cal a kiss. I'd never seen him so euphorically happy.

After I closed the car door, as I took the cut-through alongside the Patterson's house, I glanced back. Probably to see why Calvin hadn't pulled away.

He was kissing Dana again, and she was kissing him back.

It was a full-on Hollywood clinch—an embrace that seemed almost life-and-death, and I remembered Morgan's dire words as I hurried home.

How many years do you really think we have before we're kidnapped and bled dry, too?

When I got to Cal's at a little before 6:30, Garrett was still sitting on the couch all by himself, looking absolutely bored out of his mind as he obediently studied the TV screen that showcased the three different views of the inside of Rochelle's house. I could see with one glance that the sofa was now empty, and there was no sign of either Rochelle or her friend Ashley in the kitchen or hallway either.

Garrett sat up as I came in. "Finally," he said grumpily, rubbing his face. "That was *the* worst day ever!"

I looked at the half-empty pizza box and the scattering of Chinese-food containers and fast-food bags that littered the coffee table in front of him. "Try it the way Cal and I did it yesterday—without any food."

"Jeez, just kill me now," he said.

"Where're Dana and Cal?" I asked.

"They've been in Cal's room ever since they got home," Garrett reported. "They ordered themselves their own private pizza and vanished with it." He added a "Bow chicka bow bow!" along with a flurry of eyebrow movement.

"Don't even," I said with heavy disgust, even though I was thinking *Oh, really...?*

"Hey."

I jumped at the sound of Milo's voice and turned to see him standing in the doorway. He must've come in right behind me. He was still wearing the same shirt he'd had on during our trip to Adventure City—and I immediately hated myself both for noticing that *and* for the rush of relief it gave me.

"Hey." I tried to sound casual as I sat down on the sofa next to Garrett. My action made it impossible for Milo to kiss me hello. That was far better than my standing there awkwardly, like an idiot, because my boyfriend *still* didn't want to touch me.

"Update!" Dana came striding out from the hallway that led to the wing of the house where Cal had his wheelchair-accessible suite. It had once been the master bedroom and bath, but before they'd moved in, his parents had had it redone for him, while they'd taken over the rooms up on the second floor.

Dana's hair was still wet from a shower, which really wasn't that strange. She and Milo frequently used Calvin's bathroom to clean up, since they often camped out or squatted in abandoned buildings without any running water.

And yet…

"Milo first." Dana was acting like…Dana. All sharply efficient and down-to-business. But I couldn't help but notice that she wasn't *quite* looking me in the eye. And? She seemed…dare I say it…? *Happy?* Well, maybe not. But certainly happy-*ish*.

"Our John Doe from the Sav'A'Buck remains at the hospital, under guard," Milo reported as Calvin quietly joined us, rolling into the playroom. He also failed to meet my gaze. But he *definitely* looked happy. And yeah, Cal's default emotion was joyful and upbeat, but this was a quieter, deeper sense of contentment—like all was right with his world, despite the battles we continued to fight.

"No word on when he'll be released," Milo continued. But then he glanced at me and cleared his throat. "As far as Rochelle…she started texting me about a half hour ago. *Can't wait.* That kind of thing."

Rochelle and Milo. Texting. In advance of their *date*. I breathed. Inhale. Exhale.

Dana turned to Garrett. "Your turn, G."

"Nice to see you again, too," he grumbled. He sat up and stretched his arms over his head. "Yeah, um, about forty-five minutes ago, hot, blond Ashley snapped out of her coma, staggered into the bathroom, peed like a racehorse for about ten minutes straight, and then left." He yawned. "Rochelle started moving around right after that. She went upstairs. There's been no sign of her since."

Dana nodded to Milo. "Text Rochelle and tell her that your car broke down, so she's gonna have to meet you at the restaurant. That way you won't have to pick her up—it'll limit your time alone with her and keep you out in public."

I shook my head because being in public wasn't going to stop a Destiny addict from jokering. The danger Milo was putting himself into was reduced only minimally. And then there was the *other* danger—that Rochelle was going to jump my boyfriend.

"I'm doing one better than that," Milo told Dana with another look over at me, his phone already out. "I've already texted her that I'm tied up at work. I've told her that I'm doing a construction job up in Palm River. I said I still want to have dinner, but that I need her to meet me at a restaurant up there, instead of here in Coconut Key." He glanced over at me again. "That buys us a solid half hour of drive time each way, along with however long she waits before she realizes she's been stood up."

Stood up, as in Milo wasn't actually going out on a date with Rochelle, which meant that not only was he *not* going to go face-to-face with a psychotic Destiny addict, but he also wasn't going to have to play kissy face—or worse—with Ms. Elderly Grabby-Hands.

Oh, thank goodness. I didn't realize that I'd said it aloud until Milo looked over at me and said, "You didn't *seriously* think I was going to…?" His words were sharper than I'd ever heard from him, and they were tinged with uncharacteristic impatience and annoyance.

He didn't wait for me to babble some inept apology or excuse, because that *was* what I'd thought. Instead he just reached across the coffee table, holding out his hand to me.

I took it without really thinking, and our connection snapped on and my head nearly snapped back from the power of Milo's emotions. He was usually so even-keeled and calm, but this was like stepping out of the house into one of those Florida late-afternoon thunderstorms where it rains sideways from the force of the wind.

He wasn't presenting me with complete sentences, but through and under and alongside of his raging annoyance with me, I felt the magnitude of his sheer disgust for Rochelle. And yes, he'd kissed her— let *her* kiss *him*, really—but he'd *hated* it and absolutely did *not* want to do it again. Never, never, *never*.

Well, how was I supposed to know, I tried to say, but my words were drowned out by a wave of something strange that instantly vanished as Milo abruptly pulled his hand away.

"Thanks a lot for your faith in me," he muttered tightly, and I realized that what I'd felt was hurt—I'd badly hurt Milo's feelings with my mistrust.

I should've felt better—knowing both that Milo wasn't going to put himself into danger *and* that he didn't secretly want to make out with Rochelle. But that icky feeling in the pit of my stomach remained. I should have trusted him. "I'm sorry," I said.

But Milo just shook his head. "I need the name of a nice restaurant in Palm River," he said as he sat down on the couch, way on the other side of Garrett. "I haven't had a chance to do an Internet search, so… hit me with one."

"The Strand." Garrett, Calvin, and I all said it at exactly the same time.

"It's upscale, on the water," I added. "She'll know where it is." Kinda the way all three of us Coconut Key—that is, rich—kids knew where it was. Why did that make me so uncomfortable?

"The Strand," Milo repeated as he typed it into his text to Rochelle. "Thanks."

I glanced over at Dana and Cal—who were now whispering to each other in the corner of the room. Cal touched Dana's arm and said something quietly, and she laughed.

Dana and Cal.

Who would've thought?

Garrett didn't seem fazed by it. In fact, he had been led to believe, for quite some time now, that Cal and Dana were an item. As far as he knew, they'd been dating for a while.

It was kinda cool actually. Like life imitating art, instead of the other way around.

"Text is sent," Milo said as he set his cell phone down on the table. "I told her to come as soon as she could. At seven, I'll text her again, telling her I won't get there 'til seven thirty, which'll buy us even more time." He pried free one of the now-cold remaining pizza slices and took a bite.

"Good," Dana replied, turning her attention to the task at hand. "As soon as she leaves her house, we'll head over there."

I caught Cal studying Dana, adoration pooling in his eyes. I couldn't help but feel a little envious. I wanted Milo to look at me the same way that Cal was gazing at Dana. We'd had that—once. But things felt way different now, and I was at least partly to blame. If not totally. Except, no. Even though the secret that Milo was keeping from me apparently *wasn't* that he had the hots for a D-addict, he was *still* the one who kept pulling away and avoiding contact.

"You can heat that, you know, in the microwave?" I told Milo, feeling more annoyed than I should have by his cold-pizza consumption. "It doesn't *have* to suck."

He shook his head, not meeting my gaze. "I'm good."

"Look!" Garrett exclaimed. "Guys!" He pointed to the TV screen.

Rochelle was on the move. She'd entered into the frame of the kitchen-cam, her eyes focused down at her phone as she sashayed across the floor in a tight black dress and sky-high heels. Before opening the fridge door, Rochelle typed something into her cell and then set it on the countertop.

Almost instantaneously, Milo's phone vibrated.

"What's it say?" Dana asked as Milo used his pizza-grease-free pinkie finger to unlock his phone and read her message.

He looked flustered as he stuttered, "Just that she's getting ready and…she'll be leaving soon." He tried to pick up his phone, but he was too late.

Garrett had already grabbed it. "Oh, come on," he said. "Share, share!

Ooh, she wrote, *Almost ready to leave, the Strand is perfect, lots of dark corners.*" He scrolled up through the chain of text messages. "Ho-ho-*holy* sharing! Dude! She texted you a bath pic? Whoa! Check this out!"

I didn't want to see it, but Garrett shoved Milo's phone right in my face, and yup. There was Rochelle in all her glory. She'd sent Milo a naked selfie. The woman was pure class.

"Listen to this," Garrett chortled. "*Wish you were here, XOXO!*" He looked at Milo. "She sends you this, and all you send her back is a *smiley face?*"

Milo just shook his head as he grimly ate his pizza.

In her kitchen, Rochelle had grabbed a bottle of wine from the fridge and a glass from the cabinet, but she picked up her phone when it chimed.

"I just sent her a panting dog emoticon," Garrett said. "She'll like that better."

Sure enough, Rochelle smiled as she typed a response with both of her thumbs.

"Dana." Milo spoke sharply, and Dana and Cal both turned their focus toward the TV, where while Rochelle texted back to what she thought was Milo's emoticon, *her glass of wine poured itself.* The bottle just elevated, the cork came out with a pop, and the liquid splashed into the waiting glass.

"Her powers are increasing," Dana said.

"Oh-my-God-oh-my-God," Garrett said, still focused on Milo's phone. "She says, *Bathroom or parking lot, your choice, sweet thing.*" He laughed.

"Ew!" I was most definitely not amused.

"*Can't wait, Mistress Nasty,*" Garrett said as he typed.

On Cal's TV, Rochelle checked her phone and gave what could only be described as an evil-queen smile. She chugged her wine, then grabbed her purse and keys, and exited the kitchen.

From the flower-cam in the living room, we heard the front door close with a solid *bang*.

Cal's house was maybe ten minutes away from Rochelle's beach house. Five, if we really hauled ass.

"Ladies and gentlemen?" Dana said. "It's go time."

CHAPTER FIFTEEN

Click!

The dead bolt on the door opened easily despite Dana's lack of a key.

"Dude." Garrett was clearly impressed by her fine-motor telekinesis skills.

Cal nodded proudly and smiled at Dana, who stayed on task, focusing now on the easier lock on the doorknob.

I looked around the big room that, up 'til now, I'd only seen via the oddly placed flower-cam.

It was half playroom, half home gym. A treadmill and an elliptical were in one corner, along with a rack of free weights. In another corner was a pool table. Over here, near the closet door, was a small sitting area with a chess set and several tall bookshelves filled with everything from heavy medical guides to bestselling paperback beach reads.

The ceiling was high, with three hanging fans that moved lazily overhead.

"Got it," Dana announced and pulled open the unlocked closet door.

Milo, who was right beside me, chewed on his gum with an almost violent intensity. I could hear his ragged breathing as we all got our first look inside. But the space was dark, and it was difficult to see.

Then there was a noise from the shadows. It sounded like a whimper.

"Someone's in there!" Milo stepped forward, past Dana and directly into the closet. The quiver in his own voice was hard to miss.

The whimper became a very clear "No! Don't! Stay back!"—and it was definitely coming from a girl.

Milo backed up fast. "No one's going to hurt you," he said.

"Jilly?" Dana called out. "Let's get some light in here," she ordered, and Garrett quickly slapped on the switch for the overheads.

The light shone into the small closet space.

It was uncanny. The narrow space, the heavy door, the darkness... I gasped, instantly brought back to that nightmare I'd had the other night—the one with the horrible man and the belt.

In the corner of *this* closet sat a fully dressed girl, huddled on the floor as she hugged her knees to her chest. She'd buried her face into her legs, and only her eyes were visible as she stared, horrified, up at us through her matted hair.

Her matted *pink-streaked* hair.

"Jilly!" Garrett exclaimed. "You're alive! You're okay. You're—*Are* you okay?" I'd never heard Garrett sound so genuinely concerned for anyone or anything.

"Don't come in! You can't come in!" She lifted her head, her eyes wild in a face that was pale and gaunt. Remains of thick, black liner were smudged around her eyes and streaked down her cheeks, like a bad Halloween makeup job for a character listed in the movie credits as *Girl in Danger*. "You shouldn't be here! If *she* comes home…"

"She won't." I tried to reassure her, knowing that *she* was Rochelle. "She's out—for at least another hour."

"Who the hell are you?" Jilly looked from me to Dana to Cal to Milo, finally landing on Garrett. "What have you done, you *fucking idiot?*"

She was terrified—that much was clear despite the tough-as-nails attitude—and Garrett tried to reassure her. He leaned into the closet. "Jilly. These are friends. We're here to help you." He reached out his hand. "Come on. It's time to go."

Jilly started to shake as she shrank away from him, and her eyes welled with tears. "Don't touch me! Don't touch me!" She looked like a wild animal cornered by predators.

I exchanged a look with Dana. What *had* Rochelle done to her?

"Give her a second," Cal suggested, although he sounded just as clueless as I felt.

Milo was less patient. He put a hand on Garrett's shoulder and leaned around him so that he could make eye contact with the girl. "Jilly. We need to get you out of here. We're going to take you somewhere safe. Far away from your mother."

"She's *not* my mother!" Jilly exclaimed fiercely, and several books from that nearby set of shelves fell onto the playroom floor with a *thwack*. Cal and I both jumped—particularly when one of the larger books skittered across the floor and crashed into the side of Cal's wheelchair. It looked like a medical journal—the word *Phlebotomy* was on the cover.

"Whoa," Cal said.

"Your aunt then," Dana said. She turned to Garrett. "Get this girl some food. She's starving. Go into the kitchen, see what you can find."

"She's not my aunt," the girl said as Garrett dashed away. "She's not my sister either! She's a monster!" From deep inside the closet, we all heard another thump, and this time Jilly was the one who jumped. "*Now* look what you made me do!" She stared at us with those giant, crazy, accusatory eyes. "Get out! Get *out*! Just go—*now*! I don't need your stupid help!"

But Dana was staring into the closet. "What's back there?" she asked, reaching in to feel along the wall.

I thought about the man with the belt from my dream. "*Who's* back there?"

"Nothing!" Jilly insisted. "No one!"

"Cal," Dana said. He'd already gotten out his cell phone and turned on the flashlight app. But as he handed it to Dana, he looked at me, and I knew what he was thinking. If this girl got too worked up, there would be flying objects everywhere, maybe not just books next time. And we weren't exactly doing the greatest job at calming her down.

"There's another door back here," Dana announced.

"You can't go in there!" Jilly shouted, and more books fell off the shelf.

"Yeah, actually I can," Dana said coolly as she did just that— unlocking the hidden door as easily as she had the closet deadbolt and the doorknob. The door opened in and she went into what looked like a larger room. "Is there a light in here?"

Meanwhile, Milo had gone into the closet and knelt down next to the girl, trying to calm her down. "Jilly. We *have* to get you out of here. I know this is gonna sound crazy, but we think it's possible that Rochelle is going to try to sell you to some really bad people."

She laughed in his face as Dana found one of those strings hanging down from an overhead lightbulb and pulled it on. We all squinted in the sudden brightness.

"Holy shit," I heard Dana say, but I couldn't see what was in there.

"You think Rochelle is going to *sell* me?" Jilly repeated what Milo had said as Garrett came back from the kitchen with a bag of candy and a shriveled apple. "I wish. But she's not gonna do that. As long as she owns me, she's gonna *use* me—until she uses me up."

I looked at Cal; Cal looked at me.

"What does *that* mean?" Garrett said what we were thinking.

"I wish she'd just get it over with!" Jilly said bitterly.

Milo was focused on the same word that had stopped us. "She *owns* you?"

Dana, meanwhile, had emerged from the room behind the closet. She was carrying a hospital plasma bag filled with what looked like blood and an already-prepped syringe—similar to the ones we'd seen this morning when Rochelle and Ashley had injected D into their perfect bodies.

"This was in the fridge," she said. "There's a whole lab setup back there. Rudimentary, but…it's a Destiny lab. A *home* D-lab. Right here."

"Rochelle *owns* you?" Milo asked Jilly again.

The girl raised her head in pointy-chinned defiance. "She paid good money for me. Signed a contract. I signed it, too. So yeah.

She absolutely owns me." She turned to Dana. "And yes. She cooks Destiny back there. With my blood. These days, everyone's doing it. So put that back—it's precious—and lock both of these doors. And then get. The hell. *Out!*"

———————

"Are you *serious*?" I asked Jilly as around me, everyone started talking at once.

"*I'm* not cooking my own Destiny by keeping a girl locked in *my* closet," Cal was saying, "so really not *every*one is doing it. I'm just saying."

Milo was muttering, "This is *not* okay," as Garrett said, "I don't understand. Rochelle *bought* you?"

"From who?" Dana demanded. "Who sold you to Rochelle? And FYI, whatever it was that you signed, it's not legal. You can't buy or sell a human being here in Florida. At least not yet."

All the while, Jilly was speaking over them. "If you drop that," the girl said, her volume getting louder as she pointed to the blood bag and syringe still in Dana's hands, "and it breaks or spills, she'll just take more blood from me, which probably *will* kill me—she's already taken too much. On second thought, why don't you just fucking do it, because then at least this time I'll be dead and it'll finally be *over!*"

That shut us all up. *This time…?*

Of course that was when Garrett dropped the entire open bag of licorice-flavored Doozies. The colorful little balls clattered onto the tile floor in punctuation to our shock.

Dana spoke first. "Who sold you to Rochelle?" she asked again, as Garrett scrambled to pick up the spilled candy.

Jilly's chin went up. "What does it matter to you?"

"It matters to *me*." What do you know? Garrett had finally said something useful.

Jilly glanced over at him and her eyes filled with tears. But then her mouth hardened and she blinked them back. "Yeah, well, you're an idiot." She turned back to Dana. "*I* sold myself to Rochelle."

None of us believed that.

"Okay. But who got the money that she paid?" Dana asked with a patience that I didn't expect. "Your father? Or was it dear old Mom who sold you to be bled dry? Screw her, Jill. I'm emancipating you. Right here, right now. You're officially free—you owe your parents nothing. So come on. Let's blow this Popsicle stand."

Jilly's face got even tighter, and even though it was clear that Dana's guess was dead right, I knew that Dana's tough-guy approach wasn't going to work on this kid.

Sure enough. "I'm not going anywhere," Jilly said tightly. "Screw *you*."

And suddenly, I knew what was keeping her there. "You have, what, a brother or maybe a sister?" I asked.

"Brothers," she answered sullenly.

"What are their names?" I asked. "Older? Younger?"

"Ronny's my twin," Jilly said flatly. "And Jack…" Her face crumpled, but only for a second before she was back to her default almost-bored expression. But the crack in her voice gave her away when she said, "He's only two." She shook her head, correcting herself. "Three, by now."

I remembered that family I'd met in the Sav'A'Buck parking lot—gaunt and shivering in the cold morning air. Their hunger evident in their empty eyes… "And your mom and dad were both out of work. Maybe even…homeless?"

"*Maybe.*" She mocked me. "What do *you* know about it?" She included Garrett in her scathing look. "Stupid rich kids."

Milo pretended he believed that selling herself to save her family had been her idea as he asked, "So you sold yourself to Rochelle in order to feed your brothers?" And who knows? Maybe it had been Jilly's idea. But the fact that her parents had actually let her do it…? That was *not* okay.

Jilly shook her head, and when she answered Milo, I could tell that she trusted his quiet calm and she opened up a little. "I was sold to a D-farm. The farm rents me to Rochelle. She's my second mistress. The first one jokered pretty fast. It happened while she was at work, so I survived."

"And when she died—your *first* mistress—you didn't somehow earn your freedom?" Milo asked, and Jilly just laughed her disgust at what was clearly now *his* stupidity, too.

"Or try to escape?" Calvin chimed in.

"That wasn't the deal," she told us grimly. She could see we didn't understand, so she made it super simple. "The D-farm owns me, and they rent me out to the client. If the client dies—*when* the client dies, because they all die, they're stupid Destiny addicts, right? But if I happen to survive when the client, my mistress, finally jokers, then I have to go back to the farm. They get me into shape, fatten me up, let whatever injuries heal—and then they rent me out to someone else— another addict. Lather, rinse, repeat."

"So Rochelle pays, what, *monthly* rent for you?" Dana clarified, exchanging a glance with Milo. I knew what she was thinking. That explained why Rochelle pawned her jewelry and left an envelope of cash in her car's wheel well—in exchange for what had seemed like nothing in return.

But was, in fact, a rental payment for the blood from this girl who was her slave, locked in a closet in her house.

"I don't know how it works." Jilly shrugged. "I don't care. What does it matter?"

"So…when *will* you be free?" Milo asked.

"Never," Jilly said. "The contract was for life. Most of us don't live long."

"So just don't go back," Dana said. "When Rochelle finally dies."

In response, Jilly held out her hand, and there, on the inside of her forearm, about halfway between her wrist and the inside of her elbow, was a small bump.

"It's a tracking device," she told us, and she was so pale that I could see its greenish light flashing from beneath her skin.

"But you told me that was a blood-sugar monitor," Garrett said.

Jilly gave him a withering look of disdain as Dana said, "It's not very deep. Someone give me a knife. I'll cut that shit out of you right here, right now."

"No!" Jilly pulled her arm back, cradling it against her chest. "If I do that—if I break the agreement, they'll kill my family."

"And what will your parents do?" Dana asked harshly. "When they run out of money again? Sell Jack? Or maybe they'll have another baby and hope it's a girl with G-T powers so they can sell *her*, too?"

Jilly flinched. "They got enough cash to start over. Buy a place to live. My dad got a job as part of the deal and…" She shook her head. "They wouldn't do that."

"Yeah, because they're such upright citizens," Dana countered.

"Just go," Jilly said wearily. "Get out of here. You don't understand."

She was right. We didn't understand. We couldn't. But then Milo surprised me by quietly saying, "*I* understand." He looked so sad as he sat down on the floor, his back to the wall of the closet, just like Jilly. "What if we reach out to them?" he asked her. "Your family? Maybe they have enough money saved now—maybe they could buy you back."

"Get real, Miles." Dana scoffed at that. "You honestly think that's gonna happen?"

But Garrett latched on to the idea. "Maybe they feel awful. Maybe, even if they don't have the cash, they'd be willing to, I don't know, maybe…go into hiding so that you can escape…?"

Jilly was unmoved. "You're a moron, Garrett. I'm already dead to them. Besides, *I* have no idea where they are. It's not like we exchange birthday cards."

"I can find them," Cal said. "I just need your last name."

"Fuck you," she said.

"Is that with an *F* or a *P-H*?" Calvin tried to make it into a joke, but Dana had had enough.

"Okay," Dana said. "I'm done. Let's just grab her and go. We'll cut that thing out of her arm after we're out of here. Garrett, Skylar."

"No!" Jilly said as both Garrett and I went into the closet—more out of reflex than an actual desire to manhandle the girl out of Rochelle's house.

But the moment I stepped inside that claustrophobic little space, I was immediately hit with waves of nausea. It was more than just a memory of last night's bad dream. Whatever I was feeling was psychically enhanced.

And even though the last thing we needed here was more drama, I was so overwhelmed that I fell to my knees. Somewhere, Morgan was rolling his very green eyes.

But it was beyond weird—like I was suddenly back in that nightmare. I was in that closet, feeling sheer terror as I waited there for the man with the belt to come back and beat me senseless.

"Who is he?" I blurted as both Dana and Milo rushed to help me. I shook them both off—although it was entirely possible that Milo recoiled with horror. Again. But this time, at least, I understood why he'd let go of me as if I'd burned him. My head was filled with images from that awful dream.

"Oh, my God," Milo breathed as Dana got in Jilly's face.

"Cut that shit out," Dana ordered. I could tell she was ready to kick Jilly's butt—thinking it was something that the girl had done that had brought me to the floor.

Jilly got defensive. "I'm not doing anything. I'm not allowed—it's in the contract. No G-T behaviors while under the client's care."

"Who is he?" I asked again, this time aiming my question at the younger girl.

Jilly looked at me, her eyes quizzical. "I don't know *what* you mean."

"Sky, no," Milo said, but I spoke over him.

"The man," I continued. "With the belt. Does he work for Rachel? Did she hire him to come in here and hurt you?"

There were a variety of special hormones and enzymes in a Greater-Than's blood. I don't know the exact details of the science, but I *did* know that adrenaline, which was created by fear and pain, produced more of those hormones and enzymes. In plain English, that meant if you terrified and tortured a G-T right before you drew her blood to use it to cook Destiny, you ended up with a way more potent batch of the drug.

But Jilly was staring blankly at me. "There's no man," she said. "I don't know what you're talking about."

"Sky," Milo said again, but again, I was already talking over him.

"The man," I repeated. "The one who beats the crap out of you." I turned to Dana. "I *saw* him in my dream!"

"*Skylar.*" I finally looked over to find Milo gazing at me, shaking his head. "There's no man with a belt. Not here. Not now."

As I stared at him, I realized…whatever this was that I was feeling, it was…coming from *him*…?

"That was *my* nightmare," Milo told me quietly, and I didn't need to be touching him—I could tell he was ashamed. In fact, he looked like he actually might start to cry. But his gaze didn't waver as he locked eyes with me. "The man with the belt and the scabs on his knees? That was my stepfather."

"The one with the dog?" I whispered.

Milo nodded. "Yeah, he had the dog, too," he told me. "He

238

sometimes made me feed him, which…sucked. But at least he let me out of the closet to do it, right?"

He was trying to make a joke, and I felt my eyes fill with tears. Last night's dream had been *Milo's* nightmare?

"I spent seven months locked in a closet about the same size as this one," he told me as he looked around the tiny space. "It was after my mother died. It started because he didn't like it when I cried. At first, he'd let me out when I stopped, although sometimes he forgot. It became his default punishment—the beating was optional."

We were all silent, Jilly included, so Milo kept going. "When I was nine, someone broke into the house and stole his stash, and he blamed me for it. For seven months, he only took me out of that closet to beat the crap out of me or to, you know, feed the dog—and myself. I ate dog food for about that long, too. *When* I ate." He turned to look at Jilly. "This is not okay. I know you signed a contract, and you think that means you have to stay here, in Rochelle's *care*—"

She cut him off. "I know you think I'm crazy—"

Dana cut *her* off. "You're not crazy," she said. "You're a victim of some serious abuse, and you can't think clearly. You're starving; you've lost too much blood—so I'm gonna do your thinking for you. You're going to have to trust that we'll find your family and at least get your brothers to safety."

"What are you doing?" Jilly asked, panic in her voice as Dana used her telekinesis to lift the girl up. Her arms were still wrapped around her knees. Dana had her pinned there—she couldn't get her arms free or straighten her legs. "Stop it! Don't! *Don't!*"

I scrambled to move back out of the closet—Milo and Garrett did, too—as Jilly began to howl. It was a primal noise, unlike anything I'd ever heard, and we all clapped our hands over our ears. Except, Dana, that is, who was blasting out her TK as Jilly struggled to get free.

Books exploded out of the bookshelf and we all ducked, but I got slapped in the face with a battered and ancient paperback copy of the first Harry Potter book. There was symbolism there. I just wasn't sure what it was.

I nearly tripped over Calvin's chair—he alone was moving closer to Dana, as if he could somehow help.

"Dana, you need to calm her down," I warned, shouting to be heard over Jilly's wailing.

"Gee, thanks, Bubble Gum," Dana said from between gritted teeth. "I never would've thought of that."

I'd experienced Dana's G-T version of a straitjacket, and I'd barely been able to move my head. But Jilly must've had some serious countering skills. As I watched, she got first one leg free and then other, and then suddenly both of her arms. She flailed wildly as Dana still managed to keep her hovering about two feet above the ground.

The ceiling fan directly overhead kicked into overdrive and started to creak, its lights flickering on and off, as if an electrical surge was threatening to shut down the power entirely.

"*Jilly!*" Dana exclaimed. "Stop this!" I could see the vein pounding at the side of Dana's temple.

But then, Dana levitated, too—but instead of hovering, she flew backward and crashed against the wall, her back hitting with a loud and painful-sounding *thunk*.

She landed gracefully, both feet on the tile floor—but so did Jilly, who'd broken free from Dana's control. For a moment, both G-Ts looked freaked. But then Dana's expression changed. And she switched to full-on pissed off in two seconds flat.

"Enough," Dana hissed as she stared intently at Jilly. Her eyes were narrowed, chin down. I knew that expression well by now. Dana was trying to mind-control the younger girl.

But whatever G-T powers Jilly owned, they were stronger than Dana's mind control.

Because Jilly didn't tilt her head to the side and comply, walking out of the house with us. Instead, she crossed her arms over her chest and glared back at Dana in the same fashion, even as she very slowly and deliberately backed up, right into that closet.

It felt like the very air around us was vibrating.

All of the lights were flickering now. I looked up, because as the fan blades spun faster and faster, the base began to loosen from the ceiling. Books were one thing, but I didn't want that crashing down on us.

But then, without warning, the closet door slammed shut. Jilly was trying to lock herself back inside.

Dana used her own TK to yank the door open, and it creaked on its hinges.

"*Stop!*" Dana hollered.

"*No!*" Jilly shrieked.

The groaning creak of the door was enough to make me believe that, if the two girls kept it up, the wood would crack in half, right down the center.

Overhead, the ceiling fan was still picking up speed. One of the bulbs from the light fixture exploded, and tiny pieces of glass rained down onto the floor as we all ducked.

"This needs to end!" Milo shouted, and I knew it was time for me to step in and help Dana, who was still using that closet door as a G-T tug-of-war.

I knew that I could use my liquid-based TK to move people—human beings were essentially walking bags of H2O. I'd done it before. In fact, I'd saved Garrett's life with my power just a few months earlier. I just wasn't very good at it, especially when I was stressed.

Like right now.

Still, I focused on the water and blood inside Jilly's body. I *could* do this. I knew I could move the girl, and with Dana's less finicky TK, we could get her out of here and…

Keep her locked up where?

Okay, *that* wasn't helping. I had no idea what we were going to do with Jilly after we got her out of Rochelle's house, but I trusted Dana. She'd figure it out. Right now I had to focus on the water inside of Jilly. And so I focused. And focused…

And, with a blast of energy, the closet door opened with a huge bang, because Jilly came flying out of the closet. Jilly—and a crapload of other things from that back room. I couldn't even tell what was happening at first—but I knew that I was the one who had moved it all.

And then I saw the bag of plasma that Dana had been waving around earlier. It came right at me, and I ducked.

"Holy—" It was Cal who spoke first.

"*Calvin!*" Dana's voice rang out this time, and it was filled with a combination of despair and horror.

I realized that my eyes were squeezed tightly shut, so I opened them. And I saw that I was crouching down, in a position similar to the one we had found Jilly in when we'd first opened that closet.

I couldn't process what I was seeing at first—other than the fact that there was broken glass from that lightbulb everywhere, and that Dana was lying on the ground, *covered in blood.*

It's not her blood. Milo was next to me then, helping me up, and his thoughts came through with his gentle touch. *Are you okay?*

I am. Are you? I realized that the bag of plasma had hit Dana and broken. As we watched, she scrambled up to her hands and knees, skidding in the gore as she headed for Calvin, whose wheelchair had been knocked onto its side.

"I'm all right," Calvin said. "I'm all right. Really."

"No, you're not," Dana said, even though he'd already sat up.

"Oh, Jesus," Jilly said, shock in her voice. Garrett had caught her when I'd pulled her—or rather the fluids in her body—out of the closet. They were crouched down on the other side of Calvin's toppled chair.

"Yeah, I'm really okay," Calvin insisted, showing Dana that he wasn't badly hurt by pushing himself onto his knees in order to right his wheelchair.

And that's when I saw it.

The syringe, sticking out of the back of Cal's neck, the needle stuck deeply into his skin like he was a pincushion.

"Cal?" I said.

"Dude, what are you doing?" Garrett chimed in. "I mean, *look at* what you're doing!"

Cal looked down at the way he was using his legs to kneel there. "Whoa."

"No. No no no no no *nooooo*!" Dana wrenched the syringe out of Calvin's skin and held it up to the light. It was completely empty.

Beside me, Milo's face was ashen. I could barely breathe, fear squeezing my chest, but he managed to say the words I couldn't get out. "Tell me he wasn't injected with Destiny."

Dana shook her head. Was that *no* Calvin wasn't, or *no*, she couldn't tell Milo that Cal wasn't?

"Um, guys?" Calvin said, his eyes still wide as he looked around at us. "Guys? I'm feeling pretty freaking awesome right now. Um, was that...? Did I just...? Holy shit, I think I can..."

And then, without any further hesitation, my paraplegic best friend stood up.

As I watched, Cal walked over to Dana, pulled her up to her feet, and put his arms around her.

"Do you know how long I've wanted to do this?" he whispered.

And she burst into tears.

CHAPTER SIXTEEN

Dana was sobbing.

That, in and of itself, was terrifying. On the crying front, the most I'd ever seen her surrender to was a tiny sniffle that could have been mistaken for allergies before she'd stomped away to be alone. She didn't let her guard down in front of people. Ever.

And yet she was doing just that as she sobbed into Calvin's shoulder, as the empty syringe she'd been holding clattered to the floor.

Calvin—who was *standing there* on his *own two feet*, without any assistance from Dana's TK.

He'd walked over to her like he'd been doing it every day of his life. Like he was magically cured.

No, like he'd just been injected with a miracle drug that had fixed his paralysis...and also happened to be so addictive that the likelihood of his death from withdrawal was one hundred percent.

And *that* was why Dana was sobbing.

I started to cry, too. Because it was all registering now. I had tried to move Jilly. And I'd succeeded. Oh yes. I'd moved her, all right. I'd also moved everything else containing liquid, like the bag of plasma.

And the syringe.

It had shot through the air like a dart. I could picture it now. I'd dodged it right after the blood bag. It had all happened so fast, but that image of the flying D-dart was emblazoned on my brain like a terrible dream.

But this was real. It had happened. This was happening.

I'd just killed my best friend.

"I'm so sorry," I said, but those three little words were the most inadequate in the English language. "I didn't mean to—" But the words fell hopelessly short—so much so that I couldn't possibly finish the sentence. *I didn't mean to inject Calvin with a deadly drug. I didn't mean to shorten his already limited life.*

Dana looked at me over Cal's shoulder, but there was no anger in her eyes—only grief and utter hopelessness. I'd never seen her so defeated.

"It's not your fault," she told me quietly as she forced herself to stop crying. She wiped her nose with the back of her hand. "It's as much my fault as yours—I left that syringe on the counter instead of locking it back in the mini fridge."

"Because you came to help me," I pointed out. I'd fallen to my knees when I'd walked into the closet, and Dana had been right there, fast.

"Because of *my* nightmare," Milo countered. "It's my fault, too."

"And mine," Garrett chimed in. "We're only here because I wanted to help Jilly."

"And I didn't duck," Cal turned to face me. "So I'm just as much to blame."

Everyone but Jilly was trying to make me feel better by taking at least part of the responsibility. But really, *I* had done this.

I realized then that the girl was busy sweeping up the mess from the broken lightbulb. And when she'd gone to the kitchen for the dust pan and brush, she'd gotten a bowl and a sponge, too. She'd already squeegeed up the biggest pool of blood from the tile floor where Dana had fallen after the plasma bag had hit her and broken open. When she saw me looking at that bowl of blood, she defensively said, "I have to make it look like the bag broke while it was in the lab fridge. If she finds out you were here, she'll kill me."

Perfect.

Jilly, whom Calvin had given his life to save, *still* didn't want to be saved.

Dana had been staring at Calvin, but now she turned to look at Jilly.

"You," she growled.

Jilly's face flushed and she swallowed hard, taking a step back—which ironically put her back into her closet-slash-jail-cell.

"You're going to have to stay here," Dana told her.

"We can't just *leave* her," Garrett protested.

"Yes, we can," Dana said.

Jilly looked like she actually might start to cry. But she nodded righteously. "Thank you," she said. "All I wanted was for you to leave me alone."

"We're on it," Dana told her. "Believe me." She looked from me to

Milo to Garrett to Calvin. "Jilly's not our biggest problem right now. Everyone, help her clean up this mess. If she wants to stay here, this is where she'll stay—for now. But if Rochelle comes home and finds this mess, yeah, she *will* kill Jilly."

Garrett and I immediately got to work putting all those books back onto their shelves. Milo came over to help, but first he placed a steadying hand on a wobbly Cal.

Dana had broken away from their embrace, and Cal had been left standing there, shifting his weight from left to right and back, as if testing his legs.

"You okay?" Milo asked Cal, who nodded his response.

He was now staring down at his legs as if waiting for himself to fall to the ground, or maybe to wake up from this crazy dream.

"What now?" Cal asked. It might've been my imagination, but I thought I could actually see the blood vessel in his temple pounding. He was breathing heavily, too.

"Does it hurt?" I blurted, my voice cracking.

Cal looked up at me, surprise in his eyes. "What? Hurt? No! I feel… Well, I actually feel *great*."

"We need to get Calvin someplace safe," Dana said. She was helping put the books back, too.

"I can get my own self someplace safe," Cal pointed out, marching a little in place as she picked up that tattered copy of *Harry Potter*.

"Dude," Garrett asked Cal. "This is so cool. Are you a Greater-Than, now?"

Dana hit Garrett with the book.

"*Ow!*"

"He's *not* a Greater-Than," Dana told him as she put *Harry* back on the shelf. "He's a fricking instant Destiny addict who, yes, will probably develop some freakishly uncontrollable powers before he dies a hideous and awful death."

Cal nodded. "Well," he said, "my life expectancy was shorter than most people's anyway. *He walked again at the very end*—they can put that on my gravestone."

He was trying to be casual, but I heard the quaver in his voice. "Stop it," I said. "Both of you! There's got to be something we can do to…to…fix this!"

There's not. Dana didn't say it aloud, but I knew she was thinking it, because there wasn't. A Destiny addiction equaled death. Period. The very final end.

"We'll go back to Calvin's," she said instead. "Do research, and figure out at least where we're going to get his next dose of Destiny. He's going to need more in about a week. Two weeks if we're lucky."

Calvin walked over to me—it was going to take me a while to get used to that—and he hugged me, patting me on the back reassuringly. It was weird. In the past, hugs from Cal involved my bending over his chair. I realized then that he was taller than me. That was weird, too.

"This wasn't your fault," he told me, but we both knew that it was.

"I'm going to fix this," I told him.

Like Dana, Cal thought that was an impossibility.

Meanwhile, Milo was talking to Jilly, who'd come back out of the closet after dumping the bowl of blood into the lab fridge, along with the empty plasma bag. Garrett took the bowl and sponge from her, running it back into the kitchen to rinse it in the sink.

"We're going to leave you here," Milo told the girl. "But you need to promise that if we can locate your family and if we can figure out a way to keep them safe, you'll let us help you break out of this place."

Jilly laughed, and it made me wonder what she knew that we didn't. "Absolutely," she said. "But good luck with that."

"Help us out. What's your last name?" Milo asked again.

"Fuck you," she said again, and pulled the door to her makeshift prison closed, using her TK to throw the bolt.

And that, really, was the final proof that she absolutely wanted to stay there. If she could lock the bolt like that, she could also unlock it to get out. When I turned to look at Milo, I could tell that he was thinking the same thing, and the expression on his face was an awful mix of anger and vulnerable pain. I wanted to reach for him and silently ask about his horrendous seven months (seven months!) of abuse as a child, but I knew that he'd pull away from me. He wouldn't want to get into that here. We had no time—because I'd just killed my best friend.

"We can find her info on my dad's office computer." Garrett spoke up in the sudden silence, surprising us all by being extra-useful. "He has access to National Medical Records. Jill or Jilly with a twin named Ron and a brother named Jack? That should be enough data to get their last name and even a phone number."

"That's assuming they went to see a doctor in the past year," Milo pointed out grimly.

Garrett shrugged. "I'm sure they did. With a three-year-old?" He wasn't kidding. He honestly didn't get it. In his world, people didn't have to choose between a toddler's visit to the doctor and their next week of meals.

Milo didn't attempt to educate him. He just shook his head as he came toward me.

"I *am* going to fix this," I tried telling Milo this time, and his eyes softened with both grief and sympathy. I knew he was in Dana and Cal's camp. Like them, he believed that was an impossibility. He reached for my hand and sent me a wave of sorrow-laced *Still thoughts*, and this time I was the one who jerked my hand away.

Still thoughts weren't going to save Calvin, but just *maybe* crazy, outrageous, outside-of-the-box thinking could come up with something that we'd missed. I dug my cell phone out of my pocket and scrolled through my contacts as Dana said, "Let's go."

I found the number I was looking for and hit Connect as Calvin picked up his wheelchair and carried it out of the house.

———

"That's a myth," Dana said flatly.

"No," Morgan countered. "It's not."

"So there's hope," I said eagerly.

Dana turned on me. "No, there's not," she said, biting off her words sharply. "Even if what Morgan's saying is true, the last thing we need here is some stupid false hope—"

"It is true," Morgan said. "I'll say it again, more slowly, so that even *you* can understand, despite your anger issues. Two people, both male, both normies like Calvin, survived being detoxed from Destiny. It was dangerous—the treatment involved stopping their hearts and putting them into a medically induced coma—but they're both still very much alive. And addiction free." He turned to me.

"But as far as hope goes, darling," he continued, "you might want to review that math before you start planning Calvin's next birthday party. Only two people out of thousands have survived. Most don't make it past the stop-their-heart part of the procedure, and the rest never wake up from the coma. So while Cal's chance of dying from his Destiny addiction isn't a hundred percent, it's flipping close. Ninety-nine point nine-nine-nine-nine."

My heart sank as I watched Dana reach out and hold tightly to Calvin's hand.

We were sitting in Cal's playroom. His mom was still out of town, and his dad had left a note on the fridge saying he was pulling another all-nighter at the office.

And yes, as we were leaving Rochelle's, I'd called Morgan and left a message begging for his help—saying only that we'd had an emergency, and that if he could come out here tonight, we'd pay him an extra thousand dollars. I had no idea where we were going to get the *first* thousand we were supposed to pay him for visiting Sasha—but the promise of a second had just fallen out of my mouth.

To my surprise, the G-T had actually shown up at Calvin's door moments after we ourselves arrived. He rang the bell, and I'd checked the security cam to see him standing there in human form—fully dressed, thank goodness—in staid khaki pants and a muted blue polo shirt.

"I was already in town," Morgan told me when I'd opened the door, "since the meeting with Sasha is scheduled for early tomorrow morning, and I'm *really* not a morning person."

I was confused when he'd said that, because we'd left it that we were going to get in touch with him after the meeting with Sasha was scheduled, and it still hadn't been scheduled. He just smiled as he walked past me into the house, saying, "Check your messages on your phone, Bubble Gum."

And indeed, as I closed the door with my hip, I saw that I'd missed a text from my mom, who loved cutesy shortcuts: Mtg w Sasha 2morrow @ 8:30am!!! OK w U? Cn Cal drive U, I hve 2 wrk. ;-(

OK and TY sooooo much!!! :-) !!! I quickly typed back, responding with her mom-approved three-exclamation-point excitement, complete with many extra *O*s in *so*, in part to make up for her ridiculous lack of vowels. I looked up to glare at Morgan. "Did you bug my phone?"

Morgan laughed. "Yes, because your life is *sooooo* exciting," he said, obviously sarcastically. "Trust me, darling, I wasn't eavesdropping on you. I simply know these things."

But that was when he spotted Calvin talking to Milo on the other side of the room, and he immediately stopped laughing—recognizing instantly that Cal was now a Destiny user.

"But I didn't know *that*," Morgan added under his breath. He glanced at me. "I assume this is your emergency? Funny, I didn't take Calvin for the reckless type."

I nodded, but then shook my head. "He was injected by accident," I said.

"Nothing's ever *really* an accident, is it?" Morgan mused as he studied Cal.

"This was." We both turned to see Dana, and one look at the thundercloud that was her face was enough for Morgan to back down.

He nodded. "How can I help?"

"Aside from time traveling back a few hours and telling me not to let Calvin go with us into Rochelle's house?" Dana said. She shook her head and lowered her voice. "We're beyond help, but thank you for asking. That's...very generous of you."

Morgan glanced at me. "Sky offered me an extra thousand dollars to come here tonight. This is purely business."

Dana shot me a WTF look, then shook her head in disgust. "Of course it is. What was I thinking?"

"Morgan! How're you doing, bay-bay?" Cal had spotted the Greater-Than, and he strode over and gave him a bear hug. "Welcome to *mi casa.*"

"You seem cheerful enough." Morgan pulled back to look at him with narrowed eyes. He glanced at Dana and me. "Has drug-induced delusion already set in?"

Over time, Destiny gives users a deluded sense of superiority as it erodes their ability to empathize. It eventually even turns them sociopathic. As their powers increase, they begin to believe they're invincible, too. Unstoppable and perfect. *Better than*—as opposed to Greater-Than—with absolutely no compassion for anyone.

That was when you got the D-addict who killed his or her own baby because they wanted a little quiet in the house. Of course, a *jokering* addict would add some serious crazy to their problem solving. A jokering addict might not just kill the kid to shut him up, but also cook and eat him for a snack.

But Dana answered Morgan's question with a quick shake of her head. "It just happened. His first dose. It was only about an hour ago."

"And he can already walk?" Morgan's eyebrows were up. "That must've been some extra-potent D. Of course, everyone responds to the drug differently." He turned to ask Cal, "Have you noticed any other powers? Aside from this intense self-healing that your body's been doing?"

Cal looked from Morgan to me to Dana. "You mean, can I move shit with my mind? No. And believe me, I've been trying."

"Don't try too hard," Morgan warned. "Let the D in your system do its thing on its own time."

"Yeah, and when did *you* get your medical degree?" Dana asked Morgan, folding her arms across her chest as she gazed coolly up at him.

"About a year ago," he told her, completely seriously. "And no, I didn't attend an accredited university. It was purely self-study, so I'm only the equivalent of a medical doctor, but right now I'm all you've got." He turned back to Cal. "You *do* understand how serious this is, don't you?"

"I'm just living in the moment," Cal said, nodding yes. "BTW, I feel *great*. You don't know how shitty you feel until you realize you don't feel shitty anymore. So I'm just going to enjoy that while I can, if that's okay with you. Oh! We should dance. Who wants to dance?"

"Cal," Dana said tiredly.

He took her face in his hands and leaned down to kiss her sweetly on the mouth. "I love you," he said, then told Morgan, "I've decided to tell her that every five minutes. She's very freaked out by this whole thing."

"As she should be," Morgan said.

"When I was nine," Cal told him—told all of us—suddenly super-serious, "right after the accident, I wasn't expected to survive the night. But I did. And then I survived the year, and all of the years after that, through the reconstructive surgeries on my legs and my back. And I finally got to a place where I could breathe on my own, and then into my wheelchair, and finally I went back to school.

"They'd fixed me enough so I could roll around on my own, but they couldn't fix the damage done to my heart. And they always sent me out of the room—the doctors—when they talked to my parents about my life expectancy, but I knew what they were saying. I listened in. And frankly, it's been a miracle that I have reached eighteen—that I made it this far. Thirty was a crazy goal. Forty, unheard of.

"So if I get to spend the last day or week or month or however long it is that I'm gonna live feeling like *this*, able to walk and yes, *dance*, with this amazing woman right here, who loves me…?" Calvin smiled. "Well, I'm gonna take that as a win. And? FYI? I just found a website that gives detailed instructions on how to manage a Destiny addiction. There's a ton of information—"

"You're going to try to manage your addiction." Morgan laughed as he shook his head. "That's extremely delusional."

"Yeah," Cal said, "but right now, it's all I've got."

"No," Morgan said, "it's not. There's another option, and yes, it's an incredible long shot, and the truth is that you probably *are* going to die, but it sure as hell beats killing your friends when you joker—and you *will* joker, Calvin. You can't *manage* that. It's really just a matter of time."

And that's when we all got cozy on the couch and Morgan gave us the news that two (yes, the single digit that comes after one) former Destiny users had been cured of their addiction—out of all of the many thousands who'd died.

There were a lot of nines in the ninety-nine point mega-nines number that Morgan gave us, and my heart sank all the way down to my toes.

"The procedure was done up in Boston," Morgan told us, "at a place called the Obermeyer Institute."

I'd heard of OI—through Dana, in fact. It was a little-known research lab where neural integration was studied—*neural integration* being the scientific term for Greater-Than superpowers.

I looked over for her reaction, but she didn't seem impressed. "Do you have proof?"

Morgan widened his eyes at her. "Yes, because I always carry around proof that obscure medical procedures work." He exhaled his disgust. "I can show you online reports, and I can tell you that over the course of my medical studies, I had a conversation with one of the survivors. He's definitely alive." He looked at Cal. "But he was a former Navy SEAL. He was in excellent physical shape before he used Destiny. We can't say the same about you."

The news was just getting worse and worse.

Still, I clung to my teeny spark of hope. "So, road trip to Boston?" I suggested.

Calvin looked at me with disbelief. "You want me to spend three of the last days of my life in a car, driving to Boston?"

"No! I want you to go to Boston so you'll *live*." But as I looked from Cal to Dana and Garrett and Milo and even Morgan, I realized that I was the only one of us who held out any hope that Calvin could survive this. "Point zero-zero-zero-zero-one is *not* zero," I exclaimed, but the conversation had moved on.

"You were talking earlier about managing your addiction," Morgan told Cal. "That's just not possible."

"Each time you inject yourself with Destiny, you risk jokering," Milo reminded him. He didn't need to add the part that went, *And when you do finally joker, you risk killing us all.* Or maybe he should've, because it was possible that Calvin was starting to forget about that.

But before I could say it for Milo, he shifted to pull his phone out of his pocket. It was set on silent, but it must've been shaking, because he accessed his messages. Whatever he read there made his jaw clench.

"Rochelle?" I asked, unable to, well, *not* ask.

"No," he said, "I already sent her an *Oops, I got arrested, can you come bail me out, it'll only cost ten thousand dollars* text. As expected, she did not respond." He looked over at Dana. "No, this is the police alert that Calvin set up for us. Our John Doe's release from the hospital is pending."

"Get over there." Dana threw him the keys to her bike. Milo was already standing up and he snatched them effortlessly out of the air.

"Trail him. I wanna know where he goes, what he does, who the hell he is."

"I will," he said, shrugging into his jacket.

"Keep us posted?" Somehow that came out as a question, so I added, "Please."

I'd hoped to have a chance to talk to Milo privately tonight. Not only did I want to try to convince him that there was hope that Calvin could survive this, but I also wanted to know more about his time in that awful closet, about his stepfather, about all of his childhood. I knew very little—only that his father had died when he was tiny, like five or six, and that his mom had remarried, but she'd died soon after *that*.

His stepfather had also either vanished or died. I didn't quite know which, but it was possible the man had been arrested after locking his stepson in the closet for *seven months*, so Milo had gone into foster care. That had been awful, too—I knew that—but that was where he'd met Dana.

Oh, and I also knew—not from Milo, but from something Dana had told me—that there was a warrant out for Milo's arrest. Apparently when he and Dana had run away from their foster home, Milo had taken some money that his birth father had left him but that his foster parents were attempting to claim for themselves.

"And be careful," I added that, too.

"I will," Milo said, holding my gaze from across the room. He nodded once, and then turned and left.

I looked over to find Morgan watching me. Dana had leaned over and quietly given him the rundown on our John Doe—everything from my encounter with him at the Sav'A'Buck to his alleged amnesia after the cops found him unconscious in the parking lot.

"Oh good," Morgan said now. "Because things just aren't exciting enough, we also have a professional G-T bounty hunter on Skylar's trail."

"Professional bounty hunter," I repeated, because yes, that's exactly what our John Doe was. He found G-Ts, grabbed them, and sold them for serious money. Those girls went into Destiny farms—or maybe they ended up like Jilly, rented out to some D-bag-addict, locked in the closet...

"Five five four three!" Calvin said suddenly, and we all turned to look at him. He seemed as surprised as we were, and he added, "Excuse me," as if he'd burped.

"*Five five four three* what?" Dana asked, but Cal made an *I don't know* face.

"Destiny addicts who are prescient are *extra* dangerous," Morgan said. Now we were all looking at *him* in some surprise, so he added, "It sounds like Cal might be nursing some seeing-the-future skills. Which, I'm sure you can imagine, can be dodgy."

"Let me see that website that you found about managing the...you know," Dana said to Calvin.

"Yeah, I want a look, too," Morgan said, and I inwardly seethed, because it was clear to me that they were already putting Calvin into hospice-type care.

"What should *I* do?" Garrett asked. "Should I go to my father's office and use his computer to try to find Jilly in the National Medical

Records database?" His focus was still on the girl we'd left locked in Rochelle's closet.

Morgan looked at Garrett as if seeing him for the first time. "Your father's a doctor?" he asked, and Garrett nodded. "With an office." Another nod. "With a medical scanner?"

"It's a doctor's office," Garrett said impatiently. "It's got a lot of shit—whatever he needs to do outpatient surgery. He's a plastic surgeon. He nips; he tucks; he rakes in the cash."

"Good to know," Morgan said. "We won't need to go to Boston after all. We can detox Calvin right here."

Cal was already shaking his head. "I never said I was willing to—"

"And you're going to be less and less willing as time goes by," Morgan told him. "That's part of the addiction—the monster grabbing hold of you."

"Monster or no," Cal said, looking from Dana to me and back, "it'd be hard enough to put my life in the hands of *real* doctors, let alone Mr. Homeschooled over here."

"That's *Dr.* Homeschooled," Morgan said.

"Let's just get through tonight," Dana said. She turned to Garrett. "We need someone to monitor the Rochelle-cams—keep an eye on her when she gets home. We'll get that info on Jilly tomorrow. Your dad's still out of town for a while, right?"

"Until next week," Garrett confirmed. "At least."

I stood up. I needed to go home and pretend to be a normal seventeen-year-old for a few minutes with my mother. After which I'd pretend to go to bed and then sneak back out of the house—where once again, I'd be the G-T who'd just killed her best friend.

"I'll be back later," I said, but Calvin was the only one who noticed. Everyone else was already glued to various computer or TV screens around the room.

"I'll walk you home," Cal said and then smiled. "And this time, I'll actually walk instead of roll."

––––––––––

It *was* odd. Going home along the dimly lit sidewalks with Calvin walking at my side.

"Does it feel weird?" I asked him as two sets of feet smacked the concrete, replacing the quiet hum of his chair. "I mean, to walk again. Do your legs hurt?"

"What's with all the focus on *Am I hurt?*" he asked.

I shrugged, then admitted, "I'm scared."

He nodded and whispered, "I am, too." But then, more loudly, he said, "It doesn't hurt. It feels weird though." He looked down at his jean-clad legs. "Looks weird. Must look weird to you, too."

I nodded.

He rubbed his thighs through the thick denim. In the time that I'd known him, Calvin rarely wore shorts, mainly because he was embarrassed about letting people see the muscle atrophy. His legs were super-skinny, even with constant physical therapy.

"At first, I thought it would be kind of hard to balance, considering I haven't put any weight on my feet in such a long time," he told me. "Even that time Dana used her telekinesis to make me walk…it didn't feel the same as it does to move myself using my own muscles."

"So it's hard to balance?"

"Well, that's the thing." Cal smiled and did a little shuffle step to the side and then back. "I thought it would be. But it's not. And maybe it's my imagination, but I feel like I'm already gaining strength and muscle tone." He rubbed his thighs again. "Pants are getting tighter."

"Maybe it's not your imagination. Maybe that's the D working," I said.

"Or that."

We were silent then, just walking in the darkness.

But then Cal sighed and said, "My vision's crazy good right now. I don't think I've ever been able to see so well, even in the dark. I keep thinking, this must be what it's like to be you. Or Dana. And that thing with the numbers? That would be insane if I could just burp out winning lottery numbers."

"If you're prescient," I reminded him, "you don't get to pick which numbers you *burp out*. Five five four three could be the combination on Hobo Joe's bus station locker. Congratulations, you just won a pair of socks that haven't been washed in twenty-eight years."

Cal laughed but then quickly sobered. "There's a pretty intense Would You Rather question happening here."

"Hobo socks or the lottery?" I quipped. "That's not a hard one for me."

"No," he said, "I meant, *Would you rather get injected with Destiny, walk again but die young, or live in a chair and still die young?*"

I didn't respond. I couldn't. Not without bursting into tears.

"Man, would it be bad if I said that I wish I could stay like this?" he asked me.

I cleared my throat because crying wasn't going to help. "I'd think there was something wrong with you if you *didn't* want to stay like this," I told him. "But you can't. Not exactly like this. Not without turning into something…bad." When I looked at Cal again, I knew he was thinking about Rochelle, too. Or maybe more precisely, about the awful lack of humanity in the D-addict's eyes.

"But maybe," I continued, "if you do the thing that Morgan wants to try, the detox procedure, you get to keep some of it. Not the numbers-burping prescience. And maybe not even the sharp night vision. But maybe the Destiny has healed your back. Maybe, after detox, you'll still be able to walk. Maybe you'll get to keep that."

Cal was already shaking his head. "I don't know why, but I don't think so," he told me. "Or maybe I just don't believe I'll survive. I won't walk after detox because there's no *after detox*. At least not for me."

I didn't want to question him, certainly not about any prescient signals he might be receiving. I knew firsthand what it was like to have people not believe me when I said I knew something was true, with nothing more than a gut feeling to back me up. Instead I asked, "But what if that's just—how did Morgan put it—*the monster* talking?"

Cal was silent at that, looking over at the single wan porch light on what had once been the Rodriguez house, where little Sasha had lived with her parents.

All of her father's awesomely artistic and brightly colored sculptures had been removed, and the house had been repainted a far more staid beige. A "For Sale" sign lurched crookedly on a bent wire frame jammed into the shells of the newly xeriscaped front yard, and I noticed with a pang that someone had recently added a bright-red "SOLD" banner to the bottom.

It was the death knell for my hope, and tears filled my eyes.

Cal put what I was thinking into words. "You knew they weren't ever coming back," he said quietly.

I nodded because he was right. I had known that, deep down inside.

"You'll get to see Sasha tomorrow," he reminded me. "Say *hi* for me."

He'd been planning to go, too, but I realized now that he couldn't. Sasha would know from just one look that Cal was now a D-addict, and that would terrify her.

Shoot, it terrified the crap out of *me*, and I wasn't nine and on the autism spectrum.

"You really think…" he started to say, but then stopped.

"Just say it."

"You think I'm a monster?" His voice was so low I could barely hear him.

"No," I said, stopping and turning to face him. "Lord, Cal! No! But I think—no, I *know* that Destiny will turn you into one. That's just how it works." I kept going because I knew he was really listening. "And I also know your only chance is to at least find out more about this detox thing. I trust Morgan—I don't know why, but I really do. I trust him more than any doctors up in Boston. I trust Dana, too."

When I said Dana's name, Cal's face erupted into a megawatt smile.

"Promise me you'll leave the option open," I pushed.

He nodded. "Okay."

And then, as we started walking again, I changed the subject because even with all this crap happening, Cal was still my best friend. "So. You. And Dana."

I didn't think it was even humanly possible. But Cal's smile actually grew wider.

It was contagious, and I actually grinned, too.

"Me," he said as he nodded his head. "And Dana."

"I *knew* she had a thing for you," I confided.

"And you only share this with me now...?" Cal's voice went up an octave.

"I'm pretty sure I told you," I countered.

"I thought you were kidding! I mean, you never said, *Calvin, I am not kidding!*"

"Well, it *was* more of a *guess* than a hundred percent *know*," I admitted. "I mean, she's *Dana*."

"Yes, she is," Cal said. "And I sure as hell didn't think I stood a chance with her—especially since, up until recently, I couldn't stand at *all*—literally."

"Are you kidding?" It was my turn to do the higher-voice thing. "Dana never saw the wheelchair when she looked at you. All she saw—all she sees—is you. And you're awesome."

I could tell he didn't believe me. "Well, now she doesn't have to pretend not to see the wheelchair."

"I'm sorry," I said, stopping again, this time in front of my next-door neighbor's house. "*When* was it that you and Dana shared your first very, *very* special pizza? I do believe that was *before* you started walking around. Let's check the video, John. Why yes, yes it *was*. Check out the way neither Dana nor Calvin can quite look me in the eye as they come back into the playroom after enjoying said *special pizza*."

Cal was laughing again. "That pizza was private," he protested. "I can neither confirm nor deny—"

"You fooled exactly no one," I told him. "Okay? And it's very gallant that you won't share details, but as your best friend, I just have to make sure that in addition to, ahem, pizza, ahem, consumption, you and Dana actually had a conversation. I mean, beyond discussion of personal preferences for things like, oh, extra cheese?"

Calvin was cracking up. "This is getting way too creepy, but yes, we've talked. A lot."

"And you're both on the same page?" I asked.

"Thank God we've moved from pizza to books. And yes, same page. Same paragraph, in fact. But no, I'm not telling you anything else about anything, other than the fact that the *page* we are both on, together, completely, is wonderful and great—and that I might be a tiny bit in love with absolutely everything about her."

I smiled. "I know exactly how you feel."

"Wait." Cal narrowed his eyes. "If you try to steal my woman, I will unleash the full fury on you, with superfast lightning speed!"

I laughed. "What I *meant* was that I know how you feel because that's how I feel about Milo."

Cal nodded, his eyes still narrowed, as he played out the joke with a little *I'm watching you* hand gesture.

"Bottom line?" he continued, his tone still light. "If this Destiny crap ends up killing me, it's not like I haven't done pretty much everything I've ever wanted to do."

My heart lodged in my throat. "Except live happily ever after with the girl of your dreams, who really doesn't care whether you walk or roll, as long as you're alive," I pointed out.

"So why is it then," Cal said, suddenly quiet and intense, "that you're trying to kill me?"

I didn't know what to say to that—in fact, the expression on his face took me aback. But then it was gone or maybe I'd imagined it, because he smiled with his regular warm Calvin smile as he added, "That's what detox is all about, right? Stopping my heart? You guys kill me and then bring me back, allegedly Destiny free?"

"I guess so," I said.

"Although my chances of surviving are zero point zero-zero-zero-zero-zero-zero one," he said.

"That's way too many zeros," I said.

"Any zero is way too many," Cal pointed out. "These odds are not good, but I know you, and you've got to cling to hope, so go big and cling with your clingingest clingosity. But you also need to know that whatever happens, I love you, and I don't blame you for this. It wasn't your fault that I got injected. It wasn't Dana's fault; it wasn't even Jilly's—if it's anyone's, it's Rochelle's for cooking Destiny in her closet."

I nodded, trying hard not to cry.

"But I meant what I said before," Cal continued. "I love feeling like this. I feel healthy, I feel good, nothing hurts, and God, I *really love* walking. I'm in control; I'm still me; I'm still okay, so promise me you won't let Morgan kill me too soon, a'ight? Because I think that's really what his *procedure* is. It's a kind of…what's it called? Assisted suicide. I agree to do it, knowing that I'mma die, but that at least I won't die ugly, all jokering and nasty-ass sociopathic—killing you guys, too."

I shook my head. "You're wrong. It's your only chance to live!"

Cal chuckled quietly. "You still have hope that the detox will work. That's kind of adorable, and whoa, that came out a little asshole-ish, but I didn't mean it that way. I really do appreciate it. I just don't think it's very realistic and… Look, I better get back." He bounced on his toes, once, twice, three times, and said, "I'll wait here while you go inside. Don't want to freak your moms out by walking you to the door."

"Yeah, we definitely don't want that," I agreed, and as I walked up my driveway and then up the stairs to my front stoop, I glanced back to see Calvin doing a little dance on the sidewalk.

"It *will* work," I called to him as I unlocked my front door. "I know it."

He shrugged expansively. "And I know it won't. You're not the only one who *knows* things like that. Not anymore." He sent me a salute before turning and running back to his house.

"Sky? Is that you?" Mom called as I locked the door behind me.

I resisted the urge to call back, *No, it's a serial killer*. "Yup," I said instead as I wiped my eyes and braced myself for an hour or so of pretending that my life was normal.

CHAPTER SEVENTEEN

"I'm assuming you have the money you owe me in cash, in small bills," Morgan said quietly to me the next morning as I sat between him and Garrett in the waiting room of an obstetrician's office, on the eastern edge of Coconut Key, out past the interstate.

The fact that we were meeting Sasha in the medical office of a doctor who specialized in delivering babies had created some confusion when we'd first walked in—not just for us, but for the receptionist, too.

"Are you here for your first prenatal appointment?" she'd chirped as we'd approached the front desk, looking expectantly from Morgan to Garrett and adding, "With the baby's father…?"

Garrett and I had responded with loudly exclaimed horror. I'd shouted *Omigod no!* He'd shouted *I'm not the father! I swear I'm not!* Morgan stayed calm and leaned in to say quietly that we were here to see Sasha. He then led us over to a line of chairs where we all sat down to wait.

I realized then that we were here because Sasha's parents weren't comfortable giving out the address where they were staying, not even to me. With the enormous media coverage of Sasha's disappearance and the false murder accusations hurled at her father, they were all still in hiding from the press.

And then, of course, there was the need to keep Sasha safe from future abductions. We didn't talk openly about that or the fact that the little girl was a Greater-Than, but I'd stressed to Sasha's mom— over and over again on that day Cal and I had brought Sasha home— that it was vital the Rodriguezes kept Sasha hidden.

It was actually kind of nice to know that I'd been taken very seriously. Because no one would expect to find Sasha here.

I swore under my breath at Morgan's mention of payment. "I knew I forgot something. Dana has the money. I'm sure. It's just that, in the chaos, with everything happening with Calvin—"

"The deal that Calvin and I agreed to, via email," Morgan said coolly, "was cash in my hand, half in advance"—he held out his right hand— "and half"—he held out his left hand—"at the meeting with Sasha."

Both hands were noticeably empty.

"Plus there's the matter of the money you owe me for last night," Morgan added. "I didn't push it because of the 'chaos.'" He made air quotes around the word.

I glanced over at Garrett, who was staring in horrified fascination at the posters on the wall depicting the female reproductive system, as well as the cutaways that showed a baby in various stages of development in an ever-expanding womb. Sex ed had been banned for years in most schools. And although the Academy still covered the very basics of human reproduction in honors biology, I was pretty sure

Garrett wasn't in that class. It was possible he was getting his very first look at a uterus.

I nudged him. "Dana has the money, right?"

"What? I don't know," he said.

"The money from the other day," I reminded him, "when you pawned all that stuff from your attic…?"

"I'm pretty sure we used the last of the cash," Garrett said very unhelpfully, "to buy that GPS tracking device that Milo wanted."

"What GPS tracking device?" I frowned. Nobody had told me anything about any GPS tracking device.

Garrett shrugged. "Do I look like I know? All I know is Milo asked and Dana handed it over, saying something about how that was it, that our stash of cash was gone."

"This doesn't sound at all reassuring," Morgan said.

"We'll get the money," I told him. "I'm sure, when there's time, Dana and Garrett'll make another pawn-shop run."

"Nah, we stripped the attic," Garrett contradicted me. "We even cleaned out the closets—but things like ski boots and baseball bats don't bring in more than a few bucks at most. That sucked. But anyway, my house is done. We take anything more, and my dad'll hit me with his shit stick when he gets home."

Morgan sighed heavily.

"We'll get you the money," I told him. "I promise."

"Your promise won't mean much after that bounty hunter catches up with you," the G-T pointed out. But he didn't get up and walk away.

And Garrett leaned forward and said, "That's not gonna happen as long as I'm around."

Garrett's proclamation surprised me—that was probably the nicest thing I'd ever heard him say—but Morgan didn't blink. In fact, he mocked the other boy. "Yeah, look at how *that* worked out for your friend Jilly. Good job keeping *her* safe, Normie."

Garrett's face flushed. "At least I *have* friends, even though they're weirdos and freaks. I don't go around making people pay for things that should be done for free."

Now was probably not the best time to remind Garrett that he'd enlisted Calvin's and my help via blackmail—and that Dana had also blackmailed me.

Morgan shot back with "Talk to me after all your friends die. Let's see how eager *you'll* be to make new ones, so you can watch *them* die, too. It's no fucking fun, and I don't need more of that, no fucking thank you!"

A very pregnant lady had come in while we were sitting there, and she now looked up from her magazine in alarm at all those exploding f-bombs.

I realized that Morgan and Garrett were glaring at each other, bristling across me, so I sat forward, hands up, and loudly said, "The paternity test will end this argument once and for all," and the woman quickly turned away, clearly embarrassed for me. More quietly I said, "For Sasha's sake, let's not make a scene, okay?"

Both boys sat back, arms tightly folded across their chests, as I thought about the strange fact that Garrett McDouche considered me to be his friend, and that Morgan *didn't* because in *his* world, friends always died. Of course, that made me think of Calvin and then Dana, and then the fact that we were here today because Dana hoped that her little sister, Lacey, *hadn't* died, but instead had been abducted and imprisoned by horrible people for close to ten years.

And I suddenly had a flash of memory of Sasha's terrified face when we'd found her in that decrepit barn in Alabama. She'd been horribly traumatized by just a few weeks of captivity on a Destiny farm.

What would a girl be like who'd been imprisoned for nearly a decade?

"I can feel you getting tense," Morgan said to me. "Look, I'm already here, so I'm not going to leave. We'll work out a payment plan, but I have to warn you, the interest rate is going to be high."

"Thank you," I said. "I think."

"When we go into the room with Sasha," he continued, "I'm going to need you to keep your angst to a dull roar. I know you haven't seen the girl in some time, but truth is, if she's struggling with PTSD, she might not look too good. Try not to react to that, okay? If you let yourself get upset, you'll create static and make it harder for me to connect with her. Also, she's a little kid, so if you stay calm, she'll stay calm. And that's important, too. Last thing we need is for her to go ballistic and make her mother kick us out."

I nodded, drawing in a deep breath and letting it out in a rush. What he was asking was easier said than done. My heart was already pounding.

Morgan leaned closer to me. "Just…focus on the mantra that your boyfriend always repeats to you. What is it?" He closed his eyes for a moment and concentrated. Then he opened them and smiled at me. "*Still thoughts.*"

"How do you know that?" I asked, but he didn't answer, because here came Sasha's mother, Carmen, out of the door that led to the exam rooms in the back. I barely had time to stand up before I was enveloped in a wonderful-smelling hug of pure love and affection.

She greeted me half in Spanish, peppered with terms of endearment and words and phrases I didn't know, but also a very clear "I thank God every minute of every day that you were there to help my Sasha when she called you from that awful place!"

That was our official story. That Sasha had escaped from her kidnappers by herself, and all Cal and I had done was drive eight hours to pick her up and then eight hours back to bring her home—after she'd had the presence of mind to call Calvin's cell phone to ask for help.

"Where is Calvin?" Carmen asked, looking from me to Garrett to Morgan, who'd also stood up.

"Oh, he's, um…" I started. I swallowed hard, thinking about the real reason Cal couldn't be here right now.

Morgan said, "Cal's a little under the weather. It's nothing to worry about, but he didn't want to expose Sasha to his germs—or his negative energy."

Carmen was nodding. "Tell him I hope he feels better," she said. "But it's just as good. Sasha is still very frightened of strange people—men in particular. I think it's best that Sky goes in alone."

"Oh, but…" I said as my hopes dissolved.

Morgan cut me off. "That's smart," he said. "It's best to be careful."

He held out his hand. "I'm John. I'm a 'friend' of Skylar's." He didn't put emphasis on the word *friend*, but after that last conversation, I could hear his invisible air quotes.

"I own a service dog," Morgan continued as he held on to Carmen's hand. "A dachshund named Morgan. He's waiting out in the car. Sky was hoping to bring him in with her. He's very gentle and sweet. In fact, he's great with little girls."

"Dachshunds are Sasha's favorite!" Carmen turned to me, clearly thrilled. "Sky, you are so thoughtful. By all means, bring the dog." Back to Morgan, "Is it okay if it's just the dog, if you wait outside?"

"Of course," he said. "We'll go get him."

"Wait," Garrett said, clearly confused. "A dog...? What? We don't have—*Ow!*"

I'd stepped on his toe—hard. "I'll be right back," I told Sasha's mom, as Morgan and I pulled Garrett out the door to the parking lot.

―――――――

"Still thoughts," the little dog in my arms reminded me in a whisper as we followed Sasha's mom to a door labeled "Birthing Room Two."

Apparently, Morgan didn't have to shape-shift into a pit bull. Apparently, he could turn himself into any breed of dog—or any type of animal for that matter. And no, it wasn't an accident that he was now a dachshund—Sasha's favorite. He'd pulled that info from Carmen's head when he'd shaken her hand.

As for Garrett? His face as Morgan got into the backseat of his car, and then as I reached in to pull this incredibly adorable little dog out from the pile of clothing had been *nothing* compared to his face when the dog said, "There's a tagged collar and a service-dog vest in my messenger bag. Size small for both, I think."

It was very clear that Morgan had come here prepared to be shut out as a human—but not in his dog form.

"This is crazy shit," Garrett had said. "I need a nap."

We left him in the car and went back inside where Carmen greeted Morgan with more Spanish endearments and a barrage of kisses on top of his now-little doggy head. I saw his tail wag—it was impossible to not love Sasha's mom.

She led us into a room that was larger than I expected. It was set up like a living room, with sofas and chairs that were slouchy and comfortable, and with regular lighting instead of the traditional doctor's office fluorescent panels overhead. And yes, there was a hospital bed in the corner, but it was behind a curtain—clearly only meant to be used at the very end of the natural birthing process.

The room was dim compared to the brightness of the hallway, and it took a moment for my eyes to adjust. But I saw the small figure curled up on that big couch. And I recognized that face immediately.

Sasha. She had her favorite teddy bear with her—the one with the chewed-up nose. She was holding tightly to him, and her posture reminded me a little bit of the way Jilly had sat hunched in the closet when we'd found her yesterday.

Rochelle hadn't gone into the closet after she'd gotten home from her non-date without Milo—we'd monitored her via our cameras—but that didn't mean she wasn't in there right now, tormenting the girl or bleeding her dry.

"Still thoughts," the little dog whispered to me again.

But I was worried. Worried about Jilly, worried about Calvin, worried that we were somehow going to make things worse for Sasha—worried, worried, worried.

As we went into that room, I could smell Sasha's fear. It lingered in the air, a pungent, fishy odor. She'd been anxious about being left here alone. And she was anxious about who might be coming in the door.

Her mother couldn't smell the fish but knew enough to allay her daughter's nervousness. "Look who's here!" Carmen announced gaily.

"Skylar!" As soon as Sasha saw me, she put down her bear and bounded off the sofa, crashing into me and wrapping her arms around my waist. "Skylar, it's *you*!"

"It's me!" I said as Morgan jumped from my arms and onto the cushions of the couch, so I could hug the little girl back just as tightly.

He managed to give me an *Oh no you don't* look, despite his dog-face, so I worked as hard as I could to keep my tears from escaping.

Sasha held on to me for another long moment. Then she let go a little, enough to gaze up at me and smile. "I'm so happy you're here."

She looked weary and worn. And her body felt thin—too thin, even for her slight frame. But her hair was beginning to grow back again, enough so that, as her smile grew wider, I couldn't help but compare her current look to that of a tiny female elf.

Sasha's kidnappers had done many terrible things to all of the little girls we'd rescued. And, whether it was to stop an outbreak of lice or simply to dehumanize their tiny prisoners, their captors had shaved their heads. When we'd rescued Sasha, she'd been barely recognizable.

Now, standing in front of me, I was able to spot a glimpse of the girl I'd babysat so many months before. But even the trip from the sofa had been too much for her. She was breathless and clammy as I led her gently back to the couch.

"I brought a friend to visit you," I told her, and her eyes widened when she saw Morgan.

"A hot dog!" she said. "Oh, I love her! Can I have her? Is she mine? Mommy, Mommy, Mommy, can I keep her?"

"She's a he," I told Sasha, laughing as she hugged Morgan. "And I'm sorry, but you can't keep him. He belongs to a friend of mine and he's just here to visit you. His name is Morgan. He wanted to meet you."

"Careful, not too tight," Carmen warned.

"Oh, he's giving me kisses!" Sasha giggled, because sure enough, Morgan was doing an awesome imitation of a happy little dog, right down to licking the girl's nose and chin. She caught his face between her hands and gazed into his eyes, proclaiming, "I love you, too, Morgan!"

"Are you okay alone with Skylar and Morgan?" Carmen asked Sasha, who couldn't hide another burst of fishy fear at the idea of her mom leaving her, even with Morgan and me.

But I could tell that Sasha wanted to keep petting Morgan more than she wanted to go with her mom, so she gathered her courage and bravely nodded her head yes. But then she smiled more genuinely and said, "Morgan says we'll be fine."

Carmen smiled. "If you need me, at all…?"

"Push the call button," Sasha responded obediently, lifting a remote control that contained a single big, red button. She showed it to Morgan and began to explain to him what it was. "See, if anything bad happens, or even if I *think* anything bad is going to happen, all I have to do is push this button and Mommy will come…"

"Are *you* okay alone with Sasha?" Carmen pulled me aside to ask me quietly. "If not, it's okay, I'll stay with you, but if it is, I have an appointment with the doctor." She made a face at me and put her hand over her stomach, and I realized she was talking about seeing the obstetrician. Apparently, Sasha was going to be getting a brother or a sister.

"Does Sasha know?" I said soundlessly. Carmen shook her head no and put her finger to her lips.

"So many things upset her," she whispered. "We're still waiting for the right time…"

"She seems…good," I said, but I was lying. The little girl was hyper-vigilant and a jangling mass of anxiety and nerves. And if Morgan didn't do this right—or maybe if he *did* do it right—we were going to make her remember the excruciatingly awful details of her abduction, and quite possibly make her even more terrified.

Again, Carmen shook her head. "The nightmares," she told me. "They're awful. And they're not stopping."

"Morgan's a great service dog," I said lamely. "Maybe this visit will help…?"

"Maybe," she said, but I knew she didn't believe it. Still, she gave me one more hug and a quick "Thank you so much for coming" before she left the room, closing the door behind her.

Sasha spoke up immediately. "Lock it," she said. "Please, Sky?"

"I don't think it locks." I went over to look.

"Yes it does," Sasha said. "Up at the top."

Sure enough, there was a hook-and-eye lock up toward the top of the door. It wouldn't do much to keep anyone out—at least not anyone who truly wanted to get in. But if it made Sasha feel better...? I locked it. "You have good eyes," I said.

"Morgan does," she said. "He told me it was there."

Sasha had settled back on the sofa, her legs stretched out, with Morgan securely settled on her lap. She was stroking his ears, and she seemed less anxious and brittle. Calmer. Peaceful almost.

"He says to tell you *still thoughts*," Sasha added, her voice sounding very drowsy. As I watched, her body relaxed even more. Her eyelids drooped a little, and the smile on her face became one of utter content-ment. That expression was one I'd seen before. She looked like the Sasha I used to tuck into bed after a tall glass of chocolate milk and a good-night story. It was my sweet Sasha, getting ready to slowly fade into a peaceful sleep.

Except she didn't sleep. She kept her eyes open. Calmly, slowly, she looked down at Morgan and nodded. And Morgan nodded his little dog head back.

They must've been communicating silently.

For a very strange and brief moment, I wished that I could trade places with the little girl—just long enough so that Morgan could use his magic to take away all of the worries that crowded *my* thoughts and kept me from feeling like anything would ever be all right again.

———

While we were visiting Sasha, Calvin texted me, letting us know that his dad was coming home for a nap, so we should meet over at the old twenty-plex to debrief.

I'd also gotten a series of group texts from Milo—a status report that he sent to all of us.

Morgan and I got into the car where he re-humanized in the backseat. I wanted to give him some time to get dressed before I grilled him on what he'd learned from his mind meld with Sasha, so I read the texts from Milo aloud while Garrett drove us toward the abandoned mall.

"*Followed JD.* That stands for John Doe," I interpreted. "*Went via bus to Sav'A'Buck, then back to CKPD's*—Coconut Key Police Department's—*impound lot. Believe he's looking for his car, came up empty.* Yeah, because I gave his car to the family of the girl he tried to kidnap. Of course, he was unconscious when I did that, so how would he know?"

I kept reading, "*Then went via foot to North St church. Must've had a locker there, came out wearing suit & tie & carrying computer bag.* Okay, I think we can be pretty certain his amnesia was an act. *Then went to 24-hr car rental, drove out of lot in full-size gray SUV.*" Milo included the plate number in his text, and I rattled it off, adding, "So gas money's not a problem for him." That, too, was good to know. Well, it was good only on one level—that we knew about it. It was, in fact, *very* bad news that the bounty hunter who was going to start actively looking for me had a credit card that worked.

I kept going: "*Followed him into Harrisburg, he did business with*

*man in pickup truck in dive bar parking lot—my guess is JD's now armed
and dangerous. Then back to Coconut Key to all-night CoffeeBoy, where
he spent hours on laptop. Tried, but I couldn't hack in via wireless. Also
he sat by window near his SUV—I couldn't get close enough to place GPS
tracker.* And *that* explains what the tracker's for."

"*Stayed there all night. Looks like he's just starting to pack up his
computer. I gotta be ready to move.*" The very last part of his message
was to me, so I didn't read it out loud. Skylar, this man is dangerous, and
he's coming for you. Stay inside if you can, cover your hair if you go out, in
case he did catch a glimpse of it at the Sav'A'Buck. And keep your phone on
and accessible. I love you.

I love you, too, I typed back. I wish you'd told me about the closet and
your stepfather. I feel like you didn't trust me, and that hurts. Probably feels
a lot like me not trusting you with Rochelle, and I'm so, so sorry about that. I
hit Send quickly, before I chickened out, and of course, I'd forgotten
that any reply I made would go to the entire group. Oh, dear God.

Garrett's phone pinged, and because we were stopped at a light, he
glanced at my text. But instead of smirking and mocking me he said,
"You know that went to—"

"Everyone, yeah." I shook my head. "I'm more tired than I
thought." I glanced into the backseat, expecting some raised eyebrows
from Morgan, but the G-T had fallen fast asleep.

The good news was that he'd put his pants on first.

And it occurred to me, if *that* was today's good news? We were
definitely in trouble.

"They must've already gone into the 'plex," Garrett said.

As we pulled up, Calvin's car was parked outside the chain-link fence that surrounded the mall, but he and Dana were nowhere in sight.

Morgan was already stretching and yawning.

As curious as I was to find out if he'd gotten a lead from Sasha on the whereabouts of Dana's sister, Lacey, it seemed only fitting to wait and let Dana get the news first.

"That was hard—spending all that time in Sasha's head," he admitted as we all got out of the car. "Thanks for letting me sleep."

"Dude." Garrett's voice was loaded with admiration. "What you did? Was unbelievably cool."

"You didn't even get to see the best part," I told him. "The way that Sasha responded to him? It was amazing." When I'd carried Morgan out of the room, she was calmly telling her mother that the hot dog had told her that her mommy was going to have a baby, and she was so excited to be a big sister, and that everything was going to be okay.

But Garrett-the-Douche was back as he frowned and said, "No, I meant being able to turn into a dog. Chicks *love* dogs, especially the stupid little ones. You give 'em those puppy eyes, and *boom*, you're sleeping in their bed." He delivered his sleazy trademark laugh as punctuation. "Tell me the truth, have you ever used this G-T trick to hook up with, like, a supermodel? Please say yes."

"Seriously, Garrett," I started, but Morgan cut me off.

"I keep my *G-T tricks* separate from my dating life," he said. "But I *have* dated a supermodel."

Garrett's jaw dropped. "For *realzies*?"

The corner of Morgan's mouth lifted a bit, but other than that, he managed to answer with a straight face. "For realzies," he verified.

"Oh, please tell me everything," Garrett begged as he followed Morgan through the hole in the fence. "Her bust size, height, favorite position…"

It was then that I noticed that Calvin's car was unlocked. He'd just left his wheelchair there behind the steering wheel, like a discarded thought. He needed it to drive—it doubled as the driver's seat—but once he'd arrived, he'd apparently just walked away from it. I opened the door and hit the button that would lock the car manually, and then closed the door tightly.

It made me feel uneasy—the idea that Calvin, who was usually so careful about everything, would make such a big mistake. *An unlocked car was a stolen car.* How often had that been drilled into us, starting back in nursery school? And a car like his, tricked out for his physical challenge, wouldn't be easily replaced.

Of course, Cal probably didn't think he'd need it for much longer, on account of his impending death.

I hurried after Garrett and Morgan just in time to hear the G-T say, "He wore a size forty-regular jacket, was a little taller than me, and his favorite position was shortstop. You do mean baseball, right? He played in the minor leagues before he signed with the Moss Agency."

"Wait, dude," Garrett said. "No, I meant… What?"

"His name was Billy," Morgan said, "and he had the nicest ass I've ever seen in my entire life. Washboard abs. And those cheekbones. To. Die. For. He was hot, the sex was molten, but sadly he didn't have all that much to say and had *terrible* taste in music, so we broke up. End of story. Roll credits."

I glanced back at the parked cars and it occurred to me that Dana might've distracted Cal, and they'd hurried inside to...

I got out my burner phone and texted both Cal and Dana. We're here!!!

Meanwhile, Garrett had gone silent as he did the math. "So, you're, like...?"

"Gay?" Morgan finished for him. "Yes, darling, I'm a dude who likes dudes. Are you cool with that, *dude*?"

Cal's texted reply came back quickly: Waiting for you in theater 6.

Garrett took a little longer, and I cringed, waiting for the inevitably douche-tastic homophobic remark as we went inside the dimly lit mall and headed toward the former cinema.

But instead, Garrett shrugged. "Yeah, man. I mean, whatever floats your boat is cool, I guess." He laughed. *Heh-heh.* "Leaves more hot G-T chicks available for me, right?"

"Absolutely," Morgan said, even as he looked at me and widened his eyes in an unspoken *Did you know you were in that hot G-T chicks subset?*

I responded with an eye roll—there was no time for more than that, because Dana came out of the theater to meet us with her flashlight and with a barrage of questions. "Did you have any trouble? Did you get to see Sasha? Did you find out anything? Is Sasha okay? Does she remember seeing Lacey?"

"No, yes, yes, yes, and maybe," Morgan told her.

It didn't surprise me that Dana had followed all that. "She *maybe* saw Lacey?" she pushed. "Did you find out where Sasha was when she *maybe* saw my sister?"

Morgan hesitated. "It's tricky," he replied. "You see, when I went into Sasha's head, I saw her memories of her abduction—even some of the ones that she's since tried to block. But memories are based on perception, and perceptions are different from facts. For example, she has a *very* clear memory of a monster in that barn in Alabama—a very big man who carried a club that literally dripped with blood."

Cal had come out of the theater, too, and he now put his arms around Dana.

"There *was* a guard in the barn where she was being held. He used a baseball bat that was bloodstained, and he was definitely monstrous," I said. He'd nearly killed Dana.

"Was he half-bear, half-Bigfoot, with a hairy face and sharp, pointed teeth?" Morgan asked.

"No, he was human," Dana said grimly.

"But evil," I chimed in, shuddering as I remembered his telltale stench. "He had scruff on his chin, but it wasn't even really that much of a beard."

Morgan said, "Unless there was more than one guard who was also a giant and carried a club—"

"There wasn't," Dana said.

"Sasha's monster had hair covering his face," Morgan countered. "Even on his cheeks and forehead. *That's* what I saw when I was in Sasha's mind. That's how *she* remembers him."

I wondered if the man had put on some kind of mask to scare the girls he was guarding, but then I realized it didn't matter. Morgan's point was clear. Sasha's memory of the guard with the bloody club was of a hairy beast-man. Which meant her other memories could be equally creatively altered or enhanced.

Cal spoke up. "Why don't we bring this inside?" he suggested, pointing over his shoulder to theater six. "You all can sit down and... let Morgan start at the beginning, okay?" His last words were aimed at Dana, who nodded.

"Yeah," she said. "Let's sit. We're all tired."

She and Cal led the way and I was right behind them. There was another flashlight already in there, on the slanted floor, and Cal turned back to grin at me. "Look what I can do," he said and pointed at the flashlight.

A tiny bolt of electricity left his hand and raced toward the flashlight, and the bulb glowed brightly.

"Whoa," I said, taking a step back.

The light didn't stay lit for long. "It's nothing much," Cal said, but all I could think was, *Look what I can do! Look what I can do!*

Our very first encounter with Destiny, just a few short months ago, had been when an addict jokered in front of us at the Sav'A'Buck. It had been awful and violent, and the entire time she'd done hideosities like pull out her own teeth and throw them in bloody globs onto the floor, while gleefully proclaiming, *Look what I can do!*

But Cal had either forgotten, or maybe he just no longer cared.

"Yeah, we have to talk about that, too," Dana muttered to me as we sat down on the floor. Garrett and Morgan sat beside us, forming an impromptu circle—like we were getting ready to play duck-duck-goose. Meanwhile, Cal chose to stand rather than sit, leaning against the wall outside our circle, half of his face masked by shadows.

"So do you think Sasha actually saw my sister?" Dana asked Morgan. "Or did she just dream her or maybe see a photo or…?"

"I know that Sasha met someone named Lacey," Morgan replied. "Lacey spoke to her—they had a conversation, but Sasha was confused. And terrified. It's possible she was drugged at the time. Or maybe just low on blood."

"Was this up in Alabama?" Dana asked. She was shaking. I could see her hands.

"I don't know for sure," Morgan said, adding gently, "I'm sorry, darling. I hate guessing, but if I had to, gun to my head? I would say that it wasn't. My guess is that this happened close to immediately after Sasha was kidnapped, but her memories of that time are…a jumble at best. Wherever this conversation with Lacey happened, it wasn't anywhere near the barn where you found her. *That* she remembers very clearly.

"In the mysterious place where she met Lacey, there were dogs barking. Lots of dogs," Morgan continued. "Big dogs—Sasha was scared of them, but she was more scared of the *bad people*. Her internalized words, not mine. And then Lacey was there and she told Sasha to run. *Run*. So she ran, and she remembers that Lacey was holding her hand, with those dogs barking and barking. It was night—everything was dark, and again, Sasha's memories are disjointed and blurred. They might've been using dogs to track down girls who'd somehow escaped, but I'm guessing here."

"Or it happened while they were being held at one of the Doggy Doo Good warehouses," Dana said. "We know that Doggy Doo Good trucks are sometimes used to transport girls to Destiny farms."

Morgan nodded. "I've heard that rumor, too."

"It's not a rumor."

"Okay," Morgan said. "I heard a shred of a memory of voices both calling and whispering Sasha's name—that might've been a nightmare, but then there was a bigger shard of Sasha trying to hide behind a palm tree before being grabbed by an angry woman who probably knocked her unconscious. It went from sheer terror to pain to black. I dug at it as best as I could, but I don't think Lacey was with Sasha when that happened—if it even really happened."

"What did she look like?" Dana asked suddenly. "Lacey." I could see how difficult this was for her.

Still, to have confirmation that Lacey was still alive! After so many years, the girl was still out there, at least as of a few months ago. And that meant that we could find her. We'd brought Sasha safely home—we could do the same for Dana's sister. I *knew* we could.

Morgan looked like he was trying to find the right words. "She was…okay. Considering. She looked a lot like you, darling. It was uncanny."

"But she was uninjured? Healthy? At least relatively?"

Morgan didn't hesitate. "Yes."

Garrett had remained silent up until that moment. But now he glanced uncomfortably at Dana, and then at Morgan. "Not to sound like a dick, but why would they keep Dana's sister alive for so long?

I mean, wouldn't the constant bleeding thing get to be too much for her after years and years?"

Dana shot Garrett the evil eye. "When people say *not to sound like a dick*, it's always followed by a dick comment. And you *are* a dick, by the way."

From behind us, I heard Cal giggle quietly. "She says that with love in her heart, bro," he told Garrett, and I was struck by the weirdness of Calvin attempting to soften Dana's verbal blow.

"Garrett's question is a good one," Morgan said. "But a more pertinent variation is *how* could they keep her alive for so long? Obviously, anyone making money off these girls would want to keep them producing blood for as long as possible. The *why* of that's a no-brainer. But a D-maker needs to balance those costs of keeping girls healthy with the need to scare them shitless through beatings or worse, in order to produce a purer product, right? Eventually, in the course of any one girl's life, the cost of her medical expenses will become too high, and it'll become simply good business to bleed her dry and start fresh with a new girl."

The awfulness of murder being *good business* plunged us into a rather darkly grim silence.

"ORANGE CIRCLE BOULEVARD ORLANDO FLORIDA GAAAH!"

We all jumped—Cal's voice was so unexpected and so loud.

Dana turned around first. "What are you screaming about, Scoot?"

But Calvin had covered his mouth, clearly startled, too.

"Five five four three," I remembered. He'd done this before—just blurted out random information. *Look what I can do...*

"Wait a minute. That address sounds familiar." Dana pointed at

Garrett, but Calvin was already on top of it. He'd gone over to the one place in the room where we had enough cell service to access the Internet, and he'd typed the address into his phone.

"5546 Orange Circle Boulevard," he reported, looking up at Dana, "is the Doggy Doo Good warehouse in Orlando. *Ding*."

"So what's 5543?" she asked.

He checked whatever map had come up on his phone, but shook his head. "I can't tell. Looks like it might be another warehouse, but it's not labeled." He looked up. "It could be abandoned. One of the nearby buildings looks like it might've burned down—the jungle's pretty much swallowed it up."

"Jungle as in palm trees?" I asked, thinking about Sasha's memory of hiding behind one.

"Looks like it from the satellite map," Cal said.

Dana nodded, and I didn't need telepathy to know what she was thinking. We'd have to go there ourselves and check it out. Although I could also tell that she wasn't thinking reconnaissance. If she had her way, we'd kick down the doors and do a Rambo on everyone inside.

It made sense, in a desperate way. We were looking for Lacey, and Sasha saw Lacey in a place where dogs were barking. We knew they bred puppies at Doggy Doo Good, and *blam*, Cal blurts out an address that's essentially next to the DDG warehouse in Orlando.

I wanted to go check it out, too. Or I would have if I weren't so worried about Calvin.

He'd begun to pace—a sight I'd never seen before—or thought I would ever see, for that matter.

"Was there anything else you found out during your time with Sasha?" Dana asked Morgan.

"And I'd like to know," I chimed in, "what you actually said to her or, I don't know, *did* to her...? Because she was way less anxious when we left." I looked at Dana. "It was amazing. Sasha was practically serene."

Morgan answered me first. "I helped her process her memories," he said. "And I even, well, I didn't remove them, not exactly, but I softened the memories of things like that monster-man. I also enhanced her memories of when you came to set her free and of her return home to her parents. Now when she thinks about the ordeal, even if it's triggered, the very first thing she'll remember is being saved—and being safe and loved."

"Thank you," I said.

"You paid for my services," he reminded me, except we hadn't. Paid. Not yet anyway. But if it was easier for him to think of his relationship with us in terms of payment plans and services rendered, that was okay with me. He might not want to admit it, but he was one of us now. Like it or not, we'd become friends. But he'd already turned back to Dana. "There *was* one more thing. A tattoo."

Dana raised an eyebrow. "A tattoo?"

"It was actually an image that I recognized," Morgan said, "and I was wondering if it was maybe yours, and Sasha saw it on you and somehow connected it to her ordeal. I tried to find a face—you know, of the person whose tattoo it was, but..." He shook his head.

"I have a lot of tats," Dana said.

"I know," Morgan said. "Believe me, darling, I noticed. It's impressive for a G-T to have that much control over her self-healing abilities."

Most Greater-Thans couldn't keep tattoos. Their systems viewed them as injuries and "healed" them—and within hours of getting inked, they vanished. But Dana had taught her body *not* to do that. It *was* impressive.

"Describe it," she ordered Morgan now.

"I can do better," he said. "I'll draw it. Anyone have a marker?" He looked at me, eyebrows up.

"Fresh out," I said dryly. Really, he'd thought I'd carry around a marker?

"Here." Calvin handed over his phone, open to his drawing app, and Morgan used his finger to draw two lines. It was an equal sign, and he put a greater-than sign, like this <, in front of it, and a less-than sign, like this > after it, so it looked like this: <=>

And then he drew an oval entirely around it.

Dana was already shaking her head long before he finished. "No," she said. "Nope. Not mine."

"Anyone else?" Morgan looked around, stopping on me. "Angst-Boy, maybe?"

"His name is Milo, and no," I said.

"It looks kind of like an eye," Cal noted.

"It's a symbol used by an underground Greater-Than rescue group called GTFU," Morgan told us. "And that *FU* stands for exactly what you think it does. They're based mainly out of Atlanta. I didn't realize they had a cell here in southwest Florida."

"Cell, like terrorist cell?" Cal asked.

"Yes, except they're not terrorists," Morgan told him. "Although they *are* badass. Their mission statement is to liberate girls from Destiny farms. They run a series of safe houses for G-Ts—like an underground railroad. I've camped out with them a time or two, with the group in Atlanta. Again, I didn't know there was a local group. I mean, if there even is. For what it's worth, all of the normies in GTFU have that tattoo." He pointed to his picture. "The G-Ts tend to draw it on themselves with permanent marker."

And *that* was why he thought I might have a marker. He'd thought we might be part of this regional G-T rescue group. It was kind of flattering, actually. *Badass*, he'd called them.

"If Sasha didn't see this tat on one of you," Morgan said, "then she saw it somewhere else." He looked at Dana. "That's good news. It's actually possible that Lacey was rescued months ago."

But Dana was already shaking her head. "No. If Lacey were free, she would have found me. You said it yourself. *Months ago*. At the very least, she would've contacted my dad's lawyer and *she* would've contacted me."

Dana's and Lacey's father was in prison—on death row—framed for the murder of his daughter. Who wasn't dead.

The sound of Calvin's sneakers against the floor as he paced back and forth was worrying. Why couldn't he stand still? Why, for that matter, hadn't he sat down with us?

Morgan was looking over at him, too. "Hey, Calvin," he said. "How are you feeling?"

Calvin froze, and I could sense the tension in him, even from over here. "I feel great," he said. "But I probably shouldn't've had that last cup of coffee. I'm a little jittery."

"Too much caffeine can do that," Morgan said, nodding. He turned back to Dana. "I was thinking that now might be a good time to take him over to Garrett's dad's office."

"Whoa," Cal said. "*Whoa whoa whoa!* I didn't agree to do that detox thing!"

"I meant for a simple medical scan," Morgan said.

But it was as if Cal didn't hear him. "I'm not ready!" he insisted.

"Dude, no one's saying you should attempt the detox right now," Garrett spoke up, and Cal turned so that he was towering directly over him.

Cal's body language was pure aggression—so much so that Garrett threw his hands up, arms crossed in front of his face, as if to brace for a blow.

"You'd like that, wouldn't you?" he snarled at Garrett, and it was beyond weird, because he almost seemed like he was starting to glow. "With me dead, you'd have Dana for yourself."

"What?" I scrambled to my feet. What happened to *She says that with love in her heart, bro?*

"Calvin!" Dana exclaimed, standing too. "What the *hell*?"

"Or maybe you just want me back in my wheelchair, rolling through school like a sitting duck, while you wait for the perfect moment to humiliate me?" Cal continued, and there was no doubt about it: he *was* glowing. Little sparks seemed to fall off him as he moved, fading before they hit the floor.

"I don't," Garrett said, his voice shaking. I could smell the fishy whiff of his fear. "Dude, we're friends now. I wouldn't. I'm just trying to help figure out a way to, you know, fix you."

"*Fix* me?" Calvin's eyes were molten lava as the sparks falling off him increased. "You wanna *fix me?*"

"Calvin!" Dana said again as Garrett said, "No, man, that's not what I was... I meant, *help* you, *help* you! I want to help you!"

"*Well, maybe I don't want your help!*" Calvin shouted as around us the entire movie theater lit up like a Christmas tree before exploding in a shower of sparks.

After that? Pitch-black.

CHAPTER EIGHTEEN

"Is everyone okay?" Morgan's voice rang out through the dark cinema.

Correction—it was more than dark. The blackness was *thick*—so much so that I was unable to see my hand as I held it directly in front of my face. "I'm good," I said.

"Me, too, um…I guess?" Garrett answered.

Cal and Dana didn't offer their two cents. But I could hear Cal's ragged breathing and Dana's quiet words to him, "You're okay. It's okay. It's gonna be okay." But he didn't sound too good.

There was a gravelly scratching sound, and then a flickering light illuminated the room.

Morgan held a match in front of his chest, cupping a feeble little flame. Still, after that pitch-darkness, it was enough to make me need to squint as I turned to look for Cal.

He was hunched over against the side wall, with Dana kneeling beside him as he laboriously worked to catch his breath.

"Did he just joker?" Garrett asked.

"If he had, we'd all be dead," Dana said as she helped Cal sit beside her, their backs braced against the wall.

"I don't know what happened." Cal tried to smile reassuringly, but he looked a little green, and I could see his fear in his eyes. "I'm sorry I snapped at you, dude," he told Garrett. "I don't know what came over me. It was weird, like I was outside of my body, watching it all happen. But I'm totally okay now. I just feel a little…breathless."

Dana kept pressing her flashlight's *on* button with her free hand—but the thing was dead.

Even the emergency exit signs in the theater had gone out entirely.

"Control of electrical currents is a powerful ability," Morgan said, as he sat down on the other side of Calvin. He let go of the glowing match, and it hung there in the air, burning itself out as he lit another, and then another. They hovered just above his head, the small flames dancing and crackling quietly. "Right now, the current you can throw isn't much stronger than a shock from static electricity. But that's going to change with time. You're going to have to learn to manage it. You can't just go off like that."

"I know," Cal said. "God, I'm tired."

"You just expended a lot of energy," Dana told him. "Literally."

"I'm sorry," he told her. "I didn't mean to—"

"It's okay," Dana interrupted. "Nobody's angry. I'd just like to understand what triggered this, so we can make sure it doesn't happen again."

"You said you felt jittery," I chimed in. "You were pacing—you didn't seem to want to sit."

"Jittery and irritable," Cal said and then shivered. "I'm still feeling..." His voice trailed off.

"Like what?" Dana pressed him.

"Okay. I'm going to sound crazy here," Cal told us. "But...you know when you're really *really* jonesin' for chocolate peanut butter ice cream? Like, it's the only thing you can think of, and everything else is kind of just a blur until you go have that big huge bowl of chocolaty awesomeness?"

I nodded. "I get cravings like that for s'mores sometimes."

"Yeah!" Cal exclaimed fervently. "Perfect example. Skylar and her s'mores. She craves s'mores like nobody's business. Well...that's how I feel right now."

Garrett raised one eyebrow. "Dude. You can't stop thinking about chocolate peanut butter ice cream, so you almost tore my head off?"

Cal shook his head, clearly frustrated.

Morgan's face was grim as he said, "It's not ice cream he wants."

Calvin nodded. "I don't want ice cream," he said, "but...I really *really* wish I had more...Destiny."

Dana let out a little sound that was one part sigh and two parts pained moan. "This is the start of withdrawal."

My stomach did a somersault.

"Wait. What?" Garrett said.

Cal frowned, too. "No. I mean, I can't be. Not yet. It's supposed to take at least a week for that to happen." A pause. "Isn't it?"

With the exception of Garrett, we had all done a fair amount of homework learning about Destiny. Cal and I had spent hours online, poring over D statistics, facts, and even myths. We'd wanted to know everything we could—even before Calvin had been injected. The more informed we were, the more we stood a chance at helping other people. People like Sasha and Jilly and Lacey. And, as silly as it sounded, I felt that I stood a greater chance of being able to keep *myself* safe, too.

One thing I knew for sure was that most people didn't begin to withdraw from Destiny for at least seven days. But that was a rough number. Everyone was different. Plus…

"Your injuries," Dana said, the realization hitting her at the same time it occurred to me. "Cal, maybe your body's absorbing the D at a much faster rate because of the extent of your injuries."

Morgan was the closest thing we had to a doctor, and he pursed his lips as Dana glanced at him for confirmation of her theory. "That's entirely possible," he said.

"So…what does that mean?" Cal barked out a laugh, but the sound was laced with fear. "I know it means that if I don't get more Destiny, I'll die, but…once it starts, does it happen fast? How worried should I be?"

"The symptoms become severe," Morgan said. "The jittery feeling will intensify. You'll start to shake…"

"And puke," Dana said. "Once you start with the puking, *then* we worry."

"Yay?" Cal said.

"Why don't we just buy more?" I blurted. I knew it was wrong. I knew that injecting Calvin with another dose of Destiny was just increasing the chances that we would all get hurt. Cal could joker at any moment, but odds of it happening would increase dramatically if—when—he shot up.

And as hopeful as I was that Morgan's detox procedure would work, Cal's words from last night echoed in my head. *Assisted suicide. I agree to do it, knowing that I'mma die, but that at least I won't die ugly, all jokering and nasty-ass sociopathic—killing you guys, too.*

Was that really what it was—simply a way to control when and how Calvin died? Was that why Morgan had suggested it, so that no one else would get hurt when Cal inevitably jokered?

Two survivors out of thousands *were* terrible odds.

And right now, all I could think was that I wasn't ready to lose Calvin. Not yet. "How much money do we have?" I asked. "Maybe if we pool what we've got…?"

"I've got fifty bucks on me," Garrett spoke up first.

Dana reached into the pocket of her bomber jacket and pulled out a wad of bills. "I've got another forty."

Morgan shook his head as he lit a few more matches to keep the room from going dark. He'd been doing that regularly while we talked. "I don't carry cash. And I pretty much live hand-to-mouth."

Also? We already owed him two grand, although this time he didn't bring it up, and I knew from the way he refused to meet my gaze that I was right about him. Like it or not, he cared about us and was unwilling just to walk away from us now. I also knew to keep my mouth tightly shut and not let any words of thanks escape. It was better to just pretend he was in this for the money.

I dug in my own pockets and pulled out an old tube of lip balm, along with two grubby-looking quarters. I'd made absolutely zero money since I'd stopped babysitting Sasha. And while Mom allowed me access to a debit card, she rarely placed more than the equivalent of a few school lunches on it at a time. "Gee. I'm a *huge* help."

"I have access to maybe a few hundred," Cal said. "More, if I tell my parents what's going on."

"If you do that," Dana said, "we should all say good-bye to you first, because we won't ever see you again. They won't have a clue how to help you, but they sure as hell won't listen to us. I guarantee it." Her expression was dark. "No. We need to handle this ourselves."

"But you said that Destiny costs five grand a hit," Garrett pointed out. "And we have, what? Three hundred bucks?"

For a moment, as Dana looked at him, there was so much grim determination in her face that I wouldn't have been at all surprised if she announced that she was going to go rob a bank to get the money Cal needed.

Instead, she stood up, and one sleeve at a time, she removed her bomber jacket and tossed it onto the floor. Then, with one swift movement, she reached into her waistband and pulled out a knife. And she sliced the inside of her forearm, just above her wrist—just enough to draw a thin line of blood.

"What'd you do *that* for?" Garrett all but shrieked.

Dana didn't flinch. Instead, she turned to Cal and held out her arm. "I have what you need," she told him. "It's inside of me."

Cal's eyes filled with tears as he gazed up at her. "I can't make you do that," he whispered.

"You can't stop me either, Scoot," Dana replied. "I'm done losing the people in my life who mean something to me. I'm through with that. Do you understand what I'm saying?"

Cal shook his head as he gazed up into her eyes, but she didn't back down so he finally nodded.

Morgan broke the silence. "Good luck with that."

Dana knew he was being sarcastic, but she chose to pretend his words were sincere. "We'll need all the luck we can get, thanks. And we won't turn down help, if it's offered. So…are you offering?"

"Noooo!" Morgan laughed as he said the word. "I'm outta here."

I laughed, too, because he was a terrible liar. "No, you're not," I said. It was the wrong approach, because he immediately bristled.

"Oh yes, I am," he said.

"Well, I appreciate the help you've given us so far," Dana said. "We'll pay you what we owe when we can. Have a safe trip back to Adventure City." Just like that, she dismissed him, turning to me and Garrett. "You two head over to Garrett's dad's office. I think it's a good idea for Calvin to have a medical scan. I'm pretty sure we can figure out the equipment on our own."

She turned to tell Cal directly, "It's smart to get a baseline at the very least." Back to Garrett and me. I was watching Morgan and he was just shaking his head. "But I also want you to do as much research as you can on the Destiny detox process, see if we have access to the rest of the equipment we'll need. If we're going to do this—"

Cal made a noise.

"I said *if*, Cal," Dana repeated. "It's only an *if*, but *if* we're going to do it, we're going to do it right. Oh, and while you're at it, Sky, see if you can't use Dr. Dick's computer to track down Jilly's family—give 'em a call to find out WTF."

"Got it," I said, gesturing for Garrett to follow me.

But Morgan blocked our path. "Oh, gods, yes," he said. "All right. I'm offering my assistance, sweet baby Jesus help me."

Dana smiled, and it was beautiful. "Thank you," she said graciously. "Go with Garrett and Skylar then. Cal and I will be in touch as soon as we can."

"Wait, where are you guys going?" Garrett asked. It was kind of amazing that he didn't know—that he hadn't figured it out. But then again, this crazy world was still new to him.

So Dana spelled it out. "Harrisburg," she said. "We need to pick up some lab supplies—things that Garrett's dad probably won't have in his office." She looked down at the cut on her arm, and I watched it disappear as she swiftly used her G-T healing powers to mend herself. "If Rochelle can cook her own Destiny in a closet, then so can I. I had a look at her setup. Remember back when people were cooking meth at home, in soda bottles?"

I didn't, but Cal and Milo both nodded. "That was seriously a thing?" I asked.

"Yep," Dana said. "Cooking D is easier and way less dangerous. For the cook, that is—but not for the blood 'donor.'" She made air quotes. "There's a big difference between Rochelle's lab and mine. I'm not stealing some innocent's blood to cook Destiny." She lifted her chin in defiance. "I'm going to use my own."

———

Garrett had been shaking his head back and forth since we'd gotten back into his car. Fifteen minutes later, as we turned onto the private road that led to his dad's castle-like beach house, he was *still* shaking his head.

"A Destiny lab. In the trunk of Calvin's car," he mumbled. "Un-friggin-real."

"It's not at all like a meth lab," Morgan tried to reassure him from his seat up front. I'd let him ride shotgun. "The ingredients aren't combustible."

I leaned forward. "It won't blow up," I translated.

"I know what combustible means," Garrett said, glancing at me in his rearview mirror. "But the main ingredient is blood. One, gross. And (B) doesn't that make Destiny addicts kinda like vampires? Feeding off innocent little girls?"

Clearly, Garrett had paid attention when Cal had spouted some of his theories. I sighed as he continued, "Also, I read that D-addicts are hard to kill, because not only does the drug heal their injuries, but they don't feel the damage, so you have to go big. Cut off their heads. Sound familiar? I wonder if a wooden stake through the heart would do the trick."

"Probably," Morgan said. "Because the splinters would get in the way of the addict's ability to close up the hole in the organ. But a double pop to the head with a nine millimeter would also cause irreparable and immediate damage to the brain—and that's really what you want to aim for. The head. I've seen jokering addicts take bullets to the chest and keep wreaking havoc right up to the nanosecond that they bleed out. But crush their skulls...?"

"Good to know," Garrett said.

"I can't believe we're talking about this seriously," I said. "*Crush* their *skulls?*"

"As a Greater-Than," Morgan told me, "with a known bounty hunter on your trail, you should be aware that in order to incapacitate you, your John Doe will go for your head. A solid blow to knock you out, so you can't use your powers against him. *And* if he accidentally hits you too hard and kills you, no biggie. You've still got all that blood inside you. A quick exsanguination, dump your body in a landfill..."

"Gee, thanks for that image," I said.

"Always protect your head," he told me as Garrett pulled into the long driveway that led to the house.

Lately, Garrett had been managing to drive like a responsible human being—but when we reached the circular end to the drive, he sped up and peeled into his parking space with a squeal of tires. No matter how many improvements he made on the real-human-boy front, there was always a little bit of douche-ness lingering in the background.

"Wow," Morgan said, and I wasn't sure if the G-T was reacting to Garrett's abrupt and ridiculous impression of a stunt driver or the gargantuan mansion.

"We just renovated," Garrett said as he led us not to the front door, but to a second entrance back around the garage. A sign said: "Dr. Richard Hathaway." "Dad moved his medical office out here to lower overhead, because why not, right? That's why we painted the parking space lines on this part of the driveway—because now his patients come here to get nipped and tucked."

There was a keypad lock on that door, and he quickly typed in a code, then flipped on the lights as he led the way into a small waiting room decorated in classic Florida seashore—blues and aquas and whites, with tail-walking dolphins aplenty. Instead of a receptionist's desk, there was an in-wall computer, complete with keyboard, with a sign saying "Virtual Check-In" beneath it. There was another door, also with a keypad lock, and Garrett quickly opened that for us, too.

"Dad's genius-smart, but sometimes he can really pull a dumb move. His password is my name, all caps. Might as well have made the password *password*."

He turned on more lights as we followed him into a pristinely empty hallway. There were two open doorways, and a third door that was closed with another of those keypad locks. Garrett pointed to the open door on the right.

"Dad's office," Garrett said, and Morgan and I looked in to see a room paneled in rich, dark wood. Windows looking out onto the ocean lined one wall. Bookcases covered two other walls, extending from floor to cathedral ceiling. A library ladder on wheels leaned against the edge of one of the bookcases.

A huge desk that held an expensive-looking computer was in the middle of the room, and I recognized it from the first—and last—time

I'd been in Garrett's house, a few months back when he'd thrown a huge party. I'd attended with Calvin and Dana and Milo, hoping to literally sniff out a connection between Garrett's dad and the local Destiny drug ring. Of course, we'd come up cold, because although the douche was strong in both Hathaways, neither was involved with the bad guys.

Frankly, it was kinda crazy. So much had changed in the months since that party. And although he wasn't a bad guy, I would never have imagined that Garrett would find his way onto our official team of good guys. And yet here we were.

"The exam room's over here," Garrett said, pulling our attention back to the other open door as he reached in to turn on the over-head lights.

That room was a pretty standard medical examination room. It held a padded table with one of those rolls of paper on the end. There was a little footstool in front of it, to assist the shorter patients. A sink was in the corner with a set of cabinets above it. A stool on wheels was tucked under a desk, and another chair sat in the corner. A plastic case for a box of nitrile gloves was attached to the wall, along with a very large flat-screen TV.

"You said your father had a medical scanner," Morgan said as he opened the cabinets above the sink. Inside were bandages and gauze, and more boxes of those gloves.

"It's on wheels. It must be locked in the new operating room." Garrett led us back into the hall, toward that closed door. It was metallic and reminiscent of the door to a fridge rather than a room.

Beside it, on the wall, was another keypad. "This one's *garrett*, all lowercase." There was silence for a moment, then the keypad lit up green, and the door beeped.

Garrett opened it. A swoosh of cold air came rushing out, then we all stepped inside.

"Whoa!" I exclaimed. The room's automatic sensory lights clicked on, illuminating the area. It was like stepping into a legitimate hospital operating room. There was a shining metal operating table, along with an array of fancy, high-tech equipment and computers of all shapes and sizes, including, yes, a medical scanner on wheels. Complicated-looking illustrations of bisected humans lined the walls—along with several ginormous computer screens. The floor shone with an intimidating sterility.

For a moment, I pictured Calvin laid out on the table while Dana leaned over him and ordered me to pass the scalpel. I was suddenly very glad Morgan had offered to help.

"Relax," Morgan murmured to me. "The detox procedure is relatively noninvasive. No cutting Calvin open anyway. We'll use various drugs and electrical currents to stop and then try to restart his heart."

"Try?" I asked, but Morgan had already turned away.

"So, here's the deal," Garrett announced. "You guys can use anything you want, but you have to clean up afterward. And…? No stealing anything."

I grunted. "Yeah. You know me and my nasty bedpan-stealing habit."

"I'm just saying," Garrett replied defensively.

Morgan was looking at the scanner. I knew what it was even though I hadn't seen one up close all that often. I rarely went to the doctor because I didn't get sick. My annual checkups were all done by my mom's doctor friend—I called her Dr. Susan. And she didn't use a scanner, preferring the old-fashioned methods for taking blood pressure and pulse.

But I'd seen enough medical shows on TV to know that a scanner gave doctors easy access to those vital stats as well as far more intricate info like imaging of internal organs and X-rays of lungs and bones. The biggest bonus was that the scanner analyzed blood without breaking the patient's skin.

Medical scanners also—according to Dana—revealed telling information about neural integration. In other words, if you were a Greater-Than, and you were scanned, your G-T-ness would show, provided your doctor knew what to look for.

And, huh. As I stood there, watching Morgan drool on Dr. Hathaway's state-of-the-art scanner, it suddenly occurred to me that maybe it wasn't an accident that my personal doctor was a non-scanner-using "friend of the family." I suddenly remembered how upset—crazy upset—my mother had been when I'd been rushed to the ER after a bad car accident. The doctor there had scanned me again and again, amazed that I'd walked away from the wreck without a scratch. This was back when we'd lived in Connecticut, right before we moved to Florida…

Huh.

But announcing *I think my mother might have known I was a*

G-T long before I knew it myself wasn't going to help us save Calvin. Here and now we had better things to discuss. Like, "How does it work, the Destiny detox? And what did you mean, we'd *try* to restart Calvin's heart?"

Morgan glanced up at me as he moved from the scanner to the operating table, where he checked what looked like a series of leather restraints, probably there to make sure the patient didn't roll off mid-procedure. "We're going to need more than this," he said. "Chains. In case he changes his mind or gets scared."

"Because chaining people who are scared helps them...how?" I asked.

"If he leaves, mid-procedure, he'll die," Morgan said bluntly. "The concept—how the detox works—is pretty basic. It uses the theory that as a D-addict dies, as he or she is actually physically dying, their body burns off all of the Destiny in its system, in kind of a hail-Mary self-healing move to try to stay alive."

I was following him, but he glanced over to see Garrett frowning so he said, "Picture a Destiny addict. Rochelle. Say she starts to joker while she's at the mall, so she goes on a rampage, and she's just going crazy and people are dying because she's flinging them around, off the balconies. Right? And the SWAT team shows up, and they shoot her, right in the chest, and she goes down. She's bleeding—she's basically got a hole in her body. But the Destiny in her bloodstream kicks in with its self-healing abilities—kind of the way Cal got injected and can suddenly walk?"

Garrett nodded.

"So the drug is working to rebuild Rochelle's damaged tissues and organs and blood vessels," Morgan continued, "but the injury is too severe. Still, the Destiny won't give up and it works and it works and it works. And she's still moving around, too, and maybe even accessing some additional powers—like maybe she can breathe fire—which uses up even more of the drug. Everything's accelerating—it happens really fast when you throw a catastrophic injury into the mix. And suddenly, there's no more Destiny in her system. She's burned it all off, but *boom*, then she's dead, because she's got a bullet hole in her chest, which is something that can't be fixed with a snap of your fingers."

Morgan turned back to me. "Autopsies done on former addicts revealed that more often than not, there's absolutely no trace of the drug in their bloodstream. That's one of the reasons why the people who are lobbying to legalize Destiny claim it's not dangerous. Yeah, the users died, but how could D be the cause of death if they weren't using it when they died? All other drugs and toxins leave a trace. But not Destiny.

"So what we're going to do with Calvin," he continued, "is strap him down and stop his heart. The Destiny in his system will kick into overdrive, trying to fix something it can't possibly fix. We use the scanner to monitor the level of D in his blood, and as soon as it's down to zero, we'll zap him with electricity and, hopefully, restart his heart."

"So we'll kill him," I said, to make sure Garrett understood, "so to speak, but then we'll bring him back to life."

"Hopefully." Garrett had caught that word, too.

"There are no guarantees," Morgan told us somberly. "The odds are not good. But we'll try our best." And then he added the words I was hoping not to hear: "And the worst-case scenario is far less bad than it would be if Cal jokered and died on his own terms. This worse-case scenario only needs one body bag, as opposed to half a dozen."

Garrett exhaled hard. "I don't know, dudes, I'm not sure I'd agree to do it, if I were Cal."

"Good thing you're not Cal then," I said, except I was thinking *I'm not sure I would either.*

Morgan continued to explore the OR, while Garrett and I went into his dad's office to access his computer—to attempt to break into his National Medical Database account.

When I touched the mouse, the screen came to life, so I sat down in the big leather chair behind the ginormous wooden desk. Garrett leaned over my shoulder. "Check his browser history. He never clears it. It's like he just doesn't care."

"Or maybe he just doesn't watch any porn," I suggested. And there it was—a bookmark for the NMDB. I clicked it open and a sign-in box popped up. The user name was filled in, DocHath, but the box beneath, marked Password, was empty. Inside of it, the blinking icon waited for me to type.

I took a deep breath and typed *GARRETT* in all caps.

It was amazing. Doctor Hathaway *was* the dumbest smart person in the world.

"Bingo," I said, watching as the database opened for us.

For the past several decades, starting back before I was born, the whole HIPAA deal—where doctors weren't allowed to divulge any information about patients to anyone non-consenting—had become obsolete. Anyone who worked in the medical field, including nurses and techs—or anyone who pretended to work in the medical field—had access to any and all medical records. It had started as a way to monitor women in particular, in response to personhood laws. And it had gone south, fast. It was a total invasion of privacy. But today? Easy access to medical records was actually working in our favor.

I pulled up a search box. The simple search function required the patient's name, date of birth, and/or NID—National ID number. I found the advanced search, where I typed in *Jilly, Jack, Ron*.

No results was the result.

I tried *Jill, John, Ronald*.

And suddenly there were more than twenty thousand matches. I clicked through to a few and realized that, in many cases, *John* or *Ronald* or *Jill* was the first name of the doctor involved in someone's treatment.

We needed a way to narrow down our search. "What more do we know about them?" I mused. I looked up at Garrett. "You told me Rochelle went up north and then brought Jilly back with her. Do you remember where—which state?"

He shook his head. "I don't think she ever said, but…" As his voice trailed off, he looked like he was deep in thought. Which was kind of scary in a way. Then, all of a sudden, he started jumping up and down. The move was so abrupt, it made me jump too.

"What? What is it?" I asked.

"The number on her arm!"

"Number?"

"Yeah!" Garrett stopped jumping and pulled his phone out of his pocket. He scrolled through it for a few seconds and then tapped on the screen excitedly as he held it out for me. "See that? That's a selfie that Rochelle made me and Jilly take, back when she was still pretending Jilly was her daughter and we were gonna be one big, happy family. You can see Jilly's arm—she's holding the phone out. And see that number?"

In the photo, Jilly's hair was streaked with bright orange and yellow. And sure enough, a series of numbers and dashes was written on the inside of the girl's forearm, next to the little bump that we now knew was a tracking device. The color of the ink and size of the print reminded me of photos I'd seen of the concentration camp ID tattoos that Nazis gave Jewish people during the Holocaust.

"At the time, I just thought it was one of her weird goth moves," Garrett continued. "She'd write it on her arm on some days. Other days it would be scrubbed off. Anyway, I was thinking about it, and...I'm pretty sure that's her National ID number."

"Holy crap," I mumbled, because he may have been onto something. It *was* the right number of digits to be her NID.

We all had one. Everyone in the country did—which, yeah, was pretty creepy.

I didn't waste any time. Yanking the phone out of Garrett's hand, I enlarged that part of the photo and went back to the original search screen where one of the options was for the patient's NID. I typed in the numbers, realizing that I didn't even need her name. I just pushed Enter.

The computer thought for a moment.

Then?

"Holy crap, it *worked*!" Garrett was jumping up and down again.

I'm not ashamed to admit that I squealed, too.

Morgan heard us and came in.

I read out loud. "*Jillian Teller. Deceased.*" What? I looked up at Morgan and Garrett. "Somebody's claiming that she's already dead," I said. I clicked over to what was definitely a death certificate for Jillian Margaret Teller, age fourteen at the time of death. "As of ten months ago. It's signed by a doctor, who was obviously lying, but what if her parents think she's really dead?"

"Go back, go back," Garrett said, and I returned to Jilly's main page.

"*Parents: Cynthia and Ronald Teller,*" Garrett read from the screen. "*Twin brother: Ronald, Jr.; younger brother: John, age three.* I thought he was named Jack."

"Jack is a nickname for John," I told him. How could he be eighteen years old and not know that? But there was no time for even an eye roll, because...

"There's an address here," Garrett told Morgan. "And a phone number."

Jilly's family lived in Virginia, just outside of Richmond.

I reached for my phone. But Morgan was already holding out his. "Better use *my* burner," he said. "After you make this call, we're going to have to smash it, and I know you're waiting to hear from Milo."

I was. "Thanks." I took it, dialed the number, then set the phone on speaker.

It rang once, twice, and then a woman answered.

"Hello," she trilled. Her voice sounded cheery. Singsong. Not the way I imagined the voice of a woman who had lost her only daughter not too long ago would sound.

"Um, Mrs. Teller?" I asked in a careful tone.

"Yes? This is she."

I cleared my throat. I needed to sound confident. "I'm calling with news about your daughter."

I paused, and there was silence on the other end of the line, although I could tell that Jilly's mom hadn't hung up.

I continued. "I wanted to let you know that Jilly is not dead. She's safe. Well, she'll be safe soon if—"

"Who is this?" she whispered. She was no longer cheerful. "How dare you call like this! Haven't we suffered enough?"

"No," I said. "I mean, yes. But that's why I'm calling—your daughter's *not dead*!"

This was where she was supposed to fall to her knees, the way Sasha's mom had when we'd brought Sasha back home to her. This was where she was supposed to cry and sob, *Oh, thank God, thank God!*

But this woman said nothing. There was absolute silence from her end of the phone.

So I said, "She's being held prisoner, and we're going to set her free, but she needs to know that you'll be there for her when we—"

"Don't you dare!" she said again, her voice sharp. "She's already dead to us. We've already grieved, so just stay out of it! Stay away from her!"

What? I glanced over at Garrett, who looked as shocked as I felt.

While I'd been talking, Morgan had leaned over my other shoulder and had typed something into the computer. I realized now that we were looking at a satellite map of the Teller's suburban address. Morgan zoomed in on the highlighted house, and we all realized that not only was it huge, it had a swimming pool in the back.

"How much money did you get for her?" I asked, suddenly wildly angry. "And maybe you've already *grieved* for her, but she's still out there being tortured. Did you know, when you sold her into slavery, that she would be *tortured* before she was killed?"

"You have no idea how hard it was!" Mrs. Teller interrupted. "My husband has a job now! My boys have food on the table! Do *you* know how hard it is to watch your children starve? Do *not* throw judgment onto me for even a moment, because you have no *idea* how much I have sacrificed to protect my family!" The words came tumbling out of her mouth in rapid succession. When she was done, her breathing turned ragged through the phone.

It was my turn to be absolutely speechless. How much *she'd* sacrificed?

"Don't you dare call back again!" she hissed. "And stay the hell away from Jilly! If you go near her, or if you so much as contact me again, I'll have them track *you* down, too!"

"Who's *them?*" I asked, but there was a click, and the line went dead.

———

Garrett was oddly silent after that.

Morgan took his phone from my hand, pulled out the battery, and then dutifully went about taking it out to the driveway and running over it with Garrett's car.

After that, Morgan spent about ten minutes on the computer, laser printing articles and reports from the Obermeyer Institute on their ground-breaking Destiny detox procedure. He knew without asking that Dana was a hard-copy kind of girl, but he also forwarded the links to Cal's email address, so that we'd have access to the information that way, too.

I spent the time silently willing Milo to text me again, but his sole response to my Y'ok? was Yes, TY.

Finally, we had everything that we needed to reconnect with Dana and Calvin in Harrisburg and see if we could help them get the supplies they needed for that makeshift D-lab.

I made a quick pit stop, and as I was coming out of the bathroom, I heard Garrett say to Morgan, "No, you know what? Just take my car. I'm not going to go."

"Okay," Morgan said evenly. "I appreciate your trust with your wheels. We'll be back in a few hours to scan Calvin and—"

"No." Garrett cut him off. "You're gonna have to find someplace else to do that and your detox, too. I'm out. I'm done."

"What?" I couldn't believe what I was hearing.

He turned to me. "I'm just...done. If we try to save Jilly, then *you're* in danger, and then you *both* die. We bring Calvin here, he's just going to die, too. And we're going to be the ones who kill him. Let's be real about this bullshit. We're fighting a losing battle!" He voice got louder. "And I didn't sign up for *any* of this. So just leave. Just fuck it. Fuck everything! And just...*leave*."

Neither one of us moved.

Garrett leaned forward and got right into my face. "*I said leave! Get out! Get! Out!*"

Morgan reached out to place a sympathetic hand on Garrett's shoulder. But Garrett shrugged it away. "Hands off, Gay-Boy!" he exclaimed and stomped past both of us to fling open the door that led out to the driveway. "Go!"

Morgan didn't flinch at the insult. But his expression was one of utter sadness.

"Close the door behind you when you leave," Garrett said and started back past us to his father's office, where there was a door and a stairway leading up to the main part of the house.

I blocked his path. "If you quit on us now, if you just walk away from this fight, then you're no better than Jilly's mother."

He flinched, almost as if I'd punched him in the face.

By this point in my crazy life, I'd been pretty damn certain that nothing could ever shock me again. And yet, the next thing that happened sent my jaw to the floor.

Garrett Hathaway burst into tears.

It was messy and noisy, the sobs wracking his body in waves.

I didn't know *what* to do. So I stood there awkwardly, while Garrett leaned against the door and cried. I reached out to touch his arm, and he took that as an invitation to envelope me in a soggy hug.

I looked at Morgan over Garrett's shoulder, sending him a silent, *Did you do this with your truth-telling voodoo?*

Morgan shook his head and silently mouthed the words, *Not me.*

So I stood there, awkwardly patting Garrett's back as he cried himself out. To be honest, if it were me, I'd've kept sobbing for a whole 'nother hour. But he finally quieted down. And he eventually let go of me, turning away from us as he wiped his eyes. "That was stupid of me," he said in a muffled voice.

Neither Morgan nor I responded. I wasn't sure which part Garrett was talking about—telling us to leave or crying his eyes out.

"I'm sorry about that," Garrett continued. He wiped his nose on his sleeve. "I don't do that ever."

"You don't have to apologize," I told him. "I cry like that every week or so."

"Yeah, but you're a girl," he said.

"So what?" I countered. "Being a boy means that you're not human? That you don't feel things?"

Garrett was silent, so I kept going.

"I know you think this is all hopeless—detoxing Calvin and helping Jilly, but I for one am not going to quit. I'm not going to let that lady scare me off. I don't care what she thinks she can do. I'm going to figure out a way to save Jilly even though she doesn't want to be saved—I don't know what, but I know we'll think of something. And working together, we'll make it happen. And I know this sucks and it's hard, but we need your help. We need to use your dad's OR, and yeah, it may not work, and you're right that Cal is probably going to die, but if we just give up, then he'll *definitely* die."

"My mother died last year," Garrett said quietly. "She got cancer and she fought it and she should've survived, she did everything right, but she fucking died."

"Garrett," I said softly. I'd had no idea. "I'm so sorry."

He nodded. "I didn't tell anyone. She and my dad were divorced since forever, and she lived in Harrisburg—by choice. She ran a food bank, and I was ashamed of her, so I just never talked about her. And I just keep thinking that she would never do what Jilly's mother did. *Never*. So how come she's dead and Jilly's mom lives in a big house with a swimming pool?"

I couldn't answer that, and I looked to Morgan who just shook his head.

"Life rarely makes sense," he told Garrett. "Best you can do is give it—all of it—a big *fuck you* and keep going. Keep trying, keep fighting."

I nodded. "Please say you'll help us, Garrett. We need you on our team."

Garrett sniffed and glanced from Morgan to me and back again. His face was blotchy, and I knew how embarrassed he probably was.

So I led him back to more familiar-to-him, douche-tastic territory by adding, "If Dana were here, she'd say the same. And I know you can't resist two hot chicks, both *begging* for your help."

"*Heh-heh*," Garrett said. "*Heh*. I guess I can't. But the question remains, can either of you fly?"

I sighed and rolled my eyes. That was my own fault. I'd opened that door. Nevertheless, he'd gone charging through it.

No doubt about it, even the best version of Garrett was still Garrett.

CHAPTER NINETEEN

Stay put at Garrett's. Cal and I on our way.

The text came in from Dana before Garrett, Morgan, and I had a chance to leave Doc Hathaway's OR.

"Dana wants to meet us here. Is that okay with you?"

Garrett had already excused himself, no doubt to spritz cold water on his face and regroup a little bit more after losing it in front of us. As he came back from the bathroom, he nodded. "Yeah, that's cool." He casually rolled up the sleeves to his polo shirt, no doubt to reveal his muscular forearms as he crossed them over his chest.

Morgan was playing around with the scanning machine again, and I used the time to check my messages. "I wish Milo would send an update about his stakeout of our John Doe." My heavy emphasis on *Milo* was for Garrett's sake.

I texted Milo via the group he'd set up earlier, hoping it would come across as businesslike teammate instead of needy girlfriend. Update?

For once, the reply came back quickly: Spent the morning shopping. John Doe's been valeting his car so I can't get close enough to plant GPS device.

Shopping? I asked. For...?

Looks like clothing but also camping gear and MREs. Best guess is he had lots of equipment in his car. He's doing a resupply.

Good. Hopefully the family of his Sav'A'Buck kidnapping victim had found it all before they ditched the vehicle in Orlando.

A new text popped up: WTF are MREs? It was Garrett, who was following our conversation from the other side of the room.

Meals Ready to Eat, Milo texted back. Military-style food, easy to store and keep.

He'll also need more ammo, I texted.

Yes I'm certain he replaced that too, Milo responded. Also bought a legit hunting rifle.

Great.

Right now he's @ lunch, Milo reported. @ the fish tank. Car again valeted. Can't get close enough.

The Fish Tank was an upscale restaurant in Coconut Key Village, not far from the richie-rich mall.

Do u think he knows he's being followed? That was Dana chiming in from Cal's car. Bcuz of all the valets?

It feels more like an FU to someone, Milo sent. Maybe his bosses for leaving him in the hosp for all that time? Buying underwear and camping stuff from an upscale mall instead of Big W or Outdoor Emporium. Lunch here. He's on someone's payroll, using their credit card. He's sending them a message = my guess.

Hope ur right, Dana texted back, adding, Fifteen mins from you, BG.

BG was me. Bubble Gum. We're here, waiting, I told her.

And then, because I was in wait mode over here, and Milo was in wait mode outside the Fish Tank, I sent a private text, just to his phone.

I've been thinking about that closet and ur stepfather, and while I wish you'd told me about it, I also wish that I'd asked you. I knew something was wrong and I didn't. Ask. And I'm not going to do that anymore. I'm not going to not ask if I think something's wrong, or if there's something I want to know about you. I love you, but this won't work AT ALL if you think I need to be, I don't know, protected or shielded. Like a child.

I hit Send before I chickened out and erased the whole thing.

And then as I flashed both hot and cold, I quickly typed, I'm tougher than both you and Dana think.

I really am sorry, he sent back, followed by: I know.

I got a message that he was typing more, so I waited.

I didn't want to tell you bcuz I was ashamed. I'm still ashamed.

Why on earth are you ashamed? I started to ask, but his next text came in before I could hit Send.

I never tried to escape, Milo told me. He told me I deserved to be punished, and part of me must've believed him because I never tried to get away.

You were a little boy, I texted, whose mother had just died!

I know, he replied. And I also know that when you get told something over and over again, you start to believe it and he hammered me with the fact that I was worthless. That it was my fault my mother died. I know he's wrong, but I still sometimes hear his voice in my head.

Oh, my Lord. Milo was the *least* worthless person I knew. I wanted to travel back in time and kick down that closet door and hug that poor, sweet little boy that he'd once been.

Before I could respond, the screen of my phone shifted slightly as a new text appeared.

Outside.

What? Oh crap, that wasn't Milo—it was from Dana. She and Cal had arrived.

"They're here," I announced as I went back to my conversation with Milo and quickly typed, Thank you for telling me that. I love you. I hit Send and was in the process of typing But Cal and Dana are here, when Milo sent back, Love you too. Gotta go. JD done w lunch & on the move. Sry sry sry

"I'll let them in," Garrett said.

For a second, I forgot about Cal's situation, and I almost asked Garrett how he intended to maneuver Calvin and his wheelchair up the stairs that led to the outside office door. But then I remembered.

Calvin's workable legs were going to take some serious getting used to.

The door opened and Calvin came into the operating room first. "Whoa!" he exclaimed. "This is, like, legit!"

Garrett was right behind Cal and back in bragging mode. "Yeah. It's a nice little multimillion-dollar extension to my dad's practice."

Dana was the last to step into the room. And even though I was still preoccupied with the conversation I'd been having with Milo, I knew that something was very, very wrong as soon as I saw her.

Her face was ashen, her normally pink cheeks a sallow shade of gray. She carried a small canvas bag across her back—a load that normally wouldn't have fazed her in the slightest. But at that moment

Dana might as well have been lugging a stack of bricks—her temples were shiny with sweat. She glanced at me before setting the bag on the floor and then finding a chair in the corner and sitting down fast.

"Are you—"

"I'm fine!" Dana barked before I could finish my question. She turned to Garrett. "This is exactly what we need. This room. It's perfect. Thank you so much."

Garrett nodded, and I knew visions of flying Greater-Thans danced in his head. "You're welcome," he said. "Did you, like, draw your own *blood* or whatever to make the...you know?"

Destiny. Yes, we all knew.

"I'm fine," Dana said again. It was becoming her personal aloha, used for both *hello* and *good-bye*, or in this case, *yes*. "We've got a batch already cooking in the trunk of Cal's car." She turned to watch Morgan, who'd already waved Calvin over to the scanner.

At second glance, Cal was looking pretty crappy, too. His hands were shaking, and his face held a tint of green.

"How are you?" Morgan asked as he helped Cal sit on the metal operating table. I knew, from last year's visit to the ER after the accident, that you didn't have to lie down to be scanned. You just had to sit still—and not even completely still, just mostly still. Calvin surely knew that. With all of his surgeries and checkups, he probably knew more about scanners and being scanned than any of us.

He shrugged casually and smiled at Morgan. "Never better," he said in a nonchalant tone. "Although...would you rather have a med scan done by a hot gay guy or your even hotter girlfriend? Hmm, I think I'd go with girlfriend."

I knew he was trying to be good ol' funny Cal. But this was serious.

Morgan shut him down. "Yeah, well, the hot gay guy knows how to work the scanner so... Kinda hard not to notice your tremor there." He pointed at Calvin's hands.

Cal looked down before clasping one hand in the other. "Yeah," he admitted. "I mean, the shaky hands rank high on the suck-o-meter. Other than that, I'm golden." He used his head to gesture over to Dana and lowered his voice. "She's the one you need to be helping right now. She's stubborn as all hell and keeps saying she's fine—but she's not. Apparently, not even G-Ts can use their self-healing mojo to immediately replace a significant loss of blood."

Dana's face was hidden in her hands as she leaned her elbows atop her knees. "I can hear every word you say," she grumbled through her fingers in a grumpy voice. "G-Ts have really good hearing. And FYI, I'd feel a crap-ton worse if I weren't a G-T."

"I know," Calvin replied cheerfully as Morgan gestured for him to lie back on the table. "I'm just reiterating the fact that you're hurtin' more than me right now, even though you won't admit it."

"I'm *dizzy*, Scoot. You're withdrawing from *Destiny*." Dana leaned back and turned her palms up. She pretended to be a scale of importance. "Dizziness?" she said, looking at her left hand as it lowered, "Destiny!" Dana lowered her right hand even more dramatically.

We all got the point.

"So how long is this gonna take?" she asked Morgan.

"You mean the scan I just gave Calvin, or the backup scan I'm doing right now with him lying down, both to focus on his spine and to double-check the readout?" Morgan asked.

"State-of-the-art," Garrett said. "Superfast scanner."

"Actually, this model's already obsolete," Morgan said, giving Cal's leg a pat in a *You can sit up now* signal. "There are new scanners on the market where the subject doesn't have to stay still in order to be scanned."

"It could at least beep or make lights flash or something," Dana complained. "I mean, how else do you know when you're being scanned?"

"You don't." Morgan pointed to the huge flat-screen on the wall that had come to life with a brilliant-blue background while a single word—Processing—flashed in the center. "Although this would be what we call a clue. But it's definitely more of a clue for the scanner as opposed to the scan-ee."

"So you could just scan any one of us, without us knowing it," Dana realized.

"If I were unscrupulous, yes," Morgan said.

"And with the newer scanners..." she started.

"I could set up a scanner at the mall and get a full medical readout on everyone who walks through the scanning field," Morgan finished for her, adding, "And, again, if I were super-unscrupulous, I could use those results to pick the G-Ts or the little girls with G-T potential out of the crowd. Make a nice little wish list with photos and descriptions of the targets to give to my buddies, the G-T bounty hunters, so they could deliver the girls to me, so I could make millions from their blood."

The blue screen turned into a display that was labeled *Results: Young Adult Male. Weight: 170 lbs. Height: 5'11".*

"Lucky for us those newer scanners cost as much or more than this entire office," Morgan continued, "along with the house and ocean-front property."

"Yeah, but how long until that kind of scanner gets made into an app that anyone can download onto their phone?" Dana shook her head. "Something tells me it's gonna get much harder to be a G-T in the future." She swore. "And I thought it was hard now."

"One way to fool a scanner," Morgan told her as he used the touch screen to scroll through the results of Cal's scan, "is to always be in close proximity to another person. Walk through the mall with your arm around someone's waist, and the readout will register as an error."

"Or we need to create an app that'll alert us whenever a scanner is being used," Cal said as he slid down off the table to get a closer look at his results. As he stood there, he shifted back and forth from foot to foot, and I knew his constant motion was an attempt to hide the fact that he was shaking.

That was *so* not good.

Morgan was using the touch screen to scroll through the results, making little *hmm* and *huh* noises.

"What's it say?" Garrett asked eagerly.

"Good news?" Dana's voice was more demanding than hopeful, as if she was trying to intimidate Morgan into making the news good *or else*.

"Good news...*and* not-so-good news."

"Good news first," I said. "Please."

"Okay," Morgan said, scrolling back to the top of the readout. "Calvin's heart." He turned to Cal. "You said there was some kind of damage done to it in the explosion?"

Cal nodded. "I took a piece of shrapnel to the chest, and they didn't find it right away, and…long story short, I had a heart attack, which messed me up pretty badly. That's the kind of damage that you can't fix."

"Well, right now," Morgan said, "you have the heart of an eighteen-year-old. It reads as one hundred percent healthy. No sign of any previous trauma."

That was amazing news!

Calvin laughed. "Wait. It's…fixed?"

"Your heart is. Completely. Yes." Morgan tried to smile back, but I could see that there was a serious *but* coming.

"So what's the not-so-good news?" I asked.

As Morgan scrolled through what looked like a series of images from the second scan when Calvin was lying down, Dana came over and put an arm around Cal's waist—in part to hold him up, but also just to hold him. It was weird seeing the two of them like that, but it was the perfect kind of weird.

"The damage to your back," Morgan said, stopping on what looked like an X-ray of Calvin's spine. "Appears to have been catastrophic."

Cal nodded. "They had to go in and clean up the parts that were crushed."

Morgan nodded back, pointing to the screen. "Like your lower vertebrae. Some parts of the lumbar section were removed entirely and replaced with a combination of steel and medical plastic."

"Yeah," Cal replied. He was still smiling from ear to ear about his repaired heart. "The doctors were surprised about how well I recovered from that. The initial prognosis was grim. But I worked really hard. Went to rehab diligently. Still do, as a matter of fact. Although—" He glanced down at his legs as if they held answers to a secret. The leg gaze was a move that was becoming habitual for him. "I don't really know how much rehab I'm gonna need in the future."

Morgan pursed his lips. "Here's the thing, Cal. The damage to your spinal cord hasn't been repaired by the drug. Not like your heart."

Dana didn't change her expression, but her hold around Cal's waist grew tighter. "I don't understand," Cal said slowly. "I'm on my feet. I can walk."

Morgan let out a long, slow exhalation. "Right now, the Destiny in your system allows the rest of your body to compensate for this injury. Your muscles, ligaments, connective tissues—they're all strengthened substantially because of the drug. But, without it…that will go away."

"So…what you're telling me is that I need Destiny in my bloodstream in order to keep my walking legs walking. Without it, I'm back in my chair?" Cal glanced at me and I knew what he was thinking. Somehow, he'd already known this.

Morgan nodded. "Yes."

Garrett looked stricken. "Man, that's so messed up. Isn't there a way around that?"

Morgan shook his head. "I think this might also explain why your body is burning through the drug so quickly. Your system is using the Destiny to try to heal something that won't heal. *Can't* heal."

"So…I stop taking D," Cal was trying to make sense of what he'd just heard, "*if* I survive detox, and that's a big *if*, then *boom*, I'm back in the chair."

"With a healthy heart," I pointed out.

This time, he barely glanced at me, and I recoiled because his eyes were suddenly hard and cold, as if we were strangers. "Well, yay," he said, obviously sarcastically. "So, great, I can live until I'm ninety— sitting in a freaking chair."

"That *is* great," I said.

"Excuse me if I don't feel the same way," Cal said.

"Cal," Dana said quietly.

"What?" he said. "I'm supposed to be happy at this news? I'm not."

We were all silent for a moment, but then Cal blurted, "I'll manage the addiction."

Dana turned to look at him like he'd just sprouted a second nose. "We've already talked about that. You know that's absurd."

"Well, no! I mean, listen, most D-addicts start *out* greedy. They want as much as their bodies can take. But not me. I don't need all that. I don't want to be the prettiest, or the youngest, or the strongest. Hell, I don't even need to walk all that *fast*. But…just…there *has* to be a way to keep me walking. I know I won't need that much D to make that happen." Cal smiled, but his eyes held a level of desperation that I'd never seen in him before.

I looked at Morgan and frowned. This was exactly what the G-T had predicted—that Calvin would start to lose sight of reality. If we didn't act fast, Morgan had told us, then Cal would descend into a place where the lines of morality became blurred and even eventually ceased to exist.

Morgan had started scrolling through the readout again, and now he pointed to a series of numbers on the screen. "Right now, you have remarkably little Destiny in your system," he said, "considering when your first dose was injected. My best guess is that even just to *manage* your addiction with the smallest amount of the drug as possible, you'll still need a dose of D every twenty-four to forty-eight hours."

"What?" Dana went another shade paler, and I knew she was imagining having to draw blood on that same timetable. Of all the bad news we'd received, that was the dead worst.

"I can help you," I murmured, but she just shook her head.

It was then that Cal blurted, "Seven! Nineteen! Twenty-one! Thirty! Fifty-four!"

"Um. What?" Garrett asked as I got out my phone and made a note of the numbers.

"Oh, man, I think I'm gonna—" But there was no time for Calvin to finish his warning as he raced across the room and threw up into the trash can.

"Oh my God, Cal!" I rushed toward my best friend, but Dana beat me over to him. She knelt down beside Calvin and I hovered nearby, as he retched and choked over the side of the garbage pail. His normally chocolate-hued skin lost almost all color. He looked up at me for a second, in between heaves. When his eyes met mine, I felt like I was being stared at by a corpse.

"Guys, it's time," Dana said.

"We're not ready to try the detox," Morgan warned, and Dana nodded.

"I know," she said. "That's not what I meant. But we're not injecting Cal here. We're heading back to the Twenty to do it."

And I realized that the only thing that could save Cal right now was the one thing that would also end up killing him.

"It's time, Calvin," Dana said more gently as she helped him to his feet. "For more Destiny."

———

When we got back to the twenty-plex, Milo was waiting by the hole in the fence, astride Dana's motorcycle.

I wasn't expecting him, and my stomach did a somersault into my throat at the sight of him in his leather jacket, with those long, jean-clad legs, his hair windblown around his face—as if it had come out of his ponytail holder but he'd been in too much of a hurry to get here to stop and fix it. He found me instantly, there in the front passenger seat beside Garrett, and his dark eyes met mine.

"I texted Milo to meet us here," Dana explained. She was sitting in the back with Calvin and Morgan. Cal was looking even worse, but Dana appeared to have plateaued. She still looked, though, as if she could use a long nap. "Precautionary stuff."

Garrett had offered to drive Cal's car so that Dana could focus on Cal, and it had been a bumpy ride. Garrett was, after all, a far cry from a Greater-Than, and he'd had a hard time figuring out Cal's wheelchair-friendly hand controls. By the time we turned into the twenty-plex parking lot, I'd grabbed the *holy shit* bar above my head more times than I could count.

But I'd also taken the drive time to tell Dana and Cal about my depressing phone conversation with Jilly's mother. Garrett was in the *Let's just go into Rochelle's house and drag Jilly out of the closet whether she likes it or not* camp. But Dana was quick to point out that the girl was a G-T, and the last time we'd tried that, it hadn't gone well.

So some of Garrett's driving may have been a passive-aggressive response to being completely shut down.

Now, he cut the engine with one final jolt. "If we wait too long to save Jilly, then she'll be dead. Of course, if she's dead, then she won't have to go back to her owners, on account of being dead, but then again, she'll be *dead*, so…"

"First things first," Dana said. "And first is Calvin. We'll get to Jilly, I promise."

"But if we wait too long—" Garrett said again.

"We get it," I interrupted him, not wanting to hear him say the word *dead* another twenty times.

"Here," he said, turning around to hand the car keys to Calvin in the backseat.

"I'll take those." Dana grabbed the keys out of Garrett's hand before Calvin could get to them.

Calvin frowned.

"Precautionary stuff," Dana repeated as we all got out of the car. She tossed Cal's keys over to Milo, then opened the trunk, pulling out both the bag she'd brought into Garrett's dad's office and a larger duffel. I assumed it contained the cooking batch of Destiny and all of the paraphernalia needed for Calvin to get the drug into his bloodstream.

337

The reality of the situation was setting in big-time, and Dana's mention of *precautionary stuff* over and over was making it all the more real. She truly thought there was a chance that Calvin might joker.

Which was why, I realized with a sinking feeling in my chest, Dana had made sure that Milo was here. He was Dana's *Whoops, Cal Jokered and I'm Suddenly Dead* Plan B.

Meanwhile, Cal was arguing with Dana over the absconded car keys. "I mean, for real. It's not like I'm gonna just fly off the deep end here."

Dana's eyes were intense. "Babe. No offense. But, worst-case scenario, that is *exactly* what you'll end up doing."

"First things first. There is nothing more awesome than when you call me *babe* instead of *Scoot*. You should never not do that. Also? I feel fine—" Cal suddenly jerked and spun and then doubled over and puked just back beyond his car.

Dana set down her bags and went to help him as the rest of us tried to give them privacy. Which, frankly, is very hard to do when someone is violently dry-heaving a few feet away from you.

Garrett checked his email on his phone, while Morgan leaned against the front of the car and simply closed his eyes.

Milo came to greet me. Still no kiss hello though. But maybe that was because he was chewing his nicotine gum. Of course maybe he was chewing gum as an excuse not to kiss me. Or...

He broke into my current swirl of crazy overthinking by saying, "I got the GPS marker on our John Doe's car. When Dana called, it was kinda now or never, so I did it en route. A fifty-mph marking can be ugly, so I'll have to go back. Make sure it's secure. Kinda driving me crazy—the idea that we might lose him. But this is important, too."

It was an unusually long speech for Milo, and I could smell that he was nervous. Of me? That didn't make sense. I tried to focus on his words, which didn't quite make sense either. *En route?* "Wait. Fifty *miles per hour?* You seriously put the GPS thing onto his car while you were going *fifty miles per hour on the bike?*" I had to work really hard to keep my voice from sliding up to octaves that only dogs could hear.

Milo nodded. "I had to. It's stupid and dangerous, I know, but letting him just vanish would've been even more stupid and dangerous, so…"

"Seriously, Miles," I said.

"He's coming for you, Sky," Milo told me, "and I'm not going to let that happen."

Now my heart was in my throat. "But first you had to come here to make sure I wasn't the one who had to kill Calvin, if Calvin jokers and needs, you know, killing." I looked at him hard. "That wasn't Dana's idea—that was yours, wasn't it?"

Milo nodded.

"You're always trying to protect me," I said. "But you don't have to. I'm strong—"

"And tough, and capable," he said. "I agree completely. Could you handle this—if Cal jokers? Yes, I know you could. Absolutely. But you shouldn't have to. Nobody should ever have to kill their best friend, Sky."

"Great," I said. "Thanks. Except he's *your* friend, too."

"But I've seen enough addicts joker," Milo told me quietly. "Yeah, he'll have Calvin's face, but I won't have any doubts at all that he's not Calvin anymore. I'll be okay." He corrected himself. "More okay."

We were talking as if it was a given—that Cal was going to joker, kill Dana, and then die at Milo's hand. My face twisted as the shock of that hit me, and I almost burst into tears, but Milo grabbed me and hugged me hard.

And yes, our connection clicked on. *God, Sky, I love you so much and I wish to hell I could fix this!* He wasn't so much thinking it in words as he was feeling it with every cell in his body.

Still thoughts, I sent back for both of us. *Still...*

Just then, the alarm for Calvin's car went off—the horn blared and the lights flashed, and Milo and I sprang apart.

"Ow! *Merde!*" Morgan jumped up from where he was leaning on the front hood. "Hello! I just got a shock!"

"Sorry! Sorry!" We all turned to see Calvin backing away from the car, his hands out. Dana gestured to Milo to give back the car keys, but Cal beat her to it, silencing the car by pointing at it and sending it an electrical current direct from his hand. It would've been cool, except it wasn't. It was scary and weird and awful.

"Sorry, that was me," he apologized. "I was leaning against the car and I must've... Sorry." He looked at Dana and added, "I'm okay. Sorry about reprising my role as the Vomit King, but I'm done. And yes, I know I've felt *better*, but—" He shook his head feebly. "I'm not great. I'll admit that much. But I do know that I'm in complete control."

Dana's expression was grim as she looked at him, especially

considering he'd just sent an accidental electrical current through the car that he'd been leaning against. "You think that now. But if something goes wrong and you joker—you could do things. Terrible things. And it won't be *you* anymore, Cal. It'll be the drug, making decisions *for* you."

Calvin's jaw clenched. I had never seen him look so solemn. "I would never hurt you, Dana. I swear it."

Dana nodded as she gazed into his eyes. "I know you *believe* that, babe. But Destiny is stronger than you. It's stronger than love. It's stronger than anything."

She picked up both bags again, slinging them over her shoulder as she used her other arm to help support Cal.

Milo took a step toward them, his brow furrowed in concern.

"I got this," Dana said, looking at him—her longtime friend who I knew she loved as much as I loved Calvin. She pointed to the collar of her bomber jacket, and I saw she'd clipped one of those Minicams there.

Milo nodded and held up the tablet we'd been using to scope out the inside of Rochelle's house. He must've had it in his jacket pocket. "Turn it on," he said, and she did even as she started to lead Cal through the fence and toward the abandoned mall.

I leaned in to look, and the picture had already come on line. I was both relieved and horrified that, even from a safe distance, thanks to that camera, I'd have a front-row view of my best friend getting injected with Destiny.

And then maybe killing Dana.

I loved them both so much. This whole thing was like one big nightmare that I couldn't wake myself up from.

I couldn't stand it. I bounded after them. "Wait!" I exclaimed.

Calvin and Dana both turned around, their frowns identically quizzical.

"Just let me give you both a hug before you go inside," I said.

Dana didn't hide her eye roll. But Calvin grinned. "Lend me some sugar. I *am* your neighbor!" he exclaimed, stealing a quote from an old-school song he liked to sing when he was in one of his goofy moods.

I felt way more like crying than laughing. But I managed to smile before wrapping my arms around him. "Be careful," I said.

"Always," he whispered.

I let go of Cal and turned to Dana. "I know you think I'm cheesy, but I really need to—"

"Just get it over with, Bubble Gum," she interrupted me impatiently, spreading her arms wide as I rushed to hug her. "Christ," she added in a gruff voice. But she hugged me back, hard.

———

"When we're done here"—Dana's voice came through the Minicam's microphone, loud and clear, as Garrett, Morgan, Milo, and I got back into Cal's car to avoid the mosquitoes—"let's take a road trip to Orlando and scope out that address you were screaming about. The one near the Doggy Do Good warehouse. Okay?"

Milo took the driver's seat—he had the car keys. And Garrett and Morgan climbed in the back, leaving me the seat beside Milo. He propped the tablet on the dashboard so everyone could see. He also put his cell phone in the cup holder between us. Except it wasn't his cell phone. It was different. That was weird. I shot him a *What's that?* look, but his full focus was on adjusting the screen of the tablet.

"Yeah," Calvin said from inside the mall, his voice clear, too. "That's a good idea."

"She's good," Morgan commented from the backseat. "Dana. She's setting up a reality where Calvin survives the injection without jokering. It's good he goes in believing that."

"Wouldn't it be great if your sister was just…*there*," Cal said as Dana helped him through the door to our familiar theater six. She was holding a flashlight and the light bounced around the big room. "Like, we kick down the door, and she's the first girl we see? I mean, everything's always so hard. It'd be nice if *something* was easy."

"I hear you," Dana said. "That *would* be nice."

"Then we could all go to Hawaii and live happily ever after," Cal said.

"Hawaii?" We heard the sound of her putting her bags on the floor, heard a zipper unzipping as she briskly opened the larger one.

"Yeah, I've always wanted to go. Take a hike through the jungle to see a volcano. Maybe make out beneath a waterfall…"

"You have a thing for waterfalls, huh?" Dana teased.

"I have a thing for *you*," Cal told her.

Dana must've turned to look at him, because Calvin's face appeared on-screen, his eyes shiny as nickels against the glaring beam of the flashlight. He looked like a cat gazing into the dark, and I shuddered. But then he smiled and he was back to being Cal again.

Dana said, "Wait a sec, let me…" And the image was dizzying for a moment as she plucked the camera off her jacket. She somehow stuck it against the wall, giving us a clear view of the whole room.

Calvin was sitting against the far wall of the theater. He deliberately focused his gaze onto the camera and waved.

Garrett, genius that he was, waved back.

"Here hold this for me," Dana ordered, crossing to Cal and handing him the flashlight.

He obediently aimed the beam down onto her two bags as she took out what looked like a syringe. Yup, it definitely was.

"I wish I could turn on the lights for you," Cal said pointing up at the theater's overheads. Last time we were there, he'd used his Destiny-induced power to make them explode. But now, little more than tiny sparks jumped feebly from his fingertips. *Look what I can do, look what I can do...*

I shivered again. And I wanted to reach for Milo, hold his hand, but *not* reaching for him had become our new normal, so I didn't. Instead I gestured to the phone in the cup holder, mostly to distract myself while Dana prepped that syringe. "Don't tell me your phone died again and you're already using the backup."

"No," he said. "That's...not..." He cleared his throat. "No."

"It's a trigger phone," Morgan said from the backseat. "Isn't it?"

Milo glanced at me as he nodded.

"A what?" I asked.

Milo sighed and then answered by taking my hand. Our connection snapped on, and I felt the sudden rush of being shown one of Milo's memories. He was with Dana. They were both out of breath—they'd been fighting...someone...?

A Destiny addict who jokered. It was before we met you, and it was ugly, Milo told me, as in his memory, he opened the trunk of the now-dead joker's car. "Whoa," he'd said aloud, and Dana came to look, too. "Whoa," she'd echoed.

The trunk contained four homemade bombs, all wired to be triggered by a cell phone. I watched Dana reach into the trunk to pick up the phone—it was the same one that was now in the cup holder.

Dana didn't want to sell them, Milo said. *She was afraid they'd end up in the wrong hands. We blew one up*—he shot me another memory, this time of a deserted and overgrown orange grove, similar to the ones out to the east of the interstate, where an explosion ripped through the overcast morning sky—*just to see how it worked—if it worked.*

Obviously, it had.

He shifted to another memory then—this one of Dana stashing the three other bombs beneath the piles of rubble inside the twenty-plex's theater six.

Now, inside that same theater, Dana looked up at the camera and spoke. "This thing still on?"

Milo took his cell phone—his real cell phone—from his pocket, and quickly typed All good.

The sound of an incoming text made Dana's phone chirp and she glanced at it to see that, yes, Milo was giving her the green light. We were ready to blow Calvin up if he jokered and killed Dana.

Dear Lord.

"All right, boys and girls," she said under her breath.

Milo used the zoom feature on the tablet to bring the camera to a relative close-up of Calvin.

I felt my heart rate quicken. This was it.

Still thoughts. Still thoughts. Milo's voice filtered through my mind. I realized he was still holding my hand. And, despite the fact that I could sense those walls he'd erected—the ones that kept his various secrets from me—I knew that he wanted to be there for me, as much as he could be in that moment.

I, however, wanted to cry.

Don't cry, Skylar. Just breathe.

On the tablet screen, Dana helped Calvin by tying one of those giant rubber bands around his upper arm. His veins popped up, and she tapped them, feeling, exploring with her fingers, then wiping with a little antibiotic swab before settling the needle on his arm.

"I love you," Calvin told her. "I love all you guys."

"We love you, too," I whispered.

"I'm going to do this slowly," Dana said. "Try to stay as still as possible. If you can, keep your heart rate down."

Still thoughts...

As I closed my eyes, squeamish or maybe just unwilling to watch that needle puncture Cal's skin, I remembered my recent flurry of texts with Milo and my promise that if I had any questions for him, I'd *not* not-ask.

So I asked. *What is it, exactly, that you still don't want me to see?*

Milo got very still, and then almost as if opening a floodgate, he did it. He actually dissolved those walls. I was suddenly hit with hundreds of vividly sharp memories—a brown-eyed young woman singing, me getting off the bus at school, an enormous dog lunging and snarling before being jerked back by a chain, that awful moment in Alabama when Milo'd thought I'd been shot and I thought he'd been shot, a hawk wheeling against a bright-blue sky…

The giddy, dizzying rush of the street beneath the wheels of a motorcycle—I fell hard into that memory. I knew instantly that it was from this afternoon. The street hummed beneath those wheels as Milo got closer, closer, *closer* to a gray SUV. At the speed he was going, it was heart-stoppingly dangerous, and I actually gasped. But then I felt him kick that memory away. *Not important.*

Don't, I tried to tell him, but then I was sucked into another memory, just as vivid, but much, much older. The closet, his stepfather, his stepfather's rage…

Just like in the dream I'd had, I was Milo, seeing through Milo's eyes.

"You want to go? Then go!" the man shouted at us, spittle flying as he flung the closet door open. "Get the fuck out of here!"

I could feel Milo's nine-year-old self crying, sobbing: "I'm sorry! I'm sorry! I have nowhere to go!"

He—we—shrank farther back into the darkness of the closet as his stepfather laughed—and left us there, the door unlocked.

I could feel Milo's shame that he hadn't run away. He'd stayed.

You were nine! I told him.

But I didn't try to escape foster care either, he said as he showed me a memory from when he was fifteen. Bigger. Stronger. We sat, head down, at a table in an unfamiliar kitchen. Hands almost as big as Milo's were now clasped together in front of us as yet another man screamed at him. "You worthless piece of shit!" and "How will he ever learn if you coddle him?"

I knew from being inside this memory that Milo had taken his stepmother's punishment for leaving the light on in the bathroom—a beating that should have gone to a younger boy who'd only just arrived and was still deeply grieving his real mom's death.

I didn't leave, Milo told me, *until Dana showed up*. We lifted our head in that memory, as Milo's foster father raged on, and there, sitting across the rough wood of that table was a teenaged Dana. With long hair and no makeup, she looked very different, but the fire that burned in her ice-blue eyes was exactly the same.

If it weren't for Dana, I'd probably still be there, Milo told me.

Then thank goodness for Dana. She'd put a crack of doubt in Milo's well-forged belief that he truly was a *worthless piece of shit.*

"Almost done," Dana now murmured to Calvin from theater six. "Just keep breathing, babe."

It was then that it happened.

Calvin's eyes snapped open. And all the previous absence of color came rushing back to his face, like a wave of life crashing into his body.

He smiled—and then he made a horrible, hideous face, teeth bared. "*ARGH!*"

Electricity seemed to crackle around him, and—*bang!*—all of the lights went glaringly on in theater six.

The camera had been set for low light, so we instantly lost the picture to extreme overexposure, but I heard Dana scream, heard something clatter—the syringe—as it hit the floor.

"Oh my God!" Garrett shouted from our backseat. "Is he jokering?"

The car was awash with the smell of fear, anger, and grief as Milo dropped my hand and reached for the trigger phone. Morgan lunged for the tablet, working to adjust the settings so we could see what was happening, as over the microphone I heard Cal laughing.

"Hey, hey, hey," Cal said even as I caught Milo's wrist. "Easy, easy there! I was kidding, I was *kidding*! I'm fine! But, girl! Your face! I punked you! It was *crazy*!"

"That was *not funny*, Calvin!" we heard Dana say raggedly. "I could've killed you!"

"Yeah, I don't think so," he said and Morgan got the picture back just in time to see Cal shoot what looked like a lightning bolt from his finger. He laughed again. "I'm *so* cool!"

Dana turned to look into the camera, and the expression on her face was a million shades of grim. "Calvin is fine. He *punked* me. He was just kidding," she told us.

She had reason to be grim. The fact that Calvin didn't recognize just how messed up it was to pretend to joker was a sign of his growing lack of empathy.

Morgan said what we were all thinking. "So that was definitely not good." And then he asked the question we were all wondering, "So where do we go from here?"

CHAPTER TWENTY

We went to Dr. Hathaway's office "to regroup." That was how Dana put it.

But we all knew she was hoping to convince Cal to attempt the dangerous detox procedure sooner rather than later.

Milo took off on the motorcycle to check up on John Doe the bounty hunter. He'd left without kissing me good-bye, which had made me shake my head. *Didn't you recognize how glad I was that you shared those memories with me?* I wanted to shout after his receding taillights. *Don't you know how much I love you?*

It occurred to me then, in a flash of clarity similar to Cal's trick with the lights in the movie theater, that maybe Milo *didn't* know. What if his shame was so powerful that it made him literally unable to feel anything else?

But as we pulled into Garrett's driveway, Dana asked Morgan, "How long will it take you to set it all up? The detoxing? From the moment Calvin says *go*."

"I haven't said *go*," Cal was quick to point out.

"Maybe an hour?" Morgan said. "I'll want to defrost another batch of instafreeze adrenaline to have on hand. Dr. Hathaway has some in his medicine fridge, but not enough."

Adrenaline was one of the drugs Morgan would use to try to restart Cal's heart. After we killed Cal by stopping his heart.

"Also," Morgan added, clearing his throat, "I want to make a quick run to the hardware store."

To pick up chains, because he believed the leather straps on the OR table wouldn't be enough to hold Calvin.

Cal was oblivious about that little uncomfortable detail. "I thought we were going to Orlando," he complained.

"We were," Dana told him, "but then you were a giant asshole."

"I said I was sorry." Cal sounded affronted, but then must've realized that he could win Dana's heart more easily with sugar than vinegar, so he added, "And I *am* sorry, babe. Right now I just feel *so* great. And I know you're gonna try to talk me into letting y'all stop my heart, and since the purpose of that is to get the D out of my system, then doesn't it make sense to wait until I have less D in my system? If Morgan's right, it's only gonna be a day or two before I start puking again, so why not let me have this time?"

It *was* a compelling argument. Plus it was then that Milo called.

It seems he'd lost track of our bounty-hunting John Doe. Milo was going to find the man—but until he did, he wanted me to go into deep hiding. Preferably somewhere outside Coconut Key.

"Orlando's outside Coconut Key," Calvin pointed out.

Which is how we found ourselves in Cal's car on yet another road trip, when instead we should've been strapping my best friend to a table and stopping his heart.

———————

Dana and Cal did a sneak-and-peek of the huge warehouse's perimeter, while Morgan, Garrett, and I crouched in the lengthening shadows beside the car.

During the three-hour drive, Cal had pulled up a map of the area and we'd all studied it, although now that we were here, Garrett was still confused.

"We're at the back of the warehouse," I told him, gesturing with my chin toward the door, where a feeble streetlight flickered to life in the growing darkness, its bulb popping and buzzing as it cast weak shadows across the deserted and overgrown parking lot. "This must've been an employee entrance. The front is the part with all of the cargo bays. You know, where trucks can pull right up and load in or out?"

Those huge garage-like doors were made of battered, ribbed metal. As we'd pulled up and driven slowly past the address that Calvin had burped out, we'd all made note of the heavy padlocks that kept the three doors securely shut. There had also been a fading sign out front: "For Lease, 80,000 square feet in the Heart of Orlando's Thriving WestPark Industrial Center!"

It had been quite some time since the word *thriving* could be used to describe this industrial complex. In fact, *ghost town* seemed more fitting. As far as I could tell, out of five separate warehouses positioned around a giant truck-sized cul de sac–type circular driveway, only the largest—the Doggy Doo Good—was currently in use.

"That's the Florida headquarters for Doggy Doo Good," I told Garrett as I pointed toward the only slightly brighter lights that came from the gargantuan DDG building two warehouses down from us. If we were at twelve on a clock, DDG was at four, with the burned-out hulk of a decaying and only partially boarded-up building between us. We couldn't see more than the glow of DDG's lights from here—but likewise, anyone over there couldn't see us.

I told Garrett, "We know that their trucks are used to transport kidnapped girls like Sasha to Destiny farms. And we suspect both the local police and the FBI are involved. At the very least, they're looking the other way. See, after the thing with Sasha, we made some anonymous tips about the kidnapping ring using DDG's trucks, and Dana watched them go into this very warehouse, but they didn't find anything. So either the kidnappers knew the police were coming and moved the girls or..." I looked again at this seemingly deserted building that bore the numbers 5543. "Maybe they've been keeping the girls off-site but somewhere nearby, like, oh, say, *here*."

With five empty warehouses to choose from in this complex, the people who kidnapped G-Ts and sold them for their blood could stash those girls anywhere. The bonus was the distant but incessant echoes of dogs barking and howling. The Doggy Doo Good warehouse included a horrible puppy mill, and the noise of the dogs would no doubt hide any stray screaming and crying from the human victims.

I caught Morgan gazing at the burned-out warehouse next door. "This is awfully familiar, Skylar," he murmured. "Both the visual *and* the soundtrack. Sasha was here. Definitely."

"But that was months ago," Garrett pointed out. "Wouldn't Lacey have been sold to some creepy Destiny addict by now?"

"Maybe it's like what Jilly described," I suggested. "Maybe they bring the really powerful, older girls back here—the ones who survive. And they get them healthy and back in shape before they send them out again." But even as I said it, it sounded really unlikely. Most girls like Jilly probably died when the clients—their mistresses—jokered. They'd be lucky to survive. Or *unlucky*, as Jilly had implied.

Garrett, however, must've thought that was possible, because now he was pondering other big questions. "Why didn't you do your creepy morph-into-a-dog thing, instead of sending Dana and Calvin out into the void?" he asked Morgan.

"(A) It's not a void," Morgan said. "It's twilight. It's spooky and shadowy, and spooky and shadowy is good when your goal is to not be seen. And (B) Doggy Doo Good has canine sensors outside the warehouse. I spotted them when we drove in. Trust me, I've learned to recognize them. They're set to sound an alarm if a dog gets loose. So, don't be a dog, right? I don't know their range, and I didn't want to accidentally set them off." He looked at me. "They're also probably set to sound an alarm if the sensors are triggered by small humans. Small females, around Sasha's size and age…?"

I nodded. Still, Morgan had given in a little too quickly when Cal had announced that he and Dana were going to surveil the warehouse.

"You guys wait here," Cal had ordered.

There had been something about Morgan's face as he'd clamped his mouth shut that told me he was actually hesitant to disagree with Calvin.

Was the super-G-T seriously *scared* of my best friend, I now wondered.

Morgan did his read-my-mind-without-actual-telepathy thing. "Not scared, darling. Cautious," he said quietly to me out of the corner of his mouth.

Still, it was enough to make me think. Hard.

How *were* we going to convince a kind of scary Calvin to submit to the detox procedure? I just couldn't imagine him volunteering to be strapped onto that operating table in Garrett's dad's office.

And as Garrett went into Calvin's car to get his jacket—it was getting nippy—I whispered to Morgan, "Do you honestly believe there's a chance that the detox will work, or are we just using it as an excuse to put Calvin down, like a rabid dog?"

"Good analogy," he said. "There's no cure for rabies, either—and it makes dogs both terrified and insane. If your dog got rabies, wouldn't you want to be humane?"

It wasn't quite an answer—and yet it was, and my heart sank. "But Cal's not a dog," I whispered back fiercely.

"So we should treat dogs better than we treat people?" he asked, one eyebrow raised.

I didn't respond. I didn't have time, but even if I had, I'm not sure how I would've answered that.

But not only did Garrett rejoin us, but Cal and Dana also came running back to the car, their footsteps soft and quick on the pavement.

"There are definitely people in there," Cal said, sounding a little too gleeful, considering just how dangerous this was. If we got caught, Dana, Morgan, and I would be kidnapped and sold as slaves, while

Cal and Garrett would be murdered where they stood. Of course, if we survived, we had *Convince Calvin that we're going to save him while really we kill him before he jokers* at the top of our to-do list. In light of that, slavery and murder seemed almost acceptable.

"Three people in a small room, here in the back," Cal continued. "There was a skylight on the roof that we looked through, and we think we saw her."

"What? *Her?* You mean, Lacey?" I asked, looking sharply at Dana.

Her face was impassive. "I'm not positive. We can't be sure…"

Calvin made an impatient sound. "It was her," he insisted. "Seriously. It had to be."

"That girl—the second girl—was wrapped in a blanket, and we only saw her face for a moment," Dana started.

"But she looked exactly like Dana. Identical eyes," Cal said. "Plus she was the right age."

Dana nodded carefully.

"The second girl," I repeated. Cal had said there were three in this back room. "Who's the first girl? And who else is with them?"

"This is where it gets extra crazy," Cal said. "The first girl was April. For real, Sky. It was April, from school."

I frowned. "Wait. *April* April? As in, crazy April from last year?"

Calvin and I had become friends under extremely stressful circumstances—to put it mildly. I'd been the new kid at Coconut Key Academy, and Cal and I had bonded over lunch—just in time to save each other from a disgruntled student named April who had started waving two very lethal-looking guns around in the middle of the school quad. The consensus had been that she was attempting to commit suicide-by-cop, and for some weird reason had decided that I should also die that day.

Long story short, everyone had lived, but April had been arrested. I'd always assumed she'd been transported to some court-ordered psych ward. Although the mysterious circumstances surrounding that whole ordeal, and the ominous words April had whispered to me—*You. You're one of us*—before the cops took her away, had recently made me wonder if April was a G-T.

Cal nodded. "Yup. That April. But it's weird. She looks…better than she did before. Like, not so crazy. Like she has her shit together. I dunno. That doesn't make sense if she's being rented out to Destiny addicts. Although maybe her last owner was nice—"

"Cal," Dana interrupted him.

"Yeah, that's right. Sorry. I forgot that Destiny addicts can't be nice. My bad."

"Three people in the back room," Morgan said, bringing us back on track. "I assume the third's a guard?"

"Looks like it," Dana reported, "although I didn't see any weapons. Doesn't mean she doesn't have one."

"The guard's a woman?" I asked.

Dana nodded. "Older woman. Midfifties," she said in a tone that was carefully devoid of emotion. She sounded like she was reciting a laundry list. "Short, gray hair. Military apparel, but again, not visibly armed."

"How about the rest of the warehouse?" Morgan asked. "Anyone else there?"

Cal nodded. "We couldn't see inside, but Dana used her G-T mojo. She could feel that there're a dozen people in the front of the warehouse."

Dana turned to me. "When we were looking through that skylight, we saw a series of pipes that makes me believe there's a water source—a bathroom or a kitchen—in the next room over from where the guard is with the two girls. If we can flood that area fast, the three in the back will come out the back door while the guards in the other part of the warehouse go out through the doors in the front."

I nodded. That made sense. For at least a short time, April and the other girl—maybe, please God, it *was* Lacey—would be alone outside with a single guard. And us. One against five G-Ts plus Cal and Garrett were odds that I liked. Provided we could get the two girls into the car and zoom out of there before the twelve people from the front of the warehouse stopped us.

Still, I glanced at Cal, remembering the last time I'd used my water-based TK to try to help. "You sure you want me to—"

Dana cut me off. "Just do it."

———

It was a good thing that adrenaline was my best friend when it came to channeling my G-T abilities. Because at the moment? Adrenaline and I were having a serious bonding session.

I could feel my heart racing as I pictured Dana's helpless sister inside that warehouse, and my heart pumped even faster.

It was now or never. I could sense the water inside that warehouse, too. A lot of it. I could *feel* the pulsing rhythm of the water traveling through the pipes, just as surely as I could *feel* my own blood working its way through my veins.

Thum-THUM. Thum-THUM.

All of these girls, taken and used—for what? Why did this need to happen to innocent people? Why did Cal—my best friend and one of the greatest people I'd ever met—find himself sentenced to almost-certain death because of greedy, selfish people like Rochelle? *Why?*

I was ANGRY! SO ANGRY! SO! *ANGRY!*

Maybe a little *too* angry, come to think of it.

Water burst out of the pipes with such force that the first-floor windows exploded outward, sending shards of glass flying through the air.

For a moment, my mind sent me back to that day in the school quad with April—the day that Calvin had saved my life and I'd saved his. The day that April had been taken away in a police vehicle. Windows had shattered on that day too.

This time? I knew the destruction was my own doing.

I took a step away and covered my head with my hands to keep any flying fragments from hitting me. Dana had draped her body over Cal's, while Morgan shielded Garrett. Water roared out from the building and onto the pavement, picking up bits and pieces of debris as it dispersed into smaller rivulets on the slope of the driveway.

The next sound was the back door as it burst open.

Twilight had surrendered to true darkness, and the light from the open doorway illuminated the pitted ground. By now, Cal, Dana, Morgan, Garrett, and I were all tucked off to the side, huddled behind a rusted and long-forgotten blue mailbox, our figures blending into the dark outlines. Around our feet, water rushed and twisted as it seeped downstream toward the storm drains.

"Careful! Step carefully!" It was the voice of the guard—the older woman, barely audible over the roar of the water. She held the door open, and I could see that her boots were soaked through as water rushed around her calves and escaped out the doorway.

A teenage girl splashed through the doorway behind her, brown hair mashed against her wet face. Her T-shirt stuck to her chest, and she swung her arms wildly to keep her balance as the flooding water whipped around her legs.

Calvin was right. It was definitely our old friend April.

"Where's Ell?" the guard asked her.

April squeegeed her hair back from her face. "What? I thought you had her, Miss Aurora!"

"I didn't. I don't!" They both turned to look back into the building.

Dana drew in her breath sharply and said, "Lacey's still in there!" She moved, as if to charge through the door and into the flooding building.

But Morgan said, "Wait! Let me."

"Who's out there?" the older woman demanded as both she and the girl turned sharply toward us.

Meanwhile, Morgan had started…undressing? He pulled off his shirt and yanked off his jeans and his underwear, too.

"Seriously?" Garrett said, but I knew what Morgan was doing, and I tried to help him.

"Hold this," Morgan said, thrusting his clothes into Garrett's arms.

He dropped into a four-legged position and, without hesitation, morphed into animal-mode. But this time, instead of a pit bull or a dachshund or even a Portuguese water dog, Morgan opted for a...*horse?*

If we were surprised, I can only imagine what it looked like to April and her guard. An enormous horse—and I'm talking majestic white stallion—just suddenly appeared from behind a relatively tiny mailbox and galloped toward them.

"*What the hell!*" April hollered. She pushed the guard out of the way as Morgan rushed into the building, his hooves clip-clopping and splashing through the flooded walkway.

And that really should've been a clue. Along with calling the so-called guard *Miss Aurora,* April had just kept the older woman from being harmed. So...maybe Miss Aurora *wasn't* a guard?

But Miss Aurora was now completely spooked and probably believing they were under attack. She fumbled in her jacket and pulled out a small but deadly handgun as she moved toward our hiding place.

Calvin either wasn't paying attention, or he hadn't done that particular math equation (respectful title of *Miss Aurora* plus April saving Miss A's life most likely equals Miss A is neither a guard nor one of the bad guys), because before she could point the weapon in our direction, he let out an animallike growl and leaped onto the top of the mailbox. His movement was stealthy and graceful and terrifying as he extended his legs and balanced effortlessly atop the slope of the metal box. Dana and I stood up too, although something inside of me kept me from reaching out and touching him.

"Calvin, don't," I started to say, but he'd already blasted Miss Aurora with his crackling, blue-tinged electrical current, and she screamed in pain and fell onto the ground, the weapon flying out of her hands.

Dana was there instantly, and she scooped the gun up, mostly because April was frozen in place, staring at Cal.

April's expression quickly morphed from pissed to scared. "Oh my God, you're an addict!" she shouted at Cal.

At that same moment, the truth of what was happening here registered with Dana, too, as she looked from April to Aurora. "Oh my God, you're *both* G-Ts!" Dana shouted at them.

It was then, in that eureka moment of *Hey, we're almost all G-Ts here, except for the kindhearted Destiny addict who's still and admittedly kinda creepily perched up on that postal box*, that Morgan came galloping back out of the warehouse with a blanket-covered girl on his back. She was clutching his neck, his horse mane blowing gracefully in the wind like they were on the cover of one of those historical romance novels my mom liked to read, where everyone always wins their happily-ever-after at the end. Always.

But before Dana could win at least a part of her HEA by finding out if that girl riding Morgan really was her long-lost sister, Garrett said, "Heads up!"

Because a whole pack of people came rushing toward us. It was the dozen who'd been up at the front part of the warehouse. No doubt someone had heard Miss Aurora scream when Cal zapped her. Or they'd heard Morgan's galloping feet, or…

Let's face it, this little rescue operation had left its stealth status behind a long time ago.

But chances were that whoever was sharing this warehouse with three unguarded G-Ts was probably also not part of an illicit Destiny ring.

Sadly, Calvin still hadn't figured that out. The sky lit up blue, and the world erupted.

"Cal! Don't!" I heard Dana shout, although my ears rang so loudly, I wasn't sure if I'd really heard her or if I'd just read her lips. She'd swiveled and changed directions, running toward Calvin. Watching her was like watching a movie scene in slo-mo. She crossed and uncrossed her arms over the front of her body as she signaled him to cut it out. She shook her head and bellowed "*No!*" over and over again—to no avail.

Because, when I turned to look at Calvin, he wasn't looking at Dana. His eyes weren't even open as he turned his face to the sky and pointed his hands rod-straight in front of him, extending his fingers into the air like ten makeshift gun barrels. Most awful of all was that Calvin's lips were curled up into a menacing smile as he unloaded his terrible Destiny-induced power into the crowd.

Blue lines shot from his fingers, the stringy, thin angles of the laser-light trails reminding me of a Taser blast. And I knew that the damage he was causing was amplified by all the water on the ground. Currents were traveling along the pavement, carried along by the floodwater. All twelve of the people rushing to the rescue fell down and writhed on the pavement. April fell too, her body convulsing as Cal's power lapped through her in nauseating waves. As I watched, horrified, the blue electrical trail found its way to Miss Aurora as well, and she fell to her knees.

I was safe, standing behind Cal. So were Morgan and the girl atop his muscular equine back. He'd galloped a good distance away from the madness, and looked poised and ready to move even farther away.

But Dana? She was receiving some residual shocks simply from standing in a puddle. And, despite her efforts to nullify them with her own G-T abilities, I could tell that she was hurting.

"*Cal! Stop it!* You need to stop!" I barked even as Dana breathlessly exclaimed, "They're good! Cal! They're good! Our side! They're on our side!"

But it was like Calvin was under a spell—a terrible one that he was actually *enjoying*. Dana tried to step toward him, but she jumped back as soon as she realized that she'd be stepping into a world of pain. The blue current surrounding the mailbox was worse than anywhere else, thin blue lines snaking their way around the metal like fluorescent tapeworms, slithery and awful.

I focused my attention on the water that was still swirling out from the warehouse and TK'd the crap out of it, sending it up into the air with the force of a fire hose—directly into my best friend's face.

The water alone didn't stop him. But it caught Cal's blue current and he ended up zapping himself. It didn't knock him off the postal box, but it jolted him badly enough to make him stop.

In the sudden silence, Cal glared down at me from his perch on the mailbox. The expression on his face was terrifying.

His pupils filled up his brown eyes almost entirely as he bared his teeth at me. He looked like a monster—in the shape of my best friend. The thing that made him Calvin—the lightness and life in his eyes—was all but completely gone.

Something else had replaced him. Something terribly evil.

"Cal!" Dana said sharply, and just like that, he changed back into Calvin. Or almost-Calvin. There was still something…off in the way he was looking at me. And he made it worse by making that same *watching you* gesture with his hand that he'd made in jest, just a few hours earlier. This time, though, I didn't think he was kidding.

But now Dana had already turned and given a hand up first to Miss Aurora and then April, hauling them both to their feet.

"We're all on the same side," Dana said again. And the fact that she gave that handgun back to the older woman, butt first, made her words ring even more true. It also made the gang of twelve from the front of the warehouse breathe a little bit easier. Sure enough Miss Aurora made a *stay put* motion toward them, but they definitely made sure we knew they were armed as well.

Of course, we were armed, too, with Calvin still perched on the postal box.

Dana turned to April. "We thought you were being held prisoner. Cal and Skylar recognized you from their school in Coconut Key."

April gazed at me from underneath her wet mop of hair. I knew she remembered me. She nodded but then looked at Cal and shuddered. "You should kill him before he kills you."

Cal, of course, bristled, and Dana was back to calming him down as April turned toward me and asked, "Why would you come all this way to save *me*? And how'd you even know I'd be here? And why now, after all that time?"

"Well, we didn't. Know," I tried to explain. "Cal's got a little weird prescience thing happening with his...condition—"

"He's a freaking addict," April said flatly. "It's not a condition."

"Yes, I know, but—"

This time Dana cut me off. "We've been looking for my sister. I thought she was dead. She was taken years ago when she was small, but we just found out that she might still be alive. Another girl saw her here, and...her name's Lacey. Lacey Zannino?"

Miss Aurora stepped forward and reached out to tip Dana's face more fully into the wan light from the still-open doorway. She nodded. "Yes," she said. "It's remarkable. The resemblance."

Hope flared in Dana's eyes.

It was then that Morgan came clip-clopping back toward us. He was still carrying that blanketed figure, who was now sitting up straighter atop him. I could see a shock of blond hair as Miss Aurora said, "We call her Ell. And yes, it's short for Lacey. She doesn't remember her last name, but she's been with us for about six months now. The transition back to freedom's been particularly hard for her."

Next to me, Dana let out a sound that was three parts gasp and one part sob. She brought her hand to her mouth as she turned to look up at the girl.

"It's definitely her." Morgan the horse spoke aloud to the group. And, as weird as it should have been, he somehow made the whole talking-horse thing much more elegant than Mister Ed. Maybe it had to do with the words he was uttering.

It's definitely her.

"Lacey?" Dana breathed.

Miss Aurora went to help the girl dismount from Morgan. And as she slid off the big horse, the blanket slid off her shoulders.

The girl who stood there was Jilly's age—fifteen years old. Her eyes were crystalline blue and heavily hooded with a curtain of dark lashes in a face that could've been Dana's. Her hair was longer than her sister's—just touching the tops of her shoulders—and she was a few inches taller, but the resemblance *was* uncanny.

Except for the fact that little Lacey was hugely pregnant.

"Lace. It's me," Dana said, her voice little more than a whisper. "Dana."

"Dana?" the girl repeated. She placed a protective hand around her round belly before stepping forward and squinting disbelievingly. "You can't be. You're lying! Dana's dead!"

Then, Lacey—Dana's long-lost sister—fainted at our feet.

———————

When Lacey came to, she started to scream. Morgan quickly morphed from horse to dog, and when he leaned up against her leg, she immediately clung to him and calmed down.

Dana backed way off, but I knew that she was horribly freaked out. She'd clearly upset her sister—badly.

It wasn't the worst thing in the world that both April and Miss Aurora—it was hard to tell which of them was actually in charge of this crew—wanted to do something called "bug out." Immediately. They were rightfully worried that with all of the noise and weird blue lights and exploding windows and water, that the gang over at the Doggy Doo Good would send someone over to see what was causing the ruckus.

So instead of standing around and making Lacey even more upset, we bugged out. Which basically meant we got into our cars and drove away.

The gang of G-Ts had a couple of ancient cargo vans hidden in the burned-out warehouse next door. They all piled into those vehicles, and we got back into Calvin's car. Morgan-the-Dog went in the van with Lacey, and April went with us in a kind of impromptu "hostage" exchange.

It was then, as we drove to a safe location on the other side of Orlando—it took us about a half hour to get there—that April answered most of our questions.

Who the hell *were* they?

April's first response to that question was to pull a marker pen out of her pocket and draw <=>, surrounded by an eye-shaped oval, on the inside of her left arm. I recognized the mark—it was the one Morgan had showed us, back in the twenty-plex.

It turns out that Morgan was right, and we'd stumbled upon a local rescue cell from GTFU. This group of G-Ts and allies had set up camp right in the proximity of the Orlando Doggy Doo Good complex in order to intercept shipments of kidnapped little girls.

April had become part of the group after they'd saved her life.

Apparently, last year, after her breakdown at school, she'd been snatched from the hospital by some very bad people who sold her to a Destiny farmer. But the truck she'd been in, heading north to God knows where, had been stopped by this rescue cell, and she'd been saved.

Turns out she'd found not just a home but a calling.

Some months later, she'd been part of a daring raid of a Destiny prison near Gainesville. This little group of G-T freedom fighters saved three dozen girls in that op—and one of them was Lacey.

Unlike in most Destiny production rings, those girls had been cared for. Periods of torture and imprisonment were juxtaposed with weeks of food and shelter and health care—all of which must've felt like sheer luxury—before they were sent back out "on the line" again. That's what they called it when they were chained to a bed or sometimes just to an anchor in the floor, and forced to bleed into bags while being threatened with beating and death.

But the girls got harder to control when they reached puberty because their powers increased. When the girls in this particular farm turned thirteen or so, they got taken off the line, April told us, and put into a breeding program.

Yeah. That's as awful as it sounds.

Dana's little sister, Lacey, was pregnant because the people who'd owned her had decided it was time for her to make them more G-Ts. But not just regular Greater-Thans—*super* G-Ts.

That was pretty horrible, but the thing that made Dana start to cry was finding out that this was not her sister's first pregnancy. According to April, Lacey's first baby had been born about a year ago—and immediately ripped from her arms. She had no idea where the girl was or even if she'd survived. And yes, Lacey had had a daughter.

Apparently there was a way to ensure that "Breeder Girls" had female babies, since most of the time males wouldn't do their owners any good.

I wanted to throw up. I knew that the people who produced Destiny were evil, but this was… Lord, I couldn't even.

As we all absorbed that info, we arrived at a crumbling hotel in a part of Orlando that looked like it had been abandoned thirty years ago. This place was dark and boarded up—except for one window that we crawled through to get inside.

Morgan was waiting for us—back in human form and fully clothed, thank goodness.

"How is she?" Dana asked him.

He nodded. "She's, um…in really shitty shape. I don't want to lie to you."

"No," Dana said. "Don't. I don't want you to. I wanna know."

"She believes with a deep conviction," Morgan said, "that both you and your father were killed in a car accident. She, well, she saw it happen."

"But it didn't! How could she…?" Dana asked.

"Someone planted a false memory of your death in her mind," Morgan said. "I've seen that done before—nothing like this, though. Whoever did this is…brilliant in a really evil way. The memory is anchored in there in a way that'll be hard to fix. Even for me. It was implanted years ago—my guess would be that she kept trying to escape when she was first kidnapped.

"Whoever owned her recognized the potency of her blood," he continued. "They used the implanted false memory to instill a feeling of hopelessness in her—which seemed to work. With you and her dad gone—dead, in *her* mind—she had nowhere to go. About the same time they did that, they wiped her memory of her last name. She really has no clue what it is."

Dana nodded. "That explains why she didn't come looking for me when she was rescued."

"Yeah," Morgan said. "Look, you should go in and see her. Let her get used to the idea that you're not dead. But I wouldn't try to move her. Not right now. She feels safe with Aurora and April. I'd let her stay with them, for a while at least." He lowered his voice. "Also, Calvin really freaks her out, so—"

"I heard that!" Cal said.

I spoke up. "We'll stay out here while you go see Lacey," I told Dana. "Take as long as you need."

Dana nodded. "Thanks." She looked to Calvin for support, but his head was down as he was looking at his phone. So she asked me, "What do I say to her?"

I hugged her. "I'd start with *Hi, I'm your sister, and I'm definitely not dead.*"

"Thanks a billion, Einstein."

"Sometimes it's good to go with the obvious," I said as she went down the hall with April, leaving Morgan, Cal, Garrett, and me to entertain ourselves.

I quickly shot a text off to Milo: We found her! But it's weird.

"Hey!" Calvin said. "Holy shit! Holy *shit*! You guys! You remember those numbers that I kinda burped out at the twenty-plex? Seven, nineteen, twenty-one, thirty, fifty-four? If we'd used them to play the lottery, we'd've won seventeen million dollars! Am I the bomb, or am I the bomb?"

He started singing and dancing, right there in that mildewy hallway in Orlando, completely unconcerned that the girl that he loved really could've used his support.

We were losing Cal. It was happening right before our eyes. And as I remembered the way he'd looked at me, teeth monstrously bared, from his perch on top of that postal box, I heard an echo of April's voice. *You should kill him before he kills you.*

CHAPTER TWENTY-ONE

We left Morgan in Orlando with Lacey, with an unspoken plan for him to return to Coconut Key in the morning to do Cal's detox procedure then.

It was easier for me to think about it that way—as our attempt to save Cal. But in truth, my best friend was going to die tomorrow.

I wasn't sure how we were going to do it—how we were going to kill him. And I don't mean the stop-his-heart part. *That* I knew. What I didn't know was how we'd get him strapped down on the operating table so that we *could* kill him.

It seemed extremely unlikely we'd be able to talk him into willingly participating. That left two options. Either we'd trick Calvin, or we'd have to overpower him.

Oh, wait, there *was* a third way. We could sedate him, which was kind of a combination of tricking and overpowering him. We could slip drugs into his drink or zap him with a hypodermic needle—and watch his shock and his sense of betrayal flare in his eyes before he slipped into unconsciousness.

The shock-and-sense-of-betrayal-in-his-eyes part was guaranteed, whatever method we chose.

I was aching to talk to Milo, but he'd briefly texted me back after I'd let him know we'd found Lacey. He was psyched, but his phone battery was running low. He'd let me know that he'd found our John Doe, who'd checked into a hotel, so that was good. But Milo didn't have access to a charger, so I couldn't take advantage of the long drive to have a longer conversation, which really sucked.

I wasn't the only one steeped in silence as Garrett pulled Cal's car into the parking lot of the Coconut Key CoffeeBoy—the same CoffeeBoy, in fact, where Cal and I had bumped into Garrett just a few days ago.

I know I've said it a lot lately—but it was true. Things had *seriously* changed since then.

I was riding shotgun, and I glanced in the side rearview, where I could see Dana's usually inscrutable face. Right now, grief was etched there for anyone with half a brain to see.

"Pull up here, dude! Here! Here!" Cal sat in the backseat beside Dana, and he waved manically at a parking spot close to the front of the CoffeeBoy entrance.

Garrett started to shake his head. "We need gas—"

"And I need to take a leak!" Cal barked out a laugh before jolting the door to the backseat wide open, even as Garrett still drove.

"What the eff, man?" Garrett slammed on the brakes.

"You know, the leak I take standing up now?" Cal leaned forward and slapped Garrett on the shoulder like they were sharing an inside joke. It was supposed to be a *bro* move, but the slap was executed a little too hard, and Garrett winced.

"Just get out and let me park," Garrett said.

Cal climbed out, but then waited for us to get out of the car before heading inside the CoffeeBoy.

We had all agreed that it would be best to stop for a bathroom break and something to eat-slash-drink before heading back to the Twenty to get some rest.

CoffeeBoy had been Cal's overpowering choice. I wasn't sure how safe it was for a Destiny addict to load up on caffeine—but, then again, nothing seemed safe at this point anyway. I doubted a large hazelnut was going to push him over the edge.

We all trooped inside and Dana and I went toward the counter as Garrett and Cal both headed for the men's.

"Hey," we heard Cal say. "If y'all really do try to change me back to Sir Lame-a-Lot, you should definitely get a video of me shooting electricity out of my fingers first. I mean, that shit would go *viral.*"

I shot a glance at Dana and her expression was grim as she stared up at the menu, deliberately ignoring Calvin's comment.

But then he roared with laughter, which was harder to ignore. "Dude!" he squealed. "Dude! You're killin' me!"

Garrett was the dude to whom Cal was referring. But Garrett definitely wasn't laughing.

"What's so funny?" I asked.

Garrett shook his head. "I told him that we all liked him better before he started walking," he uttered far more quietly than Cal.

The CoffeeBoy wasn't that busy, but there were a few bedraggled men in paint-spattered clothes sitting at a table in the corner, along with a mom and her two kids ordering donuts at the front of the line. They'd all turned to watch Cal out of the corner of their eyes, because his laughter was so high-pitched, it almost sounded hysterical. Literally hysterical.

But then? His laughter just stopped. Like someone had flipped a switch. And Cal stood up straight and shook his head at Garrett, his expression so cold that I swallowed hard. "No, dude. Wrong. *No one* liked me better before I could walk. You, of all people, should know that."

Garrett wouldn't meet Cal's eyes. But *I* did. "Calvin. Stop it. What do you want?"

"What do I want? To be able to stand up when I pee for the rest of my life, and to maybe be able to shoot laser beams out of my fingers without people breathing down my throat." He giggled. "Oh! You mean, what do I *waaant*? Large hazelnut. Black. Lots of sugar. Please and thank you." Calvin winked at Dana before he finally went into the bathroom.

Dana nodded to the girl behind the register. "You heard him. I'll also have four bottles of water, please. And four plain bagels, toasted with cream cheese. Anything else, guys?"

Garrett had wisely decided to let Cal have the men's room to himself and he stepped forward. "I got this," he said and swiped his credit card. Something about the way he did it was extremely sweet—a far cry from his normal condescendence.

"Thanks," Dana said, and her voice broke, just a little.

"I know it must've felt weird to just leave Lacey there," I tried to reassure her. "But the good news is that she's *alive*." It was almost hard for me to believe the words coming out of my own mouth. Lacey was alive! It was amazing news. We should've been celebrating.

"Yeah," Dana replied. Her voice cracked, and she looked down at the CoffeeBoy counter. "Alive and knocked up. At fifteen." She played with one of the coffee stirrers next to the register. "And scared to death of me." Her chin crumpled, and when Dana gazed back up into my eyes, there were tears in hers. Her face was full of resolve though, and she steadied her voice as she said, "You know, for years. *Years*. I imagined what it would be like to see my baby sister again." She laughed, just once, and the sound was bitter.

"I mean, yeah, I thought she was dead, so it was really just a fantasy. But I always imagined that I'd be somewhere—getting groceries, I don't know—and I'd catch a glimpse of her and I'd turn, and she'd see me, too, and we'd run toward each other and hug and laugh and cry. And she was always a little girl, the way she'd been when she was taken. And I know. I'm not stupid. I can do the math. She's not that little girl. But she's not even—" Dana cut herself off. "I know that was a fantasy, but this is a nightmare. And then there's Cal…"

The counter girl had come back to the register with Cal's coffee, the water, and the bag of bagels. Dana shook her head. "I'm sorry, can you just—" She motioned for us to get the food. "I need to get some air."

Dana strode, head down, out of the CoffeeBoy and around the corner of the little brick building. Garrett grabbed the bagels and I got the coffee and the water, and we followed to make sure she was okay.

We found Dana bent over in tears, her back against the outside wall of the store.

"Dana," Garrett said carefully. "I mean, I know I don't know you that well and all. But Lacey's your sister. She's had some rough shit happen to her, but she'll come around. I mean, really. I know she will."

It wasn't the most eloquent speech. But Garrett was making a serious effort.

And it occurred to me that, right now, Garrett McDouche was more aware of Dana's feelings than Calvin.

Dana looked up at Garrett. "Do you really think so?"

"I know so!" Garrett replied. "She's family. And, with Morgan doing more of his weird gay voodoo on her—"

Dana managed to laugh through her tears at that.

"His voodoo comes from him being a G-T," I pointed out.

"Whatever," Garrett said. "Bottom line, Lacey's going to be okay."

"And Calvin is, too," I blurted.

"Yeah, Calvin. Too." But Garrett didn't sound as convinced.

Dana stood up and wrapped her arms around him. "Thank you," she said, wiping her face with the back of her hand. "Even if it doesn't turn out to be true, thank you for, you know, trying to give me hope."

"*Hey!*"

Calvin had come around the corner.

Garrett glanced up and spread his arms out wide, still holding the bag of bagels in one hand, as if to signal that he meant nothing by hugging Dana.

Dana, however, was so overcome with emotion that she didn't let go of Garrett. And didn't let go.

"Shit," I said quietly.

"I knew you were a douche! You've always been trying to steal my woman!" Cal roared and marched toward Garrett, who tried to swivel himself so that Dana wasn't directly in Calvin's path.

But Cal pushed Garrett, hard. The sudden move knocked Dana off her feet. She landed on the sidewalk, on her butt.

"*Stop!*" I yelled. "*Calvin, what the hell!*"

But his rage was too thick, and he couldn't hear me—or maybe he was just choosing not to. Blue currents shot from his fingers, landing squarely on Garrett's chest.

Garrett went down, convulsing almost instantly.

"*Stop it! Calvin, you'll kill him!*"

Garrett's body moved jerkily, involuntarily, as Calvin pushed wave after sickening wave of electricity into the other boy's body. I watched as Garrett's head made contact with the pavement.

Cal really was going to kill him if he didn't stop now.

"*Calvin!*" My best friend may have been super-powerful, but Dana was stronger. She jumped up from where she had fallen and tackled Calvin to the ground, and his crazy power stopped.

Garrett groaned, stunned but still conscious, thank goodness.

"What? Wait, what just—" Cal was equally stunned, apparently.

"You must stop this," Dana said and reached out to cup Cal's cheek. "Please. You must."

And Calvin's eyes softened as he gazed into Dana's. "Oh God. Oh my God, what was I doing? What did I do?"

His expression was one of utter shock—like he'd just woken up from a terrible nightmare.

Then he turned and looked up at me, his eyebrows raised helplessly. And he burst into tears. "I'm sorry," he sobbed.

Dana crouched down and put her arms around him. "It's not okay," she told him. "I can't tell you that it is, because it's *not* okay. You can't be doing this."

I was grabbing Garrett's arm to pull him away and give them privacy when Dana's burner phone rang. She pulled it from her pocket while still hugging Cal. She glanced at it before handing it to me. "It's Milo."

"I'm so, so sorry." Cal was sobbing. "I won't do it again, I promise."

I answered with, "Hi, it's me. Dana's...a little busy right now. There was kind of a...thing. With Cal."

"There's a thing happening here, too," Milo told me, his voice distant over a crappy connection. "With Rochelle."

"But that's just it, babe," Dana was murmuring to Cal. "You absolutely will do it again."

Cal lifted his head at that, and there was an echo of his earlier anger in eyes that were suddenly clear and dry. He wiped his face, and then his nose with the back of his hand. "I will *not*."

Um.

Meanwhile, I was getting even worse news from Milo. "Since our John Doe seems to be in for the night," he told me, "I used the tablet to check in on Rochelle. Her friend Ashley came over and…I'm pretty sure Rochelle is jokering."

I put Dana's phone on speaker. "Guys, we've got trouble," I announced.

Milo's voice came through the phone. "I think Rochelle just killed Ashley!"

That got their attention, fast.

"She's jokering!" Dana snapped into team commander mode. "Milo, where are you?"

"I'm already outside Ro's beach house," he reported, his voice even more distorted and crackly. "I heard them get into an argument— Rochelle and Ashley—something about a stain on a dress that Ashley borrowed. But the camera in the living room is still pointed at the sofa, so I couldn't see what was happening. It got loud and extra crazy, so I came over here, but by the time I got here, the screaming had stopped. I replayed the audio from the tablet and…I'm pretty sure Rochelle killed her. Ashley. I have no idea where Jilly is, but it looks like the closet door is unlocked."

"Stay outside," Dana ordered Milo as we all piled back into Cal's car. "Wait for us. We'll be there in five minutes."

"Jilly might not have five minutes," Milo said.

"Milo, please," I said, as Garrett put Cal's car into gear, and we peeled out of the CoffeeBoy parking lot.

"I'm pretty sure Rochelle is upstairs," Milo said. "There may not be a better time to go in there, grab Jilly, and get out. I'll leave the tablet outside in case we don't get back out. I love you, Sky, I do, but God, I have to try."

"*Milo!*" Dana and I both said it in unison, but he'd already cut the connection.

"Oh my Lord," I said. Milo was going in there. I looked at Garrett. "Drive faster." Why was he going so slowly?

"Police on my tail," Garrett said, gesturing at the rearview mirror.

"Here." I turned to see that Calvin was holding out his phone to me. "I hacked into the video feeds from the cameras in Rochelle's house," he told me. "I got them to come up on my phone, so you can see what's happening inside the house."

"How did you do that?" I asked, realizing that along with his ability to burp prescient-ish information and his crazy electricity-shooting-from-his-fingertips thing, the Destiny was also making Cal scary-smart. He was smart to start with, but this was evil-genius smart.

"It's complicated," Cal told me, a little heavy on the douchi-ness, considering he'd just been begging us for forgiveness. "You wouldn't understand."

As I watched on the screen of Cal's phone, the camera that was pointed toward the living room sofa spun to reveal Milo, who had gone inside. He'd moved the flowers so that the camera now showed us the living room. "Ashley's definitely dead," he reported, his whispered voice coming through much more clearly than it had via the cell-phone signal.

"Oh my Lord!" I said again. The walls were sprayed with the

woman's blood. This wasn't just a murder scene; it was a psycho-murder scene.

"Jesus!" Cal said when he saw the carnage.

"Rochelle *is* upstairs," Milo said. Clearly he expected us to rewind and watch the footage when we got to Rochelle's house—he had no idea we'd hacked into the signal and were watching him, live. "I can hear the sound of the shower."

"He needs to get out of that house!" I said but I knew Milo wasn't going to leave—not without Jilly.

Meanwhile, we were driving at Great Aunt Matilda speed. I turned to look behind us, and the police car was still *right* there.

Hell, I could've *run* faster to Rochelle's house.

No. I really could have.

But, of course, *that* would catch us a lot more attention than we needed right now. So instead I stayed in my seat, fists clenched, watching through Calvin's tiny cell phone screen as Milo came back into view via the flower-cam in the hallway—as he walked toward Jilly's closet-slash-prison.

The door wasn't just unlocked at this point; it was hanging wide-open.

Dana and Cal leaned forward to keep tabs from the backseat. Dana's expression was stoic, but I saw her eyebrow twitch, and I knew she was as anxious as I was.

"Jilly?" Milo called the girl's name quietly, as he picked up the bouquet with the camera and held it in front of him so that we could see what he saw.

With his foot, Milo nudged the door open farther. The lighting was dim inside, but there was enough illumination from the lamp in the hallway for us to see the outline of feet.

Jilly, lying on the closet floor.

"Jilly!" The flower-cam got jostled for a second as Milo set the bouquet down next to him on the closet floor.

Her limp body came into view, her face and neck the color of spoiled milk. Her eyes were open, but she wasn't moving—and for one horrible, sickening moment I actually thought she was already dead.

But then, she blinked. And her left arm twitched—her arm, which was, at the moment, being squeezed tightly above her elbow by a rubber tourniquet.

An IV needle was sticking out from the map of blue veins beneath her paper-thin skin. Tubing filled with dark red liquid led down to a nearly full bag of blood. No doubt about it, Rochelle was bleeding her dry. Thankfully, the D-addict had messed up and left that tourniquet on, so it was happening slowly.

Jilly spotted Milo, and her expression changed. She didn't look angry this time. Her eyebrows raised high, and when she met his eyes, she actually appeared relieved.

"Don't move," Milo said softly. I watched his muscular forearm come into view. It was such a contrast next to Jilly's malnourished limb. He leaned forward and ever so gently pulled the needle from Jilly's arm, careful to apply pressure with a piece of cotton he'd found in Rochelle's home D-lab.

Jilly nodded and mouthed the words *thank you*. Her de-needled arm flopped down to the floor, as though she didn't even have the strength to keep herself upright.

If Milo expected Jilly to leave Rochelle's house with him, he would need to carry her out. It wouldn't be the kicking-and-screaming variety this time—but she wasn't going anywhere without some serious help.

Out of the corner of my eye, I spotted a glint of movement.

"Guys? You see that?" Calvin spoke from the backseat.

Garrett had been reciting four-letter words in a little rhythm the entire time he'd been driving—and he still hadn't stopped. Because the police vehicle was still behind us. And that meant Garrett was required to maintain the speed limit—which felt, right now, like the pace of a snail on Valium.

"What?" Garrett asked. "See what? What happened?"

At first I didn't know what Cal had seen. And then, I did.

Rochelle.

I spotted a glimpse of her as she came into camera view in the living room. She was done with her shower, and now she was back downstairs.

"Oh my God," Dana muttered. "No. No."

"Milo has to get out of there!" I said for what felt like the trillionth time.

Rochelle was stalking around the room, taking her sweet time to observe the damage she'd done when she'd brutally murdered her best friend Ashley. She stopped at one blood-spattered wall and paused for a moment to wet her index finger before scrubbing gently at the edge of a silver frame holding one of her beloved self-portraits. Ashley's blood smeared slightly, but it didn't come off. The blood had already solidified into dark streaks against the cream-colored wallpaper.

Cal sighed heavily from the backseat. He didn't say a word.

"Come on come on come *on!*" I willed Rochelle to turn around and head back upstairs. Surely there was something she needed up there. But, instead, she kept inspecting the scene of her crime, her face disturbingly blank as she emotionlessly studied the carnage.

Milo was taking too much time as well. If he would just get his act together, he might still have a chance to run out through the garage without Rochelle seeing them. But he had to leave *now*.

"This is bullshit," I said and pulled my own cell phone out of my pocket, even as I continued to watch the play-by-play on Cal's. Quickly, I dialed Milo's number.

And then?

It had been an inside joke between Milo and me. Whenever my name came up on Cal's phone, Sir Mix-A-Lot's decades-old single "Baby Got Back" played. It was apparently my official ringtone, and every time I heard it, it cracked me up. So Milo had downloaded it onto his burner phones, so when I called *him*, it played, too. The first time it happened, I'd laughed so hard I'd almost peed my pants.

Right now though, I wasn't laughing.

Because Milo's phone was turned to top volume. He must've had it set like that so he could hear if I called him while he was on Dana's motorcycle. And right now that ridiculous ringtone was playing, the bass bumping loudly, even through Milo's cheap cell-phone speakers.

Tell her to SHAKE that (shake that) SHAKE that (shake that) SHAKE that healthy butt!

Rochelle had been kneeling over Ashley's body, and when the music started to play, her head whipped up fast, her pupils filling her entire eyes.

Dana looked at me and gasped. "Hang up!"

"What's happening?" Garrett finally turned onto Rochelle's street, his eyes on the rearview to see if the police car was following.

"Dude, that's my jam," Calvin said to no one in particular from the backseat.

"Hang up!" Dana barked at me again.

Shocked, I pressed the End button and then dropped my phone like it was a spider. "Oh my Lord!"

Meanwhile, Milo had been fumbling with *his* phone, trying to turn the ringer off. But the moment he'd attempted it, the volume had only increased.

And, anyway, it was too late now.

Rochelle was bounding toward the hallway—toward the closet—toward Jilly and Milo. She was out of sight for a moment as she exited the range of the living-room flower-cam.

Meanwhile in the car, Garrett finally hit the gas and we surged forward, but we were still at least a half a mile away.

Over the cameras, I could hear Rochelle's voice as she shrieked. *"What are you doing? How dare you!"*

I should say, I could hear her *voices*. She screamed the words in three very different octaves. One was high-pitched, like a baby crying.

The second was midrange, and the third was a low roar—like a lion. It was terrifying.

I saw Milo's arms, still in the view of the flower-cam as he reached for Jilly.

But before he could pick her up, Rochelle got to Milo.

He tried reasoning. Tried to sound as if he belonged there, quickly turning the flower-cam to face her as she glowered at him with some very crazy eyes.

"I'm here to help Jilly," he said evenly. Calmly. "Rochelle, if she dies, you'll be out of Destiny."

But reasoning didn't work with a jokering addict, because then, God, Milo was in the air, flying across the room like he was being carried by a hurricane-strength wind, and I realized that Rochelle was using her TK on him—as effortlessly as if she were tossing away a rubber ball.

Milo hit the opposite wall with a sickening *thunk* before he landed in a heap on the floor.

"Oh my God," Dana breathed.

"Is he okay?" I shrieked, although I knew that no one in this car could answer that question for me.

I tried to see, through the image on the screen, if Milo's chest was rising and falling. But the camera was too far away and he didn't move and he didn't move and he didn't move...

"Get up, Milo," I whispered. "Please. Get up."

Garrett's jaw was clenched as he continued to race toward Rochelle's house.

My heart pounded. This felt exactly the same as the night Dana had pretended that Milo had been taken. Except, this wasn't a drill. *This* was really happening. And *this* time I *knew* that Milo was hurt—that he was in danger. I knew it, because I could still see him, slumped on a jokering Destiny addict's floor.

Get up, Milo. I need you to get up. I need you to be okay.

I need you.

"That bitch," Dana snarled.

In the closet, Rochelle had turned her attention back to Jilly. She was jamming that needle back into the girl's vein.

"Almost there," Garrett said softly, determined. "We're almost there."

I breathed. *Still thoughts. Still thoughts.*

But the mantra did nothing to calm me.

All I could think about was getting to Milo. And this time, I couldn't screw things up. This time I would rescue him. I would save Jilly too. I would get them both to safety. I would.

If I got there in time.

Hold on, Milo. Just hold on.

I reached out to him, despite the distance, and I hoped that some part of his unconscious mind could hear me before it was too late.

CHAPTER TWENTY-TWO

Dana kicked in the front door, using her TK along with her steel-toe-booted foot, and the sheer force tore the thing off its hinges. It hit the floor with a crash.

"So I guess the plan isn't to use stealth," Calvin said as we followed Dana inside.

"The plan is we kill the bitch," Dana said, "and then we get Milo and Jilly out of here."

"Holy shit!" Cal's foot must've hit a puddle and he slipped, nearly going down onto the tile floor. "*Holy shit!*" As he scrambled to keep his footing, he realized that it was blood that had made the floor slippery—it was everywhere and it was even more awful seeing it in person. The gory splatter sprayed the walls and the furniture as well as drenching the floor. "*Holy shit!*" he said again. "But they were friends!"

Ashley's body was on the floor next to the sofa, her legs sticking out into the room. I looked at her through my eyelashes, and even then I didn't look too closely. A butcher knife—the murder weapon—was nearby. I didn't look too closely at that either.

And yes, she and Rochelle *had* been friends.

"This is what jokering addicts do to their friends," Dana snapped.

Calvin turned, leaned over, and threw up, and at first I was afraid he was starting to detox again, but then I realized that his was the right response to seeing this carnage. Garrett puked, too, and I probably would've done the same, if I wasn't hell-bent on finding Milo. *Please, God, let him be alive!*

I was right behind Dana, who was already leading the way toward the playroom. She caught my arm as I tried to hurry ahead of her. "Me first," she said. "I'll distract her, while you get to Miles."

I didn't have time to do more than nod, because there we were. In the playroom. And Rochelle, who'd heard the door crash open, was waiting for us.

"Welcome, girls," she said in that weird three-octave voice. She'd been kneeling beside Milo, but now she stood up. "I smelled you come in. What a lovely surprise! Have you come to help me?"

After seeing what she'd done to Ashley, I'd expected something different—maybe a screaming and incoherent she-monster flinging kitchen knives at our heads. I would've stopped short, but I saw Milo there on the floor behind Rochelle and I lunged for him.

Dana caught my arm again, holding me back as she returned Rochelle's faux politeness by asking, "Help you do what?"

Milo was still not moving, crumpled there, facing away from us. To make things worse, Rochelle had—Lord! She'd *bitten* him. Her teeth had broken the skin on his arm, and she had some of his blood smudged next to her mouth.

"What did you do to Milo?" I blurted, even as Rochelle told us, "I'm making the biggest batch of Destiny ever."

Dana's fingers tightened around my arm in warning, but Rochelle didn't take offense. In fact, she seemed to think my question was worth answering, too.

"His blood's not any good," she said. "But yours is. I can smell it from here."

It was then that I saw it. Milo's finger moved! Just his first finger, and just a little. Just enough for me to recognize that he was alive and awake and ready for us to kick Rochelle's butt.

The relief that ripped through me nearly knocked me over, and I had to lean on Dana to keep from sinking to the floor.

Dana nodded to me, very slightly, and I knew that she'd seen Milo's movement, too, even as she kept this weird conversation going. "I guess you didn't want to share that giant batch of Destiny with your friend, huh?"

"With Ashley? No. She annoyed me." Rochelle's eyes were pure crazy, and the smile that curved her mouth was hideously evil. Now that I wasn't quite so frantically focused on Milo, I could smell a thing or two myself—and I caught a nasty whiff of sewage. Despite her recent shower, this joker couldn't wash off her malevolence. It clung to her and made her reek.

And it reminded me that even though Milo wasn't dead, Rochelle could still kill him, easily, without any thought or remorse. She could easily kill Garrett and Calvin, too. They were lurking just outside the playroom door, and I made a motion behind my back that I hoped they'd interpret as a very solid *Stay back*.

"What are you going to do with it?" Dana asked Rochelle. "The giant batch of D?" She narrowed her eyes, just a little—and I knew that she was trying to mind-control the woman.

"I'm going to bathe in it and drink it and *become* it!" she told us.

I realized then that she was dressed rather oddly in a blue pair of men's boxer briefs—maybe something Garrett's dad had left behind—and a brightly patterned top that she'd pulled on both backward and inside out. The tag was right up by her throat, and the loose neckline draped down her back. She wore mismatched shoes on her feet—one expensive and black and four inches high, the other strappy and bright yellow with a slightly lower heel. If I'd had any doubt at all that she was jokering, her complete disregard for fashion would've convinced me that she'd snapped.

She took an unbalanced step toward us, telling Dana, "And, by the way, I can feel you creeping around in my head, little girl. It's not working, whatever you're trying to do. I'm stronger than you—stronger than you'll ever be!"

"Yeah, I don't think so," Dana said, adding, "Milo! Go!" as she let loose with the same kind of blast that had opened the front door—the same kind of blast I'd seen her use just a few months ago on that Alabama Destiny farm. She'd sent a sociopathic guard literally flying, saving the day in an incredible show of power and strength.

I was pretty certain that not only was this conversation over, but that Rochelle was now toast.

Milo sat up at Dana's *go*, and I began to move, too. I knew his focus would be on Jilly—he wouldn't leave without her. I had no idea how badly injured he was, so I shouted for Calvin and Garrett to come and help us, *now*.

Except Rochelle *didn't* go sailing back across the playroom the way I'd expected. In fact, she barely moved more than a steadying step, and I skidded to a stop just a few feet away from her, with Cal and Garrett nearly crashing into my back.

They both retreated, ducking for cover more quickly than I did— probably because I was so stunned that Rochelle had the ability to absorb Dana's blow. I just stood there stupidly staring at her.

"Is that really the best you can do?" Rochelle asked Dana as, with a flick of her finger, she used her own power to launch me up and into the air.

"Skylar!" I heard Milo shout over my own screaming as I fully expected to die. This was it. My life was over. But then I realized that Rochelle had only used her TK to fling me away from her—I was no longer under her power. If I had been, if she'd had abilities like Dana's, she would have used the force to slam me against the ceiling— crushing my skull and breaking my neck and back. As it was, only my body weight and motion made me crash into one of the overhead fans and then hit the cathedral ceiling with a far less lethal crunch. I realized in those slo-mo nanoseconds while I flew through the air that this was the reason Milo was alive, too. Rochelle's TK was limited. That was good to know.

But now I screamed again as I fell back toward the tile floor. That ceiling was more than two stories high, and my impending landing would probably break both my legs—if it didn't flat-out kill me. *I was water, I was water*—I tried to find the H2O inside of me and float it above the ground the way I'd done first to the bubble and then to the flowing stream of water at Adventure City. And at first I thought it was working, because I slowed waaaay down. But then I realized that Dana was saving me with her powerful TK. She may not have been able to stop Rochelle, but she was definitely helping me.

And then, as I was still about seven feet in the air, looking down at Milo and Jilly—I could tell with just one glance that she was nearly bled dry—I realized that I alone had the right kind of G-T power to save the girl. Assuming, of course, that Rochelle didn't kill me first.

"Don't," I called to Milo, who was again about to yank the IV needle from Jilly's arm. Blood could flow in as well as out, and even though I didn't have the exact right medical equipment to give Jilly a greatly needed transfusion, I had the two most important things. Her blood—and my unique ability to control liquids.

And yes, that ability was definitely temperamental, but I'd already reached out and felt the blood in that collection bag, so I started pushing it back up that tube and *into* her veins. It required precision and delicacy, which demanded way more effort and concentration than just flinging water around, like I'd done in Adventure City and at the warehouse. I had to do this carefully. *Gently*. Still thoughts, *still thoughts*... I could do this. *I could save this girl*...

Meanwhile, Dana shouted, "Fry her, Cal!" and Calvin let loose with a blue-tinged blast that surrounded Rochelle with jumping and crackling currents of electricity.

As my feet finally touched the tile, I immediately dove toward Milo and Jilly, not wanting to get hit with Cal's erratic newbie superpowers. I was certain that upon Cal's blast, Rochelle would drop to the floor where she would flail and thrash. Silly me.

Milo came toward me, grabbing my hands and pulling me closer to the wall where Jilly was huddled.

"Are you okay?" he asked even as I breathlessly asked him, "Are *you* okay?"

Our connection had snapped on, allowing me to *know* that he *was* okay—but that Rochelle's bite had really freaked him out. It had been hard to play dead when she'd done that. No kidding. I flashed him a visual shorthand version of what I was trying to do to help Jilly, and he thought I was brilliant and he loved me madly, but he was also extra not thrilled that I was in danger.

Ditto on you and the danger, normie, I shot back at him, and he laughed and kissed me—just a quick smack of his lips against mine— before turning back to Rochelle.

This is bad.

I turned to see that Rochelle was neither flailing nor on the floor— this was not only bad, it was also getting very, *very* old.

She stood there as if absorbing or maybe even feeding off Cal's electrical current, moaning and groaning as she jolted and jerked. It sounded like she was having the best sex of her life, which was just too disgusting to think about.

"The power! The power!" she cried in that freak-show triple voice. "I love the power! Give me more! Give me more!"

Dana was flinging everything she could find at Rochelle—using her TK to pummel the joker with the books from the shelves, the fan blades I'd broken, the easy chairs, and an end table.

But Rochelle shattered it all into pieces before it could hit her and knock her down—pieces she sent sailing back at Dana, forcing the G-T to bob and weave.

The remaining ceiling fans were spinning and even smoking, and the roar from Calvin's power was nearly deafening. I saw Dana gesturing to Calvin, telling him to keep going—but the effort was surely making him burn through the Destiny in his own system. I wasn't sure how much longer he could keep this up.

Let's get Jilly out of here, I told Milo, who agreed. I added, *Take her and go—*

He cut me off. *Yeah, I'm not leaving you here.* Milo looked around for… "Garrett!"

I was looking at Rochelle, and even though Milo's voice could barely be heard over the din, her eyes flashed open and she looked right at us as Garrett scrambled over to help. He was terrified. I didn't blame him—I was terrified, too.

I'd never been gazed at with such molten hatred before, and I wondered if Rochelle somehow knew that Milo had played her and stood her up the way he had because he was my boyfriend.

"I know about that and other things, too," she said, and I realized she wasn't moving her mouth. Not only had she read my mind, but her thoughts were being projected and vocalized without her having to speak them aloud.

"*That* is extra freaky!" Calvin shouted as he kept up his assault.

Dana sent one of the heavy wooden bookshelves launching at Rochelle.

"She's telepathic!" I warned them, instantly realizing *oh God oh God oh God. Don't think about Jilly, don't think about Jilly.* I didn't want her to know that I was putting the blood back into the girl's body instead of draining it out, except...

"I already know," Rochelle intoned as she demolished the bookshelf. "I know everything about all of you!"

Milo had put the girl into Garrett's arms, but Garrett was hesitating, clearly aware that the jokering woman was watching us and not at all convinced that the current Calvin was hitting her with would keep her from coming after him. I wasn't convinced of that, either.

"It can't stop me. It won't stop me," she intoned. "Don't you dare move!"

"Get her out of here, now! Get her into the car and drive!" I shouted at Garrett, and he finally scrambled for the door with Jilly in his arms.

"*Stop!*" The triple voice was so loud then, I thought my eardrums would burst.

And Garrett froze.

"*Don't stop!*" Milo and I both shouted at him. "*Keep going! Go, go, go!*"

"*I can't!*" he shouted back, his voice almost as high as Rochelle's highest octave. "*I can't move! I can't move!*"

And then—holy crap—*I* couldn't move. And then Milo couldn't either. And—double crap—he'd let go of me for a moment to help Garrett with Jilly, so we weren't touching and now we couldn't communicate with just our thoughts, which probably didn't matter since Rochelle knew what we were thinking anyway. But still, I didn't want to die like this, all alone, and dear Lord, for the first time I realized that we were all probably going to. Die. Here. Now.

"But your glorious blood will live on in me," Rochelle intoned.

"She's got some kind of super-telekinetic powers," Milo shouted to Cal and Dana, who were both still moving. Dana sent the second of the bookshelves at Rochelle, who blasted it into splinters. "She's holding Sky and Garrett and Jilly and me. We're frozen in place!"

It was remarkable—the amount of power that a jokering D-addict could access. Dana had a similar ability—to encompass another person in a telekinetic straitjacket, so to speak. But she couldn't use it to control more than one person at a time. She certainly couldn't lock down four of us like this.

"Oh, fuck!" Dana said, and I saw with a sinking heart that Rochelle had frozen her now, too. She was unable to dodge the spray of wood and dust that the joker sent back at her, and the force knocked her down and pushed her back until she hit the wall. And this time she didn't get up. "Damn it! I can't move! Cal!"

"I got this!" We were down to Cal. Our last best hope was a D-addict himself, and for once I was grateful that he was wearing his scary face, head tilted down so that he gazed at Rochelle from beneath furrowed brows, his teeth barred in a snarl.

But Rochelle just laughed, and that, too, was so loud it hurt my ears. "You think you're so dangerous," she intoned. "But you are *nothing*!"

And with that, she somehow turned Cal's power back on him, zapping him with his own electrical current. Just like with Dana, the force sent him backward until he hit the wall. He slid down so that he was sitting several feet from her. Now he couldn't move either.

Without Cal's electrical current buzzing, the fans spinning overhead were creaking noisily, and Rochelle looked up and exploded first one and then the other. After the dust finished raining down onto the tile floor, the silence was deafening.

Milo spoke up. "What now?" he said. "Sky? Dana?"

"Now? There is nothing you can do to escape," Rochelle said as she moved toward Garrett, who was still holding Jilly.

I expected her to kill us. All of us. Right there, the way she'd killed Ashley, but Rochelle turned to me and said, "What, and miss the fun?" And I knew instantly that this joker was one of those who, as Dana put it, *enjoyed playing with her food.* She was going to kill us, but she was going to do it slowly.

That was both good and bad. Good because it gave us some time, and time was definitely on our side. Bad because of the whole killing-us thing.

Meanwhile Dana ignored Rochelle and answered Milo's *What now?* "I don't know. I'm working on it."

I knew she was doing the same thing that I was—going down my entire list of G-T abilities to see if I had anything in my pocket that could help us here. I could run really fast, but not while in this TK body hold. I could still move liquids, maybe burst the pipes or create a giant wave to crash into the house, but I'd have to stop saving Jilly's life to do it—I couldn't do both at the same time. I didn't have that kind of power or control. Also? If I flooded this place with water while none of us could move, it was far more likely that we'd drown long before Rochelle.

All of my other powers—my ability to home in on a person I'd met, my ability to smell evil, my psychic-ish dreams and visions, my eidetic memory, my self-healing skills—were useless to us now.

Except…my super-memory meant that I remembered everything that Morgan had told me about D-addicts and the detox process—the idea that stopping Cal's heart would make the Destiny in his system burn itself out…

"We need to get her to burn through the D in her bloodstream, so she'll go into withdrawal and, you know…" I called out to my friends, even as I strained against the hold Rochelle had on me. I didn't want to say the word *die* and piss her off. "This can't be easy—holding six of us in place like this. We need to figure out a way to make it even harder. Maybe if we all struggle? Maybe one of us can get free!"

Rochelle was looking hard at Jilly, at the bag that was emptying instead of filling. She turned and looked directly at me with her crazy eyes. "Stop doing that," she ordered. "I want her blood!"

"Let's all talk," Calvin suggested. "Maybe she'll overload if she tries to gag us, too."

"Absolutely, let's try it," Dana said as Cal began reciting the alphabet, and Milo said, "I love you, Sky, you know that, right? And we're gonna get out of this, I know we are. And then I'm going to let you see my entire childhood, in real time if you want to…"

"I wanna go home, I wanna go home," Garrett chanted as I alternated between telling Milo, "I love you, too," and saying, "Everyone push back on three. One…two…*three*! One…two…*three*!"

Rochelle spun to glare at each of us in turn as we spoke, and I could tell she was trying to use her powers to shut us up, but she couldn't. Of course, that didn't mean she wouldn't develop the ability to gag us eventually. A jokering D-addict's powers often got stronger and stronger, just continuing to grow—until the joker's head exploded. Often literally. Please dear Lord, make her head explode soon…

"*Silence!*"

We didn't shut up, and she started to scream, a wordless, plaintive wail that got our complete attention. And when we shut up and she finally stopped, she glared again at me. And pointed to Jilly. "Stop! That!"

"Nope," I told her. "One…two…*three*!"

It worked—it worked! For a fraction of a second it had worked. I saw Rochelle stagger and I'd moved my arm—just a bit. But I'd definitely moved. "Dana?" I asked.

"Yup," she said. "Let's keep it going. One…two…*three*!"

Rochelle just laughed and turned on her unequal heels—but again, she'd wobbled just a little as she went into the closet.

"Don't push her too hard," Milo said to me quickly and quietly. "She'll lash out and she'll kill you."

"No, she'll lash out and kill *you*," I whispered back, my heart hammering in my chest. "She wants *my* blood."

And sure enough, Rochelle came out of the closet—out of her home Destiny lab—with IV tubing, a needle, and an empty plasma bag. She wasn't carrying them—she was floating them telekinetically beside her as if to emphasize how unconcerned she was by our attempts to tax her abilities.

In her mind, her powers were limitless. But I knew better. She was starting to sweat. I could see it beading on her upper lip and along her hairline.

"One…two…*three*," I whispered, and we all pushed hard.

Rochelle just laughed again, and the rubber tourniquet wrapped itself around my arm, which she'd used her powers to jerk straight. And yes, there were my veins. Ouch. The needle pricked as it slid in and my blood began to flow out.

"So who do you save now?" Rochelle taunted me. "Jilly or yourself?" She turned to look at Dana as another blood bag and IV tubing came dancing out of the D-lab closet. "Or maybe…your precious Dana?" She smiled that awful smile at me. "I know your TK powers are limited and that you can't save more than one of you at a time, you poor, pathetic little waste of powerful and delicious blood. So who, exactly, is it going to be?"

———————

I was frozen—and not just because Rochelle had me in that TK body lock.

But then I realized that this was what she wanted. She wanted me paralyzed—and not actively fighting back and forcing her to use up more of the D in her system.

Dana and Milo were both hammering me with variations on, "If you die, everyone else will, too."

Dana said it best. "Always put the oxygen mask on yourself first."

Still, I knew if I stopped sending that blood back into Jilly, she was in serious danger. I could handle losing a bag of blood. I looked at it again. It was a *very* big bag.

But I also knew that Dana hadn't recovered yet from donating blood into Calvin's private Destiny fund. It wouldn't be long before I was going to have to choose between Jilly and Dana, and I'm sorry, but I was going to pick Dana. But I was going to hate myself for the rest of my life—I knew that, as well.

But then Cal spoke up. "Bitch, *please*," he said. "We all know Skylar's gonna choose herself—because that's what we all do, right? When it comes down to it? We always choose ourselves. So why don't you let me get the hell up, so I can go and get that batch of D that's cooking out in the trunk of my car—add it to what you've got going here. Because if you're making Destiny with all three of these girls' blood? That shit is gonna *rock*. And I want in."

Dana started to cry. "Oh, Calvin, no," she said. "Please, no, don't make me kill you, too."

Rochelle had turned to stare at Calvin, but now she looked hard at Dana. "She's lying," she reported in her crazy triple voice as she turned back to Calvin. "She will never kill you. She is not able. But you... *You* are *not* lying."

My heart sank. I had been so certain that Cal was playing her— convincing her to set him free, so he'd suddenly... I didn't know what. Save the day? Somehow. We desperately needed *someone* to save this extremely awful day.

But now...

Rochelle stepped closer to Cal. "You...*want* to help me. I see this in you."

"That's right," Cal said, and my heart was in my throat because his eyes looked as crazy as hers. It was worse, because he was *Calvin*. Except he wasn't. Not anymore. Oh, dear Lord... Was jokering contagious?

Except he wasn't looking at me. His full focus was on Rochelle and only on Rochelle. His gaze didn't waver, like she was the only person in this room he could see.

"Calvin, no," Dana sobbed.

"Dana won't have to kill you, Cal," I spat out through gritted teeth as I strained against Rochelle's hold. "I will!" He flinched—just a little—but he *still* didn't look at me.

"No," Milo said quietly. "*I* will."

Rochelle did her truth-o-meter thing, looking first at me—"Lying"—and then Milo. "Not lying."

Calvin laughed—the tiniest chuckle in the back of his throat as he kept his gaze glued to Rochelle. "Thanks, Miles. Good to know. Come on, sweet thang," he implored the woman with a great big smile. "Cut me loose. Let's have us some *fun*."

Rochelle nodded and did it. I was waiting for her, and as I pushed and strained against her hold on me, I felt her control give just a little bit. Just enough for me to get my hands free and to rip that IV from my arm. *Ow!*

She whirled to face me at that, crazy eyes sparking, her focus on locking me back down as behind her Calvin sat up, released from her hold. It was only then that he finally shot me a look—a slight widening of his brown eyes in an expression that said *Seriously?*—even as he reached for Dana, wrapping his arms around her as he shouted, "Now, now, *now*!"

He wasn't on Rochelle's side after all! I was right! I was right!

And it was insane what happened then. It was as if by touching each other, Dana's power somehow combined with Cal's, because the force they blasted out toward Rochelle was tinged with Cal's blue electricity, but it was bigger; it was better; it was *super* Greater-Than. It picked up Rochelle and it flung her all the way across the room and slammed her against the far wall with a crash that shook the entire house.

And just like that, the TK hold Rochelle had on us was gone. Garrett sank down onto the floor, with Jilly still in his arms.

I could move again, and I reached for Milo, who also grabbed for me.

Are you all right? I am. Is Calvin...? He was lying to her! How in God's name did he manage to lie to her?

But Cal and Dana weren't done. They sent another bolt of their combined power at Rochelle, who was lying motionless across the room, and then another and another, until Dana finally spoke. "Cal! That's enough. That's enough, babe. That's enough."

And then they lay there, arms still around each other, both breathing hard.

Garrett asked what we were all thinking: "What the *hell*...?"

"Apparently one of my new abilities is some kind of telepathic blocking," Cal told us. "And that whole weird knowing thing? Different than the numbers or addresses I blurt out, although... twenty-two! I don't know what that means, but twenty-two. I got a big honking twenty-two echoing in my head—do with it what you will. But I somehow knew that I could do it. That she'd believe me even though I was lying. Kinda the same way I knew that if I grabbed hold of Dana, our powers would combine. And can I just state for the record? That. Was. *Awesome*."

I asked the next important question. "Is she really dead?"

Dana pushed herself up off the floor and—still holding tightly to Cal in case they needed to blast her again—went over to check. "Yes."

"Whoa," Garrett said. "Whoa, whoa, whoa!"

Alarmed, I turned to look, wondering what new monster had appeared that we'd now have to fight, but saw that it was Jilly who was making Garrett go all *whoa*. She'd roused—apparently enough of her blood had returned to her system for her to be able to regain consciousness. She was trying to pull the needle from her arm.

"It's okay," Garrett told her. "The blood's going back in."

The bag was almost empty. "I'll see if there's any more in the back, in the lab," Milo said and went to do just that.

But the girl was still disoriented and upset. Garrett had to hold her hand to keep her from removing the IV. "It's all over," he tried to reassure her. "You're safe. Rochelle is dead."

Jilly started to cry. "Oh Jesus, oh no!"

"Rochelle being dead doesn't make Jilly safe," I reminded Garrett. "She thinks she has to go back."

"Because I do," Jilly said, sobbing. "I have to go back. And then it all starts again! Please, *please* just let me die."

"Okay," I said. "We will. We're going to. You're going to die here. Today."

Now Dana, Calvin, and Garrett were all looking at me as if *I'd* jokered.

But Milo had recently spent time in my head, and since I'd been thinking about this for a while, he knew exactly what I meant. And as he brought another bag of Jilly's blood out of the closet, he said, "Skylar has a really good idea. It was from something Garrett said. About how the only way Jilly will ever be free is if she dies." He knelt down next to the girl and told her, "So we're going to make it look like you died. Here. Today, just like Sky said." He looked up at me. "We'll have to burn the place down."

I nodded. "I figured Cal could start an electrical fire. It'll be an accident. Rochelle's body will be found, along with her dear friend Ashley, and the body of a teenager that Garrett can identify as Jilly. That, plus we'll leave behind the tracking device from Jilly's arm..."

Dana was following, partly. "Hello. This means we need the body of a teenaged girl." As she said the words, she, too, figured it out. "We'll go into Harrisburg. And buy one."

I nodded as I put the new plasma bag on the end of Jilly's IV and gently sent that blood back up the tubing.

Most people in Harrisburg were desperately homeless. They couldn't buy food let alone pay for burial costs when a loved one died. So a truck went around every morning, picking up the dead. Some of the cadavers were sold to the university and colleges up in Palm River.

The others were buried in the local landfill. It was awful to think we could buy a dead girl, but if it meant saving Jilly…

Jilly looked from Dana to me to Garrett, and for the first time, she had a spark of hope in her eyes. "But…I don't have anywhere to go."

"You can stay with me," Garrett said, not entirely gallantly.

Dana shook her head. "That's not a good idea. Your father's eventually gonna come home. I think she should go to Orlando. Stay with April and the others. They're doing a good job taking care of Lacey…"

Calvin took her hand. "That's a really good idea."

"For now, anyway," Dana said.

Garrett cleared his throat. "I'll go into Harrisburg and get the, you know, body. That's something I can do. You guys have been carrying most of the weight today."

"Thanks, G," I said. "That would be great. Meanwhile, we'll get Jilly ready to travel."

Garrett cleared his throat again. "But I kinda need…money. Sorry. I'm broke, and I'm betting the guy with the bodies won't take my plastic."

Dana nodded. "You and Cal go upstairs, see what Rochelle has in her wallet. If there's not enough cash, go shopping in her jewelry box. We don't want to take it all. We don't want anyone to think there was a robbery here—just an accidental fire that burns itself out."

And it would burn out. Coconut Key's skeletal fire department would, at best, only be called in to prevent the neighboring houses from igniting.

"Let's do this," Dana said. But before Cal followed Garrett upstairs, she pulled him in for a long, lingering, *thank God we're alive* kiss.

And I realized then that this dangerous day wasn't over.

We still had to deal with Calvin's addiction. The words he'd told Rochelle echoed in my head.

When it comes down to it? We always choose ourselves.

I knew he was lying when he said it—that he didn't believe it, because it *wasn't* true. We were all still alive because we always chose each other, because we worked together, because we relied on and protected one another.

But as the Destiny took a tighter hold on him, Calvin *would* forget.

CHAPTER TWENTY-THREE

Jilly signed on to our plan by doing it herself—cutting her own arm and removing the tracking device that her Destiny farm owners had implanted beneath her skin. Like most G-Ts, she had an ability to heal superficial wounds rather quickly. Her massive blood loss, though, would require a longer period of recovery, so after she did her little self-surgery, she curled up and took a nap.

Dana and Milo were in the closet, making sure that Rochelle's home Destiny lab would be completely destroyed in the fire, when Calvin approached me.

I was still shaking from the fight with Rochelle, but I was trying my best to help—going through the piles of laundry that were in the hallway. I pulled out Jilly's clothes and packed what I found in a series of leopard-print suitcases. I'd tossed in the video game player, along with a small collection of games—but not enough to make anyone think there'd been a robbery. Still, I figured that since I'd recently flooded out the rebels, they might appreciate whatever Jilly could bring with her.

"Hey," Cal said as I tucked Jilly's sneakers in next to a pile of T-shirts.

"Did you find what you needed?" I asked. He'd wanted to cover both Ashley and Rochelle with sheets. I think the sight of them—particularly Ashley—royally freaked him out.

"Yeah," he said. "I did. Upstairs. Thanks. Although this does seem to be laundry central, doesn't it? I guess it saves time if you can get dressed while walking down the hall."

"You know, I didn't *want* to believe you before," I told him, just bluntly changing the subject.

Cal nodded. "I know," he said. "It's okay. I'm pretty scary these days."

He'd meant that as a joke—at least I think he did. But I didn't laugh. Or deny it.

"She killed her best friend," he said. And I knew he was talking about Rochelle who, yes, had jokered and murdered her bestie.

"Yup," I agreed.

"Pretty awful," he said. "Extra brutal, with the whole butcher-knife thing. I mean, you'd almost understand it if it were an accident. If they were arguing, and Ashley slipped and hit her head… But Rochelle stabbed her and chased her and then stabbed her some more. That's, um…"

I nodded. It was very *um*.

Cal took a deep breath. "So, I called Morgan," he said. "We're doing the detox tonight."

I wanted to cry at that news, I was so glad that we weren't going to have to do with Calvin what we'd just done with Rochelle. But I was scared, too. I didn't want him to die.

And then there was the fact that the best-case scenario put Calvin back in his wheelchair for the rest of his life. Worst and most likely case, of course, was that we wouldn't be able to restart his heart.

Twenty-two. The number Cal had blurted out earlier popped into my head as I hugged him hard. I had no idea what it meant—or even if it meant anything at all.

"Thank you," I said, then pulled back to search his eyes. "Does Dana know?"

"Yeah," he said. "I told her first."

"Of course," I said.

"I also told her that I wanted to make sure that I don't, you know, back out, chicken out, whatever. I'm afraid that I might," Cal admitted. "That the D might make me, you know—be a douchebag. And I just wanted *you* to know that I, um, gave her permission to, um, make me. Do the detox. So if she does whatever she does? Like hold me in place or drag me to the operating table and lock me down? I want her to do that. I do. I might not sound like it in the moment, but I definitely want it. Okay? So back her up. It's going to be hard for her, and she doesn't need you bringing any extra doubt to the party."

I nodded again because I couldn't speak.

Tears filled Calvin's eyes. "Because here's the thing: I will *not* do to you or Dana, or even Milo, what Rochelle did to Ashley. I *will not*. I would rather die."

"I love you," I managed to choke out.

"Yeah," Cal said. "I know. That's why I'm going to say this to you, because I can't bring myself to say it to Dana, but, Sky, if my heart *doesn't* start again, after you guys stop it? It's not because I don't want it to. I need you to promise me that you'll tell Dana that. And that you'll also tell her that it was worth it. Remind her, regularly, that my life was perfect, and I regret nothing—not a single minute. And that I loved her madly."

I was crying now, but I nodded. "I promise."

Twenty-two. There it was again.

Cal pulled away from me, because Dana was back. "Everything okay?" she asked.

"*Absolument,*" Cal said with the hokiest faux French accent I'd ever heard. "I was just asking Sky, would she rather have a rare condition that made her fart uncontrollably every time she saw a hot guy, or have a *different* rare condition that made her quack like a duck every time she entered a quiet room? And she just burst into tears at the trauma of having to decide."

Dana knew Cal was BS-ing her, especially when she looked at me and we both said, "Duck," and then started to laugh. It was either that or keep crying, maybe forever.

"Huh," Cal said. "I didn't think it would be *that* easy."

As they walked away from me, hand in hand, I knew that strapping Cal onto that table was going to be the hardest thing that Dana had ever done.

"Twenty-two," I whispered. It meant something. I *knew* it did. But what?

———

We were ready. And when I say *we*, I meant *Morgan* was ready.

He'd reinforced the leather straps on the operating table in Garrett's dad's OR with some serious-looking chains. He'd also mixed up an extra-large batch of the adrenaline he'd need to restart Calvin's heart as well as prepping the defibrillator.

Whether *Calvin* was ready was anyone's guess.

But "It's time," Morgan told me, and I went outside to get Dana and Cal.

Milo had gone in a separate direction after Garrett had returned with the body from Harrisburg—after we'd lit the fire at Rochelle's house. He'd taken off on Dana's bike to check in on our John Doe from the Sav'A'Buck. Milo and I were both in a much better place—I believed him and I definitely trusted him—but these next few minutes would've been a whole lot easier to get through with Milo by my side.

I paused in the doorway, just watching Cal and Dana. They were out on Garrett's driveway, slow-dancing to an ancient, romantic big band song, in the headlights of Cal's car.

This was it, Calvin had told her. His one chance to get to dance with Dana like this. If he survived, he wouldn't be able to do this.

When he survived, Dana had corrected him, even though neither one of them believed it. She'd also told him that she didn't care how he rolled.

"But I do," he'd said.

He'd already called his parents—leaving them *I love you* voice-mail messages. Because he also knew that two survivors out of thousands meant he didn't stand much of a chance.

Now, he lifted his head and looked up, as if he'd sensed me standing there. "It's time," he said, using Morgan's exact words.

Cal kissed Dana sweetly, deeply. And then together, arm in arm, they walked toward me.

"You good?" Dana asked, looking up at him.

He shook his head. "Nope," he said, as easily as if his answer had been *yes*. "I love you. And I need you to do your thing now."

And that's where it got ugly. Or it would have, had Dana not been ready for Calvin to try to back out of the procedure.

She put him in a TK body lock that must've felt a lot like the one Rochelle had used on us just a few hours earlier. And together, she and I hurried Calvin into the OR.

He started screaming, "*Wait! Wait! I changed my mind! I don't want to do this! I don't want to do this!*"

But Morgan had known that he might resist, and the G-T didn't flinch. He just calmly strapped Cal down on the table with those heavy-weight chains.

"*Please!*" Calvin shouted, looking at Dana. "*Please!* Baby, I know what I said, but I didn't mean it! I didn't mean it! I love you! I love you, don't do this! *I don't want to die! I don't want to die!*" But when she didn't release him, he got ugly—cursing her out and snarling and even spitting—and trying to use his electrical powers against us.

But Morgan was ready for that, too, and he injected Cal with a sedative. And then, right before Calvin lost consciousness, his sweet self returned, and he looked right at Dana and said, "I'm *so* sorry. I love you." With that, he was out.

I held Dana up as she gave in to her grief. "It's going to be okay," I said.

But she just shook her head.

I have no idea exactly what Morgan did during the first part of the procedure—the part where he stopped Calvin's heart. Yes, I was there, but it all happened fast, and it was mostly a blur. I do know that I held Dana's hands, and she clung to me so tightly, I had little finger-shaped bruises for about a week after.

I also know that the usually unflappable Morgan was sweating. He kept the medical scanners going the entire time, and he announced important moments, like exactly when Cal's heart stopped beating and when the Destiny was finally gone from Cal's system. He also told us what he was doing, like when he tried to jump-start Cal's heart first by using that good old classic CPR.

He practically knelt on Calvin's chest as he applied pressure, again and again and again. "We just need his heart to start moving; then we can use the defibrillator," he said.

But the medical scanner delivered only an ominous-looking flatline.

Morgan didn't give up. "Come on, Calvin," he said. "Come back to us!"

I stared at the screen, willing that line to move, to pulse, to do *some*thing.

Twenty-two...

Morgan still didn't stop, but now he was shaking his head. "Adrenaline," he ordered, and Dana picked up the giant syringe and handed it to him.

"Needle going in!"

I closed my eyes. I didn't want to watch. *Please, please, please, Calvin...*

"His heart's still not beating," Morgan grimly announced as he tossed the empty syringe onto the counter and went back to trying CPR. Those were not the words I wanted to hear.

Dana wildly looked around the room. "More adrenaline," she said. "Where's the rest of the adrenaline?"

"There is no more," Morgan told her as he kept nearly pounding on Calvin's unresponsive chest. "There's a risk of brain damage if we use too much."

"Right now, the biggest risk to Calvin is *death*!" Dana shouted.

Morgan shouted back at her, "We knew going in that he was probably going to die!"

"He's already dead." Garrett spoke up through tears that were running down his face. "You guys, just stop, because it's over."

"No, it's not!" I was the only one who turned on him, and that shocked me.

But then it didn't, because I knew that Dana and Morgan both had already lost so much in their lives that they expected to lose again.

But I still had hope, and Lord help me, but that tiny seed bloomed into something brilliant and colorful when Garrett told Morgan, "You need to stop, man, and mark his time of death. It's sixteen minutes past—"

"Twenty-two!" I shouted, startling everyone. "Keep going," I ordered Morgan. "Don't you dare stop! We are going to keep doing this, we are going to keep fighting for Calvin until twenty-two after, and maybe even until twenty-two minutes after that." I pointed to Dana. "Get that defibrillator ready, because this is *not over!*"

For once, Dana didn't argue. For once, she followed my command.

"Cal is *not* going to die," I shouted. "I *know* that he is not going to die! Not today!"

I could see that Morgan was exhausted, but despite that, he didn't let up. Still, I could tell that he needed a break, and I'd been watching him for long enough to feel confident that I could take over. "Let me," I said, placing my hands on Calvin's chest.

"Press hard," Morgan told me, watching closely to make sure that I was doing it right.

I leaned into it, feeling Cal's muscles beneath my hands as I stared down into his slack face, imagining his heart inside him, willing it to move for me, thinking of the blood inside his body, a body that was mostly water, a *heart* that was mostly water, which I knew I could manipulate if I focused...

very...

very...

carefully...

"Come back to us, Calvin," Dana whispered. "Please, babe. I don't know what I'll do without you around to make me smile..."

THUM-thump.

"*Defibrillator!*" Morgan shouted. "*Skylar, move! Clear! You need to get clear!*"

But I didn't move.

THUM-thump.

I kept my hands on Cal's chest. I wasn't even pressing that hard anymore. "Wait!" I ordered, and they actually obeyed me.

THUM-thump, THUM-thump, THUM-thump, THUM-thump.

Calvin's heart was beating.

"Make sure the respirator's working," I ordered.

"It is," Morgan reported. "But he doesn't need it." He laughed his surprise. "He's breathing!"

I looked up at the clock on the screen, expecting to see that it was twenty-two past the hour, but it wasn't. It was only eighteen after.

Calvin was still unconscious, of course, but his heart was beating steadily.

"He's now in a coma," Morgan told us. "So far, so good. Now, he'll either wake up or he won't."

"He'll wake up," I said. "In twenty-two…hours." I was guessing. Hoping, really. I said it again, more firmly. "Cal's going to wake up in twenty-two hours. I know it."

No one argued with me this time. In fact, Dana did the opposite of argue. She hugged me hard and whispered, "Thank you."

After that, we got ourselves cleaned up and then sat down next to Calvin, to wait.

Twenty-two hours is a long freaking time to wait for anything. Add to that the fact that I was praying I *was* right, and that it was hours and not twenty-two days or weeks or even months.

People could stay in comas for a very, very long time.

The first few hours passed relatively quickly because there were things to do.

Morgan volunteered to drive Jilly to Orlando, where he'd connect her with the G-T rebels. He wanted to spend a little more time with Lacey, and he seemed convinced that getting Jilly settled ASAP would be the best thing for the girl.

But before they left, he kept checking his phone, and he finally told us that Milo had called him. Apparently, Milo had a package he wanted delivered to Orlando, too, and he was hoping that Morgan would wait for him to get back to Garrett's so he could take it with him.

When Milo finally arrived, it was in that same gray rental SUV that I'd caught a glimpse of when I'd seen a flash of his memory of putting the GPS tracker on our John Doe's car. And yes, there in the back, unconscious and in handcuffs was none other than the man who'd nearly killed me in the Sav'A'Buck parking lot. *He* was Milo's "package."

"I was sitting outside his motel room," Milo told us apologetically, "and all I kept thinking was: *We're going from one disaster to the next. It's never gonna end.* I know he was planning to come after Skylar, and I suddenly thought, *Why wait?*" He looked at me. "If we wait, he'll find you, and he'll be armed when he does, and someone's going to get hurt. This way, he's out of the picture. And I figured whatever information he's got about the local Destiny rings, well, that G-T group in Orlando can probably use it." He looked back at Morgan. "I thought you might as well take the car, too."

"They won't...hurt him, will they?" I asked.

Dana laughed. "What do you care? He was going to kill you—or worse."

"I just don't want to be like them—like the people who make Destiny," I said, and even though she rolled her eyes, I knew she agreed.

"Whatever," she said and went back inside, where Garrett was sitting with Cal.

Milo put his arm around me. *You're not like them. You couldn't be.* Aloud, he said, "Morgan will make sure they don't hurt him."

"Right! Because I'm the miracle worker!" Morgan rolled his eyes—he and Dana were more alike than either of them would admit—and climbed into the SUV. Jilly was already slouched in the front seat. "I'll be back before your twenty-two hours are up," Morgan said. And with that, they drove away.

I shook my head. Jilly had said practically nothing to me. Not even *thank you.*

Give her time, Milo told me. *She's still getting used to the idea of not being dead. Life can be scary when you're finally free—when you move from the darkness into the light. You have to learn how to be human, sometimes for the very first time.*

I knew that he was talking about himself as well as Jilly. And I also knew that he was wrong. *You didn't have to learn those things,* I told him. *You just had to remember.*

But Milo shook his head. He had almost no walls up anymore, and I could see the way he saw himself. He believed that he'd been shaped into something severely broken by his stepfather's abuse. And I didn't doubt that he'd been damaged. It was hard to imagine any child surviving what he had without paying some awful cost in self-esteem or self-worth.

But everything that he was—my kind, generous, thoughtful, gentle, sweet Milo—had been part of him from the start.

He laughed at that. *Gentle and sweet. I'm not sure John Doe would agree.*

I didn't try to argue. Boys can be weird when you use words like *sweet* to describe them, even though it was one of the things that most women looked for in a guy. I just mentally took his hand and led him, in his mind, back to a long-ago memory that I'd first glimpsed when he'd torn down those mega-walls.

In this memory, he'd been tiny and tucked into a bed in a small, dark room. But it wasn't a scary room like the closet had been. The door was open a crack, and the light from the hallway was bright enough so that he—we—could see walls that were decorated with beautifully hand-drawn pictures of cars and airplanes and smiling teddy bears. There was a big bookshelf along one wall, and it was filled with books and handmade toys.

What is this? He was surprised and I realized it was a memory that he'd forgotten. It had gotten lost in all of his anger, sorrow, and pain.

In that memory, the door was pushed open, and a young woman came inside. She was trying to be stern, her finger up to her lips, but she smiled with genuine joy as she sat on the edge of the bed.

"You saved your cookie for me," she said, her cool fingers pushing our hair back from our face. It felt unbelievably good. We were glad she was finally home—that we knew she was safe.

"It's your favorite kind," we told her earnestly, then asked, "How was work, Mommy?"

She was tired, but she smiled again. She worked as a waitress at a restaurant and tried to get the breakfast and lunch shifts, but sometimes had to go in at night. "It went quickly, no big problems—thanks for asking." She narrowed her eyes, but that smile still curled about her lips. "Did Daddy forget to give you a bath? I think he did. Do you know how I know, Mr. Milo? Because you are so, *so* stinky."

We giggled as she tickled us, but then she snuggled close to hug and kiss us despite any stinkiness, and we felt so, *so* safe and content.

"How about we share that cookie tomorrow?" she asked us with another kiss. And then she started to sing. Her voice was pretty but nothing special, except it was, because it was *hers*. And the song she sang was a made-up melody about Milo climbing up a tree and finding a bird in a nest and a bug on a leaf, and we knew it was a song that she'd sung to us a thousand times before. And we relaxed and floated, safe and secure, as her face and her voice and the love in her eyes faded away as we finally fell asleep.

And there on Garrett's driveway, outside that doctor's office where Calvin was clinging to life, Milo was trying not to cry as he kissed me. *Thank you for that.*

You were loved, I told him as I kissed him back. *But then you weren't. But now you are again. Okay?*

He nodded and kissed me even more deeply.

Also? I think it's kinda hot to have a boyfriend who's sensitive enough to cry when he feels emotion.

He broke off our kiss to look down at me and smile. *That's something I'm going to need to work on.*

I smiled back at him, reaching up to trace the adorable dimples in his cheeks. *Take your time. I'm not going anywhere.*

The moon was out, and its reflection on the water was beautiful. It was a gorgeous, balmy, romantic night, and all should have been right with the world.

Except for my best friend in a coma, and my *other* friend whose long-lost little sister was eight-freaking-months pregnant, and—

Still thoughts, Milo said and kissed me again.

———

A few minutes later, at around two in the morning, Milo and I went inside to check on Calvin. "You want us to sit with him?" I asked Dana. "Take a turn?"

I could smell her tension mixing with both her fear and her hope.

"Feel free to sit," she said. "But I'm not going anywhere." She motioned to the chairs that Garrett had pulled into the room.

I realized that he was in there, too—curled up and asleep on pillows he'd tossed into the corner.

And while that wasn't the strangest thing I'd seen today—not by a long shot—the concept of Calvin's arch nemesis, Garrett Hathaway, sitting vigil at Cal's bedside was pretty darn weird.

Milo sat down in the softest-looking of the chairs and pulled me onto his lap.

"Feel free to tell me to shut up if you'd rather sit here quietly," I said to Dana, "but I read somewhere that people in comas can hear when people talk to them." I looked at Cal. "So, Calvin. Would you rather have a tattoo of a dog pooping on your back, or a tattoo that says *Long Live Goat Cheese* on your forehead?"

Silence. Because, of course, Cal couldn't answer. Dana's back was to me as she held tightly to Cal's hand, and she didn't move.

Garrett sat up in the corner. "What kind of dog? I mean, I think that would probably matter to Cal. Pit bull, yes. Terrier, probably no."

"Unless he wanted to make it as small as possible," I said. "Then a terrier makes sense, or maybe a teacup Pomeranian in that four-legs-together crouch...?"

Dana cleared her throat and finally turned to look at me.

I went proactive with the apology. "Sorry."

"No," she said. "These are definitely questions Cal would want answered. Like, he'd also want to know what font. You know. For the *Long Live Goat Cheese.*"

I laughed—a short burst of surprise and gratefulness. "Comic Sans," I told her. "Definitely."

"That's a tough one," Dana said. "Because Cal does love Comic Sans."

I laughed again, and this time it felt good. "Then let's go for the forehead tattoo in Comic Sans. Unless Cal wakes up and says otherwise...? Nope. Cal obviously doesn't object. Good. It's definite. Next question." I looked at Milo.

"Would you...rather be a pirate afraid of water, or a cowboy afraid of horses?" he asked.

"Oh, that's easy," Dana scoffed. "Pirate."

"For sure Cal would want to be a pirate," I agreed. "With a service horse that he rides on the deck of his pirate ship, to help him with his fear of water."

Dana laughed. "Nice."

426

"Garrett, your turn," I said.

He frowned, then said, "Would you rather have a Lamborghini or a Porsche?"

Clearly, he didn't get the rules of the game. "Good try, but no," I said. I turned to Dana. "Dane?"

"Would you rather go skydiving over an ocean filled with sea monsters or...go hiking in the woods near the chupacabra's lair?"

"Chupacabra!" I said. "Calvin, you really need to wake up, because Dana just said *chupacabra*!"

He didn't, of course. But we did have to explain to Garrett that a chupacabra was Spanish for "goat sucker," a legendary bear-and-or-space-alien-and-or-lizard-like animal (depending on who claimed to see it—sometimes it was a mix of all three) that left livestock exsanguinated. And then we had to explain that exsanguinate, in this case, meant left in the middle of a mountain field without any blood—like not a drop, which, yes, was weird.

And *then* we had to discuss whether Calvin's new *Long Live Goat Cheese* tattoo on his forehead would make the chupacabra target him in particular, so we decided that, just to be safe, he'd better skydive into sea monsters instead.

Would you rather be a vampire allergic to blood, or a werewolf allergic to dog hair?

Would you rather have normal teeth and a horrible unibrow, or normal eyebrows and one huge buck tooth?

Would you rather throw up while giving your high school graduation speech, or get caught picking your nose at your wedding?

Would you rather eat fried monkey brains, or drink eel pee?

All through the night, we went through a long list of questions, deciding all of them for Calvin as Dana held tightly to his unresponsive hand.

CHAPTER TWENTY-FOUR

I went home before dawn, so I could pretend that I'd been in my bed all night. I showered while I had the chance, then went into the kitchen to endure the usual annoying breakfast ritual with my mom.

The one where she tried to start a conversation as I tried to eat as quickly as humanly possible.

"There was a fire out by the beach last night," she told me as she scrolled through the local news.

"I know," I started to say, but swallowed it and instead said, "There was?"

"It started in some faulty wiring," Mom reported. "The place burned to the ground and three people were killed."

"Yikes," I said, as inwardly I was glad that the fire had been deemed an accident.

"I think I'll call an electrician. Make sure our house is safe."

"I think we're probably okay," I said, rolling my eyes. Count on Mom to go into full screaming-terror mode.

Except even *that* wasn't as annoying as it usually was as I thought about Milo's distant memory of his mother. I'd always thought that I had too many memories of my mom coming into my room and sitting on the edge of my bed. Now I knew that there was no such thing.

In fact, I kissed Mom on the cheek on my way out the door, which surprised the crap out of her. "Will you be home for dinner?" she called after me.

"I don't think so," I called back.

"You know, you can invite that boy over," Mom said, stopping me short halfway out the door. "The cute one with the long hair? What's his name, Milo?"

"Okay, yeah," I called back, at first thinking *no freaking way*, but then thinking maybe Milo would actually like that. Dinner at my house. With my mom. "But not tonight."

"Whenever!" Mom called back. "I love you!"

"Love you, too!"

Nothing had changed with Calvin.

The medical scanner gave us a continuous readout of his condition, and when Morgan checked in via phone, I read him everything on the screen, and he seemed confident that things were going as well as they possibly could.

At this point, Dana was doing some heavy-duty movie marathoning, watching one movie after the other and describing the action to Cal—continuing with the assumption that he could hear us.

Garrett ordered pizza both at noon and in the evening, and normally I would've objected to a double pizza day, but by dinnertime we were approaching that twenty-two-hour mark, and it didn't matter what I ate. My appetite was gone.

At around 9:15—just a few minutes before I was certain Cal was going to wake up at 9:18—Morgan poked his head into the room where Dana and Milo and I were sitting next to Calvin.

"Just wanted to let you know that I'm back. And I'm right outside if you need me," he said. "And just for the record, darlings, if Cal *doesn't* wake up, that doesn't mean—"

"Yeah, we don't need to hear that right now," Dana cut him off.

"Fair enough," Morgan said and left, shutting the door tightly behind him.

We were down to counting seconds now, and as the clock on the computer screen finally flipped from 9:17 to 9:18, I turned to look at Calvin.

Who didn't move.

Nothing had changed in his vitals either. His heart was beating slowly and steadily, his blood pressure was the same.

But he didn't wake up. His eyes didn't open; he didn't laugh; he didn't move—he just lay there. Still in a coma.

Then 9:18 became 9:19 and 9:20 and then 9:21.

And I realized in that moment just how desperately and completely I'd believed it—that Calvin *was* going to wake up, and everything was going to be okay. And the panic that I felt when he *didn't* wake up nearly overwhelmed me.

"Calvin," I said sharply. "Come on!"

Milo's arms tightened around me.

"It's okay," Dana said quietly. "Twenty-two hours isn't just a single point on a time line. I mean, yeah, it *can* be, but maybe his prescience rounded it down. It's twenty-two hours from now through the next fifty-something minutes, until it's twenty-three hours, at ten eighteen, right? So let's just give him some space." She spoke directly to Calvin. "We're right here, babe, whenever you're ready to wake up."

For Cal, timing was everything. And of course, he chose that very moment to come back to us, by whispering, "Love it…when you… call me…*babe*."

"*Get Morgan! Get Morgan!*" Dana shouted, and I rocketed up and threw open the door.

"*Morgan!*" I looked back to see that Cal had opened his eyes, and he was smiling weakly up at Dana, who'd started to cry.

"Hey," I heard Cal say. "Hey, hey, hey, it's okay…"

Morgan rushed in and gave Calvin a quick scan and made sure he had water to drink, but then he ushered us all out of the room to give Dana and Cal some privacy.

As I went into the hall, I realized that Morgan had brought Dana's sister, Lacey, back with him, and I was struck by the strange coldness in her eyes as she watched Dana kiss Cal right before the door closed.

"How could she love a D-addict?" Lacey asked.

"He's not an addict anymore," I told her, and she focused those icy eyes on me.

"Once an addict always an addict," she said. "But whatever. If he hurts her, I'll kill him for her."

"Yeah, you really won't have to kill anyone," I said, but she'd already turned away, watching as Milo, Morgan, and Garrett all high-fived down at the end of the hall, in the lobby.

"Who's that?" she asked. "He's cute."

"Who, Garrett?" I asked. "This is his dad's—"

Lacey cut me off impatiently. "No, stupid. I've met Garrett. He's an idiot. Who's the cute one, the one I haven't met?"

"That's Milo," I told her, and it was weird—the next words came out of my mouth before I could stop them. "He's mine."

Lacey laughed at that, and all of the little hairs on the back of my neck went up, particularly when she said, "Yeah, that's not how it works, bitch," and then walked away.

I was about to follow her into Dr. Hathaway's office when Dana opened the door to the operating room. She was looking extremely happy—like she was having the best day ever. "Morgan said he brought Lacey? That's amazing that she felt comfortable enough to come out here."

It *was* amazing, and I decided to chalk the name-calling up to jealousy combined with years of torture and abuse. This was definitely a happy ending—the return of Dana's long-lost sister combined with Calvin being cured of his addiction.

Plus, we'd saved Jilly's life. We were on a roll.

"Can you go sit with Cal for a sec," Dana asked me, "while I say hi to Lace and make sure she has whatever she needs?"

"Of course. She's…" I pointed into Dr. H's office.

"Thanks," Dana said. But then she caught my arm and said, "I don't think I've said it yet, but…"

She hesitated, so I shook my head. "You already thanked me," I reassured her. "It's okay."

"No," she said. "I wanted to say that you kicked ass last night. Morgan and I, we both gave up, but you didn't, Bubble Gum. You refused to quit. And you took command and, well, Cal's alive because of you." And then she said the words I never, ever thought I'd hear. "Good job."

She hugged me again, adding, "Don't get used to that."

I wasn't sure if she meant the hug or the *Good job*, but regardless, I was smiling as I went in to see Cal, who was sitting up in bed.

"Hey," he said. "Rumor has it you started my heart with your freakishly freak-show G-T ability."

"Someone's been spending too much time with his new friend Garrett," I said. "And as much as I'd like to, I'm not sure I can take total responsibility. Right before your heart started beating again, Dana was all *Come back to me, babe!*"

"Huh," Cal said, trying to hide his smile. "Funny how she didn't tell me that part." He held out his arms to me.

I went in for a hug. It was one of those old, familiar hugs where I had to bend down for it. It was how we were going to have to hug from now on, since his walking days were over. That made my heart twinge, and I had to work it, hard, not to cry.

"It's okay," he said, patting my back. In a typical Cal move, he was trying to make *me* feel better. "My heart's still healthy. So that's good, right? The way Dana put it, if I had to choose only one, it was better to fix the thing that keeps me alive, right? Be a bummer to be able to walk around only to drop dead from a heart attack in a year. This way, I get to live to be old and cranky."

"Dana's very smart," I said, pulling back and sitting on the edge of his bed.

"But not when it comes to her creepy little sister."

"Hey," I said. "Lacey's been through a *lot*."

"Be empathetic, be sympathetic," Cal told me, "but promise me you won't trust this girl. At least not right away."

"I trust her about as far as I can throw her," I told him. And I knew he wasn't talking about anything having to do with the way she'd just looked at Milo, but I certainly wasn't going to trust her around my boyfriend, either.

"Thank you," he said. "So. About this *Long Live Goat Cheese* tattoo on my forehead. In Comic Sans, my *favorite* font…?"

I laughed with delight. "You heard that?"

"Every word," he said. "Chupacabras, unibrows, nose-picking at weddings. It was impressive. But I remain the Would You Rather master. Behold! Would you rather take a weeklong bus journey with a dozen evil clowns and a bathroom that doesn't work, or spend an hour in a bed with a dozen tarantulas?"

"Evil clowns?"

"On a strict vegan diet of cowboy beans," he said. "The tarantulas, however, haven't been fed in two weeks. Still, if I had to make a guess, I'd bet the evil clowns were angrier and therefore more dangerous."

I rolled my eyes. "Cal, you're ridiculous."

"You love me so much," he said with a smile.

I smiled back at him. Because I so did.

ACKNOWLEDGMENTS

We would like to thank our agent, Steve Axelrod, and the entire team at Sourcebooks—especially our editor, Aubrey Poole!

Thank you to Aidan; to Jason Gaffney and his Mr. Right, Matt Gorlick; to Fred and Lee Brockmann; and to Dexter, Little Joe, and Buster. And a big shout-out to the Melanie Mania gang, and the cast and crew of *Russian Doll*!

But most of all we thank our partners in life and love: Ed Gaffney and Vern Varela for their fierce and relentless support!

ABOUT THE AUTHORS

Suzanne Brockmann and her daughter, Melanie Brockmann, have been creative partners on and off for many years. Their first project was an impromptu musical duet, when then-six-month-old Melanie delighted Suz by matching her pitch and singing back to her. (Babies aren't supposed to do that.) Since then, Mel has gone on to play clarinet and saxophone, to sing in a wedding band, and to run seven-minute miles. She is one of Sarasota, Florida's most sought-after personal trainers. Suz has driven an ice-cream truck, directed an a cappella singing group, and can jog a twelve-minute mile if chased. She is the multi-award-winning, *New York Times* bestselling author of more than fifty books. *Wild Sky* is the mother-daughter team's second literary collaboration and the sequel to *Night Sky*. Their next collaborative project is an indie movie called *Russian Doll* in which Mel will star, while Suz executive produces. Each strongly suspects that the other is a Greater-Than.